BESSIE

BESSIE

Lawrence Bush

SEAVIEW/PUTNAM

NEW YORK

The author gratefully acknowledges permission to reprint lines from the song "Exactly Like You" by Dorothy Fields and Jimmy McHugh, copyright © 1930 by Shapiro, Bernstein & Co., Inc., New York. Copyright renewed 1957 and assigned to Shapiro, Bernstein & Co., Inc., New York, N.Y. 10022. All rights reserved, including public performance for profit. Used by permission.

Designed by Tere LoPrete

Library of Congress Cataloging in Publication Data

Bush, Lawrence.
Bessie.

I. Title.
PS3552.U8213B4 813'.54   82-80372
ISBN 0-399-31001-0

Printed in the United States of America

to the women of my family

PART ONE

Chapter One / 1900

"I was his favorite, my father's, 'cause I was the youngest. I lived in his lap. But I didn't have—how do you say it?—sophistication. I was demanding like a baby. If something comes to me, some idea, I say it. And maybe that helped make me a fighter—I didn't know how to bargain.

"I'll give you a f'rinstance. You're not supposed to cook on Saturdays when you're a good Jew. So on Friday they take meat and potatoes and beans and onions and they stick it in the stove, like a great big baker's oven—they got lots of coal and wood in there and they put a light to it. And they cover the whole pot so it cooks for twenty-four hours. That's *tsholent*, they call it, and it's very greasy, all fat. But I don't like fat stuff, I don't even eat the skin of a chicken if I eat chicken. So I wouldn't eat, and my father used to beat me every Saturday, 'cause it's wrong to fast on *shabbas*, he says. It wasn't a real beating to make me hurt, but just so I should be sorry.

"It's not okay to fast on *shabbas*, but it's okay to beat, huh? This made me mad, y'see. And one day I decided, It's enough now, I'm going to pay him for it. It was on Saturday. My father went to shul, and he invited some important people to come back and make kiddush—that's when they pray over wine and cake. We had a little couch near the window, and as soon as I see them coming I lay down on my belly and I put my *tukhas* way up in the air. And the men come in and my father says, Why do you lay there like that? And I say in front of everybody, 'Well, you know you have to beat me now, just like every *shabbas*. But first I want to know: How does one Jew beat another Jew on *shabbas*?'

"After that, he never did it again, not even with a feather. And I never ate *tsholent!*"

❀

It was usually easy for Buzie to fall asleep under the dining table. The room was sunny all afternoon and warmed by the wood stove in the kitchen until well after sundown. The footsteps of her family members, the banging of her mother's pots, assured the girl that her life, and all that was familiar, would go on without her for a while. The red lace tablecloth, draped nearly to the floor all around, would blanket her with soothing shadows as she lay on her side, twirling the end of her blond braid inside a ticklish ear and counting the red snowflakes, looking among them for the little stains and loose threads that were the endearments of her hiding place.

Within this airy room, at this old oval table, Buzie's father Rov Laib Kharlofsky counseled and gave judgment to the Jews of Mogilev-Podolsk. He was the younger and more liberal of the city's two leading rabbis, a yeshiva scholar who for a year during his boyhood had traveled with an older brother throughout the pale of settlement and beyond to avoid Czar Nicholas I's twenty-five-year military conscription for Jewish boys.

Such exposure to life beyond the claustrophobic limits of the pale had greatly lessened the insularity of his religious training. By 1895, as the rabbi of an unimportant *shtetl*, Little Chernowitz, twenty miles north of Mogilev-Podolsk and the Dniester River, he had gained a widespread reputation as a modern Jewish thinker and had received an invitation to transplant his practice from the prominent Jews of the Mogilev-Podolsk community, who felt that their modernizing town, with its new railroad station and small but growing factories, deserved a forward-seeing teacher. They had greeted the new *rov* with high expectations, and soon he had supplanted his elder colleague, Rabbi Mandelstam, as the final judge of long-standing conflicts or of questions requiring deep and subtle readings of the Talmud. Within his own congregation, of course, Rabbi Mandelstam kept the honor of supervising family and religious rituals, or of resolving bad feelings between a husband and wife, or between a merchant and his conscience as to whether two kopecks from a pocketful of twenty was sufficient to give to a Jewish beggar in the market-place.

Drinking a glass of hot berry tea from the samovar, listening intently to a woeful tale from another Jew, Laib Kharlofsky might shift his position in his chair and suddenly find his boot lodged against his six-year-old daughter, who lay sleeping beneath the table. More likely, though, Buzie would be squirming to dodge her father's roving foot so that she could remain hidden, huddled by one table leg, to eavesdrop. Little of what was said actually interested her, most of it being colorless adult talk, and she took for granted her father's erudition, but what thrilled Buzie, besides the very mischief of eavesdropping, was figuring out the appearance and identity of each visitor solely by his or her voice and smell and by the manner in which her father spoke.

The most identifiable, yet by far the most infrequent, were the *goyim*—gentile peasants, come with grievances against Jews—who spoke only in Ukrainian. They were usually ushered in by the rebbetzin, Raisl, who had been approached in the marketplace for an introduction to her reputedly fair-minded husband. The *rov* chose his words carefully with such petitioners, while Buzie sat still, almost breathless, within the shadows of the tablecloth. Laib maintained a humorless dignity, neither eating nor drinking nor crossing his legs when sitting with a peasant, and always assured him—once and one time only—that he took the complaint seriously and that justice would be served through his offices.

Among other visitors were the *oyfgekumeneh*, those newly wealthy Jews who came regularly in the spring-suspension carriages to the Kharlofsky home on the outskirts of town, bringing even their pettiest problems simply to gain ennoblement from the presence of their rabbi. "For their leisure," Laib would explain to Raisl, "we all suffer—even their horses." But he exacted a price for his aggravation by meting out stern judgments for their small sins and vanities. They would come with pious smiles and leave with headaches, frustrated by the rabbi's inattention and by the interruptions that he tolerated from his children, even from the little wraith beneath the table.

Buzie had been pilfering food for her friend Tsil throughout September and early October, delivering armfuls of sour apples, tiny cantaloupes, cucumbers, and other harvest goodies that were stored in their cellar to the cobbler Shmulke's gaunt daughter, who waited expectantly like a hungry goat alongside the stack of firewood at the top of the cellar stairs. "Psst. Tsil! An egg, you want it?"—from the basketful that Haim the poultryman had given to the rabbi's family. "Hey, Tsil, I got herrings. You want?" —from Raisl's briny barrel. Buzie grew giddy from her freedom of choice, so well stocked was the basement during this season. "Shh, don't say thanks, Tsil, you make too much noise. You should only see what we have down here. . . ."

She had kept their activities hushed not from fear but from common sense. Discovery, she knew, would mean that Tsil and the two or three sisters with whom she shared the treats would have to go without. So Buzie kept Tsil out of the basement and hushed their voices as she hushed her doubts, and as the weeks had passed and their regular thievery had gone unnoticed, her confidence had grown. Nothing bad was happening to her; she concluded that she was doing nothing bad. She was flabbergasted, therefore, when her twelve-year-old sister, Ruchel, discovered her one afternoon juggling cabbages in the cellar and set upon her with accusations: "You thief! You steal from your own family! Ooh, you're such a little pig!"

Ruchel was always the haughty one, and now carried her anger so prissily, with her chin raised high, that Buzie smirked, thinking it a tease. Cautiously she said, "I just need a little for Tsil upstairs—"

"I know who's upstairs!" Ruchel shrieked. "Poppa's upstairs! And I'm telling him that you're a thief!"

Buzie cringed. "But it's for Tsil!" she argued. "You've got to see, Ruchel, she doesn't have like you and me. So many kids, and they all live in such a hut—"

But Ruchel was already clopping up the stairs, spanning two at a time with her spidery legs. Buzie dropped her cabbage into a basket of onions and clattered after her, falling once, twice, on the heel-worn staircase. In a second her sister was out of view. "You'll be scared to tell, you're such a liar!" Buzie cried.

Tsil's dour eyes pointed after Ruchel, cuing Buzie to dash past the firewood pile and make a horseshoe turn into the dark corridor that led to the dining room. Her sister stood ahead, fidgeting alongside the sunlit table where their father sat occupied with pencil and paper. Buzie nearly shouted a confession then and there, with a curse for Ruchel and her nastiness. But first her father looked up, not at Ruchel but at Buzie in the shadows—as if he already knew! He licked his lower lip to speak, then seemed to think better of it, straightened up tall in his chair, and, twirling the point of his tightly woven gray beard, switched his gaze to Ruchel, who huffed nervously.

Buzie's courage collapsed. She backed off through the hallway and shuffled over to Tsil, Tsil with the mournful face. "C'mon, we gotta go. Don't look like that—nobody died." Buzie grabbed two green apples that they had set aside atop the logs, but held the fruits to her chest until they were safely outside. "Here. Take your apples." She squinted up at her friend, then down at the mud that was warming their feet.

"You want to come to my house?" Tsil offered.

Buzie envisioned Tsil's ramshackle quarters behind the cobbler shop, all the noise and business that attended her family, and shook her head. "Nah, I got to eat supper here. Otherwise I gotta go in and tell them." She shrugged. "You better go now, Tsil."

She watched her friend walk toward town, then ventured out to the broken cobblestone road and headed in the opposite direction, stepping alternately on the road and its mud-caked shoulder. For a few yards she was consumed by worry, hearing in her imagination Ruchel's scratchy voice, seeing her father's disapproving frown, and wincing at the thought of his flying slaps. But the sunshine was too fresh, the breeze too exhilarating, the road and surrounding fields too filled with distraction for her to remain oblivious. Her attention quickly wandered to events at hand: to a raven flying low over a field of newly sown rye and the midday smoke from the distant stovepipe of a peasant's shack. (Maybe Yeshua would come home for supper and he and poppa would holler themselves pale like the last time, and not even notice her, and then she could hide under the table until bedtime. . . .)

The cobblestone ended, curving into a dirt road just beyond a wooden church, one-third of a mile from her house. Behind the onion-domed building was Father Potrovich's house, white plaster on wood, backed by a small, scrubby apple orchard. Buzie stood for a moment and listened for sounds of activity. The father had a daughter slightly older than she, who told thrilling tales about the *leshi* spirits of the forest and the playful *domovik* who lived in the white house, made noises in the walls, and caused the roof to leak because the grown-ups would not believe and appease the ghost with food offerings and kind words. . . .

Not a sound emanated from the house or grounds. The church, too, was still, its stained-glass windows dark, patterns indistinguishable. Buzie frowned, but lingered with her disappointment long enough to spot one of Katrinka's cornhusk dolls lying in near-perfect camouflage among the yellowing grasses in front of the house. She fetched it on the run, alert to a possible encounter with a marauding *domovik*, then cut across the lawn to the soft dirt road that descended into the fields.

She held the fibrous figure at eye level. "Soon I'm gonna go to school like your mommy," she lectured it in Ukrainian. "Then nobody will pick you up, you bad doll, you'll just lie in the grass and be all wet! . . . Okay, I'll ask if I can bring you to school. First we go across the bridge, and then we see the river and where the train runs. . . ." She repeated all that she had overheard of a conversation between Father Potrovich and Laib: that the priest could arrange to enroll her in the school at Otek, the grape-growing village across the Dniester, since the Mogilev-Podolsk school had already filled its quota of Jews. Her father had been gleeful at the news. "I have three daughters," he had proclaimed to the father. "Two are good-looking and one has brains. So the two will get their heads shaved"—they would be married and don the marriage wig—"and one will get her head filled!"

Filled with what, Buzie wondered. She already could read a scant bit of Hebrew, from her first year in girls' *kheyder*, and plenty of Yiddish, from staying close to her father and his newspapers. But there would be no Hebrew or Yiddish in the school, Katrinka had warned her. Only Russian. Russian grammar and geography and history and arithmetic and . . . and and and! She held the doll by the legs and knocked it against her head as she walked. "You don't know anything," she muttered, now in Yiddish, her words trailing into a silent scold: You don't even have a name, silly doll. Stupid! Stupid, stupid doll!

"Buzie Kharlofsky, Buzie Kharlofsky, march, march, march." She lifted her knees high. "Going to school, going to school, march, march, march. See the river, see the choochoo, halt!" She stomped twice in place, slumped her shoulders as she imagined weary soldiers would do, and trudged downhill from the road to perch upon a fencepost.

Giant sheaves of unthreshed wheat sat in this field, waiting to be hauled into drying sheds. Buzie began counting them aloud, reaching nine before a strong gust of wind stole her words and tempted her, with its coolness, to breathe deeply. It blew the sun's sparkle from the air; she saw that the clouds were gathering gray in their underhangings, a crisscrossed darkness like blood on a scraped knee. Wind swept the field again, loosening the strands of hair from her braid and touching the nape of her neck, causing her back to ripple and shoulders to roll from chill.

She had dropped the cornhusk figure onto the sandy dirt at the base of the fencepost—onto an anthill! Quickly she hopped down for a look. The tiny black insects seemed to multiply before her gaze. She stretched onto her belly, bare legs across the grass, chin dug into the sand at the perimeter of the ants' jerky, relentless wanderings. It was warmer down there near the earth; she could hardly feel the wind. The sun settled on her, toasting her back as she lay watching and making up stories about the laboring ants and the desert in which they lived . . . the anthill as a pyramid, with a pharaoh ant inside who gets all the food that the others bring. . . .

She lowered her cheek to the sand and offered a finger for an ant to crawl upon. "You go, you be Moses," she whispered, driving back the insect by digging furrows in its path. "You go back and tell the pharaoh that I'm gonna come and step on the whole house if he doesn't stop taking your food. . . ."

Two sounds entered her dreams as one, and were foremost in her waking thoughts: the hollow *pock!* of an ax against bark, and the voices of men. Buzie pushed up on her hands and spied two peasants, distant in the field, loading wheat onto a flat wagon. The ax struck again, calling her uncertain attention west toward a multicolored wood, over which the sun hung low and vague behind a gray sheet of clouds. Three cows were grazing out there, with a dozen crows hopping among the dying grasses. Buzie was startled and disturbed by all the activity, especially by the indistinct sun that had coaxed her to sleep and soaked her with sweat and abandoned her to a chilly walk home.

She stood and slapped the dust and ants from her clothing and skin. The journey along the road seemed dreary, even as her crankiness gave way to a clearer sense of being awake, for now she was worried about her father's anger again. Buzie tested defenses, held dialogues in her imagination:

"I'm littler than anyone and I eat less, so it's okay for me to take!"

"We didn't hide the food or sneak it, we just took and ate. Too many snacks, okay. We're noshers, but not crooks!"

And what about Tsil, she wondered. Would she get a beating, too, at the rough hands of her father? Shmulke's hands—they're like snowshoes!

From the Potrovich lawn, where she replaced Katrinka's doll, Buzie walked swiftly, but restrained herself from running, restrained herself until her hips ached. She slowed even more when she saw Sarah Mendel's rubber-wheeled, two-horse carriage stopped before their splintery fence. Sarah stood with Raisl inside the gate—a big, stooped woman wearing a stiff straw hat and a new, shiny blue skirt. The two were chatting and holding a large sack between them. As they turned toward the house, Buzie cut toward the backyard, but hung several feet behind their notice until they were inside the door.

She was beginning to enjoy this sneaking about when she collided with the sight of her father standing alongside the well behind the house, gazing at the fields from where she had just trekked. He looked magnificent, broad-shouldered in his white shirt, his black silk yarmulke crowning his charcoal hair, his thumbs locked at waist-level behind his back. At once Buzie felt ashamed for having run from his judgment. She shivered from being overheated and wanted her poppa to hold her close. "Poppa," she called, standing away from the edge of their house to be seen as he turned. "Poppa, Sarah Mendel is here. Momma took her inside."

"Sarah Mendeleh," he muttered. "All right, so come inside and we'll say hello to Saraleh Mendeleh."

"Not Saraleh Mendeleh!" the girl squealed.

"And why not? She's a *sheyne yidene* like you're a *sheyne meydl*. If I call you Buzeleh, I can't call her Mendeleh? Hey, but you better not do it!" He strode toward the side door with Buzie running after like a puppy. She wavered nervously at the top of the cellar stairs, but he had waited inside the doorway and clasped the back of her head to nudge her along into the girls' room, where Raisl and the two sisters, Ruchel and Leah, were sitting with their visitor.

Sarah was the wife of Mordecai Mendel, owner of a garment manufactory in town. He employed sixteen workers, including Yeshua Kharlofsky as bookkeeper-accountant, in a dilapidated barn of a building, and had made a great deal of money during recent times, driving a half-dozen tailors out of business. These dispossessed craftsmen now for the most part worked at Mordecai Mendel's machines, at the sides of peasants and peasants' wives who had been forced into the factory by famine. They labored eleven hours each day, six days a week (except for those Jews who observed the sabbath, which Mordecai, a pious man himself, respected—without pay). Their wages came as twice-monthly payments of seven rubles, women receiving half that. Mordecai's other payments were to government factory inspectors, to encourage them to overlook the condition of his building, and to police spies, who kept tabs on his workers to forestall any attempts at organizing.

"Where's the younger boy?" Sarah asked as Laib greeted her. "Yeshua, I know, is at the factory—a harder worker you couldn't find! Mordecai talks of him often, rabbi."

Yeshua's employment was a sore spot to Laib. At nineteen, the boy belonged in a university, not a dingy office! "A smart boy," he replied, "will be good at whatever he does."

"Very true," she said, clearing her throat. "A smart boy—and an honest one! My husband talks about him every day."

Laib nodded sullenly as Raisl rerouted the conversation. "Our Herschel is at the gymnasium, first year," she proudly told Sarah. "His classes sometimes keep him from us until dinner."

"He always comes home with a headache," said Leah, seventeen. "Momma's got to be a doctor and a cook!"

"As long as it's classes and not Marxism," Sarah replied, "I wouldn't worry. But the students get such ideas these days!"

Ruchel had meanwhile positioned herself alongside Buzie on their bed. "If poppa doesn't give you a beating, I will!" she whispered. "Thief!"

Buzie stuck her tongue out at her sister's scowling face, then hopped off the bed and settled on the floor at her mother's feet. Raisl's hand upon her brow kept her from worrying too much and inhibited Ruchel from kicking her.

Sarah Mendel finally got down to business, drawing a smaller sack from the big one. "You know, rabbi, we keep a few chickens in our yard—maybe two dozen, a dozen, who knows? So today I had Moishe the butcher in to bring one of my chickens to the *shochet* for slaughter. . . ." But Moishe, Sarah went on, had found while cleaning the fowl a needle-shaped stone in its gizzards. Was the chicken therefore *treyf*—unfit for eating?

It was in the sack, exuding a sickly-sweet smell. "Please," Raisl suggested, "let's do this in the kitchen. It's a better place to talk about chickens." The adults filed from the room, followed by Buzie, who was not about to be alone with Ruchel.

Buzie headed straight for the dining-room table and ducked under it. "Little *shikse*," Sarah called after her, "what have you got under there, a pot of gold?" The girl closed her eyes and pretended she was already hidden. Happily for her, Laib said nothing, only plopped the chicken onto a newspaper on the table.

"Such a big chicken! It could feed a whole family!" Raisl exclaimed.

"Such a big rock," Sarah replied miserably as she drew the flinty stone from her sack. "Right in the *pipik* this Moishe says he found it. So I ask him, 'How does a chicken swallow such a rock?' 'Eh,' he says, 'it lays big eggs, too.' I tell you, if I did not trust this poor Jew, I'd think maybe he wanted a little drumstick for himself—"

"The chicken is *treyf*," Laib declared abruptly. "If it held so sharp a stone in its vitals, it is unclean."

Sarah squawked, clasping her ears. "It was healthy enough to scream like a frightened bride at the sight of that hairy butcher! How could it eat a whole rock? It's more than a pebble, this thing!"

Laib glared at her until she sighed like a decompressing spring cushion.

"All right, excuse me, I'm an ignorant woman. So give the chicken to the *goyim*. They would eat a crow."

Buzie watched Sarah's veiny ankles uncross. Laib's black boots remained flat on the floor and protruding under the red lace tablecloth. "Ach, such a beautiful chicken," Sarah felt compelled to moan one last time. "And what good does it do without an honest butcher? I'll have to hire a *goy* just to carry a chicken back and forth from the *shochet!*"

"It might be dangerous," Laib said in a low, conspiratorial voice, "to supervise too closely the work of a butcher."

"Rabbi!"

He sat upright. "I am only joking, Sarah Mendel. But you must not be careless with your suspicions. They litter the street more than a shattered window." He needed no further proverb for illustration; the reproach had already driven Sarah to the doorway, where she licked her lips and tried to frame an apology. Laib and Raisl closed in on her.

"This loss is not too great," said Raisl. "To grow one chick from the eggs of a dozen . . ."

"It will lighten your stomach," Laib added, "and make your flight to heaven that much swifter when the time arrives—may you live to be a hundred and twenty!" He yanked open the door behind her. Sunlight, cool air, and the laughter of Ruchel and Leah at the fence near Sarah's handsome horses washed their faces clean. Sarah grumbled a word of thanks and farewell and shuffled out the door, her lips flapping nonstop as if she were beset on all sides by spirits.

"I should have ordered her to fast for a few days," Laib said. Buzie heard him softly chuckle as he sauntered back to the table. Then she received a swift kick on her leg.

"Ow!"

"Out of there, *gonifte!*" he roared.

She shot out on her hands and knees, veering from his boots before scrambling upright.

"Listen to me, girl. I may not be a prophet, but I am your father."

"Yes, poppa." She kept her eyes to the floor, her body stiff.

"When a Jew does something wrong," said Laib, "but is ignorant of his wrongdoing, it is judged as a crime. He learns through his punishment and becomes a better man. And when a Jew does something wrong and *knows* he is doing wrong, it is judged as a sin. He learns through punishment of the wrath of the Almighty, and he becomes a more pious man. This I have learned in my years as a student of the Law."

Raisl set to work preparing dinner, raising an irreverent clatter with her cookery. Buzie trembled at her joints, feeling lost to the world, an orphan of her own making for having run, for having let Ruchel gain the upper hand.

Her father sat and examined her face, cupping her chin in his hand. "But what do we call it, Buzie, when a Jew does something right and yet acts like he's done something wrong? Hmm?"

She whined and shook her head. "I don't know!"

"How do you not know?" he demanded, slapping his thighs. "I've just described *you*—a Jew who places confidence not in God but in the opinions of a highfalutin sister!"

Raisl left her oven to stand behind her youngest. "Laib," she advised, "you're not talking to Sarah Mendel anymore." She touched her chin to Buzie's scalp and raised her eyebrows imploringly to her husband, then gently tugged the girl's earlobes. "Maybe these ears are filled with dust from the table where you hide, hmm? Because your mother is a terrible housecleaner!"

Laib scratched his beard. "All right," he agreed. "So she's six years old. It's the perfect age." He lifted the chicken sack that Sarah had left behind. "You think you can carry this great big chicken? If yes, then bring it to the cobbler and that tall girl-friend of yours. Tell them that it's good to eat, but not to talk about."

"Poppa," Buzie pleaded, "stop fooling, please. You said the chicken is *treyf!*"

Laib lifted her by the armpits onto the table. "Listen to me, Buzeleh. It's not enough to know and do with your heart. You have to understand the things you do, so others can learn from you. Listen to me. For two people with no little children in their house and with two dozen chickens in their yard, this chicken was *treyf* from the rock in its belly. But for Shmulke and Gertl, with ten children and not so much as a pigeon in their yard, this chicken is kosher! Now go, before they have to eat their shoes for supper. Hey!" He squeezed her toes, still dusty from her afternoon jaunt. "Don't forget to put on shoes. You don't want to insult the cobbler."

At last he turned her loose. She scrambled into her shoes, eager to get away from his confusing stream of words—and to deliver the chicken—hurrah!—chicken enough to make Tsil's eyes pop! Buzie held the sack at her chest and let her knees bang it as she ran toward the road, watching the fast-flying clouds overhead.

Ruchel intercepted her just beyond the gate. "Where are you going?"

"To Tsil's house!" Buzie screamed. "And this chicken is for her! Poppa said so!"

Ruchel took long strides to keep up with her pesky sister. She kicked pebbles at her, called her names, and made dire threats, but Buzie moved on with heart like a beaver swimming upstream to its dam. Finally Ruchel threw a cautious glance back toward the house, then cuffed Buzie on the side of her head. The girl yelped and stumbled on the cobblestone, but recovered and ran ahead gaily with increased momentum. "I'll bring you the wing, so you can wear it in your ugly hair!" she shrieked over her shoulder, then spun about and ran backward from Ruchel. "I'll bring you the wishbone, so you can choke on it!"

Chapter Two

Yeshua eventually came home that night, and, with him, four-teen-year-old Herschel, who had worried his parents by failing to show up for supper. Buzie was long in bed by the time her brothers arrived, but her afternoon nap in the field had left her alert and wide-eyed as she lay alongside Ruchel—careful not to let their bodies touch, not even a finger! She listened to the boys' footsteps as they fetched food from the cellar; she tried to shape intelligible words from the echoes of their voices as they first spoke, then argued, with their father.

Sometimes a phrase would leap out for all the town to hear, as when Rov Kharlofsky testily ordered Herschel to bed. "Spare me your profundities, little calf!" he hollered. "You are just a calf looking beyond the fence, and I will not be the one to drive you to the gate with an idle beating. Go to bed!"

Yeshua urged his younger brother to leave the table, but of this, too, their father was scornful. "Oh, great leader!" he hooted. "Banish the feebleminded to exalt the ignorant! A leader of men, you are? A leader of boys, more likely, boys with wet noses and peasants who are dumber than the machines they run!"

Buzie clung to their voices, wove them in with split-second dreams, and thrilled to her own dramatic interpretations of what was being said. Ruchel at her side woke more than once and slept otherwise with shallow breath; Leah likewise did not sleep, but sat upon her narrow pallet in the corner, hugging her knees, until Herschel passed through their room on his way to the cold anteroom where he slept. "Herschel," Leah moaned, "what's all this hollering?" But he was hot behind the ears, stung by rebuffs from both his father and brother, and could only grumble at Leah before breaking into sobs and hurrying to his room.

In the kitchen the fight flared up again. "So go to Vilna!" Rov Kharlofsky thundered. "You can go to Vilna, you can go to America, you can go to hell, because that's where you're surely headed! But I won't let you so much as speak to Herschel about your plans! One word, Yeshua, one word and you can sleep in the same woods where you hold your meetings! Do you understand me? He will finish gymnasium, your brother, and, God willing, he will be in the university and able to choose a decent way to make a living. And by then he will have learned from your pigheadedness!"

"By then," Yeshua replied in his thinner, bitter voice, "he will probably be a worker, fighting in a workers' organization! Just as well for him that the universities won't take Jews—he won't have to waste his time with useless books and obsolete languages and czarist propaganda! Czarist history, czarist philosophy, czarist economics. Let him study Marx, and Kremer, and Martov instead!"

"Anti-semites," his father snarled.

"No, father. You think you can help our people by keeping them from the rest of the world. You, wrapped in a prayer shawl, in miserable isolation from the world of ideas! You make us stale like eggs that never hatch! Until one day the czar calls for a pogrom, and then the shells get broken good!"

"There will be no pogroms in Mogilev-Podolsk!" Laib's voice plainly cracked with anger. "I have dedicated my life to this! We live among the *goyim*, we help bring them prosperity. They know they have nothing to gain from Jewish injury. Nothing! But you, it is you and your brainless friends who will call the police down upon our heads!"

"We are making a secret organization, father," Yeshua replied. "It will remain secret—especially from the police—if you just keep your voice down."

But when one quieted, the other erupted; when one was thoughtful, the other became belligerent. They were of a similar mold, an eagle and a hawk, and their likeness made their fighting fierce. The only child of Laib's first marriage, Yeshua uniquely bore in his face and character the stamp of his paternity: in his willfulness, his strength of presence, and clarity of mind. But what were ripened, natural attributes of his father were, for him, precocity, the results of discipline and single-mindedness. Physically, too, he was the tighter bundle, shorter, more rumpled, and nervous, almost furtive in his movements. His beard was scraggly, his lips thin, his neck long and vulnerable, his eyes smaller and closer set than Laib's, commanding less attention, observing more.

All differences showed in their eyes: the father's, bright with fire; the son's, clear like water. And between them, in their joined gaze, floated ashes, heaps of ashes: the dust of Muriel Kharlofsky, slit open on the floor of a cottage in Little Chernowitz, wide-eyed and dead, her naked belly ripped by the blue tip of a cossack's saber . . . and the baby Yeshua in his crib, wide-eyed and alive but silent, so silent and cold. *My God, my God, why have you deserted me? How far from saving me, the words I groan! I call all day, my God, but you never answer. All night long I call and cannot rest . . . Yet you drew from the womb, from my mother's womb you have been my God. Do not stand aside: Trouble is near, I have no one to help me! . . . I am like water draining away, my bones are all disjointed, my heart is like wax, melting inside me; my palate is drier than a potsherd and my tongue is stuck to my jaw. A pack of dogs surrounds me, a gang of villains closes me in; they tie me hand and foot and leave me lying in the dust of death.*

"Poppa," Yeshua said softly, breaking a weary silence, "I want you to know me. You do not know me."

"No, not as you are—dressed as a *goy*, talking like a maniac. You are no longer the son of your poor dead mother."

Yeshua swallowed hard. "Perhaps, poppa, I am no longer the specter of your conscience! I am no longer the silent child, the silent witness, the weak, undervoiced child who couldn't be heard in shul on his bar mitzvah day. But still I live under the sword, poppa, as always, as all Jews live—under the same sword that killed my mother."

"And that you now wield!" Laib groaned. "And so another pogrom will serve as your revolution!"

"Poppa, there is nothing in my thoughts that did not come from your teachings—"

The rabbi slammed his fist on the table. "Then cursed be the day I taught you the *alefbeys!* It was not I who taught you to fight with police! That came from elsewhere, from your gymnasium friends, the intelligentsia, who wipe their noses in silken cloths. It's very well for them to be expelled from this or that university. But for a Jew? You were one in ten thousand!"

"And because I'm Jewish I should swallow my tongue? Are we not workers? Are we not fighters?"

"Are you Judas Maccabaeus?" mocked his father. "Has God shown you a sign?"

"History has shown us all its signs! I speak of history, not of God!"

"History!" Laib shouted. "I will stuff history down your throat! Just twenty years ago the czar was assassinated by your *narodnik* madmen! And for three years after, Jews were slaughtered left and right. Your mother was neither the first nor the last! And these *narodnikii*—the same breed as your friends who murdered police in Kiev and allowed you to slip away like a rat! —the same breed, perhaps even the same men! They declared the pogroms to be revolutionary! Revolutionary, the murder of Jews!

"What will make you Kiev assassins any different? Who will change them—Jews in *goyishe* clothing like you? If I thought you were one of them, I would break your neck! I would at this moment summon the gendarmes and let them drag you off to the army with the rest of the rebel students. Do you hear?" He was standing, hollering, shaking his fist. "You are my flesh and blood, my son, and the only son of my butchered wife! Your life is the sign of my covenant with God, that there will be no more pogroms. No more! And I have protected your life, Yeshua— your life! I hid the truth from the people of this town, and from the police! I feigned illness, for weeks I deprived my people of my counsel and piled burdens upon Reb Mandelstam, just so you would have an excuse to come home, to hide the shame of your expulsion!"

"I am not ashamed of my expulsion," Yeshua muttered, his eyes cast down before the intensity of his father's tirade.

Laib sank, trembling, into his chair. "And you do not understand *my* shame. You do not know *my* fear. You think me an old, outdated man. I know you do! But it is you who are so naïve, my son. So naïve, and so uncaring. Aie, God, how can a Jew not understand that, whenever gentile blood is shed, it gets washed out with Jewish blood? Never since the original night of Passover has the Angel of Death passed over a Jewish home without paying its respects!"

For the second time in the hour, Raisl came from the bedroom, wearing her nightdress and a kerchief around her cropped skull, to plead with her men to quit their argument. This time they were too exhausted and frightened by their own intensity to resist her appeal. "Momma," Yeshua apologized, "I want only his blessing. He in his way and I in mine, we fight for the same thing. But he withholds it from me, in every gesture and word—he would starve me for kindness."

"A boy of nineteen, he wants to be part of the family," she said noncommittally while tugging her husband's arm to guide him away. As the rabbi said nothing, Raisl pursed her lips to hush her stepson as well. He was left alone at the table and discharged his frustration by blowing out the tallow lamp.

Sitting in the damp, chill room, Yeshua reviewed the argument and realized with disgust how little defense or explanation he had mustered in the face of his father's anger. Not a word spoken of Mordecai Mendel's sweatshop, of the utter unslavement of both peasants and Jews at those machines. Not a word about their study circle, grown to fourteen during the past month by the incoming of their first non-Jews, Tropim and Scharanoff, both workers from the shop; about their growing trust and realization that there were common, material causes for their poverty and unhappiness. These basic accomplishments . . . surely his father could applaud them, find some shred of respect, some link of understanding. . . .

Everywhere were comrades, throughout the Russian Empire and beyond, according to all that Yeshua had heard, read, or come to believe: that scores of articles and theoretical pamphlets were flooding the northern cities, stirring the workers to consciousness and strikes; that the Jewish Labor Bund's membership had swelled to thousands, with tremendous influence in their Vilna stronghold; that in the western pale, dozens of Socialist Revolutionist factions, inheritors of the *narodnik* populism of the 1870s, were uniting and sparking revolution in the hearts of both peasants and students. At last Yeshua could breathe with optimism, for the earth was moving, and the czar, he thought, must be trembling upon his pillow each night. Yet in his own home he could find no solidarity! He could not hold a meeting. He had to argue to exhaustion to be allowed even to store pamphlets in the cellar—or to have the right to speak freely with his own brother!

Yeshua gnawed fretfully at his lip, then pushed away from the table, resolving with the gesture to abandon all hopes for a rapprochement with his father. Let my mother's ghost come, he thought, and claim the man for the century in which his thinking is bound.

He walked briskly through the girls' bedroom into where Herschel lay. The brothers began to converse, Yeshua in normal tones, without regard for the hour, and Herschel in whispers, as if the police were surrounding the house.

In fact they did have an eavesdropper, for Buzie was still awake and very interested in the uproar. She had hopped down from her bed to take up a post at the edge of Leah's pallet, which lay right alongside the wall of the anteroom. When her dimly awake sister shooed her off, she withdrew by a few feet until Leah drifted to sleep. Then Buzie huddled in again, using a corner of blanket to warm her icy feet as she listened with an ear to the wall.

It was not so interesting now that she could hear every word. Buzie soon was dozing, rendering snatches of the overheard conversation as dreams, jerking awake whenever one of the vague, lurking *pogromchiki* of her imagination took on too clear and frightening a visage. Then the same voices that had fueled the dream would dispel all memory of it, as again she listened . . . latched on to an interesting word . . . floated with it . . .

Laib, meanwhile, was seated on the edge of his bed, brooding by candlelight, his face buried in his hands as his reclining wife stroked his back and listened for his thoughts to emerge. "You know, Laib," she finally ventured to say, "there must be a better way for us to talk."

He groaned and rested his hands upon his knees. "Of course there is. Of course. I treat him as if he were Absalom, plotting to steal my kingdom. But I have no kingdom, only a few Jews whom I try to protect. And he tries, too, in his way. He's a good boy." He eased back on his pillow and stared at the roughhewn ceiling. "He's only doing what a hundred other sons, a thousand other Jewish boys, are doing."

"Don't forget our Buzie," chuckled Raisl. "She interprets Torah by stealing food."

He turned his cheek to look at her. Raisl's lips were pressed into the faintest smile, her eyes expectant. "Ach, Raisl," he sighed, too perplexed to smile, "I can hardly keep up with it. The first year of a new century—but not according to our holy calendar, hmm?"

She laid her hand across his chest and played with the buttons of his nightshirt. "Everywhere it's the same, Laib. The ideas that have guided us, we pass them on to our children. But who knows how they'll use them?"

She watched the steady-burning candle on her dresser and felt his heart beating and the shallowness of his breathing. Then he drew air sharply and rose.

"Please," she cautioned, "where are you going, Laib? Not now."

"Let it be now," he insisted. "Everything is pressing him, now it's gotten to me, too. I don't want his heart to harden against us, even for one night."

"You're not so soft yourself. And you're very tired. Please, my husband. There's so much to be discussed and it's so late."

"Never mind," he scoffed. "Just go to sleep. I'll join you soon."

But Raisl's admonition was on the mark. Both men still carried the scent of blood in their nostrils. As Rov Kharlofsky loomed above Leah, saw Buzie sleeping in an awkward huddle against the wall, and heard the voices of his sons in their room, he recalled his injunction against such conversations and felt provoked by Yeshua's disobedience. If already the whole family seemed so disarrayed by the mere utterance of ideas, he thought, what would happen to them when Yeshua next blundered into some stupid, criminal action?

"Herschel, you're overeager," the troublemaker was saying. "The old man is right in this respect. Our activities will be increasing, and for you, with your studies . . ."

"Don't you go setting the limits for me!" Herschel complained. "Everybody tells me what—" He fell silent in midsentence as he perceived his father's figure in the doorway.

Laib spoke sternly, with a tightly set jaw. "Judging from your silence alone, Herschel, I would say you are breaking the Commandments. You do not honor your mother and father—who sent you to bed!—but you are busy worshiping a golden calf—"

Yeshua stood between them. "I would say, father—"

"I'm not speaking to you," said the rabbi. "In the morning, there will be time."

Yeshua only raised his voice. "I would say, father, that you are interrupting our conversation with pious nonsense."

Laib roared from the guts as he slapped Yeshua's face. "And I say that we should never have to hear your voice in this house again! Get out! Find a dog to lecture!"

"A dog could understand more than the great rabbi of our city!" Yeshua hissed, fists clenched.

Both men hesitated, unbelieving of their violence. Buzie began to wail in the other room. Gratefully Laib rushed to her. "What is it, little one? Shh, shh, don't pull away, Buzeleh!"

A bad dream, a rude awakening? There was no real cause besides overstimulation and the nighttime malaise of children that can turn to terror if their cloak of sleep is whisked away. Buzie was as shocked and confused by her emotions as anyone, but continued to cry even as she became more fully awake, if only to legitimize her initial upset. Finally Raisl came with a lantern, and all of the family, even Ruchel, spoke comfortingly to the pipsqueak.

Yeshua threw on his jacket, extinguished the lamp in his room, and stalked out the rickety back door.

Raisl was obviously in command. As she returned the girls to their beds, Laib withdrew into the boys' room, feeling bestial because of Buzie's rejection of his embrace. When Herschel came in, he failed to see his father in the pitch-black room, and as the boy climbed into bed, rustling his sheets, Laib found the open door.

The night was cold and windy, the sky a dark, distant blue, graced by three gliding clouds and pinned in one corner by a crescent moon. Laib wandered out to the well, tensing his shoulders against the chill breeze, heaving great sighs, then letting his thoughts go under to a mumbled prayer. Crouched

on the brittle grass by the side of the house, Yeshua was reviewing options for where he might spend a few nights away from
his family. Each man was shivering, with his face upturned toward the moon, and unaware that the other was near.

Chapter Three / 1903

"The most important thing in my life has been the revolutionary
movement, even since I was a young child without understanding.
I must have been born that way, feeling that I was with the
downtrodden, with the people that suffer and against those that
punish us because they want more money. Sooner or later you
have to start thinking about it, y'see. And it's so easy for you to
become a revolutionary if you think.

"But in Russia, you were afraid to open your eyes, no less
your mouth. If, like they say, misery loves company, then it
loved Russia. The peasants didn't have what to eat. They couldn't
read, they couldn't write, and they couldn't struggle. They
didn't know how. All they knew was God and the czar father
and how to make soup out of nothing, out of bones. And meanwhile there were people drinking champagne from women's shoes
and feeding veal to their dogs.

"If you crowd animals together in a pen, they bite and they
kick each other instead that they should all push together to
knock down the fence. If just once, in all my eighty-eight years,
everyone who had been on the good side had fought together,
instead of spending time making up their own little fights, their
own little curses, then we could have gone to bed early! But whatever's wrong with the society, y'see, you find at least a little part

of it in each person, including the revolutionaries. Competition. Greed. Racism. Anti-Semitism.

"So, in Russia: The Jewish people were not allowed to own land, so they took on jobs, like trades, or f'rinstance they sold whiskey until the government took the license from us. But we owned shops, we sold goods, we fixed things, and always we were very poor. But to a peasant, forget it, say the word 'Jew' and he spits. He might be a slave himself, but the Jews are not even human! The Jews, he says, make money off his back. The Jews, he says, won't put a finger into the earth except to dig up buried treasure. Everyone tells him this; what else can an ignorant person believe if he's hearing anti-Semitism from the priest—our priest was good, y'see, but most of them were rotten— and he hears it from the czar and from everybody else? Plus— don't forget—the Jews killed the Messiah!

"So then you get a pogrom, a riot against the Jews. The government doesn't do anything to stop it, of course. In fact, the gendarmes help to start it. It's just like the Ku Klux Klan does to the blacks in America—with the help of the FBI.

"And the Jews didn't behave much better, y'see. To a Jew, the peasant is an ox without a brain. You cheat him, and if he finds you out, you say you're sorry and cheat him again! We were better than the *goyim* and scared of them at the same time.

"There was no one to be a bridge between people. My father tried, he was a liberal man, but still, he had a mind like from a small town, a *shtetl*. 'Pray and God will provide.' And my brothers, especially Yeshua, like a lot of the revolutionaries, they forgot they were Jewish. They became assimilationists. They thought that Marx and Moses can't be served on the same plate together. So they didn't make the genuine connection with the Jewish workers until after the pogrom at Kishinev—1903. Even a group like the Jewish Labor Bund, which especially tried to organize Jewish workers in the big cities, even they didn't really get going until after Kishinev.

"Forty-seven Jews were murdered in Kishinev, in two days. After that, everyone in the world realized that the czar was using the Jews for a scapegoat, helping to make pogroms against us so the peasants should think they're achieving something by beat- ing a Jew. A lot happened after Kishinev. Many Jews went to America, some became Zionists and planned to go to Palestine, but most important was that a real progressive movement grew in Russia, with a lot of support from young Jewish people. It doesn't mean you have an end to anti-Semitism—the stronger the revolutionaries got, y'see, the more the government looked for scapegoats—but at least now you had organized groups that they could fight against the *pogromchiki* and maybe show the peasants who the real enemies are.

"Look, it's hard just to cook a noodle pudding—can you imagine how hard it was to make a whole revolution and hold it together? But I tell you, when I go back and talk about it, I really feel my blood circulating!"

❋

May 27, 1903

Dear Momma,

I have had no word from you for a month, while I've written three times. For a family of scholars, and in these times of trouble for Jews, this is a cause for fright. I've never been so eager and so scared at the same time for something to arrive—at least not since my wedding!

Ah, dear ones. I suppose you're okay and I should thank God that my troubles are near at hand and not out of reach, and that you are miles away from Kishinev, miles enough to only read about it. May our distance from such trouble always be equally as far! Still, I need to see your signatures. Send me one big letter, my eyes are starved.

I think literacy is a mixed blessing, momma. Always it's been so, since I fought going to *kheyder* with a child's stubbornness. In this New York where my Mr. Markish and I find ourselves—and lose ourselves nearly every day—to be able to read is first and foremost. It would be like sewing with a blunt needle to try to get along without my paper, the *Forvetz*. It's got everything you need: where to go, where to live, where to shop, how to dress, how to live as an American. But some of what it's got I could do without, and that is the news about Kishinev. Of course, even the oldest woman who can't read a word knows about the pogrom. Everyone is talking about it, and everywhere there are meetings, meetings, demonstrations, and concerts to raise money for the victims. Even the Chinese people have had a concert for us. Remember, momma, I told you about

Chinatown, with the pushcarts full of *treyf* food? They eat
pork like we eat beets! Or they would like to, since most of
them are poor like the rest of us.

Never mind, the point is that maybe nobody speaks
English but everybody is talking about our murdered Jews.
Even the big shots, the nobility, are having an affair in the
"Carnegie Hall" tonight and a man who used to be presi-
dent of the United States is going to speak. Mr. Grover
Cleveland. Can you imagine, a president of the United
States speaking on our behalf? When I heard this, I re-
membered poppa's old, old coin with the Hebrew inscription
and how he used to tell me that the Jewish people were
very important and respected in Poland many centuries ago.
But I don't see any Hebrew inscriptions on American dollars.
In fact, I don't see many American dollars!

Last week I read that Count Cassinki, Cassini, whatever
his name is—the ambassador from Russia—he said in the
newspaper that the pogrom at Kishinev happened because
the Jews were bankers. "Give a Jew a couple of dollars
and he becomes a moneylender." That's just what he said.
So you know what I said to my Mr. Markish? I said, "Count
Cassinki should only give a Jew a couple of dollars and
then drop dead himself!" Where are all these Jewish
bankers? I would like to know. I would have married one!

Of course, I am only joking with you, momma. We must
joke about these things or our hearts will sink right down
into the earth. Please, write a letter soon and tell me how it
is with you.

Mr. Markish is working hard, too hard, I think, at making
his umbrellas, but at 36 pennies for a dozen (less than a
ruble), I think my husband will not soon become a moneylender. Sometimes his cousin allows me to work in the store
as a salesgirl, selling umbrellas to the peddlers (5 pennies
each!), but he has his own wife to do this and gives me the
work only because he knows that Mr. Markish and I need
the few extra pennies. I'm afraid we owe too much already
to this cousin Izzy. Even our new American name, he had
it all ready and polished for us when we got off the boat.
How strange, my name has changed twice in less than a
year!

Izzy would have me working in the back of his shop with

my husband and the other umbrella-makers, but my bones
are still weak from the voyage, believe it or not, and Mr.
Markish says that twelve hours at the machine would be
too much effort for me. He wants a pretty and healthy wife,
he says! Some health! A fruit tree would have borne two
crops in the time it takes me to find myself here. With my
headaches, my cough, I don't know why they let me pass
through Ellis Island. Had I been without a good-looking
husband like Mr. Markish, I would probably still be on a
boat somewhere in the ocean. This marriage is a *mitzvah* for
you and poppa. We are as well matched as turtledoves. My
only wish is to be strong again, even amid the craziness of
New York City, so that I can contribute a little something
to our well-being. You know, a wonderful poet, Mr. Morris
Rosenfeld, recently wrote in the *Forvetz:* "To drown right
off shore is not only a misfortune, it is a humiliation." And I
think he was talking about me. But I am getting better, and
a letter from my beloved family will surely complete the
recovery.

Your daughter,
Leah

The rebbetzin might have waited to read the letter until she
arrived home, so as to cross the marketplace with her attention
properly focused on the needs of the bustling people. But she
could not wait, nor leave it incomplete once she had begun to
read. So let them think her distracted. Yes, she was distracted,
and any Jew without distraction, without fear in her heart, she
thought, had to be a fool or living far outside of Russia. Even
the air, which should have been fresh and light, seemed to Raisl
thick with the scent of blood this morning. It came not only
from Moishe's meat stall, where two cats were scrapping for
discarded chicken heads; it came from the south, from Kishinev,
only one hundred miles away, and from the breath of every *goy*
who thought that the slaughter of Jews might do him some good.
The postmaster was one such bigot. Raisl shuddered at the
thought of returning to his presence, but it could not be
avoided. Her letters to Leah were not getting through. And why
not? "What do we need to get a letter sent to America?" she
asked loudly upon entering the small brick building next to the
train depot. "Do we need an order from the czar?" She slapped

the letter down on the wormy wooden counter behind which sat Gogolin, the squat, pug-faced postmaster.

He fingered the precious letter, creasing and pinching its corners to see if it would jump. "I don't read your Jewish gibberish."

"You don't have to," Raisl said smartly, retrieving her letter. "My letters are addressed in Russian! There, you see? And if you read at all, they should be delivered to where they are addressed: America! My daughter has not received a word from us in two months!"

Gogolin retrieved a cigar from under the counter and lit it close to his face. "I'll look into it," he said through the smelly smoke.

"I will wait, please," insisted Raisl.

He shrugged, then pushed off his stool and began waddling from file to file in random order. "The address," she persisted, "is 'Leah Markhofsky'—eh, excuse me—'Leah Markish, two hundred and five Grand Street, New York City.' In America," she added, her enthusiasm tugging hard against her restraint as she gripped the edge of the counter.

"Yeah, yeah," the postmaster grunted. "Good riddance to her." He paused attentively at a large metal file drawer. "Hunh, maybe in there . . ." After a quick scan of the folders inside, he drew one up and peered into its contents without removing them, then smiled savagely at Raisl. "Your son is Yeshua Kharlofsky?"

Raisl felt her bowels drop and unconsciously tightened her body to receive a shock. "What about him?"

Gogolin thrust forward his stubbly chin. "Take it up with the police, mother. They want to know who you're writing to."

Another customer, a Jew named Trask, entered the post office just as these words were spoken. Trask was a glazier and an irreligious man who had once met Rov Kharlofsky and his family when lodging a complaint about some *kheyder* boys who had broken a window. He now recognized the rebbetzin, even as she turned, pale-faced, to the window, and, after transacting his business with Gogolin, joined her at the side counter, ostensibly to address an envelope. "Good morning," he greeted her in Yiddish. "You're having trouble with this dog? . . . It's all right, he doesn't understand our language."

"So," she said bitterly, "how does an illiterate become the postmaster?"

"How does a monster become the czar?"

But Raisl did not know how much Trask had overheard, nor who he was, and would not confide her troubles. The glazier did not press her, only reintroduced himself by name and spoke in a friendly way until at last the woman had recovered herself enough to meet his eyes. "The hatred of some of these *goyim*," he said sympathetically, "could shatter glass. This is good business for glaziers, but bad business for Jews."

Raisl murmured: "My daughter does not receive our letters—in America. She worries herself sick!" Listlessly, thinking anew of Yeshua and the police, she waved Leah's letter before her face.

Trask swayed in closer to her. "Maybe you don't give enough postage for these letters, hmm?" He waited in vain for a reply. "Do you hear me? It gets more expensive now to mail letters to America."

Her anxiety was like noise in her ears, a score of voices barking at once, and yet Trask's quiet suggestion of bribery was a call to reason. It froze her blood but stilled her thoughts. She gathered the glazier's sandy face into her gaze. "And how much would this cost? There are at least four letters lost."

Trask finished addressing his envelope with mock flourish and replied: "A little cheese will catch little mice, a little more will get the rat."

Raisl's shoulders slumped. "I have enough trouble getting cheese for my family, never mind for rodents."

Abruptly, the glazier burst into Russian. "So never mind!" he hollered, as Raisl pulled back like a startled chicken. "So you won't have a new window and I won't have a headache! Here!" He speedily pressed a one-ruble note into her defensively up-raised hand. "Have your money and goodbye!"

Trask strode out the door before Raisl could even comprehend his deed. When, with a moment's breath, she understood, her back arched with refusal—but he was gone, his absence relieving her of shame. "God bless and preserve this man," she whispered, shutting her eyes to seal the prayer.

But now Gogolin's gaze was upon her, pressuring her also to leave or face his abuse. She felt Trask's gift in her hand, moist, crumpled, and useless unless handled with courage, just as the letters to Leah would be worthless, stained with strangers' fingerprints. . . .

"*Oi vay*," she sighed. Then, in Russian: "Unless my daughter sends me more money, I'll have more trouble than this little glazier could hope to provide."

Gogolin sneered and sucked his cigar. "Your daughter sends you money, eh? You haven't got enough buried in your backyard?"

Raisl feigned indignation, as though she had not courted his interest. "I have rocks in my backyard," she snapped, "like maybe you have in your head!" Then, boastfully: "With every letter from America, I get at least a dollar!"

"An American dollar?" Gogolin clasped together his hairy hands and cracked a knuckle. "And what about this letter you showed me?"

"With this letter, she doesn't know if I'm alive or dead. If I'm dead, she can keep her dollars!"

Their eyes conspired, his flitting to the doorway and back before he beckoned her with his chin. She pressed a knuckle to her lips and stepped toward the counter, smiling obsequiously and imploring her legs not to tremble so. . . .

Hurrying out of the post office, Raisl startled a flock of sparrows into abandoning their cobblestone crumbs. "Ach, birdies," she muttered as they fanned out above the crowded, low-slung marketplace stalls, "if you could carry my heart across the ocean, I would gladly give you a ruble, too." She contemplated the two or three weeks it would take for the lone letter that Gogolin had agreed to process to reach her daughter; it was a depressing realization that, however she exerted herself as a mother, her Leah was far, so far from her protection. And now the precious letters from "Mrs. Markish" would be invaded by that grubby postmaster as he searched for dollars. *Vay iz mir!* She wanted to spit on the pavement.

A wagon piled high with lumber, pulled by a black draft horse and driven by a hairy, barrel-chested peasant, clattered slowly past, giving mild vibrations to Raisl's bones and fresh earth scents to her nostrils. She watched the animal's shaggy hooves pounding the cobblestone, its mouth fretting at the bit, the reins strewn lazily across its broad neck, and she nearly wept with longing for her daughter to be there with her, waiting to cross the familiar street. Leah would be like an angel of God at her side, dear girl, so tall and full-bosomed and gracious. "That's Leah Markhofsky," they would all say approvingly, "who now shops for her own household—ahh, but still with her momma." Dear God, thought Raisl, how much younger I would feel!

The day was damp and awash with gray light that seemed to enhance the color in people's faces or delineate, in a raw way, their haggardness. Moving from one to another of the rickety stalls, Raisl saw each face, each sad eye, each torn collar, every jot of merchandise on the pushcarts, as if through a magnifying glass. Intoxicated with sadness, she nonetheless maintained herself quietly, giving greetings with nods and squeezes instead of words, listening raptly to people's gossip, complaints, and anecdotes, but speaking none of her own. "Today, Raisl, you look like Queen Esther," said Haim as she leaned her shoulder against the wall of his poultry stand. Old Yetta was there, too, oblivious to all but the contents of her tattered purse.

"I feel this way," Raisl murmured, brushing the dead hairs of her wig back from her ears. "Like you say—I feel like Esther."

"Very good," said Haim, pleased by her mellowness. "So when you go to King Ahasueras, be so kind to ask him for a new pushcart for Haim the poultryman. Tell him that this one is rotting out at the bottom and will end up leaving eggs on the street, which looks bad, you know, all sticky. The flies . . ."

"I will remember, Reb Haim. A new pushcart. And for you, Yetta? New shoes, I think, so your feet should not have to drink the mud puddles."

Old Yetta held up a brittle finger and blinked languidly, side-long, at the rebbetzin. "Queen Esther," she announced with the suddenness peculiar to her age, "was first a concubine, mmm . . . a whore . . . for the *goyim*. And then . . ." Yetta nodded ponder-ously, lips pursed. "Then she saved all the Jews from Haman. All the Jews, she saved."

Haim appeared embarrassed and thrust a bag at the old woman. "Hey, you think you know more scripture than the *rov*'s wife? Are you blind or something, you don't see who you're talking to? Here, take your eggs. Don't drop them. Go in good health."

"Go in good health, Yetta dear," Raisl said.

"God save me from growing old," Haim said with mock despondency as Yetta moved off. He bent to his special basket beneath the pushcart to fetch some extra-large eggs as a gift for the *rov*'s family. Raisl was alert to his intentions.

"Haim, I have had charity given to me once already today."

He simply gathered the eggs more quickly. "Raisl Kharlofsky," he said, "who are you to deprive a poor Jew of gaining a little favor with the Most High?" He kissed one egg tenderly and held it skyward as a holy object. "As the prophet said unto Zion, 'By charity shalt thou be established.' "

"The prophet was not a peddler!"

"And I am not a rabbi, nor even a learned man," Haim replied. "But I want to give some pride to my little chickens, poor things. They themselves might never reach a kosher table. But at least ... See?" he said to the caged, blinking chickens at his feet. "Your eggs go to the rabbi's table. To the purest woman in Mogilev-Podolsk. What blessed creatures you are!"

Raisl tilted her head back to squeeze the ache from her neck as she trudged homeward. A cool, wet wind was nudging her from behind, pressing her skirts to her legs, as cloudbanks thickened overhead. The prospect of rain pleased her; she would be sealed indoors by the time it fell, and free of visitors a whole afternoon.

The road was busy with wagons and pedestrians, so Raisl did not notice the attention paid her by a young peasant in a slow-passing wagon until he reined in his horse and called out, "Mother, can I bring you to your gate?"

She stepped back alarmedly from the too-near flanks of the horse. She did not know this clean-shaven fellow and felt fearful of his intentions. "Who are you—who is your father?" she demanded in Ukrainian, then heard her memory of his voice and realized he had greeted her in Yiddish!

From amid the jumble of seed bags in the back of the wagon, a head poked up, lips sputtering, cheeks spotted red from sweating. Raisl startled, then cut short her cry. "Yeshua? Is it—"

"Momma, it's going to rain." He twisted out of his hiding place up to his waist. "Come in our wagon, we'll take you home. This is Dovid Ginzburg, my friend from Kiev."

"Kiev." She shrank from Yeshua's outstretched hand. Her joy at seeing him was heavily dragged by fear: of the police, of her involvement with Gogolin, of the trouble that Yeshua was sure to cause in her family, in her town. Neither he nor Ginzburg showed any outward signs of being Jewish. Both had on the rough blouses of farmers and were without beards, pink-faced, like sheared lambs to her critical eye. Yeshua sported a long, stringy moustache that reminded her of the tail of an ass. Ginzburg held the reins comfortably in his lap, his hands clean and trim. He was a pale-eyed, nimble-looking man.

"I'm very pleased to meet you, rebbetzin," he said, bowing his head.

She would not speak until she had composed herself on the wagon box, and then only to her son. "So. Where have you been for three months?"

Yeshua laughed coarsely, then fell over when Ginzburg snapped the reins and the wagon lurched forward. "I've been in the lion's den, mother," he said, gripping the side of the cart to steady himself.

"Dressed as you are," she huffed, "the Almighty himself would not recognize you to stretch forth his hand."

Yeshua laughed again to make light of her disapproval. "The Almighty has had many months in which to learn to recognize me without a yarmulke or a beard, momma. He could have asked the police captain of Kiev!"

"Hush now!" she said.

Ginzburg snickered and chucked the reins to quicken the horse's gait. They were all silent, listening to the creaking wagon wheels until Raisl again found her voice.

"You think there's no one to stalk you in Mogilev-Podolsk? You think there's no trouble for you here?"

"There are lions and lions' dens all around," Yeshua replied, staring moodily to the south. "But we are here to lay traps for them."

Minutes later they were standing before the door of their house while Dovid Ginzburg gave a feed bag to the horse and climbed back onto the wagon box to read a newspaper. Both Yeshua and Raisl were bewildered by the unpleasantness of this first encounter after three months of separation, and yet were desolate for kind thoughts. Three months of political life in the great city of Kiev as a cadre in the Socialist Revolutionary Party had so broadened Yeshua's experience as to distance him three years' worth from his Jewish hometown life, from the drudgery of Mordecai Mendel's factory and the tensions and squabbles within his family. He had found a loved one, a revolutionary woman of noble birth; he had written pamphlets, spoken to a strike meeting, shaken the callused hands of peasants, and sat down to their dinner tables. He had fashioned a disguise for himself and evaded police spies; he had lost a set of friends to the hinterlands of Siberia and even learned to shoot firearms. The walls of Kiev, he liked to think, were reverberating from the recitation of such lessons.

But now Yeshua realized that Mogilev-Podolsk and the other towns of the southern Ukraine and Bessarabian provinces had been shaken even more, to the foundations, by the tremors from Kishinev. Searching for sincere words that might fetch a welcoming light from Raisl's eyes, he felt his arrogance begin to crack. Shame seeped out from him: a sense of awkwardness in his peasant garb, of vulnerability in his barefacedness, and an intense desire to feel unharried, at ease with his kin as on a *shabbas* afternoon.

But these regrets passed without expression, displaced by tougher thoughts of his mission. There was a small printing press, covered by blankets, in the back of Ginzburg's wagon. They had come to store it in the cool cellar of the house, from there to produce pamphlets urging strikes against the owners of the town's stinking factories, attacking police repression, encouraging literacy campaigns and support for the Socialist Revolutionary party. Yet how could he even broach the subject when Raisl had refused him and his comrade her most basic hospitality? The opportunity oddly emerged as their hostility reached its peak, as Raisl roused herself into accusation and told him with withering bitterness of the confiscation of her letters by the police and her heart-stopping encounter with Gogolin. "You! All our nation suffers for your grand deeds! You're not even a Jew anymore, Yeshua! I should sit *shivah* for you before you get us all killed!"

Yeshua gawked at her, touched to the quick by her trauma and courage. "What are you staring at?" she snapped. "You with the face of a cossack!"

"Momma, did you really bribe the postmaster?"

"I'm not ashamed of it! No one will make me feel ashamed! Nothing will take from me the little bit of a daughter that I have left!"

"Ashamed? Ashamed!" He stamped his foot and whirled around as if to shout to Ginzburg this revelation. "Momma, can you hear me under that wig of yours? I love you so, so dearly!" He spoke breathlessly, hands cupped at his heart. "I had a girlfriend in Kiev, a woman of similar thought to me, and doing the same work—oh, magnificently well! She's not Jewish, momma, not a Jew, but wise, so wise, like Deborah, like all the Judges. Once she said to me—are you listening, momma? She said that the seasons have not changed until the women of Russia take off their shawls. Well, here! Today is the first day of this new season!"

Raisl waved her palms earthward and spat. "Phooey. Today is a weekday like any other on earth. And you, you are the *domovik* of our house. Go away, *goyishe* spirit, go haunt the *goyim*."

Yeshua sidestepped the abuse and launched another evangelical barrage, telling her outright about the printing press. "Let me bring it into the cellar, momma. Turn your back and we'll bury it beneath the logs until we need it. It's a source of nourishment just as surely as any cabbage you keep down there. Momma!" he pleaded as she leaned back against her door. "You have already dropped the shawl from your shoulders with the postmaster! Now put your shoulder to work with us. Here you are, deprived of speaking with Leah, deprived of your happiness, and by whom? The government! So would you deprive me now of speaking out against that government? Will you deprive me of my voice, of speaking to the masses of this countryside? Momma, this is a safe house, this is the rabbi's house, it's the perfect place for us."

Raisl's weariness seemed insurmountable. "Yeshua, you're like a hammer beating against my head. I can't take it. Go—stop beating your mother's brains. Just go."

All at once the bloated clouds lost patience with them and released a torrent. Dovid Ginzburg hopped down hastily from the wagon and raced toward the house, holding his newspaper like a wedding canopy above his head.

"Even the Almighty would wash you out of our lives," Raisl said, opening the door.

The synagogue customarily functioned as the house of prayer, study, and assembly; but during the two months since Passover and the Kishinev pogrom, the latter function had swollen monstrously, to the point where Rov Kharlofsky often desired to instruct the *shammes* to lock the doors after the afternoon prayers, when scores of pious men would linger to discuss current events. Their topics were always the same: the rescinding of the government license for the local Yiddish newspaper, which, despite censorship, had been doggedly reporting on the international outcry against the Kishinev massacre; the appearance in the Ukrainian newspaper of rabidly anti-Semitic articles penned by a local priest, Father Krushkin; and some minor looting by a gang of rowdies in the marketplace during the Easter holidays. The prospect that Kishinev's "number one export," as one joker expressed it, might soon flood the marketplace of Mogilev-Podolsk had carved new lines of worry into every brow.

The incessant debate was upsetting the social hierarchy of the synagogue itself. Too much was happening with too little understanding, theories abounding, built flimsily upon secondhand notions of Zionism and socialism, superstition and fear. The workingmen and poor at the back of the synagogue, putting in afternoon appearances at great expense to their livelihoods, were urging self-defense against would-be rioters; the rich reactionaries like Mordecai Mendel were spouting the government's propaganda against revolutionaries and urging increased cooperation with the police; the learned ones, the *sheyne yidn,* would decry the impudence of their lessers and urge the study of the holy books as their only sure defense. Even the women, segregated in the balcony behind walls with narrow windows, were banging the glass for attention and filling the shul to the rafters with their shouts.

A learned mind seemed less esteemed than a healthy pair of lungs. Increasingly Rov Kharlofsky felt himself, his family, his past judgments, even his piety, to be under intense scrutiny. Of course, no Jew would have been shameless enough to personally and publicly criticize the *rov;* but behind the veil of intellectual debate, in which no man, regardless of social status, was immune from criticism or barred from making it, the personal references were barely concealed. Just this afternoon, the face of Reb Menke Leibowitz, owner of the town's beet-sugar mill, had turned nearly as red as his vegetables as he hollered at Laib: "The *goyim* are only the agents of the Lord, rabbi! What good will it do for us to stand here lecturing about how to deal with them? The way of God has been revealed to us, long ago and through terrible signs." Reb Menke pulled his prayer shawl more tightly around his narrow shoulders. " 'I will turn against you'—this is what God said to us—'and you shall be defeated by your enemies. Your foes shall have the mastery over you, and you shall take flight when there is no one pursuing you.' Is this not prophecy? Is

this not what happens when we fail to obey the Almighty's Commandments and keep them foremost in our thoughts? But look,
now, at our young men—those who renounce the ways of Torah
—how they spit in the eye of the Almighty! It is from these few
that the evil roots!"

Mordecai Mendel chimed in from his wealthy friend's side:
"They are not Jews! They are anarchists, bundists, *shabbas
goyim,* all manner of atheist and criminal—but not Jews!" His
bulging eyes scanned the impassioned faces of the *sheyne yidn*
along the eastern wall and came to rest upon the *rov* himself, in
the spot of highest honor alongside the Holy Ark. "Even if it
means excommunicating our own sons from the community, we
must do our duty!" Mendel cried. "No man can live outside
God's law and call himself a son of Israel!"

His audacity choked off all other voices. Laib sat immobilized
and mournful like a tree stripped of its bark.

From the crowd of late-arriving workmen at the back of the
synagogue came forward Pesach Dropsky, called "Pesach the
Lip," a young cousin to Moishe the butcher known for his wit
and harmonica-playing. "Where are these nightmarish creatures,"
he asked, "that Reb Mordecai describes so well—as if he were
personally acquainted! I hear a lot about them, sure, the revolutionaries who are ruining everything—but only in the newspapers."

"Not only in newspapers," Reb Mordecai shouted back. "Why
else do we Jews suffer so? These are the troublemakers, these
ones!"

Pesach bowed in mock contrition. "Not only in newspapers, of
course not. I'm sure that your spies tell many stories to earn their
blood money. But I have received not so much as a leaflet in this
town. Believe me, I look for them! So I wonder, perhaps Reb
Mordecai believes in phantoms? Perhaps his mind is so small, like
a little Jew in a little *shtetl* who walks around with his head bowed
to avert the evil eye? Yes, bow your head, Reb Mordecai!"

Pesach about-faced to address his peers, some still in aprons
and occupational outfits. "Yet I see these parvenu pigs among
us—oh, so very visible in their fine new clothes! These men who
have forgotten the meaning of charity ever since they stopped
needing it. Those who call us animals and pray for the day that
their own hands will shed their calluses. I see these new little
bosses"—he spun back around to view his opponents—"and I

can hardly consider them human beings, let alone Jews! Though they wear their caftans to the ground and sway while they pray like a Hasid with a fever, they are merely beards without the Jew!"

The men behind Pesach the Lip laughed and exchanged insults with their bosses. Laib felt himself in a storm, struggling to get his footing amid fierce winds that wore the synagogue's walls from without and garbled words from within. He ordered the *shammes* to pound a bench for attention, but already the synagogue sounded like a lumber camp, with a dozen benches and prayer-book racks being pounded at once. Finally the rabbi raised his arms and called out in an overpowering voice. "Whose voices are these that I hear? Each Jew excommunicates the other! Are there dybbuks among us, to make such a ghastly holler? Silence! Silence! Do you think the Almighty is hard-of-hearing?"

How childlike they seemed, button-to-button in belligerence at one moment, sheepishly attentive at the next. "The spirits of *pogromchiki* have infested our shul," Laib blared over their heads. "The spirits of atheists, of evildoers, of plain fools—they have all taken seats among us. But how is it that those who would despise and destroy our synagogue have taken control? What earthly force in all of Russia has succeeded at making our holy temple into a marketplace? . . . Pesach Dropsky! Are we going to go on strike right now, here in the house of God?"

Dropsky managed a conciliatory smile. "Not until after *shabbas*, rabbi."

The boldest of his compatriots snickered, but Rov Kharlofsky patiently twirled the tip of his beard until they were embarrassed into silence.

"And you, Reb Mordecai? Shall we invite the *goyim* into our shul to beat some humility into this *luftmensch*—and anyone else you don't like?"

Mordecai Mendel meekly bowed his head. He was easily humbled, having earned so much disapproval for his prior arrogance. "Heaven forbid, Rov Kharlofsky," he stammered. "The Lord shall provide a just punishment."

"The Lord does not need your confidence, Reb Mordecai," Laib replied.

Many in the congregation murmured their appreciation of his words. Then an old man cried out, "A prayer, rabbi! Lead us in a prayer!"

Rov Kharlofsky conferred first with the synagogue's cantor, Benjamin ben-Aviv, seated alongside his pulpit near the ark. "We will give a rest to Reb Benjamin's voice so it will be fit for evening prayer, when God expects a real concert, hmm? But before we begin, let me give warning: to pray halfheartedly, with our thoughts inside your bellies and pockets, is a great sin. It was Rabbi Elazar, in a time of major conflict prior to the revolt of Bar Kochba against the Roman oppressors, who said, as it is written: 'Where there is no Torah, there is no proper conduct; where there is no proper conduct, there is no Torah. Where there is no wisdom, there is no reverence,' he said; 'where there is no reverence there is no wisdom. Where there is no knowledge,' he said, 'there is no understanding; where there is no understanding, there is no knowledge.' Ahh, and 'Where there is no bread, there is no Torah,' said Rabbi Elazar, and 'where there is no Torah, there is no bread.' . . . Perhaps now we can pray with purer hearts and quieter voices, hmm?"

Their prayer shawls went up like desert tents over their heads as Rov Kharlofsky began to improvise a service. "Hear, O Israel, the Lord is our God, the Lord is One. . . . How good, how delightful it is for all to live together like brothers: fine as oil on the head, running down the beard, running down Aaron's beard to the collar of his robes; copious as a Hermon dew falling on the heights of Zion, where Yahweh confers his blessing, everlasting life. . . ."

He read with great affirmative feeling to evoke the elemental force of faith, which would erase their names and swallow their squabbles with humbling power, as the whale had swallowed Jonah in the ancient days. Laib felt vindicated as the synagogue buzzed with high, unified emotion, scoured of pride and full of an unfathomable holiness. He read his final selection with utter conviction: "The enemy may sharpen his sword, he may bend his bow and take aim, but the weapons he prepares will kill himself and his arrows turn into firebrands. Look at him, pregnant with wickedness, conceiving Spite, he gives birth to Mishap. He dug a pit, hollowed it out, only to fall into his own trap! His spite recoils on his own head, his brutality falls back on his own skull. I give thanks to Yahweh for his righteousness. I sing praise to the name of the Most High."

All but Laib's bitterest opponents seemed placated as the *shammes* again pounded a bench for attention.

"I have made a decision regarding the present situation," Laib announced. "We can discuss it after our holy services on the sabbath morning, when all Jews worthy of the name will be here. Until then, it is only my opinion."

There was no reason to fear a pogrom in Mogilev-Podolsk, he said. The Passover season was past, and there had been no blood libel against the Jews. "They have not even claimed that a chicken, let alone a gentile boy, was stolen during our matzoh-baking," he noted. "They admit that we baked only with flour and water. And their own Easter holiday has passed without incident—"

"They stole five skeins of wool from my stall!" cried one congregationist.

"They knocked off my hat!" yelled another.

"Easter Sunday was a windy day," Laib replied. "God will forgive you the loss of your hat. The point is that nobody has lost his head!" He held up his hand to bar further interruption. "We also saw a good harvest in our region—there is not so much hunger, our barons have made plenty from their farms. . . ." Now he had to carefully gauge his words: "We've seen no significant amount of propaganda or antigovernment activity for which our community might be punished." In spite of himself, he was addressing Reb Mordecai directly. The factory boss looked smug, satisfied that his spies and propaganda campaigns were responsible for the political calm.

Rov Kharlofsky hurried to his conclusions. He suggested that a committee of citizens be formed, first to go to Rabbi Mandel-stam's congregation and all others, perhaps even in the outlying villages, to discuss matters of mutual welfare. "Then," he said, "all together, we will fix things with our neighbors and assure peace in Mogilev-Podolsk."

To "fix things" meant bribery and possible humiliations and injury at the hands of extortionist officials. Such a citizens' committee would deserve the thanks and adoration of all the community. During the week, a collection would have to be taken up for their mission, and those who gave most generously or sacrificially would be entitled to stand in the place of honor next to the holy scrolls during the Torah reading on the upcoming *shabbas*. But Laib did not choose to wait until Saturday to name his candidates.

Two were foregone conclusions: the German-born doctor,

Gideon Blum, whose medical expertise made him a privileged person in both the Jewish and gentile communities; and Yankel Kaminsky, head of the Little Dove Burial Society, the town's largest. Praises for their good names and past services to the community circulated throughout the congregation: "Dr. Blum took care of the wife of the governor of Podolia! He's got connections everywhere." "Reb Yankel knows how much everyone in town is worth. He hasn't got a pot himself, but when Reb Yankel makes the collection, no one has empty pockets."

Above the noise, Rov Kharlofsky was calling out Mordecai Mendel's name.

"He'll need no introduction to the police!" shouted one of Pesach the Lip's crowd.

"He is *my* nomination," Laib retorted. "If you would prefer another, make your case."

The shul was silent. Laib scanned faces, then looked to the doors to see if any were leaving in protest. "I see," he concluded. "Then I hope our unity will be reflected in the collection Reb Yankel will be taking up all through the week. But let there be no gossip about this work," Laib warned, "so that the *goyim* will not think that the Jews are hatching some kind of plot against them, hmm?"

He nodded to the *shammes*, who slapped his palm to a table, signaling the resumption of prayers.

Chapter Four

While everyone in town raced to complete sabbath preparations before the sunset, Laib worked in the synagogue's study room, collecting materials for the petitioning committee to present, along with their bribes, to the governor of Podolia. These included statistics derived from the government's own census of 1897, which starkly revealed the pauperism of Russian Jewry. "Your Excellency will see," the rabbi wrote in his letter of introduction, "that the violence perpetrated against the Jewish people, at present and during the previous outbursts, 1881–83, cannot correctly be attributed to any form of exploitation of gentile by Jew or incitement by our Jewish community. These upstanding representatives of our community who stand before you today are therefore requesting that Your Excellency provide us with proper protection against unwarranted violence and, if it please Your Excellency, to come out with a statement that might be favorable to the Jewish people. . . ."

Across the Dniester River in Otek, Yeshua Kharlofsky was also writing, at the table of Maxim Scharanoff, one of the few peasants who had belonged to Yeshua's fledgling underground study circle during his winters of bookkeeping for Mordecai Mendel. Yeshua's project was a series of pamphlets, the first of which would explain the initial action of the Socialist Revolutionary party in Mogilev-Podolsk. "Brothers and sisters, comrades all! The Podolia section of the Socialist Revolutionary party, an organization of militant workers and peasants, has today expropriated the funds of a certain petty capitalist who is notorious as an exploiter of the local populace. Do not allow the government propagandists to portray

our action as criminality! Ours is an act of revolution, meant to
further our work on behalf of the peasantry and working people
of the province. . . ."

Father and son knew nothing of each other's work, Yeshua
being as ignorant as any peasant of the goings-on in the shul,
while Raisl had told her husband nothing of their son's whereabouts, nor about the printing press that was now buried in their
cellar. Yet, like sleepers confined to a narrow bed, they barged
into one another's dreams, interfered with one another's rest,
while the sabbath night lengthened, deepened. . . .

Seven candles were burning atop the sabbath tablecloth, and
Raisl's eyes were still wet from the passion of her prayers, when
Laib, Herschel, and their unlikely dinner guest, Pesach the Lip,
arrived following the brief synagogue service that welcomed the
"Sabbath Bride" into their homes and hearts. The greeting
Goot shabbas was exchanged all around, and Laib proceeded to
salute the sabbath angels, praise his virtuous, competent wife, and
consecrate this day of rest, each with a traditional prayer. Only
then did he introduce his guest to his daughters.

"I remember his music!" Buzie cried. "Never mind his name!"

"Buzie!" Ruchel scolded her despite Pesach's good-natured
laughter. "You should only have a trapdoor for a mouth, so I
could lock it."

"And you," Buzie retorted, "can wear a harmonica around
your neck if you want *him* for a husband!" But a sharp glance
from her mother hushed her. Ruchel's wish to gain a husband
before her sixteenth birthday was to be respected, not belittled
by one who could not yet understand.

Laib was profuse with praise for Raisl's sumptuous table
setting, but took note only to himself of the candles—one for
each family member, yes, one for Yeshua. Well—what has been
preserved for five thousand years, he thought, is not so easily
overthrown. As it is written: Do not judge alone, for none may
judge alone except One. He glanced kindly at Pesach, whom he
was eager to question, to learn something more of this younger
generation of Jews. Pesach, in turn, was anticipating exactly that
discussion; why else would an untutored, undistinguished rascal
like him be honored as the rabbi's guest?

They had to wait for the conclusions of the rituals that opened
the meal. Finally, as Raisl served the spiced-fish appetizer, Laib
spoke. "You know, Pesach, I have not haunted yeshivas my

whole life. My learning, one might say, has been broader than
that of many others of my calling. I have lived in both tiny villages
and great cities. I have believed and disbelieved much of the
foolishness and the wisdom of the Jewish folk."

Dropsky nodded, listening intently, not daring to touch his
food.

"I have lived through times of great persecution," Laib continued. "When has it been otherwise for Jews? And I have seen
the false prophets that accompany every turn of fortune. I have
seen the world for all its fickleness, and I have tried to perceive
and honor the workings of God in all acts, great and small.
Throughout, Pesach, throughout all that I describe to you, the
wisdom of our Torah has shone through as my only reliable guide.
And so it has been for our people, the same as for me. . . . So now
I ask you, Pesach Dropsky—because you are young and well
spoken, and yet pious, perhaps you know. What is so different
today from yesterday, in respect to our share of sorrows in the
world, that has driven my—our—youth to seek answers apart
from the eternal wisdom?"

Rov Kharlofsky sat back with a great sigh to hear Dropsky's
answer, but the rest at the table were tense in their seats. Herschel
felt guilty about his own wanderlust, as he inferred a personal
reprobation in his father's words. Buzie wanted less conversation
and more eating, so that the after-dinner songs, the *z'mires*, would
sooner be sung. Raisl wanted more attention paid to her carefully prepared dishes, to gain the familiar praise that might offset
the nagging worry about keeping secrets. Ruchel was nervous on
behalf of Pesach, who looked as though he had swallowed his
tongue. . . .

Yeshua was similarly in a state of upset as he and Dovid Ginzburg, with potato sacks slung across their shoulders to enhance
their peasant costumes, walked a muddy road toward the Otek
marketplace. Desperately needing relief from the confines of
Scharanoff's hut, where they had been holed up for days with
their plans and pamphlets, they had chosen for their outing the
Jewish center of town, where their unfamiliar faces might neither
be noticed or challenged, and where the *shabbas* peace would be
the principal preoccupation. But the fresh air had rendered
Yeshua's week-long moodiness combustible, and the stillness of this

evening—in the abandoned marketplace, in the slow-fading pink sky with its sprinkling of stars and purple cirri—seemed at the moment more important than any of Ginzburg's words.

"You're sure this Mendel character leaves his safe full until Monday?"

"Even with a bookkeeper," Yeshua replied, "Reb Mordecai would never get to the bank before sundown. He's too busy driving his workers."

They were passing the synagogue, a weather-worn box shut down for the night. Yeshua pressed his fingers to his temples; a local Jew would have viewed him as a superstitious peasant shielding his eyes from a "profane" sight. But he was merely trying to relieve the pressure in his skull, to steel himself to maintain the faith and silence that their conspiracy required.

"But why must it be a Jew?" he said at last, quitting their steps and waving his hands about. "Why a Jew? The country-side must be crawling with aristocrats!"

"Hush!"

"Ach, Dovid." Yeshua broke into Yiddish. "There's not a soul out of doors and not a *goy* in this part of town!"

"A *goy!*"

"We wanted some air, but I can't even open my mouth? Talk to me, will you please?"

"First tell me who I'm talking to," Ginzburg replied. "Are you a friend of the peasants or a friend of some Jewish money-grubber?"

"I am a friend to all good people," Yeshua said.

"But for a revolutionary, my dear Kharlofsky, some friends are more important—more strategic—than others. The Jews are not an important group, they are peripheral to Russia's economy and political life. . . ."

Yeshua nodded impatiently at this familiar dogma. "We say 'peripheral,' the czarists say 'parasitic.' And if we succeed to-morrow, Mendel and the rest of the Jews will be vilified—"

"Speak in Ukrainian!" Ginzburg hissed, then waved for them to walk on.

"—as proper targets for the wrath of the peasants." Yeshua followed after his partner, shuffling his feet like a man under a weight. "And if we steal from the nobility instead, and *we* are found out to be Jews, my father is right—there would be a pogrom before they could even hang us!" The thought staggered him. "My God, Dovid! How is what we do to Mendel any different from what a *pogromchik* would do? We are repeating all of history's rotten mistakes!" He stood still again, trembling like a leaf. "Ginzburg, I need a drink. My mind is getting away from me."

Ginzburg was near despair at witnessing this dissolution of his friend's confidence. He clasped Yeshua's shoulder. "There is no inn that would be safe. It's not like Kiev, where you can just blend in with the crowd. Come, let's head back to Scharanoff's hut. Maybe he can help you to—think better."

"I've never thought of Maxim Scharanoff as such a masterful teacher," Yeshua mused.

"Maxim is an angry man, very sure of himself—just as you were in Kiev. I remember, you were utterly fearless. Yeshua— you were a great Russian bear. And now, in this worthless *shtetl* . . ."

"I'm a man again," Yeshua said.

Buzie did not like the "taste of heaven" that *shabbas* was supposed to represent. To her, heaven would not be a day of rest, but of play, free and unfettered by spotless clothes or any of her increasing household responsibilities. Heaven would be a hard, sweet apple filched from someone's backyard, not the sloppy *tsholent* that was served on Saturday. Heaven would be reading from Katrinka Potrovich's ghost book—but with color pictures!— in some dark corner of the church, where every scurrying mouse thrilled her, not a stupid rule against even carrying a book outside the house!

"Phooey," Buzie would brag to her friends as they helped their mothers in the marketplace and met to commiserate about the indignities of *shabbas* preparations. "If a taste of heaven means a taste of *tsholent*, I'll starve. And if clean hair means smelling like kerosene, I'll hide with the pigs on the nearest farm!"

Once upon a time, at least, the sabbath had meant her father's special affection and her mother's relaxed attention. Since her ninth birthday, however, Buzie had been denied her father's lap (in anticipation of her menstruation, of which she was almost entirely ignorant), while her mother had become more a taskmaster than a comforter. "Pharaoh and pharaoh's wife," she called them, each time she received a new assignment. Mostly the sabbath had become a day on which to hide: from the mandatory scrubbing and kerosene shampoo, from the boredom and the *tsholent;* in the cellar, in the yard behind the well, or even in the woods somewhere, pretending to be an animal in its burrow or a highway robber in a hideout, reaffirming her independence during each adventure and each aftermath of scoldings and threats.

Shabbas morning, especially, brought complete freedom to Buzie as her entire family, including her eligible, aristocratic sister, walked to synagogue following the fruitless search for her. This morning Buzie even managed to witness their departure from atop the house's tattered roof, a summit that she had been trying to attain throughout the spring. Bye-bye, Buzie thought triumphantly, and had to restrain herself from hurling a torn shingle at Ruchel in her new, puffy-sleeved blue dress. Say hello to the rabbi, poppa, say hello to yourself, and tell yourself that I couldn't come because I'm sick—sick of shul!

She rolled onto her back and let her tongue hang from her mouth, then considered which of her friends she cared to visit. Most of them would be home, as well, caring for baby brothers and sisters. Buzie took her time with her deliberations, considering both the personal qualities and the possessions of each, meanwhile enjoying her sunbath. Maybe Tsil? Ooh, yes—they could go play in Shmulke's workshop with all the different shoes, making a masquerade or pretending each pair were animals, on Noah's ark. . . .

"Knock, Maxim. Just knock on the door. If anybody answers, ask directions to Father Potrovich's house. I'm sure they're not home. . . ."

The voice startled Buzie, drawing her to the roof's edge. Two peasants had drawn up to the gate in a wagon, and one was walking toward the door. He knocked, waited, and rapped again, then signaled to the other, who, Buzie worried, had nearly spotted her as he glanced casually at the clouds. But why were they going *in* when nobody was home? Unless they were robbers! Or worse . . .

She held still, flat against the roof, silent even as a hot tin patch blistered her leg through her thin dress. Please, oh, please, she prayed, someone see their horse! What's a horse doing outside the *rov*'s home on *shabbas?* No riding on *shabbas!* She pressed her ear to the shingles and listened for whole minutes, hearing nothing. They must be in the cellar . . . they're waiting to kill everyone . . . but if I wait here to warn momma and everybody, then they'll kill me! Please, God, help me, she begged as she crept across the roof, resolved to climb down and run for help. Please, help me and I'll worship you forever, I'll *live* in the shul! Please, make the logs in the cellar cave in on their heads!

Her ladder was an ivy vine and two warped wallboards with edges that obtruded from the side of the house. Buzie held her breath and dropped lightly to the ground, then froze where she landed as the horse out front snorted. . . . Not out front, no! The giant animal came lumbering toward her, toward the back of the house, driven by one of the peasants. Buzie slipped inside the house through the side door, like a mouse dashing blindly for its hole, and crouched beneath the heavy linen Sabbath tablecloth.

She heard the wagon wheeling past the door, scraping the wallboards, and again their voices, their terrible existence confirmed as the horse-driver returned through the side door and called down to the cellar: "Is it working all right?" The voice held no threat, no suspicion of her presence in the room, and yet seemed familiar, calling out to Buzie's memory and multiplying her thoughts like some vaguely known melody.

"It's fine. Come on down." This, a low murmur from the cellar, as though the floor itself were speaking.

Next came a crisp, metallic sound: *clackety-clackety-clackety,* a barrel rolling across their muted voices. The mystery became keener for Buzie than the threat—what machinery was there in the cellar?

The noise continued long enough to dull her sense of time, then suddenly stopped. Logs were moved, the voices seeped through the floor again. Buzie nudged herself: Go now, run now! Then feet trudged upstairs and entered the room, and her terror rushed back into her chest like a swift wind.

"Why start a fire?" said the familiar voice, the one to which she hearkened with her head cocked. "Ginzburg and I are trained at this. We'll never be caught. It's a simple heist. Why must we start a panic in town?"

"Don't *you* panic, comrade!" said the other in an irritable, husky tone. "We need the diversion, to play it safe."

"*Why* do we need it? Who says we need it? Isn't it enough to

have to steal for our cause? Who is so evil that he deserves the
torch as well?"

"Ha! I could name dozens, not least of them Mordecai
Mendel! Not only will the whole town be preoccupied, but if we
can just get some of our leaflets circulating . . ."

"Don't be crazy! Who's going to do that under the nose of
the police, my little sister?"

Buzie's ears now lifted to Yeshua's voice like those of a dog
that has already caught the scent, yet she remained hidden,
frightened by the intensity, the insanity, of their argument.
"Never mind, Kharlofsky," growled the other voice. "Ginzburg
said you were getting cold feet! Let's get out of here before
your poppa comes and pulls your ear."

"Why don't you shut up, Maxim?"

Lugging something between them, they departed through the
side door. Yeshua walked the horse and wagon out front again,
Buzie tracking the sound. She scooted to her parents' bedroom to
glimpse through the window the strange, shaven face of her
brother just as he finished piling papers under the seat.

Buzie sat at the window for a full hour after they rode away,
the same cautious instincts that had dissuaded her from greeting
Yeshua now debating with her natural desire to tell the whole
tale to her parents upon their return. Such a disclosure would be
difficult enough: to confess, first, about her precious new hiding
place atop the roof, and leave herself a target for her father's
rage, which would be heightened, no doubt, by the news of
Yeshua's activities. . . . But to maintain the secret in silence was
to drown in it! They were going to burn Mordecai Mendel! The
other man had plainly said it. And then they were going to steal
something, and then a crowd would gather? (She would not
give out any leaflets—oh, no, not even for a hundred-ruble
note!)

If only she could figure it all out before her family returned!
Maybe she was all wrong, maybe she'd heard it all backward.
But how could she wait and say nothing and let Reb Mordecai
burn, when only half an hour earlier she'd been calling on God's
name for help? But why would Yeshua burn Reb Mordecai?
Aiee, if only she could figure it out!

Buzie paced through the kitchen to the cellar staircase, promising her temporarily reinstated God that she would never again
stay home alone on *shabbas*. The log pile at the bottom of the

stairs seemed like a mountain, and the cellar was too dark for peeking through whatever niches her fingers could find. Well, she would fetch a candle, then. Up the stairs—

"*Gonifte!* Where were you all morning?" The voice sprang at her from the stillness of the house. Buzie screamed and fell backward from the landing.

Her parents immediately confined her to bed and so completely embarrassed her with undeserved attention that her silence was sealed. Herschel came to make jokes, Ruchel to gossip, but Buzie lay without stirring, a disconsolate invalid, and when her mother inquired about her morning activities—had she eaten something to make her so sick?—she aborted the conversation by crying, then hated herself and wept more from shame.

But Raisl had already been to the cellar, following her daughter's frightful fall. She had seen the logs subtly rearranged and the oil spots in the dirt, and though she could only speculate as to what had really happened, she knew that the blame for Buzie's condition lay with her, for her dire sin of deceit. Enough: When the sabbath ended, she would tell Laib, she would tell him everything and implore him to break Yeshua's machine right over her head! Until then, she could only pray to God to act mercifully toward her innocent daughter.

"When I carried you in my belly, my Buzeleh, a bird's nest once fell from a tree right to my feet. There was a cracked egg in it, and I thought, *Oi,* now I will lose my baby! Ahh, but here you are, my Buzeleh, my sweet, even with your slightly cracked head . . . and who knows but that the spirit of a little bird is in your soul?"

Raisl sat alongside Buzie's bed all afternoon as her husband napped. She asked Ruchel to serve the afternoon meal while she fed Buzie hot tea with honey. Even as the drop-ins arrived to spin away the leisurely hours with the *rov* and his family, Raisl remained closeted with Buzie, admitting no one to the room for more than a peek and a word of consolation. Tacitly they shared their secret, Buzie reverting to girlish dependence, Raisl to her superstitions, until the daughter was asleep and the mother was prostrate on the floor, praying.

* * *

The guests who had gathered in the rabbi's home to nibble sweets and talk of happy subjects were none other than the committeemen whom the synagogue had selected to make peace with the *goyim:* Gideon Blum, Yankel Kaminsky, and Mordecai Mendel, the latter two with wives who sat separately in the kitchen, waiting in vain for Raisl. The men scrupulously avoided all discussion of subjects belonging to the week, but managed through their chitchat to begin to test one another's knowledge and force of personality. When they reconvened in the evening, following services at the shul, each had on a more careworn expression. Very obviously their *shabbas* joys were over.

They had just sat down to examine Laib's draft letter of introduction and its accompanying documents when a nearing clatter of hooves and the alarmed whinnying of Reb Mordecai's harnessed mares raised them all from their chairs.

Isaac the water carrier burst through the door. "Krushkin's church is on fire! It's going to burn to the ground!"

Reb Mordecai sat back down, smiling. "The devil claims his own, eh?"

"The devil will be a Jew!" Rov Kharlofsky hollered. "And the fires of a pogrom will consume us all!"

"Oh, no!"

"We must save the church," Laib declared, "or at least show our faces trying! Herschel! Raisl!" While his family mobilized, he rushed to a glass-doored cabinet from which he fetched a massive ram's horn with a pearl mouthpiece. "Kaminsky, you can blow this? Good. You and Dr. Blum, you go with Isaac and blow the shofar. Raise such a ruckus that the entire city will hear!"

Raisl emerged from seclusion with Buzie on her hip. "We're coming, too." The girl stared relentlessly into Mordecai Mendel's pale face.

"For what do we need a sick child?" he complained. "What can she do, pee on a spark?"

"She'll carry buckets of water!" Raisl retorted. "Ohh, never mind, you fool! Laib, I fear this night. I will not leave her alone!"

"Stay home, then," Laib said. "If the woman's curse is upon you—"

"I'm speaking of the child's blood, not mine!" she screamed, and hurried out the door with Buzie in her arms.

"The weight of so many," Mendel complained. "My horses will drop dead!"

Laib was instructing Herschel. "Take Ruchel and go to Father Potrovich. Go with him to the fire. It's a good thing for a Jewish boy and a priest to be seen together. Hurry, my boy, before he's gone!"

Throughout the clamorous journey, while Mordecai Mendel whipped his horses and hollered news of the fire to people at their windows and gates, Buzie sat mutely in her mother's lap, switching her gaze from face to face. She saw Raisl's hand reaching for Laib's elbow to steady herself on the bouncing seat. She saw her father flatten his arm against his body to avoid the touch. "I am kosher, please," Raisl said. "Hold me, husband." Laib glanced self-consciously at Buzie as his arm encircled his wife's shoulders.

Buzie saw the tension in his mouth as he whispered to Raisl: "Why did Ruchel serve our meals today? Why did you hide yourself all day from our guests? Now you say you're kosher. What are you hiding?" His throat knotted with each question, his comforting arm stiffening into a vise.

Buzie saw her mother's lips twitching, saw the secret struggling to emerge.

Then the horses neighed and fretted. She saw Reb Mordecai jump down from his seat. She saw her father reaching toward her, lifting her from under her arms. She saw Reb Mordecai standing ready to receive her. His face, like the buildings all around, was bright orange. His eyes were melting marbles. Buzie shrieked, but no one heard her over the nasty crackle of the fire.

Chapter Five / 1906

"Do you know what it means, a provocateur? A scab? Always there are these worms that they eat away at the people's movement from the inside. I don't know what kind of men they are 'cause I was never fooled by one long enough to get friendly. But I would say you should watch out for the one that he has a single match and tells you he wants to boil a whole pot of water. Watch out for the fanatics, those that they show no fear. Fear means that you're a human being.

"So this is what Scharanoff turned out to be, a provocateur, a police agent. Can you imagine, burning down a church for the sake of a diversion? And not just any church, but the one belonging to the biggest anti-Semite in the province. Some diversion you'll get—a pogrom!

"My brother Yeshua must have figured it, 'cause he and his comrade did not return to Scharanoff's hut after they stole the money from Mordecai Mendel's factory. Instead, they hid in the woods, and, sure enough, during the next day there came a roundup. All of their associates in the movement got shipped off to Siberia. The entire organization got strangled in the crib. And then the newspaper starts printing articles how it was Jewish revolutionaries that burned the church. You see how it works? You can't imagine the ignorance and the anti-Semitism in Russia at this time—they really believed the Jews had horns on their heads. I guess we were lucky it was a Jewish capitalist and not a gentile they robbed. But Mordecai Mendel didn't make it any better, y'see, 'cause he said it was the payroll that got robbed, so his workers are going to have to suffer for it! What a conniver he was! But never mind, the committee that my father organized said it was a bad plan, it would make the peasants that they worked in his factory too angry, and finally he gave in.

"Really, with all this going on, it was a miracle that the pogrom waited three more years to happen. Very nice—they gave me a chance to finish school! Part of the reason was Father Potrovich; he was very brave and he came out against anti-Semitism every time he gave a sermon. Also, we gave a nice fat bribe to the governor of Podolia, and then we had a little bit of luck: Father Krushkin dropped dead from a brain tumor. It was the right way for him to go, he was a mad dog. He should've been wearing a collar and a muzzle instead of his cross.

"He wasn't the only one to die. Scharanoff got it, too, very quick. Ginzburg paid a visit to his good friend Maxim Scharanoff, slit his throat and stole his horse and rode with it, with the money, all the way to Kiev. Now, this man Ginzburg was a real Socialist Revolutionary, y'see. They were famous for assassinations and terrorism. In fact, they were the scariest group, so far as the rich were concerned, 'cause they were throwing bombs, real bombs! 'Armed propaganda,' they called it. More than fifteen hundred government officials got killed in 1905 alone, can you imagine? And a lot of these were claimed by the Socialist Revolutionaries. Maybe it didn't organize anybody, excepting the police themselves, but it got rid of some real no-goodniks, including the big fish. Von Plehve, f'rinstance. He was the minister of the interior and the one that figured how to make pogroms and repress the revolutionary movement during those years. The Socialist Revolutionaries finally got rid of him in a train station in 1905.

"And the one that planned Von Plehve's assassination was himself a police agent! Evno Azef. He was a founder of the Socialist Revolutionary party, he headed their assassination squads, and at the same time he worked for the government. So he would arrange to kill counterrevolutionaries and give out the revolutionaries while he drank the same cup of tea. It was crazy —no one ever really figured out which side he was on, though later the Socialist Revolutionaries put a price on his head. Never mind, he lived to a nice old age.

"So if you figure that one out, explain it to me please.

"Y'see, the Socialist Revolutionaries were only as violent as their times. There was lots of blood in 1905, but the revolutionary movement was not yet ready to lead it and guide it. It's like surgery: You got to know where to cut or you just carve up the patient and you don't get rid of the disease. Everywhere in Russia, y'see, everywhere there were strikes, in all the big cities. In Petrograd, two hundred thousand marched on the czar's Winter Palace to demand bread, and they got bullets. Five hundred were killed. So they called it 'Bloody Sunday.' Before Bloody Sunday, people still believed in the czar. In fact, when they made their march they sang, 'God save the czar!' They really thought he would give them justice. 'God save the czar' while the soldiers are aiming their rifles. They ask for justice, they get death, so many turned against him. The entire city went on strike. Sailors mutinied on the ships. It went on and on like a storm that doesn't want to stop.

"And where was Buzie Kharlofsky in the middle of all this history? It wasn't history, then—we didn't have the feeling of a person that watches, an observer, like you have today with television and everything else. We didn't have Walter Cronkite to tell us how the day went. Life was more personal. You knew less, but you felt more involved. The things that made you unhappy were, like, material things: the long hours in the factory, not enough food on your table, a cold winter with no shoes—it was a struggle just to survive. Today it's different. People get fed, maybe—I say maybe 'cause there's a lot of people still don't have what to eat in the United States, and those that they do have eats, they sort of waste away in their spirit, if you know what I mean. The youth, especially—they don't have important memories to keep them going, they have no place to fit, no community, no way to feel themselves as human beings.

"It's funny, in a sad kind of a way. I—the people of my generation—we don't really understand what's going on today. We don't understand the new evils, what Marx called the 'alienation,' that modern capitalism brings. We see the young people that they look like people but they act like animals, and we don't remember our own lives. The peasants in Russia, they were animals, y'see, only they were farm animals. The city animals are a little wilder. But we forget all this, and the modern world seems so different to us, and meanwhile our friends are dying, our community is shrinking. . . . And even the youth, when they develop their own culture to save some part of themselves from the emptiness of America, still we don't understand it, it's foreign to us, and again we're afraid. So we sometimes can't tell what is progressive, what is good, and what is phony. We become afraid of people, period. Miami Beach has whole apartment developments with frightened old people that they'd rather live in the ghetto again.

"And the youth, that they're really gonna have to change the world, they're without a history, and this is like losing your memory—it makes you helpless. People don't know history no more. Young people today are so ignorant of the things that my generation did, f'rinstance. And of course they don't care for old people—where in their lives is there any message that says old people are human beings and maybe you should spend some time with them?

"I don't know if there's anything that can be done about this. Maybe someday the old and the young will live together and work together. But like they say, youth is wasted on the young, and I would also say that wisdom is wasted on the old.

"Hey, you think if I carry on like this they'll make me a rabbi?

"Anyway, back to the story—even if you had to be there.

"What happened was, Yeshua also got arrested, but with Scharanoff dead, y'see, they had no strong evidence against him, so he got out of jail in a couple of months. Maybe there was some bribery, too, I don't know. But he came home, and my father accepted him. Yeshua couldn't stand all the violence of the Socialist Revolutionaries, y'see. And my father, at heart, was a progressive, even if he was a religious man. So he couldn't exile his son. Besides, everybody was so scared that there shouldn't be a pogrom, it became very important that the family should be close together.

"My father even let the printing press stay in our cellar. Remember, in his own way my father was an organizer, too, and a printing press is a printing press, especially when there's no Jewish newspaper no more. In fact, the first thing my father did with it, he printed copies of Leo Tolstoi's statement about the Kishinev pogrom. He translated it from Russian to Yiddish and gave it out in the shul. My father loved Tolstoi, y'see. He read all his books and even wrote a letter to him once, and he actually got a reply! Boy, did he hold on to that little note! Anyway, Tolstoi made a very good statement against the pogrom, against anti-Semitism, and he was Russia's most respected writer, so it was an important thing. Sure, printing it was illegal. Everything in Russia that was worthwhile was illegal! Even the liberals like my father had to break the law to get what they wanted.

"But the unity between Yeshua and my father was fragile. It's like trying to mix oil with vinegar. They taste good for a while, but after a little more time they separate. That's how it goes with liberals and radicals. Very soon Yeshua got involved with the Jewish Labor Bund—they believed in self-defense but not terrorism—and the fighting in my family started all over.

"I began to know my older brother and to feel a part of his cause. It was my rebellious spirit, that says I know what's best and nobody else. I found a partner in Yeshua, y'see. And I began to follow him and Herschel all over. They couldn't get rid of me. Let's say I would follow them to a meeting in the woods; so they would stop and send me home and even wait by a tree to see that I should get going. But as soon as I heard their footsteps on the twigs, I would follow them some more, until they were far in the woods and I would be scared to go home alone. Eventually they started to use me, y'see, to carry leaflets mostly. They knew I could be trusted, even though I was only a child. I knew about Yeshua's taking part in the robbery of Reb Mordecai's factory, f'rinstance, but I never told nobody. If I had been a blabbermouth, they could've really gotten the goods on him!

"Maybe I didn't really understand what I was doing, not completely, not like an adult understands. But children, they have a natural kind of a justice, don't you think? It disappears with the baby teeth, maybe. And with me, it stayed, even though my teeth are now floating in a glass by the side of the bed.

"So 1905 was the last time my family was really together, excepting for Leah in America, and with plenty of secrets and lies to help preserve the unity. And by the time the winter came, then I was twelve years, and the warmth was gone from my family completely. We became very brittle. And by the time of Passover, which is Easter, which is the season for pogroms, it all melted very quick and became mud."

❀

Like a frost in early spring, the cossacks appeared in Mogilev-Podolsk at the advent of the Passover festival. Forty strong, never alone or apart from their lean-bred Arabian horses, they were

uniformly tall, mustachioed, and outfitted in the sheepskin hel-
mets, black capes, enormous sabers, and knee-high boots that, to
a Jewish eye, looked like death's own apparel. Reports of their
whereabouts—on the roads, in the train depot, near the government buildings—preempted holiday reports of visits from relatives and other community events as the busy preparations for the
seder became a bitter charade.

In public, Rov Kharlofsky had no tolerance for local doomsay-
ers, arguing that he had learned to handle the ropes of local
government bureaucracy, and so his Committee for Jewish Protection had delivered peace to Mogilev-Podolsk, even during the
tragic winter past when the Black Hundreds, reactionaries who
used the dregs of the peasantry as terrorist troops, had conducted
scores of government-sanctioned pogroms throughout the
Ukraine. "We are holding together in peace. May God do so
well with my daughters' marriages!" Laib would joke to distract
worried congregationists with reminders of his good fortune: a
baby girl named Brokha, born to Leah in America, and a swelling belly for Ruchel, now living in Odessa with her new husband,
Feivl, Yankel Kaminsky's son.

The cossacks, Laib would argue, were in town only to guard
the transport of munitions through the train depots of Podolia.
But his actions belied his confidence: He cabled Ruchel in
Odessa, urging her not to visit for the holidays; he ordered
kheyder teachers to cancel classes a few days early so that the
evening traffic of Jewish children in the streets would be reduced;
he turned over the conduct of afternoon prayers to the cantor
for three consecutive days, using the time to meet with Father
Potrovich, seek appointments with government officials, and be
at home to receive the complaints of any peasants whose anger
against Jews he might deflect from a violent course.

The only one who came to visit after three days of such
vigilance was the *shabbas goy* Ivan Yussarov, who for years had
been visiting Jewish households to perform simple tasks that were
forbidden to Jews on their sabbath, in exchange for food, coins,
and small gifts. Ivan was a man of diminutive presence, soft-
stepping, round-shouldered, with a voice as flat as the ground.
But on this day his voice was quaking. "Rabbi, it's happening this
very second, the trouble is on its way."

"What trouble, Yussarov? Sit, have some tea."

Ivan paced over to the window facing the road. "I've got to smash a couple of windows, at least on this side of the house. Then the hooligans might pass you by."

"Ivan!"

"You'll see, rabbi, I won't take a thing from you. You could leave me here alone, I wouldn't take a thing. I know you're not a rich man."

Laib blinked at him like a dim-witted beast, then hung his head and moaned as Yussarov continued, with the rapidity of one who confesses a crime and disclaims guilt in the same breath: "It's the ones from Otek that cause the trouble. They come over the bridge and think they're on a holiday. And the cossacks are permitting it, the cossacks show them how!"

Laib's legs were dissolving. He lowered himself to a chair, covered his face in the sweaty darkness of his palms, and listened to the howling of his thoughts. He felt the impulse to attack this *shabbas goy*, to pummel his face and murder his message . . .

"But the church is the culprit, if you want to blame someone!" continued Ivan, snappy and agitated. "The priests are vicious with what they say about Jews—dear God, a man doesn't know what to believe! I haven't been able to set foot in my own church for weeks. They say I live with Jews, that I'm an accomplice to the killers of our Lord Jesus. I fear for my life!"

. . . and to take the fury to the street, to curse the mob to silence, block their rampage with a blinding display of power, yes! As God's own angels had done to the rioters in Sodom, yes, as it is written! "And they struck the men who were at the door of the house with blindness, from youngest to oldest, so that they wearied themselves to find the door. . . ." But Laib sat in a stupor, his ferocity a caged animal in the hold of his heart as it tore loose from its moorings and sank deep, deep into suffocating memories.

"My God, rabbi. There's no time to pray now! Lift your head, there's no time for anything, just get your family and leave! Right now, this second, they're coming across the bridge."

"Buzie!" Laib cried, jolted to his feet by Ivan's words. "She's washing clothes at the bridge. Oh, God help us! Raisl! Raisl!" She was in the backyard, scrubbing furniture with boiling water to purify the house for Passover. Laib lurched to the side door. "Raisl!"

Ivan peered out the window at the road. "We'll have to smash at least two windows."

Squatting in ankle-deep water at the sandy edges of the Dniester River, only feet from the enormous shadow of the Mogilev Bridge, Buzie and Tsil were rinsing their new Passover blouses in the prescribed fashion, three times, while enjoying the sun, the spiced air, and the adventurous feelings that the immense, smooth-flowing river evoked. Both girls were sopping wet from horseplay and in the full swing of their friendship as Buzie told hilarious stories about Nakhum the Sea Gull, Guardian of the Bridge, a six-foot four-inch *luftmensch* who lived in a mud-pack hovel on the Otek shore of the Dniester, ate what he fished, and earned his luxuries by scavenging wood and refuse from the river, which he sold to charitable people in town.

Nakhum was the son of a Jewish woman who had been raped so brutally by a cossack that she'd barely survived both the impregnation and eventual delivery of her son. Yet he had been born with a gentle soul, around which his mother, listless and lost to herself the ten years she lived following her ordeal, had spun a cocoon of ignorance and isolation. Following her death, however, Rabbi Mandelstam had sought Nakhum as a rightful member of the Jewish community, had trained him for bar mitzvah, and had obtained, in the bargain, a pious member of the congregation and a loyal, grateful godchild—however weird his life-style remained.

Children who came to bathe, fish, or otherwise enjoy the waters of the Dniester could expect a visit from the hulking man on any sunny day, and though Nakhum was hardly a story-teller—he was shy of speech, a stutterer—he was a first-rate listener who questioned the children on fantastic subjects and took them more seriously than did most other adults. Moreover, he was a prime target for jokes and yarns; his brief visit with Buzie and Tsil today had inspired a hundred such quips in Buzie's mind:

"P-p-p-Passover means I w-w-will have to clean my house."

"Maybe you'll get a flood first, to wash it out for you. Then you just have to sweep out the fish."

"M-m-maybe."

Now that he was out of earshot, watching them from the center of the bridge, leaning over the railing, Buzie let loose her wit. "He's only a little crazy—from the neck up. . . . You know, Tsil, Nakhum swims across the river three times a day, like a Jew prays. He just wants to make sure it's as wide as before so he won't have a flood. Except, he's so big that, when he dives in, he *makes* a flood! . . . Nakhum's married to a whale, you know. I mean it, Tsil, don't laugh. She's a regular *balebusteh*—she makes kosher seaweed from the Black Sea. . . . You know, I think Nakhum stutters even when he talks to himself. That way he thinks he's got company."

Tsil had her face buried in her skirt to hide her laughter from Nakhum, which only goaded Buzie to greater efforts at breaching her friend's self-control. "Watch, Tsil, I'll show you how Nakhum goes fishing." She fashioned her skirt into culottes, then waded a few feet into the river to just below her knees.

"Hey, be careful," Tsil shouted, alarmed by the unsteadiness of Buzie's footing in the swift currents.

"It's freezing!" Buzie shrieked. "Now watch!" She lowered her nose to within inches of the water, then bravely thrust her face in as if to catch fish with her mouth. Tsil cackled out loud, with only a self-conscious glance upward at the Sea Gull.

He was gone. Tsil craned her long neck to see beyond the railing of the bridge; then realized, as her attention fixed itself, that the entire archway was vibrating with sound as if a hundred hammers were striking it. Quickly she backed off into the safety of sunlight, upset by images of the entire bridge collapsing.

"Buzie, listen! Hey, leave some fish for Nakhum!" The girl had her face underwater again.

In a moment she came up sputtering for breath. The arches of her nearly numb feet ached from gripping the mossy rocks on the river bottom. Now even her audience had abandoned her, headed up the steep slope leading to the road and the bridge itself. "Yoo, Tsil! Where are you going?" The roar of the water swallowed Buzie's cry. Then she, too, noticed the ruckus, even above the rushing currents: men's voices swarming the air, horses whinnying and stomping across the bridge's planks. She saw a pack of men grappling furiously at the center, scratching each other's faces, punching and yanking—with big Nakhum at their center, pinned to the railing! Suddenly a man somersaulted over and fell, screaming, into the deepest part of the river.

Buzie clambered to the shore, scooped up her's and Tsil's holiday blouses, and remained in a crouch, deciding which way to run. "*Gott,* it's freezing," she groaned, hugging the blouses to her belly and squeezing water from the tips of her braids. C'mon, stupid Tsil, where was she? The scuffling overhead got worse, with two more figures hurtling into the Dniester. "Where are you, stupid-head? The whole world is in a brawl. . . ." Then she spotted the horsemen and was jolted by a shiver down her spine.

Cossacks. Her bedtime bogeymen. They were riding three across in the direction of Mogilev-Podolsk, their long capes flapping like loose shrouds. Buzie huddled down, gripping the grass at her feet. Water from her hair dripped into her ear, a single, burning drop.

> The good girl marries a yeshiva boy,
> The bad one marries a cossack.
> The good girl's belly swells with joy,
> The bad one breaks her back.

Another body plummeted from the bridge, struck the surface of the water, and was snapped short by a rope tied around the neck. Buzie recognized Nakhum and screamed without a voice. The river immediately swept him under the bridge, but the rope held and twisted him around and around like a propeller blade. Buzie looked away from the grotesque sight—but the horror was relentless. . . .

Tsil was running downhill toward her, screaming as if her hair were aflame. A lone cossack was dogging her left and right with his mount, hanging low off the saddle and swiping at her heels with his saber. Buzie clawed the earth and screeched repeatedly like a wounded bird until the cossack's blade bit flesh and Tsil thudded facefirst to the ground, her left foot sliced through from heel to toe.

Buzie's hysteria crashed with her and broke into a dozen desperate impulses. (I don't want to be cut, I don't want to be cut, oh God please God!) "Oh, God, oh, God! In the name of Jesus! In the name of Jesus!" She was crying out in Ukrainian and crossing herself vehemently as she had often seen Katrinka Potrovich do.

The woolly killer peered narrowly at her from atop his sidestepping mount. The animal stepped squarely on Tsil's back—

Buzie could hear her skinny body crack—and at once reared up and away, tossing its head, resisting the bit, fetching curses and blows from its master's spurs and sword handle.

"Aie, Mother Mary!" Buzie wailed, clinging to her charade for the clearheadedness and hope for survival that it fostered.

As the cossack sheathed his blade so as not to injure his horse while reining it in, Buzie scurried toward Tsil with her head ducked low and slid on her knees at her side.

"You must not play with Jew girls," said the killer, only yards away, in a voice of jagged metal. "Unless you would share a pit of a grave with that one."

The horse snorted. Everything seemed deathly still.

Buzie gingerly touched Tsil's arm and kept her eyes pinned to the ground, a dozen curses shoring up behind her teeth, but he would leave first, dear God, he would leave. . . .

"She's a Jew, don't let her fool you. Look beneath her hair and you'll find the horns! She's bound for hell with the rest— we just help them along! Now, you, girl . . ." He cut the air with his fist. "Home to your mother! Leave the Jews to us!"

"Oh, Tsil, my dear," Buzie gasped as the demon spurred his animal uphill. "Oh, Tsil, where were you going, you stupid-head, where were you going? Now you stay here, you stay." Oh, God . . .

So Yahweh said to Satan, "Where have you been?" "Round the earth," he answered, "roaming about." So Yahweh asked him, "Did you notice my servant Job? There is no one like him on the earth: a sound and honest man who fears God and shuns evil." "Yes," Satan said, "but Job is not God-fearing for naught. Have you not put a wall round him and his house and all his domain? You have blessed all that he undertakes, and his flocks throng the countryside. But stretch out your hand and lay a finger on his possessions: I warrant you, he will curse you to your face. . . ."

Once, then twice within minutes, the sound of Katrinka Potrovich's footfalls at his back hooked Laib's attention from his Torah, as nothing else could do, for he imagined her to be Buzie, whose absence was the outstanding misery of the day. Both times he caught his error before speaking, before a spark had lit his eye or a gesture come to his hand, for the priest's daughter showed no embarrassment or awareness of his attentions. Both times also he noticed his wife, sitting, melancholy like a winter-bare vine, on a bench beneath the stained-glass window of this church parlor, but he could not construct a single sentence from the debris of his thoughts and impulses, nor stand to hear his own voice in this oppressive place.

Your sons and daughters were at their meal and drinking wine at their eldest brother's house, when suddenly from the wilderness a gale sprang up, and it battered all four corners of the house, which fell in on the young people. They are dead: I alone escaped to tell you.

Laib nodded and rocked as he read of Job's calamitous misfortunes. He felt stirrings of anger, a twinge in his legs, a tightening of his throat, but the rage fell more quickly than it rose, smothered by the constant fact of his helplessness. He could not even conjure a prayer; the Bible served only to keep him from dozing. His spirit was altogether exhausted, his thoughts stony, ill-formed. Only two images had color, constancy, and effect upon him: the first, a memory of his cold, silent baby boy and the torn, dead woman—Muriel! How deep those roots of grief ran, beneath the events of all ensuing years, beneath sunshine and frost and all transient things, to sap the vitality from them!—and the other, a vision of Buzie, a dead bundle by the river, a flower strewn on a dungheap.

Why give light to a man of grief? Why give life to those bitter of heart, who long for a death that never comes, and hunt for it more than for buried treasure? They would be glad to see the gravemound and shout with joy if they reached the tomb. Why make this gift of light to a man who does not see his way, whom God balks on every side? My only food is sighs, and my groans pour out like water, whatever I fear comes true, whatever I dread befalls me. . . .

With her mother, once, Buzie had found a crow whose neck was wedged between two saplings, a freak sight, and more grotesque than if the bird had been dead. Raisl had parted the tough young trees while instructing and encouraging her daughter to lift the half-conscious bird, lay it on the ground, and then retreat. Buzie remembered now the quivering wings, beating uselessly as she neared, and the cloudy eyes, the beak oozing a pink tongue. She remembered the weight of the bird in her arms,

its damp, warm body with shiny blue-black feathers. "Leave it
there on the leaves and come here next to momma. We'll watch
now, to see if it flies. That's for God to decide now."

God, momma—neither were with her now, and she was afraid
to touch Tsil. There would be blood under the blouse, maybe
even a bone tearing through the skin.

"Tsil, can you get up? Can you move?" Her foot was a mess
and had bloodied the rubbery grass all around her. Buzie thought
again of the crow, how it had found life enough to struggle to
its feet despite the dent in its neck, to weakly caw and receive
instantaneous replies from its friends in nearby trees. But there
was no one, though the air still swirled with violence. Even the
sky was cloudless, the bridge empty—no, she couldn't look there,
not to see Nakhum hanging. . . .

Tsil groaned without stirring, striking self-pity from Buzie's
breast. She knelt close, stroked Tsil's neck beneath her brown
braid, and made clucking, consoling sounds with her tongue.

"I'm thirsty." Tsil's lips nibbled the earth.

"What? What?"

"Thirsty . . ."

Buzie ran to the river, sloshed her unworn blouse in the water,
and brought it for Tsil to suck on. Feeding the garment to her,
Buzie began to plot and plan ferociously, as though her resolve
alone could alter reality. "It's okay, Tsil." She lay next to the
broken girl to gain eye contact, but Tsil's eyes were closed, her
face as pale as hay. "It's okay—I'll get Dr. Blum. Should I get
him now? Tsil, should I go get him now?"

Tsil's cheek twitched as Buzie touched it, and then her whole
face contorted in pain. Buzie shrieked and jerked her hands away.
The wet blouse fell from Tsil's lips, dark red with blood, her
mouth dribbling brown bubbles, brown drool smearing her chin.
Pressing her own face to the ground, Buzie screamed, long and
loud, then unfolded to her feet like a startled doe and ran, dizzy
and whimpering, to the river's edge.

She watched her footprints form and dissolve in the mud of
the riverbank, finding in their pattern a healing sense of oblivion,
until she had reached the Petrovskya cemetery, about a quarter
of a mile down from the Mogilev Bridge. It was an ancient
Christian burial ground made unfit for use by the widening basin
of the Dniester; no tombstone was dated after 1805, and all were
lopsided and loose in the soft ground like teeth in an old

woman's jaw. Diagonally from where Buzie entered the cemetery, a path led out, through woods and fields, to the eastern road into town. At that junction of dirt and cobblestone, in a grove of willow trees, stood Rabbi Mandelstam's old shul.

Buzie's guts were writhing with indecision as she touched her palm to the rough edge of a tombstone. Weeping aloud, she sank to her knees and embraced the rock like a holy scroll, wishing for inspiration, for salvation, for the *goyishe* god whose name had stopped the cossack bastard in his tracks to come now, complete the conversion: save Tsil, stop the pogrom. Her eyes were shut, her cheeks pressed to the cool granite, her muscles tense with anticipation as she invited God's touch by bringing to mind the handsome face of Jesus Christ as she remembered it from the statue in Father Potrovich's church. . . .

A minute passed before she snapped open her eyes. Her body felt no lightness or transport. The graveyard was the same, muddy and desolate. Her wandering thoughts, despite her proddings, had not been able to reach beyond images of familiar faces: Tsil laughing shyly into her collar, Tsil eating chicken like a greedy fox . . . poppa lecturing, leaning across the red tablecloth . . . Ruchel pouting and complaining . . . and Yeshua, Yeshua and Herschel as they would be at their forest meetings: sober, quick with gestures, faces lit by the fire. Buzie pushed away from the gravestone as if to banish her moment of collapse from evidence. The grave-marker crucifixes looked to her like swords stuck in the earth, daggers hurled from the sky. She cursed the cossacks to hell as she entered the shadowy woods.

The destruction of property and life at each site of the anti-Jewish riot occurred in two distinct stages. The cossacks swept through first, trampling whatever crossed their path until their horses were tracking blood through the dust. Minutes later the peasants rushed in like maggots to infect the wounds. The first few Jewish homes along the road to the bridge, including the Kharlofskys' little house, were picked apart to the foundation, along with the unfortunate inhabitants who had not known to evacuate. Isaac the water carrier was nearly drowned in his buckets, then tied to his yoke in imitation of Christ in his agony. Shmulke the cobbler put up a fight to protect his pitiful property and had his skull split with a hobnail.

Yet the rioters' boldness had been damaged by Nakhum's stout resistance at the bridge and by the superciliousness of the murderous cossacks who, on their horses, stormed through Mogilev-Podolsk at an ever-widening distance from the peasant mob. Father Potrovich thought he sensed such a slackness in their confidence when he tried to deter them from proceeding past his gate. They were only crudely and lightly armed, he noticed, and uncomfortably tight in their ranks, as if seeking anonymity despite the daylight. Most were drunk, or striving to be, with jugs of mash whiskey circulating among them, and they seemed uneasy enough to avoid looking either at him or at the holy church as they staggered past.

"My sons," intoned the slim priest to those who came nearest his white picket fence, "this is not God's work you do. God tells us to love our neighbors as we love ourselves. . . ."

One fellow, barely a man, looked through swimming eyes at Father Potrovich and began to cross himself, but a big lout behind him banged his shoulder blades with a whiskey face. "Go on, get along! Never mind this sonofabitch priest! He doesn't know God from his asshole! We all know how much he loves the Jews!" He pushed the hesitant young man stumbling ahead, then paused before the father, waving the bottle in his face. "Eh, don't worry, father, we'll convert your rotten Jews for you. We'll turn them inside out for you!"

It was enough of a threat to drive Potrovich back to his church, where he composed himself, squaring his shoulders, regulating his breath, patting his cheeks to restore their color, before reentering the parlor where the Kharlofskys sat. "They're too drunk to last for long," he announced from the doorway. "I doubt if they'll get much past your yard."

"You are a brave and a fine man, Nicholas," said Raisl.

"And a liar," her husband muttered, peering up from his holy book.

"Laib!" she gasped.

Father Potrovich crossed the room to fetch a soothing glass of tea from his samovar. "They'll hardly make it into town, I tell you. Their wives will be along to pick them up from the side of the road and clean them up for church."

Laib slammed shut his Bible. "And when will *we* be permitted to retrieve our dead? Tell me! When can we dare show our faces again? My daughter will be picked clean by the flies while we wait for your cursed messiah to be resurrected and finished with it!"

The priest swallowed his drink with difficulty. "Please, my friend," he pleaded, "don't agonize yourself. Have pity, at least, on your wife. We must have hope. We must try to have faith."

"Our faith is utterly smashed!" Laib declared. "Whether a hundred are killed or only one has his beard plucked, our trust is broken! The peace is broken!"

Raisl rose from her bench. "Laib, what are you saying? Do you hear yourself, Laib?" She carried her words closer to him. "You must be there to pick up the pieces, to reconstruct the pieces! Perhaps the worst will prevail—or worse than the worst!" She drew herself upright. "But I won't grieve in advance! I won't. And I thank you, Father Potrovich"—she nodded courteously—"for your courage and your comfort. My husband, you see—"

Laib half-rose from his chair. "Raisl! Do not humiliate me!" She knelt at the desk behind which he was standing. "What are you doing? Stand up!"

"What are *you* doing?" she replied, softly and earnestly. "Do you think that God gave you the power to prevent our persecution? You are not the Messiah, Laib! You are not the *lamed-vovnik* of Podolia. You are a teacher, a judge to your people, a source of wisdom, of hope. Hope! And you give me nothing but despair!"

"You should know," Father Potrovich added as Laib sank heavily into his chair, "I saw no more than a handful of our own townspeople among them—young boys! None from my own congregation. They're all from Otek, from the countryside, from who knows where? This is proof of our influence, Laib, don't you see? Despite the depths of hatred to which they are stirred by every influence—including my own brothers of the cloth!—despite this, our town has been humanized. We will repair the damage done on this day."

Laib shrugged, then turned away and doubled over as if taken by a cramp. "Oh, Laib," wept Raisl, reaching across the desktop to clasp his hand.

"I was thinking," he said, head bowed and sniffling, "that maybe God will take better care of our Buzie than we. . . ."

* * *

Rabbi Mandelstam's synagogue seemed as hushed and spooky as the forest from which Buzie emerged. She held back from going to its door, ducking instead into the camouflage of the low-hanging willow boughs that encircled the building. Here the filtered sunlight was soothing, restful. The woods had held no such comfort, but subtle sounds of movement and voices so distant as to seem imagined. Every grove seemed to hold secrets, but she had not once stopped to listen.

Listen! A footstep on the twigs behind her—in the stillness of the grove, there was no mistaking it. She tore from the branches' embrace and ran to the synagogue door, which she hammered and kicked clamorously. Her voice seemed to breed others, eerie rustlings in the woods and, more pronounced, a swelling clatter of horses' hooves on the main road. At last the door unbolted and she pushed inside.

She froze in the doorway, stunned by the heavy, mournful air of the synagogue. Entire families were huddled together on benches, withdrawn into one another's arms like rag bundles. There were perhaps sixty people in all, many elderly, watching her without a word of welcome. Buzie peered questioningly at the young yeshiva student who had admitted her. He rebolted the door and turned away. "You think the cossacks would prefer to find us dancing?"

Rabbi Mandelstam, in prayer shawl and *tefillin*, came down the aisle as quickly as his spindly legs allowed. "Buzie! Buzie Kharlofsky? There, I see you now, it is you! But how do you come to be here, child? Oh, I thank the Almighty that you're alive!"

Buzie lowered her eyes. "Never mind the Almighty."

The old man patted her shoulder. "Yes, yes, God is our refuge, my daughter. I will indeed thank him for your safety, and for your visit with us. We are mostly old here, but we all thank God that we can be together in His house at this hour."

Such a whining, quavering voice! Buzie looked up with murderous eyes. "You can thank God that Nakhum is dead!"

His hand slipped from her shoulder. Buzie sobbed and lunged to catch his fingers, to hold on to his comfort. The others were gliding up the aisle toward her like beggars in an alley. "Come away from the door, Buzie," Mandelstam said. "Come." He draped the edges of his prayer shawl around her shoulders. "Hear, O Israel, the Lord—"

Then the door exploded, splintered by the boot of a giant cossack warrior who heralded the entrance of four more, all with sabers drawn. The Jews shrank back toward the holy ark, crying their woe to the rafters.

"Who's got gold for us?" shouted the door-smashing goliath. "We need pay for our work!"

"Where do you hide the young ones?" roared another, hoisting his pants.

Buzie staggered among the panic-stricken Jews before dropping on her hands and knees and crawling beneath a prayer bench—no, no good, no good! She could not stand to be wedged in so! "Hear, O Israel, the Lord is our God. . . ." Buzie braced herself for Mandelstam's death shriek.

Instead the air was ripped by a volley of shots that thudded into the walls of the synagogue. She crawled forward and peered over the back of a bench, saw the cossacks in a cluster, glancing at each other with combat eyes. They moved as a bunch to the doorway, and here the big one received a shot in the face and fell dead among his comrades, his sword rattling to the floor. "Gregor!" bellowed a second cossack, kneeling by the body, only to be blown to the floor by another volley of shots. The remaining three hung back and tore down the aisles, sabers flailing, to find an alternate exit. The wailing Jews dispersed like minnows from their path.

A company of Jewish men had piled in through the front door, trampling the cossack corpses. A second group burst in through the rear doorway near Rabbi Mandelstam's study. Buzie spotted Yeshua's face among them, squinting down a rifle sight. "Get down!" their commander shouted. "Everybody down!"

Buzie hit the floor again, scraping her back on the bench bottom, jerking her fist of vengeance as the sharpshooters caught the cossacks in an ear-shattering cross fire and drove them like cockroaches to the wall. She gnashed her teeth and banged her fist to the floor again and again as the Bundists, possessing only slow-action rifles, took an excruciatingly long time to complete the execution.

Chapter Six

Arrivals, departures, and the ritualization of their grief kept the
Jews of Mogilev-Podolsk occupied during the weeks following
the pogrom. First came the troops, under the authority of the
governor of Podolia, "to restore law, order, and respect for the
czar father," according to his directive. In fact, their mission was
to break the back of the Jewish resistance, and though their
presence put a final end to the looting and beatings as well, no
arrests of gentile offenders were made. The cossacks, meanwhile,
strapped their dead to horses and departed for the East.

Tsil the cobbler's daughter, Nakhum the Sea Gull, and five
other Jews, young and old, were corpses to be buried. Their
mourners sat in darkened homes for seven days, praying, weeping,
attending to their grief, eating only what their callers brought for
them. Relatives and friends from out of town began to arrive by
train and by cart as the word of the riot went out on the telegraph wire. Ruchel came from Odessa with her husband Feivl,
and wearing a very fine *sheytl* on her delicate skull. She was a
strange sight to Buzie: a married woman, with a belly like a
barrel, and as nonchalant in her condescension toward Buzie as
any other adult. But Ruchel helped restore the house to order
and tended with a discreet touch to her father, whose sociability
and confidence seemed shattered. Buzie soon felt grateful for her
sister's presence; she herself had nothing to give her family, but
felt like a restless phantom, wandering without thought or purpose, unable to be still.

Her roving first led to Tsil's dilapidated house, where she
helped care for the children and helped nurse the half-conscious,

half-dead cobbler, Shmulke. Here she could feel with every breath the absence of her dearest friend, her laughing friend, her humble and grateful friend; Buzie let the grief mix with her sweat until she was saturated. But Tsil's death had made the poverty of her family complete. After the week of mourning, the air seemed to sour with despair. Buzie could not abide it, this fungus feeling of hopeless living; one last time she wept with Shmulke's wife, Gertl, then fetched water for her and said goodbye.

She began visiting members of her brothers' revolutionary circles who were known to her, asking about their activities and sharing rumors that she'd collected around town regarding the czar's agents and the progress they were making in flushing out the Bundists. These police spies were an obvious presence in Mogilev-Podolsk—well-heeled northerners from Moscow and beyond—but the fear of strangers that the pogrom had intensified to a phobia in the Jewish community kept them at bay, idling in taverns and brothels. Buzie found at home most of the activists she sought, and even began running messages for them, in good conscience: Their bullets, she knew, had saved her life, while the religionists had only trembled and waited to die. But she was unable to obtain information about her brothers. They were, the Bundists told her, "out of town."

Over the weeks, the social and communal life of Mogilev-Podolsk limped back toward normalcy, with the dead buried, the losses rationalized, the wounds roughly healed. Rov Kharlofsky began to lead services in his shul again. The marketplace gathered in its peddlers, and tensions between Jews and the *goyim* were negotiated as business deals instead of blows. But the Passover holiday had been aborted for the year, and this was symbolic of a deeper loss of optimism, joy, and hope for the future. Increasingly, conversations in public and in private turned to the matter of emigration to America or England. The first Zionist organization in the region emerged before the summer, and Palestine was added to the list of possible destinations. More immediately, the threat of renewed violence hung like humidity in the air, with the spies operating as cossacks in plain clothes, sowing distress by their very presence.

Then in May, a government-appointed rabbi named Meyer Zhimkoff established offices in town.

His presence would normally have presented no challenge to

Rov Kharlofsky's authority, for these government-appointed characters were common in the pale of settlement and were widely scorned, feared only for the little punitive power they wielded as czarist officials. Laib's own confidence, however, was at an ebb, as schisms within the Jewish community were more than ever manifested as hostility by the wealthy class to his liberal leadership. Zhimkoff's arrival served to mobilize this opposition and catalyze their dissent, inasmuch as he began his tenure by declaring, in a headlined column in the newly licensed Yiddish press:

IF THE SYNAGOGUE FALLS, DON'T BLAME THE WIND

by Rabbi Meyer Zhimkoff

A synagogue stands for a hundred years at the center of a thriving Ukrainian town. It seems a solid building that has withstood every storm. Then one day a slightly-stronger-than-usual gust blows over the old synagogue as if it were built upon toothpicks. Why now, after a century of fortitude? Don't blame the wind.

Blame the termites instead. Blame the parasites who have eaten away at the structure and foundation of the synagogue until it has no support, and who remain hidden, undiscovered, until the building collapses and they run for cover. Blame these, not God's winds, for your misfortune.

It is true, as the antigovernment agitators state in their illegal pamphlets, that the czar, and Czar Alexander before him, and every czar that our grandfathers and great-grandfathers have known, have denied "full citizenship" to the Jewish people. But is this cause for ridiculous sloganeering or dangerous, subversive activities? Is this cause enough to break God's own Commandments by causing blood to be spilled? The question that the thoughtful man must ask is this: What does citizenship mean to a Jew in Russia? The answer is simple: It means assimilation!

What is the benefit of citizenship in the poverty and starvation that rules this land? As Jews we have our shops, our charitable organizations for those in need, and our brethren factory owners who work not for profit and glut but for the greater good of their people. What is the benefit of citizenship in a society that is torn apart by forces of atheistic Marxism, Russian Orthodoxy, trade unionism, and all kinds of vulgar European philosophies? As the people of the Book, God's chosen ones, we are united, however varied our wealth or learning. Enough for us to contend with our own heresies, the Zionist heresies, which would have our people place their hopes for salvation in the dust of the earth instead of in the angels of heaven!

Never mind the prattlings of so-called revolutionary assimilationists. They would bring us into conflict with a government whose attention we are better off without! They would inflame the mind of the peasant to violent savagery while distracting our young men and women from their Jewish responsibilities. So if the synagogue falls, don't blame the wind. The causes of our distress are one and the same as the causes of the greater Russian ailment, and these are the nihilists, anarchists, atheists and so-called Social Democrats who are destroying the roots of our mutual well-being. Turn them out of the synagogue! Turn them out of the house! Turn them out of your Jewish hearts! Then and only then will our synagogue stand firm, tall, and steadfast, no matter what winds may blow from St. Petersburg, Moscow, or from wherever evil arises!

"And won't you be replying with a little pamphlet of your own, rabbi?" sneered Mordecai Mendel when he met Laib in the post office on the day that Zhimkoff's article was published. Gogolin's presence behind the counter forced Mendel to keep his voice low and his words Yiddish, but the threat of denunciation lurked barely below the surface of his taunts. Laib's possession of a printing press was not a tightly guarded secret in town, and his sons' membership in the Jewish Labor Bund was widely known. Reb Mordecai and not a few others had put one and one together and come to view their rabbi as very nearly an accomplice to the revolutionaries.

Laib addressed the envelope of the letter he was sending off to "Mr. and Mrs. Markish" in America. "Before the pogrom," he said without looking up, "I sent many letters of complaint to the governor of Podolia. I have complained likewise to the local police supervisor, the head of the gendarmerie, and to every official in town. It did not stop them from inciting the riot, Reb

Mordecai. I think another complaint to a government official like Meyer Zhimkoff will be just as useless."

"Even if the cossacks themselves appointed him," Mendel snapped, "he is a blessing to us! You should work *with* him, Rov Kharlofsky, to root out the vermin from our midst."

Laib brushed past the little man without offering a reply.

Zhimkoff was as active as a mole breaking ground, however, and could not long be ignored. For two weeks he conducted a whirlwind round of meetings with every important religious and civic leader in town, invariably producing at those meetings information, memorandums, and documents that were surprising even to the police, all amounting to propaganda against the revolutionary movement.

His coup de grace was a copy of a letter from the governor of Podolia to Feodor Krassily, the district police chief, dated May 14 and noting that "the continued harboring of criminals by the Jews of Mogilev-Podolsk is intolerable and will only reinforce popular notions of Jewish disloyalty to the government and motherland, which, along with the resentment of Jewish exploitation of the local peasantry, were chiefly responsible for the outbursts. . . ."

"It's like beating a hungry dog with a fat bone!" commented Rov Kharlofsky to Gideon Blum upon hearing of Zhimkoff's latest disclosure. "This rabbi's yeshiva must be located right in the heart of the czar's palace. Running dog!"

Increasingly, the *rov*'s aloofness from the news and gossip and from the endless stream of agitation that issued from Zhimkoff's pen was being interpreted as cowardice, or, worse, as sympathy for the Bundists. In his month of residency, Zhimkoff had not yet managed to net a congregation for himself—such was not his strategy—but his weekly "meetings" (harangues, actually, performed in the warehouse of Mordecai Mendel's factory) were overflowing in attendance, and not a few of the audience hailed from Laib's own synagogue. To make matters worse, the Jewish Bund had issued a pamphlet attacking the government-appointed puppet and his policies, and neither Laib nor his supporters could say with certainty that it had not been printed in his very own basement. His wife and daughters all denied having seen either Yeshua or Herschel for weeks, since before the pogrom—but had not Raisl lied before?

Laib resolved finally to ditch the illegal machine—no small

task, for it was extremely heavy, he possessed neither a shovel
nor a wagon, and there was no one whom he could bear to
jeopardize by asking for help. He was at home, scheming for its
disposal, when Rabbi Mandelstam visited one afternoon. For the
elderly man to have conveyed himself across the entire length
of the town was an exertion that bespoke important news.

"I'm afraid that our nests are built on thin branches," quipped
Mandelstam as Laib showed him to the table and fussed with tea
glasses, saucers, and muffins. "I, because the cossacks were shot
to death in my synagogue. Not that they were praying, mind
you." He stroked his stringy white beard. "And you, because of
your sons, of course. So now this Meyer Zhimkoff is shaking
our tree."

"He's a very slick operator," Laib complained. "I'm amazed
at the impact this man has had."

"The pogrom had the impact," Mandelstam said.

Laib nodded heavily. "I should have buried his influence a
month ago!"

"Never mind, Laib, never mind. Your spirit has not been
whole. The people are still with you, don't worry. Zhimkoff
merely offers them promises. Promises are comforting to a
frightened people. He offers them the golden calf. As it is written:
'Make a god to go at the head of us; this Moses, the man who
brought us up from Egypt, we do not know what has become
of him.' "

Laib sipped tea from his saucer. What indeed had become of
the fierce energy of his mind? He felt, as never before, keen
empathy with this worn old rabbi, who continued: "Laib, you
should take the initiative now. Zhimkoff has been meeting with
anybody who has a desk and a certificate on the wall. And he
came to me, this morning." Mandelstam spoke softly, as though
making a confession. "He wants to convene a conference of all
the rabbis in the area. A conference. He doesn't even know
their names! This must not be for him to decide, Laib. Such
audacity!"

"What will this conference achieve?"

Mandelstam drew his head back and laid his hands on the edge
of the table. "Have you no plan, Laib? The authorities are
screaming for blood—haven't you thought it through?"

Laib was up and pacing near the stove. "Rabbi, I am without
an idea in my head! I've been so filled up with brooding! It's

not just any revolutionaries they're after, Mandelstam—it's my
sons! Specifically those two, to get at me, to discredit all my
efforts!"

"You have been a vocal leader," Mandelstam agreed, "and the
behavior of your boys—"

"Never mind," Laib replied gruffly. "These are family matters
and I will tend to them myself, without Meyer Zhimkoff's assistance, thank you!" He rolled his warm tea glass between his palms.
"Meanwhile, this conference—it's a good idea."

Rabbi Mandelstam graciously returned to the subject. "You
should hold it in the study room of your own synagogue, so the
people will see that your doors are open."

Laib nodded, tapping his fingers atop the table. "Good. I will
meet in advance with my committee—Dr. Blum and Reb Yankel,
you know them? Of course. Both priceless men. If you would
join us, rabbi . . ."

Mandelstam sank back into his bones with a sigh. "I am not one
to be involved in making plans, my friend. My plans are all
finished. Today, everything is different from when I had my
youth."

"Nevertheless," Laib said, grasping his hand, "you have brought
me back from the dead."

"Phooey, Laib. I've only crowed a little. So now you wake up."
He raised his saucerful of tea. "*L'chaim.*" And he reached for a
second sugar lump.

Frightfully cramped under the table, Buzie was so relieved as
her father and Mandelstam went out the door that she rushed
carelessly forward and bumped her head against the table edge,
inflaming her already throbbing headache to an acute threshold.
Aie, the pounding! And the hissing in her ears, like a tailor's steam
presser. These headaches had been plaguing her since that day
of atrocities, when the gunshots in the shul had rattled her brain.
Now the pain came nearly every day, a counterweight to her
busy thoughts.

Buzie lowered her forehead to the floor and moaned, then
blinked languorously until the ache had dulled. She then proceeded to the front door with slow steps. Her father noticed
her as soon as she came outside, and excused himself from his
chat with Rabbi Mandelstam. "Buzie, come give a hand."

She stood her ground, rubbing her temples.

"Where have you been?" he asked.

"Under the table," she brazenly replied, and looked up to see his features shift with surprise.

Mandelstam flagged a ride from Avram the splinter, a lumber merchant. "Yoo, Laib! *Sholem aleichem!*"

"*Aleichem sholem!* Bless you, Mandelstam!" He watched until the wagon was well along its way. "And you, Buzie? Where are you going now?"

"For a walk, poppa. Do you need me for something?"

"Five minutes ago I did, yes! If you'd not been hiding like a criminal! We needed to fetch a ride for our visitor."

"He found it himself, poppa. I was afraid to embarrass you."

"Then why do you hide under there? You're hardly a baby anymore!"

Buzie glanced sidelong at him, as she knew he liked. "I wanted to be close to you, poppa," she said in a small voice. "This was the best way I could think of. You're so busy these days."

"And you, you're a flatterer," said Laib, suppressing his delight. "So . . . come inside now, and we'll be together. Come, brown eyes, your poppa feels much better today."

"First I want to take a walk, poppa."

"I see—before it gets dark, hmm? Is there no supper for you to prepare?"

He was, she knew, suspicious of her movements, and would pester her until satisfied. She adopted a confessional tone: "I got my headache again today, poppa—it's very bad. I can't just sit! . . . So I began to think, Maybe I would go down to where Tsil—got hurt. Maybe my head will feel better when I hear the river."

He pressed a palm to her brow. "Maybe it's better that you see Dr. Blum."

"No, poppa!"

"All right then, go." He dropped his hand, disappointed. "Go ahead! Only come back soon—I don't want you there after dark."

"I promise! And I'll bring you some spearmint!" She trotted off, ostensibly gay, but not daring to breathe until she had reached the gate. Only then, as her father withdrew into the house, did her thoughts get out of harness.

Now, to business. She reviewed the conversation between

Mandelstam and her father, sifting it for essentials that her brothers would want to know. Little of substance had been decided at that table, but Yeshua would pump her for details, especially since she had missed a visit to them yesterday on *shabbas.*

Buzie headed toward the site of Tsil's murder, as she had told her father, but then crossed the Mogilev Bridge, as if en route to school, with a hurried step and with her shawl wrapped around her face. She slipped through a thorny hedge at the side of the road and found the path leading to the riverbank and to Nakhum the Sea Gull's old hovel. She had tracked her brothers to this spot just a week earlier, after a month of constant messenger and spy work for the holed-up bundists, and only after convincing several of the group of her need to have quick access to these two most-sought of the revolutionaries. They were living miserably in Nakhum's mud hut, without even a fire for warmth at night for fear that the smoke would attract attention. Both were sluggish from poor nourishment and lack of exercise, grimy and tense, without a warm word for her as she entered through the muslin drapes that constituted the door.

"No supplies today," she announced, causing Herschel to kick the dirt. He was wearing out faster than his more experienced brother.

Yeshua was sitting on the ground against the wall, sucking a cigarette. "Sorry," Buzie went on. "Poppa's been home all day. I think he's worried about the printing press. Maybe he wants to get rid of it—he went to the cellar three, four times today, up and down. But he never turned the handle of the machine."

"It would be advisable to get our machine out of there," Yeshua said to his brother.

"Sure," Herschel said. "But if this one can't even sneak a potato out of there, how do we go about getting our machine?"

"True, you are the world's best sneak." Yeshua tousled Buzie's hair. "So what else?"

She told him of the meeting with Mandelstam. "They're going to make a conference of all the rabbis and I don't know who else. But first poppa will meet with Dr. Blum and Reb Yankel."

"The hens are conferring about the fox, eh, Herschel?"

"But that's how it is with poppa!" Buzie cried, genuinely anguished. "He's in some kind of cage, like a chicken coop, and all these other men are planning how to chop his head off!"

Yeshua patted her hip. "Our father is a tough old bird, you'd be surprised. Now, how is momma?"

"She's all right, Yeshua."

"That's all? Just 'all right'?"

Buzie backed away from his fuming cigarette. "I'm busy trying to avoid momma so she won't keep me in the kitchen or something—they're ready to tie me up, the both of them! So how can I tell how she's doing? She's all right! . . . Ohh, my head is hurting so much, Yeshua. It's full of messages for everyone, messages and questions. I have so many questions, and no one even tries to answer them!"

"Don't ask questions," grumbled Herschel. "You'll stay out of trouble."

"I'm already in trouble!" Buzie retorted. "You think I'm still six years old and doing this so I can follow my big brothers around? You're not that good-looking!"

"Shh, don't holler," Yeshua said. "He's thinking with his stomach, not with his head. Have an onion, Herschel."

"Have a heart. I'm sick of onions."

Buzie knelt at Yeshua's side. "I'll feed you if you feed me. You want to answer some questions? Tell me this: Why is it impossible for poppa to be working *with* us? Why do I have to lie to him all the time?"

Yeshua snuffed his cigarette into the ground. "Poppa doesn't believe we're going to win."

"So what? When I look around at how you live, I don't believe, either!"

Yeshua smiled and drew up his knees. "You're not really looking, Buzie. You're not looking with a worker's eye. Go ahead and look again."

"What look? There's not so much that you can't see the first time! I see mud, a stool, a table, and him—a grouch!" She thumbed her nose at Herschel and giggled.

He knelt with them and gave his sister a little squeeze on the neck. "You see only mud," Yeshua went on, "and you don't see that the mud has been shaped into a house. By one man. And if there had been a team of men, it would have been a palace."

"A mud palace!" Buzie argued. "And the czar's palace is not made of mud!"

"But the same people who built the czar's palace also built—

and live in—these mud hovels. And they will be the ones to tear
down the palace when the day of reckoning comes."

"They're not soldiers."

"And we are not cossacks, but you saw what we did to the
cossacks!"

Buzie nodded with awe.

"Look, Buzie, you've got to tear down the old house to build
the new one. Poppa is afraid of this. He sees the rubble and has
no vision of something new rising from it. He thinks that the
only way to build something in this world is to follow the blue-
prints in the Torah: You know, the tabernacle is to be twenty
cubits this way and threescore cubits that way, and with forty
sockets of silver, and just so. Any other description he condemns."

"Poppa says you're building your own gallows."

Yeshua snorted and reached to his pocket for his tobacco. "Let
me try to say something," Herschel broke in. "Maybe I'm more
like Buzie—I have more doubts, now that I have finally joined
the movement." He was tracing with a finger in the dirt. "I have
more fears than you, Yeshua."

"Not so. You just choose to share them more with your
comrades. You idealize me, Herschel."

"Let me speak!" insisted Herschel in a whining tone, then
brooded for a moment. "What I'm trying to say is that maybe
Buzie should forget some of her questions! Try not to question
so much each step of the way." He glanced at her. She saw the
leanness in his face, which suited him less than the hawkish
Yeshua; he looked ill. "We are in the minority, those of us who
are conscious revolutionaries. The rest of the world will tell us
we're crazy. If we listen to them all the time, we will become
crazy! . . . I'm trying to abandon my destiny as an individual. I
want to give myself over to a larger, better destiny, a calling
that—"

"Herschel, you're speaking like a *narodnik* fanatic," Yeshua
complained.

"Let me finish! Marxism must have inspiration, too! I would
say that to our father—you can tell him, Buzie. Tell him that
God is working this way, and the closer we get to power, to the
transformation of this mud into brick, the closer we get to God.
Tell poppa—"

"He doesn't mean to really tell him, Buzie."

"—to read his Torah and let go of his fear. Moses did not think so much! He was no great intellectual! But he heard God's calling and he went. And he became a great revolutionary! So—there's room for the religious in our movement," he concluded, winding down like a sleepy child.

Buzie felt dissatisfied and uncomfortable with all of it: with Yeshua's skeptical impatience, with Herschel's overblown passion, with their sickly appearance, and the four mud walls that offered not even an echo to enlarge their conversation. She pressed down on Yeshua's bony knee and stood. "Poppa wants me home before dark—and I have to remember to collect spearmint." With a sighing heave of her narrow shoulders, she lifted her shawl to her head. "I wish I had more for you. . . . Anyway, tomorrow I'll bring some bread and whatever else I can get."

"A piece of fruit would be worth a million rubles," said Herschel, pleading.

Buzie nodded sullenly. "Maybe I should get my hands on a goat, if you're planning to settle here forever!" She turned to leave, but knew that she could not return tomorrow without settling accounts today. "Listen, you two." She drew herself up primly before the ragged men. "You're stuck here like two dreamers—*nudniks*, never mind *narodnikii!* And the comrades are here and there and nowhere, afraid to visit you or each other —you might as well all be in prison! And me—I can't talk to anyone. I'm completely alone. Completely." She sobbed, then flared up, indignant. "None of you realize that I'm twelve years old! Even to stand here and hear myself say that, it's crazy! Poppa hardly trusts me to mail his letters, and here I am, the ears and eyes for the entire Jewish Labor Bund of Podolia! What I know, a government spy would go to Siberia to find out!"

"Buzeleh . . ." Yeshua held his hand out to her.

She stood her ground. "No hugs. You've got to think of a plan. A plan of action. A plan so my head won't hurt so much! I want to be told what to do, okay? I don't want to have to think. I don't understand things by myself. I haven't read your books, I haven't been to meetings as a real comrade. I never even saw this Marx who you all talk about like he's some kind of Messiah!"

"Lesson one," announced Herschel, scratching his back against the crumbly wall. "Karl Marx is not alive."

She would not be embarrassed, either! "Neither is my friend

Tsil, who maybe I could have talked to," she spat. "And neither, I hope, is the bastard cossack who cut her up! *That* is my lesson number one!" Buzie swallowed the lump in her throat and again covered her head with her shawl. "I need to learn lesson number two now. What is my future going to be? I don't belong to poppa's world. And I can't stand being the only one of us who goes around in the daytime! Tomorrow, tomorrow I'll get a nurse's uniform and give you both a shot in the *tukhas!*" She laughed from her belly, but the sound withered. "You see how crazy I am? It's not fair. You make me feel this way. For poppa I pretend to be three years old and I have to fit myself under the table! For you, I'm grown up. All right. Goodnight." She slipped through the doorway before either brother could speak.

The evening breeze perfumed her hair, relaxed her to weariness as she combed the grasses for spearmint leaves. (Why so angry, Buzie, why so crazy, so mean to your brothers?) How nice it was to touch the earth, how easily she could pick spearmint, spearmint and berries and flowers, pick and chew and taste it, sharp on her tongue, forever, she could do this forever. . . .

(Aie, you couldn't even provide for them—another hungry night, cold night with their scrawny blankets. You think they need your complaints? So belligerent, so uncaring, so demanding? Why didn't you hug your brother, why are you so cruel?)

Stepping onto the bridge, onto rattling planks, thinking of corpses and killers, she ran, shawl slipping to her shoulders, braids flopping, breathless to be home (because I'm scared, dear God, and without even you to pray to . . .).

Rov Kharlofsky breakfasted with his two associates from the Committee for Jewish Protection at Dr. Blum's apartment in town on the morning of the rabbinical conference. It was a bachelor's meal, nothing hot, but tasty and expensive, with cold cuts of kosher beef, golden *challah,* and several varieties of fresh fruit. But Laib ate only a sliver of an exotic melon, which led the doctor to inquire about his health. Was he simply too nervous to eat?

"No, no," Laib assured him, "though of course I expect a great deal of shouting. A Jew who has nothing to say will at the very least repeat what someone else has said. It's a social obligation! Every word will echo five, six times—"

Brushing glances with both men, he broke off the blustery speech and, mid-gesture, dropped his hands to his lap. Kaminsky and Blum bit their lips with embarrassment. Reb Yankel toyed with his fork.

"Eat!" Laib urged them. "If you don't eat now, you'll deprive me later of your strength!"

Their cutlery began to clink again. Laib stood and stepped behind them to the open window. "You have both been more than good to me, more than kind—you're real men, like I've rarely known. So—I must tell you." He patted Dr. Blum's arm and returned to his chair, but sat tentatively, with one fist clenched across his knee. "My daughter has been sneaking in and out of our house for weeks, since the riot. I am sure that she is somehow involved, perhaps to the hilt, with her brothers—if they're still in this city; this I don't know—or with the rest of the gang."

Reb Yankel knitted together his bushy eyebrows and pushed his spectacles back up on the bridge of his nose. "You mean our big Bundist heroes have been relying on a child. . . ?"

"You have no proof of this," cautioned Dr. Blum.

"I have no proof," Laib agreed. "But suspicions are rampant today, Gideon Blum, and I have mine. Every time I confront her, she acts the coy girl with me. So finally last night, she came in after dark, which I have expressly forbidden, and I took her to task for it. 'Buzie,' I said, 'if it is your brothers that you are going to see, and not just a stray kitten or the moon . . .' Let me tell you, her face was as pale as that moon when I mentioned their names, and she stared at the floor like it was going to tell her what to do! 'If it is them,' I said, 'just give them a message from me. Tell them that I must see them, tomorrow night, in our home—it is their home as well,' I said. 'Tell them that there are things of vital importance that we must discuss.'

"She said, 'Oh, poppa, you're so silly.' But she heard out my entire message. I know it in my bones, she is consorting with the Bundists!" He grabbed Reb Yankel's shoulder and pushed up to his feet again. "So you want to know what I'm nervous about? There it is! Every one of my children is crazy!"

Kaminsky and Blum exchanged glances, and then the doctor

slid his chair back from the table. "Laib, if you are right—this could be the perfect thing for us."

Reb Yankel sprang up, nodding his agreement.

"Understand me, please," Blum continued, hands on his belly. "I sympathize with your troubles, Laib. But if we can convince our associates to—well, to leave things up to us, isn't that essentially what we want? To keep Zhimkoff and his rabble out of this! Let them leave it to us to make assurances—a few payments —and then we can convince your sons, no later than tonight, to get out of Mogilev-Podolsk entirely! Let them go where their organization has strength, if this is the life they choose—to Vilna, or—"

"We could even tell the authorities," interjected Reb Yankel, "that we Jews drove the Bundists away!"

"And if I may suggest it," added the doctor, "with them should go their printing press—your sole point of vulnerability!"

They were too excited to be believed, Laib thought. Like schoolboys, as if enthusiasm alone might shoo away the complexities! Too gracious to show anger, he resorted to a simple, stubborn pessimism. "The czarists will not be satisfied with knowing that their problems have been transferred to another city, unless that city lies in the heart of Siberia! No, my friends, they have hardly begun to squeeze us. And in this district we have barely money left for a convincing bribe." He shook his head vaguely. "But if all the rabbis will unite and promise to set in order their households—and if we forget about wedding parties and Hanuka *gelt* and whatever little joys there are that steal our pennies, for this year, at least . . . believe me, Mordecai Mendel and Leibowitz and all their cronies will not give a penny more for bribes unless we turn the reins over to Zhimkoff. So to hell with them! If we keep strong the faith—this is crucial, especially among our young people—if we do that—well, they cannot squeeze much, not tears, not blood, from such a rock, hmm?"

They quietly concurred, allowing the *rov* to close out the controversy. Reb Yankel reached to his pocket for his snuffbox. Dr. Blum returned to his meal. Conversation shifted to more agreeably abstract topics until it was time to head to the synagogue. Then, too, their lack of certainty or solidarity showed in their differing postures and gaits as they passed through the streets: Dr. Blum, usually dignified and robust with a well-balanced step, stumbled twice on the heels of Yankel Kaminsky, while Laib walked some yards apart and paid no attention to his surroundings.

A sizable group had already assembled in the study hall atop the shul. They greeted the three members of the Committee for Jewish Protection with restraint and solemnity, which Reb Yankel tried to crack with jokes and handshakes. Laib hung back, scanning the faces of those who had come, to sort and rank them and poll their support.

Old Mandelstam offered his spotted hand. "Ah, my mastermind," Laib kidded him, then said in a loud, congratulatory voice: "Not only have we here the wisest of men, but they get up early in the morning to do their thinking. After all, what would have happened if Joseph had been sleepier than pharaoh and had not been awake to interpret the dream?"

Again Laib scanned the bearded faces of his fellow Jews, most of them rabbis, and nodded greetings to Father Potrovich and two other churchmen standing at the perimeter of the assemblage —ho, and behind them, Meyer Zhimkoff, that moonfaced jackass! (But nod to him, Laib, be a diplomat. . . .) And another fellow seated next to Zhimkoff . . .

Laib visibly stiffened. Mandelstam backed off, hunched up as if drenched by a cloudburst. Everyone fell silent, on cue—only Reb Yankel's tinny voice carried on for a phrase more—as Feodor Krassily, police chief of the district, rose and came forward like a hunter whose trap had sprung.

Laib swallowed his surprise and managed to improvise a respectful greeting. "Captain—welcome—but I did not expect— do not know to whom we owe this honor—"

"To your sons, Kharlofsky, all honor is due." Krassily drew a pad from the deep pocket of his coat and squinted at its page. He was a tall, stiff-limbed man with a prominent chest and jaw and a voice that found expressiveness only by varying volume. To begin he spoke Yiddish, but with clumsy impatience that soon gave out. "Yeshua Kharlofsky, age twenty-five; Herschel Kharlofsky, age nineteen. Both are wanted for crimes against the czar." He fingered the edge of the sheet, examined its back, and looked up. "And for murder, five counts."

Gideon Blum held Laib up by the elbow and stammered, "We had hoped that you would indeed visit us, captain, so we could discuss, perhaps . . . as we did three years ago?"

Krassily scowled at the portly doctor. "I don't know you,"

he declared in Ukrainian, then turned his astigmatic gaze back at Laib. "But we know you, Kharlofsky. We know a great deal about you." Again he used his pad as a prop. "We know, for instance, of a certain unlicensed printing press in your possession."

Laib seized Gideon's hand and tugged it to silence whatever response the doctor would make. Bribery, conciliation, flattery—all these were dead hopes, said the *rov* with his eyes, smiling as he truly engaged Blum's gaze for the first time all afternoon. Patting his shoulder, Laib pursed his lips and looked slowly, wistfully, around the room. "What a meeting this could have been." Not another man would meet his eyes for more than a blink. Mandelstam, especially, was wilted, aghast with shame, while Father Potrovich hung his head, hands cupped at his groin.

Laib sat on a bench. "Arrest me," he said, his lips dry.

Krassily leered at him. "No, Kharlofsky, we will not arrest you. We want to have you continue to serve as Mogilev-Podolsk's leading light. We want our Jews to have religious freedom! And for all the world to know it!" Sarcasm hardened his mouth. "We love our Jews, Kharlofsky! We only wish to see that you work loyally, along with your associate, the esteemed Rabbi Zhimkoff."

Only the sanctity of the room, especially in the presence of this suave brute, prevented Laib from spitting on the floor. "Meyer Zhimkoff is not fit to say kaddish at a beggar's funeral."

Zhimkoff pushed forward from the outskirts of the group. "Persist in your stubbornness," he cried, "and *you* will need someone to say kaddish at your funeral!"

Krassily silenced Zhimkoff with a snap of his wrist. "Rabbi, please be reasonable. Maybe Meyer is—how do you Jews say it?—*nudnik?* But maybe, just maybe, his presence has prevented another outburst by our peasants! You should think about this, Kharlofsky. There are many tensions in our city."

The threat gleamed as keenly as an unsheathed saber. "For this very reason we called this meeting," Laib replied without lifting his eyes.

"For what?" Zhimkoff hollered, stamping his foot. "To destroy my work! To bribe your sons' way to freedom, a freedom they don't deserve, with this oaf of a doctor to make your offers!"

"You little ape," snarled Dr. Blum, flexing his arms.

Rov Kharlofsky stood to interpose between them. "Captain Krassily . . ." He drew out the words with difficulty, from the recesses of his chest. "You must get this mongrel Jew out of our sight if we are to—negotiate. I cannot even consider what you are saying as long as his grunts press on my ears!"

Krassily, amused to be cast as mediator, paced with long, deliberate steps to the staircase and swiveled around. "Zhimkoff and I will both leave you and your fragile little temple. But I will return in one hour, Kharlofsky." He raised one hand, palm up, like the pan of a scale. "Either with my men, in uniform, to arrest the Kharlofsky brothers and their gang, or . . ." The hand clenched spasmodically. "We have in our jail more than a few nasty types—murderers, robbers, rapists, some who specialize in all three!" Krassily rose up and down on his toes. "Well, these fellows would like nothing more than to visit the Jewish merchants in the marketplace. Unsupervised. With clubs, or chains, or pipes. Ooh, what these fellows can do with a length of pipe, it hurts my head just to think about it! And of course, my own men would be off-duty, since you had no wish for their services. And so . . ."—he bowed, military-style—"I leave you, gentlemen. See you at the police station, yes?"

Buzie was playing, as intently as a scientist at work, on the kitchen floor with a worn, waterlogged *dreydl* that Katrinka Potrovich had dug up behind the Kharlofsky house and delivered as an enticement for Buzie's absent friendship. The top had little zest and would wobble and flop after only a short spin, but Buzie was using it for fortune-telling and found its flaw perfect for providing prompt answers to her countless queries. These she framed in thought only, for her mother was sitting right there in the kitchen, slicing potatoes for *tsholent* and boiling beets and chicken for supper.

So will my brothers come for supper, o *dreydl?* It fell with *shin* facing up, the tantalizer letter to which Buzie had assigned "maybe" as its meaning. Maybe they would come—especially if they allowed their appetites to rule! But, *dreydl,* does that mean that poppa will come home first in time to warn momma so she won't be shocked? *Noon,* said the *dreydl*—no. Then *I* should tell her? Buzie wondered. *Shin,* said the perplexing spirit—maybe, who knows?

And who did you belong to, *dreydl,* that you should know all these things? Was it someone named Kharlofsky? *Gimel,* said the

top—yes. To Yeshua? *Noon.* Maybe to Leah? *Gimel,* said the
dreydl, and Buzie smacked her lips. To Leah, from when she was
still named Kharlofsky! She must have lost you years and years
ago, my little *dreydl.*

Buzie applied saliva to her sore knees, then moved to the table
just beyond the kitchen doorway. She pushed the lace tablecloth
to clear a space and spun again without even formulating a
question. The top threw itself right off the table and scooted
back near the stove, inches from Raisl's stool.

Buzie fetched it quietly so as not to trigger her mother's melan-
cholia into anger. How dark she looked, a storm cloud across
her brow, motionless but for the mechanical movements of her
hands. Bending close to Raisl's ankles for her toy (*Gimel,* it
said), Buzie felt a craving for her mother's affection, for the
sweet exchanges that, as a Bundist tramp, she had not enjoyed for
days.

She touched Raisl's leg and blurted, "Who did this belong to?"

Raisl examined the wooden top and smiled wanly as she
straightened her back. "That's your brother's. Avram the Splinter
whittled it for him years ago, when Herschel was just a baby."
Raisl rubbed one of the top's faces with her thumb.

Buzie reached for her toy. "I like this better than the lead ones.
But"—she poked at the top with her finger—"*you* said you belonged to Leah!"

"No," said Raisl, misunderstanding her banter, "I said Herschel.
It's yours now, anyway. . . ."

"No, momma, it belongs to Herschel." Buzie impulsively
reached across the carving board. Raisl stopped cutting her
potatoes as Buzie's hand touched hers on the knife handle.

"Buzie, don't play now, I've got to finish—"

"No, momma." She took control of the blade. "I'll finish. I
can make *tsholent* to taste even worse than yours."

"Suddenly you want to help!" said Raisl testily. "I don't want
to play now!"

"I'm not playing, momma. I never get the time to play. Listen
to me." She stuck the knife in the side of a potato, pocketed her
dreydl, and climbed one rung of the stool, almost into her
mother's lap. "You should go brush your wig, momma. Herschel
is coming to get his *dreydl* tonight. Very soon. And with him
comes Yeshua."

Raisl's startle threw them both from the stool.

"It's not for sure!" Buzie warned. "But poppa said he wanted to meet with them—so I told them. They said they would come."

Raisl's icy exterior melted down dramatically as her daughter explained, with enthusiasm but discreet choice of detail, about the young men's well-being and safety. She wept in waves to match each jot of consoling information that Buzie offered, and when her eyes emerged from the folds of her apron, red-lidded but lustrous, they were riveted to the girl's face. "My God, how does it happen that you have grown up so fast, my poor darling?" She pulled Buzie to her breast. "Like a sunflower, all at once!"

Buzie snuggled up gratefully. "I miss you, momma."

"Oh, and I have missed you, dearest!" They squeezed each other, burrowing and sighing and smelling scalps, shunning words in order to prolong the reverie. "Ach," Raisl murmured at last, "if only we could set back our clock. If somehow there were justice for the Jewish people—for all people!—and not so much trouble all the time, always trouble . . ."

"If only you were rich and the czar were a Jew," said Buzie.

Raisl swayed with deep, bosomy laughter and hugged her again. Then the sound of footsteps at the side door brought a shudder to her frame.

Yeshua and Herschel looked like scarecrows, their clothes pierced by straw from the fields across which they had come to avoid the main roads. Their body odors overwhelmed the food smells in the kitchen. Yeshua's eyes, especially, were shifty, suspicious, his fists clenched. Buzie glanced fitfully from her brothers to her mother, then rose to untie their tongues. "To see their momma," she declared, as if narrating from a storybook, "they crawled through the wilderness, across half the length of Russia, braving storms and wolf packs. . . . Hey, orphans! You were braver in Mandelstam's shul than in your own house!"

Herschel rushed with a moan to his mother's embrace. Yeshua joined them, but would not lower his guard. His vigilance affected his brother and cut short the tender moment.

"Oh, my chicken!" Raisl stepped to the stove and lifted the pieces of chicken from the boiling water with a long fork. "You two look like you haven't eaten—"

"When is poppa coming?" Yeshua said.

Raisl's work at the stove had restored some calm to her. "All he said was that he would be back just as soon as Meyer Zhimkoff's beard got plucked. That's all, a joke. . . . But, Yeshua, why do you stand apart like a lost lamb? I was not expecting you, but am I insulting you?"

"We have work to do, momma," he said gently. "Poppa says he wants to see us. Fine. He'll see us. But we don't have time for a family reunion."

"I still don't understand how he found out about us," Herschel said, glaring at his sister.

She swatted his shirt sleeve. "I told you, he figured it out. He's got more brains than the entire Bund put together!"

Yeshua cut their quibbling with a gesture. "This house always has guests, momma, in and out without so much as knocking. For us that spells trouble, do you understand? We are wanted men. I'm sorry. . . . For you and for mothers throughout Russia, the overthrow of the czarist system will mark a great day. Now . . ." He beckoned Herschel. "Let's take care of our printing press."

They had brought a spade with which to bury the machine deep in the soil of the cellar. "But you must wait for your father!" Raisl insisted, with Buzie nodding her agreement. "The decision about that machine belongs to him as much as to you— and the trouble has been ours alone!"

"Will you look at this?" Herschel gloated. "The hens are defending the rooster!"

Buzie kicked his shin. Yeshua gripped his shoulder to still his reflex. Raisl again reached out to embrace her younger son. "I'm sorry," he moaned, rolling into her arms. "I'm so afraid of seeing poppa again!"

"If what you do," she murmured, "has made you afraid of your own flesh and blood, what good can come of it, Herschel?"

"Our father," said Yeshua, "is the *rov* of Mogilev-Podolsk! What the man Laib wants, his office cannot necessarily permit."

"He'll show you otherwise!" Raisl declared. "He has always sacrificed for you, especially for you!"

"Let's not argue, momma." Yeshua took Herschel by the arm and Raisl relinquished her hold. "C'mon, we'll wait in the cellar. When poppa comes home, we can come up and start all over again, all right, momma? Buzie, would you bring us some hot water?"

They spent a full hour in the basement, with Buzie running up and down for food, drink, candles, and fresh clothing. Raisl meanwhile worked furiously in her kitchen to stave off her anxiety. Mother and daughter were alone by the stove when Rov Kharlofsky finally entered. Outside, the dusk had fallen across the farmlands.

"Stay, I will speak to him first," Raisl commanded Buzie, handing her an uncut loaf of black bread to bring to the cellar. An inveterate sneak, Buzie shoved the bread onto the carving board and tiptoed after her mother, ducking low and using Raisl's wide skirt as a camouflage from which she slipped under the table, unseen. She planned to disarm her father by springing out at him like a grouse whose nest had been disturbed. His laughter would mean forgiveness; otherwise she would feel completely naked before him, with all her rotten secrets known. . . .

(And what if they fought, her brothers and father, as always? And what if he drove them away, as always? Then what, for her? Start to pray again? Or live in Nakhum's cold, muddy misery. . . .)

He said to Raisl: "They're here, then? You know?"

"In the cellar! Oh, Laib, how could you not tell me? But they're so nervous, Laib!"

"The cellar . . ." His voice dropped to a whisper. "Good. Where is Buzie?"

"She brought them a loaf of bread. Laib, you must promise—"

"Shh. Go get the girl, and hush her. Take her to our room and stay there! Shh. Ask questions later."

Shh . . . creaks and groanings outside the house, maybe mice, maybe rats? Raisl's skirts swished past Buzie's hiding place. "Buzie?"

"Sha! Can't you be quiet? Where is she?"

Shh . . . snorts and stamping by the door, maybe *domoviki*, maybe horses? Shh . . . Laib lifted up the tablecloth and scowled upside down at her. "Come out!"

"Buzeleh, come out," sang Raisl. "Come, darling."

"Poppa, who is outside? Who is it?"

Raisl lifted her head. "Outside?"

With a savage flex of his arm, Laib overthrew the table, then yanked Buzie to her feet, slapped her face, and flung her like some slippery eel at his wife. "To the bedroom!" He glanced frantically at the door behind him, then took a deep breath and stalked toward the cellar stairs.

Alarmed by the sounds of furniture crashing overhead, Yeshua and Herschel had rushed up. They halted at the sight of their father.

"Hear me," Laib growled, sweating profusely. "If you have any decency and desire for life left in your bones, you will do as I say. There are police at the door. And look!" He tore from inside his caftan a brass whistle. "My new shofar!"

Yeshua drew a pistol from inside his jacket.

"No, Yeshua!" cried Raisl.

"Put it away, fool! They'll beat and murder every Jew in the marketplace just to add to your infamy! You must sacrifice yourselves!"

Yeshua cocked the gun. "How many police?"

"You're crazy!" his father stammered, shrinking back toward his wife and daughter.

"How many, damn you! At the side door?"

"Yeshua!" wailed Raisl. "The demons have taken possession of you!"

Herschel, half-hidden on the staircase landing, leaned and muttered something into his brother's ear. Yeshua nodded, his eyelids fluttering.

"Go to the front door, poppa," Herschel said. "Tell them we're preparing to surrender."

"Dear boy," wept the rabbi, "thank heavens one of you has some sense!"

Yeshua snapped his fingers. "Go!"

"Please, try to understand. . . ." Trembling at every joint, Rov Kharlofsky shuffled to the door. "Raisl, into the back. . . . They're coming out now!" he shouted, lifting the latch.

Simultaneously Yeshua kicked open the side door. "Let Jews everywhere learn to fight!" he screamed, leaping hand in hand with Herschel.

Gunshots cracked out there, even as six policemen poured in the front door. Buzie cried out her brothers' names and tore away from her mother's grasp. "Buzie!" Raisl shouted, vocal cords popping.

Buzie's fingers gripped the doorjamb as she leaned into the night air. A bloody-chested gendarme lay moaning in the grass only two yards away. She recoiled and heard her parents crying her name from behind the overturned table where they had taken cover. The police, in a clump, entered the kitchen.

Buzie scrambled down the cellar stairs. A lone gendarme was

assigned to pursue her. She climbed the log pile and pelted the hulking officer with sticks, but he effortlessly swept them aside. Again Buzie heard her mother's voice, trampled almost to inaudibility by the boots that were pounding the kitchen floor.

"Get down!" commanded the gendarme, whose brow reached to the top of the woodpile.

"You bastard cossack!" she screamed. "Don't come near me or I'll scratch your eyes out!"

His eyes broadened with mild surprise, and then he laughed, lunged for her foot, and yanked her down. With her tumbled the entire stack of logs, and the printing press stood revealed.

Chapter Seven / 1909

"Most old people tell you about their operations, right? This is the stereotype for us, that we count our surgeries in public while we sit a whole day on benches, with nothing to do.

"You, if you're young, you don't understand old age. You see a wrinkle and you feel sorry; and if it comes on your own face, you go for the makeup kit, to cover. But I like to see wrinkles, y'see, 'cause they're like the map of a person's life. And I don't mind hearing about operations, 'cause the person who tells you is saying, 'Look, I'm alive! Still kicking!'

"It's okay for people to complain—not to *kvetch*, but to talk about our sorrows together, 'cause in this way we learn that we're in the same boat. And this is one way that we develop class consciousness. So a good revolutionary will do this: She goes among the people and she talks to them. I tell you about my troubles, you tell me about yours. You talk until you can feel the bitterness in your mouth—it's like medicine, this bitter taste. But soon you start to feel better, y'see. We can overcome our loneliness if we talk together. And I can teach you that my wrinkles are not a deformity, and also that a deformity is not a person's personality, y'see, I can teach you both these things.

"Even the president showed his operation, remember? What's-his-name, after Kennedy. I forget names, especially if I don't like you—I remember what you said and what you did, but I forget the rest. . . . Johnson, yeah, Johnson. Remember? He showed his scar from an operation to all of America, and meanwhile he covers up the wounds of Vietnam, the burned children. So we need a stereotype for him, for all the big cheeses, and not for each other.

"Anyway, I must tell you about one operation, just so you'll understand what it was like, getting arrested and sent to Siberia. So don't be impatient—I'm the one that she should be impatient—I'm old, I might drop dead right in the middle of this good story!

"I just had my second cataract operation, maybe four months ago. They told me I'm too old, I shouldn't bother, and I told them I needed eyes that I should be able to read my own tombstone. So I had the operation. And finally last week my daughter brought me to get new glasses, 'cause the doctor says it's time, my eyes are ready now. So I got them, and suddenly the whole world became so big and clear! Before that I couldn't really see. I would know it was you, but I couldn't see, like, your smile, or your eyes. I couldn't know how you're feeling just from looking. But now I can see a mile! I can see close up. I can walk better. I don't have to hold the walls or wait that somebody should come help me from the curb.

"And my point is that getting arrested and sent to Siberia was just like getting new eyes. I wanted to be independent? Now I got it good. Suddenly I was grown up. Until that gendarme took me by the collar to jail, y'see, I was only playing at being a revolutionary. I was trying to please my brothers. But I didn't have real understanding. I was a victim of circumstances, and a girl, just twelve years, and I looked like I'm eight, I was tiny. Nobody even believed they would send such a tiny bit of a girl to Siberia.

"But my brothers escaped, y'see. Yeshua got a bullet in his shoulder and had some pain for the rest of his life, but they weren't caught. And the police needed an excuse—so I became their dangerous criminal! You would think they would be embarrassed to make such an arrest. But there you have it: The gendarme carried me from my house; my mother cried like you'd think she was by the river of Babylon, if you know what I mean; and I tried to grab for my father but all I got was a fistful of beard. And the red tablecloth that I used to hide under— I took a hold on that, and I still have a piece of it today, believe it or not, 'cause I dragged it like a shawl to jail and all the way to Siberia.

"They said I was a Bundist, and they were right, but I pretended that I knew nothing and that I was just afraid, which I didn't have to pretend too hard—I was trembling to my toes! It was a miserable place, that jail, like being in a coffin and you think they're gonna nail it shut. All you see is a tiny lamp in the hallway outside the cell, and all you hear is metal, you know, clanking, and people groaning. Ach, it was too horrible, you were grateful even to go to Siberia after you were confined for a few months. I was lucky. Some people rotted in those damp cells until the mold grew on their minds.

"I guess they didn't have a torture rack small enough for me. And how can they do that? If you torture a child, even the worst reactionaries among the Jews would turn against you, 'cause they're religious, against killing. Mordecai Mendel might murder you in his little sweatshop with work, but he'll give you a bonus for Hanuka, y'see. The Jewish petty bourgeois were not the big capitalists in Russia—we had in Mogilev-Podolsk only little skunks.

"Now, the czarists did not arrest my father, 'cause he did his part of the dirty work, plus they already had who to blame for the printing press—me. But they fined him, six hundred rubles. The whole community had to go into hock to pay. I don't really know what happened to him after that—I didn't see my father again until 1918, during the Revolution, and by then he was a very old man.

"But do you see how everything changed for me, all of a sudden? It was like the snow fell and covered up all the places I ever went, all the faces and names, right up to my backyard, right up to the cardboard that covered the hole in my window, so there was not even a footprint for me to follow. All of these people that I told you about, and hundreds more—I never saw or heard of the great majority of them again.

"This doesn't happen to many people, I think, that they should be so completely uprooted, that all I kept was my ideas. Y'see, that's what makes a revolutionary—ideas. A dancer has her feet, and she can dance anywhere, so long as she watches for splinters . . . and a workman has his tools and his union, and a cantor has his voice . . . and we all have our *tsuris* . . . and the revolutionary has her ideas. Do you know the song 'Di Gedankn Zind Frei? 'My thoughts freely flower,' it says, 'My thoughts give me power. No tyrant can match them.' It's true!

"And the prison helps to make revolutionaries, y'see. It's like you put beans in a dark closet and they sprout. The separation, the hard conditions, it robs so much from you and leaves you only your ideas, which is why you're in jail in the first place. And the way they mistreat you, and the way you see others suffer—if, before, you had any questions, any doubts, now they're all gone. The government has taught you how to hate, they whip it into you. In Siberia we were surrounded by whips—'knouts,' they called them, and every guard had one: long whips with knots of rawhide at the end, so it tears the skin with every blow.

"So your sense of being a revolutionary gets hard, it gets tough. Now you not only see the monster, now you have to sleep with the monster, every single night. Oh, you learn to hate! And it was not hard to hate the czarists! So scared, they were, so violent, that if you did anything but pray and slice potatoes a whole life, you were liable to get arrested and sent to Siberia without even a trial. I'm not kidding! People spent their lives in prison or in exile for some little bit of a letter that they wrote complaining, let's say, about some official that he's taking bribes, or if it mentioned words like 'working class' or 'union.' So of course there were many, many revolutionaries and terrorists in Russia. The system manufactured them. But you didn't have to make bombs to have your whole life explode.

"What, you think it's so different in America? Here you have people that they grow up in prison, actually. Like so many young Negro men and women, the judge takes them for a little stinking crime and he puts them in jail for ten years before they can even grow up and learn a better way to behave. At least in Siberia we had each other, to hold, to talk, to help. The coldness was outside. But in American prisons it comes inside, into your soul, and as soon as you show some fire, some understanding, they put you alone in the dungeon and you can talk to yourself. And for

what? I remember Mother Jones said, 'If you steal a pair of
shoes, you go to jail; if you steal a railroad, you go to the United
States Senate.'

"Now I got another joke, so maybe we can go on Johnny
Carson. You want to hear? It's about capital punishment. If you
don't have the capital, you get the punishment. You think that's a
sick joke? I think it's a sick system.

"All right, all right, back to Siberia. There's no rush, actually—
it took us three and a half months to walk there, y'see. Yes, we
had to walk. But at least they had the railroad built, since 1892,
since then we had the railroad in Mogilev-Podolsk. So we went
part of the way in a train, in a cattle car, to Irkutsk, and we
stayed there in a forwarding prison until the springtime came.
This prison was just a big room in a barn, but crowded and
with not so much as a pail for you know what or some straw to
sleep on. And then to Yakutsk we walked, maybe thirty of us.
That's more than a thousand miles! And the men had to wear
chains, and we were given only prison clothing to wear, long
gray coats with yellow, like, diamond patches between the
shoulders, and black slippers and gray kerchiefs.

"But here's how being young and tiny helped me, y'see, 'cause
the guards took pity on me—I was the only child in the bunch
and with no parents, so they let me ride on their horses or in
the flat wagons that they had for supplies and for those that
they're already too sick to walk. Also, it was summertime, and
there was still a little grass to lie on, so I managed not to get very
sick.

"We went through so many towns, all kinds of little settle-
ments, and some people would come and give us food and maybe
a blanket, and others would come and throw rocks. So years later,
I came through these same towns with the Red Army, and I
knew where it was safe for us to be 'cause the people were
progressive, and I knew which places to avoid. . . .

"But the worst part, once I left the Ukraine, was having no one,
no one even to write. It's very important for people in prison to
have someone that cares, someone on the outside. Then maybe at
least the guards will think twice before they beat you. But I
couldn't write to my brothers, y'see—I didn't know where they
were, and you can't just send a greeting card to revolutionaries.
And my father and my mother—I don't know—I would write

them maybe a postal card, but I didn't feel like we could understand each other. Eventually I wrote to them, and to Ruchel, and
to Leah in New York. But the gendarmes read everything we
wrote, and the mail came into town and to our camp only once
a month in the summer, and only if you were lucky in the winter.

"I guess I didn't so much want to hear from my family. It was
too painful, it made me feel like a child again, and what was the
use of this? I would cry, my tears would freeze. . . . Feh.

"But meanwhile, the biggest revolutionaries, I met them in
Siberia. Vera Figner, f'rinstance. She was an aristocrat with education. They burned her with cigarettes that she should give out
the names of her comrades. We heard her screaming, but she
never gave out. But Vera Figner was only there for two months
after I came. The one I really remember is Babushka Breshkovskya. They called her the grandmother of the revolution.
She helped make the beginning of the Socialist Revolutionary
party. And she already escaped a couple of times from Siberia,
and she went and lectured in the United States, and then she
came back and got arrested again. I remember she was short,
like me—you think we can't punch you in the nose, and you're
right, so instead we punch you in the stomach!—and with a
round face and little eyes, and she had no eyelashes or eyebrows
'cause of the cold, these are sensitive parts. She always carried a
rope around her waist, inside her coat. I don't know why, I was
afraid to ask.

"Now, when Babushka spoke, you heard music. 'Cause words
were our warmth in Siberia. You couldn't have a fire in the
barracks—there was no chimney and you would choke, and the
buildings were made from old wood and they would burn up. So
all the women came together to sleep in a huddle, and we ate that
way, we talked that way. We had prostitutes and murderers
together in the same bunch with the greatest minds in Russia,
and from looking you couldn't tell them one from the other—we
all wore the same rags. But even the women that they couldn't
sign their names would hear Babushka speak and they would
understand. And even the thieves would save her a piece of bread,
and the murderers would take care of her. She was so simple in
her speech, so down-to-earth, and so confident that the revolution
would come.

"And she was really a mother to me, from the first day she

saw me. She taught me where to go and who to avoid and how to trick the guards, and how to trick a piece of newspaper to think it can warm your foot. And she told me about all the world and made me proud of myself that I am in Siberia.

"Also there was this guy I remember, from the men's barracks—Alexander. I never learned his second name. He was in the Social Democratic party, Lenin's bunch. We got him out of camp in a barrel of sauerkraut! Although we were so far from civilization, y'see, the revolutionary movement was growing, and many, many people ran away.

"Ohh, I could tell you a thousand stories from my years in Siberia: how rotten the food was, I could never eat it, and how we used to sleep on the ground with no heat. And the guards with their whips—more whips than brains, they had. And the snow, it was taller than me—I'll never forget, we had to make, like, tunnels to go through. But I don't want to exaggerate my hardship, y'see, 'cause for me it wasn't so bad. I went to a parochial school in the town; I got myself there a priest and his daughter, and with her I used to go all over. I had to sleep in the barracks, that's all. I would even feel guilty 'cause I had it better than the others.

"But the point is, when I tell people that I went to Siberia, either they say I'm a liar or their jaw drops and they treat me like a queen. But I wasn't a hero for going to Siberia, I was privileged, 'cause I met there profound people, in the most difficult circumstances, and with spirits that you'd think they were in the czar's palace eating blintzes! People that they were ready to give their lives that you and I should live better. All the wealth of Russia was here with these people. So never mind hardships. Maybe the lousy food stopped me from growing, so I'm a shrimp, all of five feet. So what? I was big enough to raise two children on my own! And maybe the cold gave me poor circulation and made it so I still have headaches to this day. So what? That way, at least, I know that my head is screwed on!

"And I lost some of my childhood, but there wasn't much to begin, being a Jew, being in Russia. You were born into hard times.

"No, all that is unimportant. I would forget it if you didn't ask. But I will never forget the things I learned in Siberia, the ideas, the love for the people that warmed me there. And I will

never drop from my hand the tools of the trade that I learned—
to be a revolutionary."

❀

The first winter had been worst, with miseries lacking analogy
from beyond the Siberian realm. Buzie remembered how the
wind had seemed a constant murder threat, barely concealed, like
the guards' whips. It whistled high and low, always angry, scraping the icy landscape and rattling every building in the compound.
Buzie had clung to Babushka in the straw each night, stirring
her to fetch a massage that would calm her trembling legs, to feel
the woman's warm breath and the near vibration of her voice:

"I know, my little rebel, even the earth is tormented here. The
czar has only to exile us, and then the wind is his barbed wire,
the snow his guard, the cold his executioner. But wait, darling,
hold on. Hold on to your smile. The seasons will change, and we
will see it together. The grass will grow again, enough to
squiggle your toes in! We women must learn from this Siberian
earth, Buzie—lying beneath the snow, waiting to feel the sun. . . ."

Merely her voice, gummy like an old woman's, could dilute
Buzie's terror to thin bitterness, while the luminous words could
be stored, picked over for long moments. In this way Buzie would
fall asleep, her thoughts racing into dreams, her ears deaf to the
wailing wind.

Now she watched with affection as her dear Madame Breshkovskya greeted the women of the barracks as they gathered
following the evening mess. It was Christmas Eve, the third for
Buzie in exile, and Babushka had again arranged for all the
women, veterans and newcomers alike, to join together for four
consecutive evenings in order to hear one another's personal
stories.

With help from Anna Oleynikov, the priest's daughter, Buzie
had secured for the ceremonies a banquet loaf of white bread, a
whole bag of apples, and a jug of vodka from friends in Ysyakh,
the settlement adjacent to the prison camp, where Anna lived and
Buzie, under the priest's sponsorship, attended school. Babushka
had given half the jug to Misevich, the drunken sergeant of the
guards, to keep him and his men occupied alongside their coal-
burner for one night at least. They could afford to relax during

the winter; to escape, a convict would need a shovel as wide as a plow and strength to dig a thousand miles.

Other women brought gifts to the gathering, though none had the splendid access to resources afforded to Buzie by Father Oleynikov, who was fanatically determined to win her conversion. One brought a sheepskin, upon which each storyteller could sit and be properly warmed and encouraged. Another had chocolate, a taste for everyone. A third had a fat bundle of cardboard for insulating boots and walls. Many of the women also wore bits of ribbon or string to enhance hairstyle for the holiday, but here again Buzie won the prize with her red lace tablecloth draped gracefully around her shoulders.

"Now, ladies," said Babushka, helping herself to her feet by pressing upon the shoulders of women seated in a circle on either side of her, "we're going to take that slop that the czar feeds us for Christmas dinner and turn it into a real nourishing meal. Do you want to know how? By speaking from our guts, that's how!" She pounded her belly with her fist. "That's where the bitterness of this life settles, and it's time, tonight, to spit it out!"

Buzie felt nearly heroic as she punctuated Babushka's welcoming speech by distributing hunks of the rich white bread to all twenty-three of the grimy women. She had feared, lately, becoming an outsider to the barracks, being exalted to aristocratic rank by the bribes Father Oleynikov incessantly offered to her "eternal soul"—the indefinite postponement of her trial, for instance, begun in August following her sixteenth birthday, then severed without a verdict at the priest's behest. With houseguest privileges granted her, Buzie at times during the winter had actually felt her blood circulating, her toes wiggling, and had been strengthened by good food, hot baths, and Anna's companionship. But seeing now how the women of the barracks received her bread and accepted her into their community, she felt cheerful about having declined Father Oleynikov's invitation to spend the Christmas holidays at his house.

Babushka was standing in Buzie's spot in the circle as Buzie completed the bread distribution. She stepped back to permit Buzie to sit, then pressed her shoes against the girl's rump and laid both palms atop her head. "This dear girl," she said, "told me something last year that I still remember, and I must use it now in my speech to impress you all."

Buzie's mouth bowed with surprise.

"Last year I began our ceremony by asking, 'Why is this night different from any other in our exile?' Who remembers my asking this? And Buzie, when she heard these words, told me that this same question is asked by the Jewish people at the start of their Passover festival, which is a magnificent celebration of freedom from slavery. It's in the Bible, this story. Now, how many of you knew this about the Jews, eh? No, because you never had someone like Buzie to tell you! You had only vicious priests to make you think the Jews did something to offend you, am I right?"

Babushka then announced that Buzie had "agreed" to sing that part of the Passover ritual in "her beautiful Jewish language." Though taken unawares, the girl gladly complied, pleased that she had actually made an impression on Babushka's memory. Leaning forward, eye-shy of the others, she sang down to the dirt: "*Ma nishtano haleilo hazeh mikhol halyelos?*"

The wind whistled and shook the bunk like a chained beast. Hannah, a young Jewish prostitute from Moscow, began to sob and weep. Buzie stopped singing, surprised to find that her own throat had constricted with tears.

"*Avodim ho-yinu l'Faro b'Mitzrayim*"—We were slaves in the land of Egypt. "*B'khol dor vo-dor khayov odom liros es atzmo k'ilu hu yotzo miMitzrayim*"—In every generation one ought to regard himself as though he had personally been liberated from slavery. . . .

"Now, I ask you," Babushka resumed, "why *is* this night different? Is it because God fathered a son with a virgin? Ha! You have to be a virgin yourself to believe that! Don't be so shocked, Sofya"—a devout peasant, she was unhappily shaking her head— "because if you're right and I'm wrong, so much the better for all of us. In hell, at least, I won't have to freeze to death!"

Babushka lowered herself to the sheepskin, one fat knee at a time, and drew her blanket more tightly around her shoulders. "But I don't wish to insult Father Christmas," she said. "I take him very seriously. Let me tell you, sisters, I have been an exile in these wastelands on and off since I was a woman of thirty and now I'm fifty-five years old and a grandmother, though I have yet to see my own granddaughter. But each year I have celebrated this holiday as my own day of rebirth, the rebirth of my hopes, the rebirth of my principles. Once I even celebrated by escaping —that's right, in the dead of winter! Three times I have escaped from these camps, and I'll do it again, don't you worry! The problem is only that I return to my work, and they know where to find me. Wherever the revolutionary movement is strongest, that's where you'll find Katharina Breshkovskya! But someday I will be the hunter, and they, the police, the czarist worms who leech from the peasant's blood, they will be the refugees!

"Those of you who know me and have heard my stories," she continued, "or those few who have survived the cold for ten years or more, like Olga, or Dvera—only the Socialist Revolutionaries survive so long, eh, ladies? Well, you know how it is, my dears. We lose not only our eyebrows, our eyelashes, our moustaches—Ha, don't laugh, Manya! My lip would appreciate a nice warm moustache right now!"

"You should go to the men's bunk," howled Manya, a husky border smuggler from Poland. "They'll give you all the moustache you need!"

The women laughed in every key, their breaths condensing in the air. "Someone fetch Manya an icicle to suck," Babushka said. "But I confess, I have dreams, too. I used to lead the upper-class life, you know, with all the indulgences. I still dream at night that the snow will turn to whipped cream and we will eat our way to St. Petersburg!" She held up her hand for solemnity's sake. "But more has been lost to us than unwanted hairs and unwanted men, my darlings. When despair comes for a visit . . . when the wind whistles right through your skull . . . when the guards show no sign of being human . . . then we realize that this grim life is no life at all. There are no comforts, no occupations, no little children, not even a worthwhile memory to indulge without paying for it with deep, deep regrets. So . . . then we have only each other, our names, our beliefs, our stories and songs. And tonight we will share these, and get a good warm feeling. Yes?"

The women murmured their agreement, but Buzie was silent, sitting tall with her eyes closed after a single, sympathetic glance at Hannah. With the bread given out and the special Passover plaudit now done, Buzie was feeling vaguely dissatisfied, an unenthusiastic spectator, and with a headache developing. A pulsebeat seemed to run through the circle of women as Babushka's rhetoric took effect, but Buzie remained aloof, withholding her attention, seeking instead the wind and the world, expanses and contexts beyond these tragic souls who had so much in common, yes, and so much to share, sure, and with acid in their spit—and with not even enough body heat to warm a corner of the room! Buzie knew from experience that none but the politicals could do more than wet the sheepskin with tears, telling tales of commonplace hardships, perhaps with some vague stringer of political analysis or some misunderstood slogan to suit Babushka's taste. And this she would applaud as a mother applauds the first dribble on her baby's chin! Buzie shunned viewing this heatless fire; it reminded her too keenly of her brothers, sitting in Nakhum's mud hut, equidistant from the czar's throne and their next square meal.

Enough bravado, enough talk! But now Hannah had sat upon the sheepskin at Babushka's prompting. She was a gaunt woman of dark, mournful looks, with sunken cheeks and finespun black curls. "What should I say?" Hannah began timidly. "I'm only glad to forget the streets of Moscow. . . ."

Dvera chimed in: "And the men who make the filth! Tell us, girl, isn't it true that a Jewish girl cannot *live* in Moscow unless she carries the yellow ticket of a prostitute?"

Hannah nodded sorrily, looking more frightened than ever. "Please," she whimpered, "I have nothing to tell, I'm nothing. . . ."

Five women told their tales that night, and everyone wept more than once. By the time they broke up for sleep, Buzie's frustration had ebbed to a vague, self-doubting anxiety. "How have I changed so much?" she muttered to herself as she huddled next to Babushka in the darkness. "The Christmas used to be so important. . . ."

Babushka's back rippled with snickering laughter. "You used to call me 'momma,' at least once when you got sleepy."

"But now it feels like I'm not even here, Babushka. I don't want to be here."

"Who does?"

"I keep drifting, thinking . . ."

"Of what?" Babushka rolled onto her back. Buzie could just make out the silhouette of her features, the luminescence of her pudgy face. "Of your girlfriend, your good food and nice house, what?"

"No," replied Buzie, offended. "I already have those things. I've had them since I was fourteen. They pull me out of the barracks and into nowhere."

"Bah. After tonight, we'll hand you over to the Social Democrats. They also like to keep to themselves."

Buzie clucked her tongue and whispered hoarsely, "Ohh, I've listened enough to you, with your revolutionary groups!" She curled up like a worm. "They can't do anything in exile!"

"Oh?" Babushka replied, her voice buoyant with derision. "But I hear that Lenin is making tremendous advances—in Switzerland!"

"You! What the hell are you talking about?"

"Vladimir Ilich Lenin. With Martov and Plekhanov and the other big shots I've told you about—little men with big ideas! You can make revolution with them like you can melt the snow of Siberia with a matchstick!"

"Breshka!" Buzie pinched her hip through the blanket. "You're babbling like you drank the whole jug of vodka! Tomorrow you can tell Dvera your theories. I want to talk about me!"

Manya, bedded nearby, begged them to hush their voices. Buzie sucked in her breath, releasing it only in rhythm with Babushka's. A single silvery star that was sometimes visible through a crack in the roof gleamed into Buzie's eye. "You carry on," she whispered, "like a wolf that has no teeth. You howl and you howl and someday even the rabbits will be laughing at you."

"Hoo, what a tongue you've got," Babushka said. "God save your enemies."

"For as long as I'm in Siberia, God is my enemy."

"You want to leave your old Babushka to rot?"

"Don't make jokes," Buzie said. "I won't laugh."

Babushka peeled the blanket from the girl's face and kissed her ear. "Then don't be bitter with me, little rebel. The Revolution is right here, right now, don't you see? If we're given guns, we make revolution with guns. If we're given only snow and sick women, then we work with them. For now, Buzie. Only for now."

The pleading tone in her voice shamed the girl. "Look," Buzie whispered, pointing at the ceiling. "Do you want to see my star? You have to look just right, there's a crack . . . Here, put your head on my belly."

Instead, Babushka caught her hand and kissed each finger. "You

think this star is going to tell you something?" she said, her voice
choked. "You think the wind is a better friend than me? Well,
Buzie, we'll have to make arrangements for you to meet that
wind, to see where it carries you. . . ."

Manya shushed them again. Buzie burrowed into Babushka's
armpit and lay without speaking. Sleep quickly closed like a
drawstring across her mind.

All activities beyond survival routines required extraordinary
effort in Ysyakh. The subzero temperatures taxed the body to
exhaustion and reduced mental activity to primitive mechanisms,
chiefly sleep. Babushka's prodigious feat of organizing these
numb, hungry women, some of them living carcasses, for four
days of cooperation and involvement showed a depth of power
that Buzie again came to appreciate as the week wore on. But she
remained more an observer than a participant in the ceremonies,
shedding the pretense of complete identification with the others
and losing, as well, the uneasiness and the headaches that had
been the dust of her idealism's retreat.

Buzie's spirit was in flight, but without direction and in the
dead of Siberian winter. The other women appeared to her as
pitiable, flightless chicks, chirping to their Babushka hen; Buzie
could not share in their peasant misery and dim expectations. Intense fantasies of escape set her to trembling more than the cold
as for the week she took up the yoke of unrelieved imprisonment.
She wrote dozens of imaginary letters that she might smuggle
past the censors to Anna Oleynikov and, through her, to the
world beyond. But the addressees themselves were imaginary, or
at best were family memories mounted upon once-a-month signatures. (Poppa is sick, Ruchel is in a family way again, Mrs. Markish has moved to "the Bronx," Momma has adopted a goat. . . .)

At night, as the women of the barracks droned on about their
misfortunes and lost lives, Buzie herded her memories like live-
stock before her, branding each event and person with a blessing
or damnation and shutting the gate to their return: shutting the
gate to poverty, to the muddy marketplace in Mogilev-Podolsk
where two beggars vied for every half-groschen; shutting the
gate to cossack violence, the violence of unfeeling men—their
sabers should melt, their knouts turn to noodles! And to religious

fakery, those disappointing fairy tales told by her own father, by Father Oleynikov, and all the others. . . . She would build a new home, far from the mud and ice, far from the lies, in a new world.

"The New World." Manya used that phrase as she took the sheepskin on the third night to speak of her life as a border smuggler. Buzie's ears opened wide to her tales of all the poor Jews and peasants who were crawling with bedding and baggage to get to Antwerp, to London, to America. "The New World." "New York." "The Bronx." A new name. A new life, and the old things would wither and die like tangled grass!

"I feel empty now," Buzie declared mysteriously to Babushka the next morning as the soup-kitchen cowbell called them to mess. "Like after the snow falls—no tracks yet. . . . Babushka?"

"Busy bee," Babushka said as she stuffed newspaper into her boots, "I can hear your thoughts buzzing."

"Listen. I don't want to take a turn on the sheepskin. I don't need to speak. I'm gone from my past now—empty. Gone from Russia."

"If only we could vanish so easily! But it's important for you to set an example for the others, Buzie. You speak so well—"

"No. No, I—" She fabricated an excuse. "I'm volunteering to work in the infirmary today."

Babushka mulled this over as she tugged at her bootlaces. "Good," she finally agreed. "We can use you there."

The plan had less than spit to hold it together. Yet Buzie held her frightened silence as Olga and Dvera crossed the barracks to accompany Babushka to breakfast. Somehow the infirmary did seem closer to America than the broken-down barracks full of hopeless women.

Her first task was to make the request to Sergeant Misevich. He would not deny her, she felt certain, for the infirmary was understocked and understaffed, a place of dying, not of healing, with a doctor sledding in from Yakutsk only once a month to fill out the death certificates. An educated girl could at least read to those patients for whom there was no other narcotic. Still, Misevich had a nasty alcoholic streak, and this would be the first time in her four years of imprisonment that Buzie would be facing him alone, without either Father Oleynikov or Babushka at her side.

The pathways between the buildings of the compound were
sheltered by decrepit wooden trellises sloped to keep some of
the heavy snowfall off to the sides. Trails were dug out beneath
these by male prisoners, with side walls of snow packed higher
than Buzie's line of vision. These arteries, called "the tunnels" by
everyone in camp, were considerably warmer and less windy
than the surface, but narrow and blind at every turn. The women,
especially, avoided them. Often the tunnels were ruined by
cave-ins and became less navigable than the hard-pack ground
above; during each partial summer thaw they yielded at least one
body of a person presumed to have escaped.

The guards' bunk, flanked by scarred whipping posts, was
nearest the women's barracks and central in camp. Beyond it on
higher ground stood the men's barracks, the punishment cells for
militant, rebellious, or insane convicts, and the long, low-slung
infirmary building; to the east, the mess hall, the ten-foot brick
wall, and the visible steeple of the Ysyakh church, drab brown
beneath a frosted sky. The thin, frigid air pinched Buzie's nostrils
as she scaled the tunnel embankment to the upper crust of snow,
nearly at roof level with her own barracks. Smoke from the
guards' quarters and the mess hall rose in straight, unhurried
columns. Buzie heard the raw scrape of shovels against the ice,
and within a few crunching steps—hurrying to keep her fears
bundled—she came upon a collapsed section of the trellis where
three prisoners were making repairs with rope and wood and
digging out the buried trail. They were standing in the tunnel,
their work motions strained by the weight of ball-and-chain
manacles fastened to their ankles. Buzie could not stand the sight,
the torture of their strength by dead, sagging chains, and
hurried past.

The tallest of the three, head and shoulders above the tunnel
wall, peered closely at her from his dense head wrappings. His
red beard was pushed up like a yoke around his neck. "Hey,
you're Babushka's girl!" he hollered at her back. "Wait a
minute!" She spun around and walked backward with her
mittened hands pressed to her face for warmth. He beckoned
her again with a wave of his shovel. "Come on, girl, you and I can
dig a hole to America!"

What kind of joke was this, plucked like a fruit from her own
wild, thorny mind? Buzie veered from the tunnel's edge, keenly
aware of the awkwardness of her gait across the ice, feeling as

though the three men were watching and conspiring to throw snowballs. She heard their shovels scraping the permafrost again, but his words, his confident knowledge of her private thoughts, continued to penetrate her consciousness with humiliating ease until she nearly turned and ran to the women's barracks, where humiliations could be countered with words or fists and this masculine brand of scorn held no sway. . . .

A skinny young guard sat behind Sergeant Misevich's desk in the guards' hut. He wore a moustache that hung like wet tobacco leaves on either side of his nose, and had beady eyes that turned Buzie's skin clammy. "I like it," he replied to her forthright request for a pass to assist in the infirmary. "Especially if we fix you up with a little uniform. How about that, girl? A nurse's uniform?"

"Better just to fix me up with a pass so I can help the sick."

He rose and stepped out from behind the desk. "You know, pretty one, it's warmer in here than in the infirmary. You could even take off your coat in here."

Buzie kept her eyes fixed on the whips hanging on the wall. There, there was the essence of his blasted, taunting soul! "I'm not so warm," she replied, "and not so pretty, either."

"But how would you know? Do you keep a mirror hidden from us? Maybe inside your underwear, hmm?"

Sergeant Misevich entered the bunk and dropped a pile of letters on the desk. "Get to work on those," he told his man. "Mail's in—should've been read by now."

"Yes, sir." The guard threw a warning glance at Buzie, then picked up the outgoing letters to censor them.

More often than not, it was Anna Oleynikov who carried the mail from Ysyakh on her sleigh. She would probably be parked in front of the women's barracks now, looking for Buzie while she waited for the return bundle. Buzie could barely contain herself long enough to gain her pass. "Here," said Misevich, scribbling. "Either get well or die, but do it without lingering!"

"She's working, not mooching, sir," said the other, winking at Buzie.

Misevich snorted. "You've got yourself a nurse, eh? A wet nurse!"

"Yessir."

"Good for you, Kuvalda. See that you don't dirty any sheets!"

Buzie backed out on their vulgar laughter with a little bow, then ran through the tunnel with an eagerness made desperate by her fear of the young guard. She was on the verge of shouting Anna's name when she again heard the scraping of shovels—she had forgotten completely about that red-haired ogre! But there was no exit now, no means of scaling the ice wall.

She came at him running, her head bowed, but he noticed her approach and, moving with speed that defied his chains' weight, dropped his shovel, grabbed her by the shoulders, and vaulted her—how she kicked and floundered!—over his head. Landing upright, her legs wobbly, Buzie could not catch her breath to scream. She felt overwhelmed by his effortless manipulation of her body.

He gave a deep, yawning laugh. "If you telegraph your fear, girlie, the gendarmes will pick you right out of a crowd. How will you get past the train station?"

The door to the women's barracks creaked open, admitting to the tunnel a mass of women with their tin cups and plates. At their head was Olga, to whom Buzie ran, casting a bewildered glance over her shoulder at the weird man who now stood flush against the wall, holding his manacled hand inside his coat as if not to offend the passing women. Olga took Buzie into the folds of her coat and turned her about-face to proceed with the rest. But then Olga herself stepped on Buzie's heels and sprawled elaborately at Red Beard's feet.

Babushka rushed forward and bottlenecked the tunnel. She boxed Buzie's ears. "Help her up! What are you, frozen?"

Buzie shuddered to be so near the prisoner's heavy, clanking chains as they both knelt to fetch Olga and her gear. "Give me that," he growled without looking up, pointing to the tin plate. He slipped under it a brown envelope drawn from his coat. These, together, he handed to Olga after she'd been raised to her feet; and while Babushka brushed her off, Olga slid the package into her coat. It was a perfectly smooth operation, completed before any of the women began even to complain about the traffic jam. Red Beard saluted them each with insults, like any common scoundrel, as they proceeded to the mess hall.

"Who is he?" whispered Buzie as Babushka leaned heavily on her shoulder.

"Shh—a friend. Social Democrat. But here we're all friends. He'll be leaving us soon."

Buzie's jaw tightened with envy. They were developing an

escape plan, taking risks, breaking their bones, for a stranger? For a brazen fool whose mouth was bigger than his brain! And she, wasn't she faced with a trial? Hadn't she rotted here long enough. . . ?

"Anna!" Buzie cried, remembering. "She brought the mail—"

"Misevich brought the mail," Babushka corrected her, "along with his supply of whiskey. Come, darling, be my cane."

Buzie hung her head as the women of the barracks squeezed past her in the tunnel. "I've got to go to the infirmary."

"Already? I'm not sick enough for you?" Babushka waddled a step ahead, then turned and beckoned her. "Well, come on, Buzie, you've got to walk to the end of the tunnel, wherever you're going! I can't lift you over the trellis!"

Chapter Eight

Dear Anna,

After you read this, please burn it. Now, I must tell you that it was a mistake for me to spend my Christmas away from you and your father, but I was in a morbid mood. You would not have enjoyed seeing my face spoiling your pretty Christmas things. If you're angry with me now, please, Anna, don't be foolish. I miss you very much, even more than I miss your tub and your warm bed . . . and that's where I'd like to be when the next blizzard begins.

Right now they're keeping us apart by giving me so much work in the infirmary that I can never get finished and never hear that you've come into camp. Can you imagine, they had nobody regular to care for the feverish, the very sick, even to take away a bedpan, until I volunteered? I have to watch over them all, clean up after them, feed them, everything.

The first two days it smelled worse than our outhouse. All through Christmas there was diarrhea in the camp. The cook said he had killed a reindeer, but some of the sick men say it was a dog. And now, every time I think of something useful to do, it means more work for me because I don't want the useful things to stop. I got the idea, for example, just a simple idea, to have a big pot of water on the stove so I could bathe the ones who smelled the worst. Now all of a sudden everyone wants a bath! Also I boil clean water for tea or chicory, whatever I can get. I spend my life now melting snow on the stove and dunking rags into it!

Rags, rags, rags for everyone but yourself. Look at Anna, fourteen years old, the little stinker, and already she bleeds—she washes and hangs her rags so her father won't see; she'd be ready for *mikvah* if she weren't a *goy*. And you, Buzeleh, you change in so many ways while your body stays frozen? Even that ugly duckling Fanya, thirteen years old, youngest in the barracks now and with a pickpocket for a mother—even this one will be fertile and whole before me!

Always wants to play, that one, the dirty-face. Ha! Better her than with Kuvalda. . . .

I have another headache here, too, an ugly gendarme named Kuvalda who's in charge of the infirmary. He follows me around all the time, hoping I'm going to lead him into a dark closet. I have nightmares of this guy—he has not left me alone since he first saw me in the sergeant's office. It makes me sick. If he would just back away and take a look at me! My skinny arms, my dirty hair, this little square, stinking body—what could it mean to him to smear his face against mine? I'll tell you what it would mean to me, Anna. I would choke! If he gets too close, believe me, I'll shave his ugly moustache with a rusty surgical knife and then we'll see how close he comes again! But I have no time to write a long letter, not about this peasant. . . .

Today he had surprised her with a gift, a new blouse, embroidered in the Ukrainian style, which he had bought in Yakutsk. "Now I start weaning you from your priest and your women, huh?"

"I'm nobody's suckling pig to be weaned, Kuvalda."

"No, except for those grimy women you lie with just like pigs in a poke!"

"You, you get to take a bath every week and still you stink!"

"Try on the blouse."

"Move your onion breath away! I've got work to do. That blouse will look better on you."

"Try it on! Or else you can wear it after I untie you from the whipping post this afternoon!"

"Very nice, Kuvalda. I'll really love you and all your ancestors then! Get back! You come any closer and I'll bite your ear off!"

(Turn and walk away now. Don't be scared.)

"Oh, Buzie, I do love you, I do. Please, please put on the blouse."

"Yeah, like a fox loves a rabbit, you love me. Go love yourself, you crazy fool." (I've got to have some tea, he puts my stomach in knots!) "Look out, I'm going to make some tea. You want?"

. . . Now Anna, if I do manage to get this letter to you without being caught, be prepared to receive others the same way. I am writing to old friends and I must send these without the guards reading them. It is nothing illegal, Anna, only private. You can even read the letters if you like. Mail them in a fresh envelope with your own signature, okay? I will pay you back eventually for the postage and everything.

Please tell your father that I miss him as well. Also that I'm as close to God as I ever was. Do you remember the crucifix he wanted to give me to wear when we first went to school together? I wonder if he still has it, a beautiful wooden cross on a gold chain. Tell him that I would like to have it now, it would make me very happy.

Please, Anna, be sure to come see me next time you're in camp. Maybe they'll try to put you off, maybe tell you that the infirmary is under quarantine, but that's a lie. You can tell them right back that Kuvalda is the only sick one here. Other than that, there's lots of fever, and I still have my headaches, but you won't find any evil spirits here, only brave souls.

Love,
Buzie

"Fanya, come here a minute."

Fanya's mother, shuffling among her blankets and piles like a clerk taking inventory, watched suspiciously as her daughter skipped over to Buzie. By picking the pockets of her bunkmates during those relaxed Christmas evenings, she had gotten both herself and her daughter completely ostracized in the barracks, though Babushka on occasion held a conversation with them, on principle refusing to abandon a soul to the wasteland. Buzie saw how Fanya's face had become hard over the weeks, how hungry her eyes grew in response to the rare summons.

"How are you, Fanya?"

"I'm hungry. What's it like in the infirmary?"

"I work hard."

"But you stay warm!"

"Fanya, I called you—"

"If I got sick, could I stay there with you?"

Buzie controlled her rising impatience and touched the girl's shoulder. "Women are supposed to take care of each other, right here in the bunk. There are only two women in the infirmary, from way before you even came here, Fanya. One can no longer control her bowels for a second, and the other has a fever that's burning her brain. You should never get so sick."

"But I will," Fanya replied, her brow deeply creased. She spat on the earth, bent slightly to examine it, rubbed the spot with her foot and then kicked it, again, and again.

"I want you to do something for me," Buzie said.

"You never do for me."

"I'll give you something."

"Something to eat?"

"No, better." Fanya's mother was moving toward them. Buzie turned her back to block her view and dug from her pocket Herschel's old wooden *dreydl*, which she had safeguarded worshipfully since her arrest. The child in her dreaded giving away such a sacred object, but she shunted aside these feelings and said, "This *dreydl* can tell the future and answer all your questions."

Fanya reached for it, but Buzie pulled it back, then twirled it teasingly by its stem above their heads.

Fanya's mother had roused Manya from a catnap. "Again, Gena! Again among my things with your sticky fingers!"

"Move aside, cow. Who wants to steal your crummy garbage?"

"I'll chop your hands off!"

"You couldn't move fast enough!"

Buzie hurriedly whispered her offer to Fanya, who seemed indifferent to her mother's trouble. "When my friend Anna comes to camp, find me, I'll be in the infirmary. You will give something to Anna for me and then I'll give you the *dreydl*. Yes?"

"Fanya!" snarled her mother, sidestepping Manya's curses.

The girl glided meekly across the barracks before Buzie could caution her to keep silent. But the big, brawling Manya had words yet for Gena, and Fanya's punishment—she waited with her head bowed—was consumed by a free-for-all shouting match. Buzie dropped to the ground to spin her *dreydl*, like a peddler showing her wares, with one eye attentive to her customer, who kept peeking at the prize.

Half an hour later, Babushka asked Buzie what she was doing on the cold ground. Buzie blushed and pocketed the *dreydl*.

Dear Dr. Blum:

You did not think that the black sheep of Mogilev-Podolsk, sent into exile for her dangerous crimes, would become a doctor, did you? But here in the camp I have been working as the only person who takes care of the sick in the infirmary, since Christmas—Hanuka. So I'm writing to you for information that might help me.

I hope this is all right with you. You were always kind to me, when I was a girl and, most important, even after they took me to jail. I cannot forget you for visiting me and examining me, right there in the squalor. And how you tried to get the gendarmes and the authorities to let me go free. For this, and for the kindness that you always showed to those who lost their health to poverty, all those hundreds of miserable souls in our town, I will never forget you.

Now, I've arranged for this letter to travel past the censors, so please don't worry about getting into trouble. Besides—I intend no disrespect—I know that you're not exactly a greenhorn in the world of trouble! Your Committee for Jewish Protection always had my admiration.

I have to ask you some very important questions, ques-

tions that I could not really ask another soul. First of all,
about the infirmary: The place is very poorly stocked, with
nothing but bandages and a little alcohol, smelling salts, and
extra rations of dried fish. They suffer terribly here from
diarrhea—two have died since Christmas—and from terrible
coughs. They breathe like they were underwater. Also there
are skin problems and wasting disease—consumption? Can *I*
get it by being near them?

I remembered how clean your hands always were, even
your fingernails, so I try to keep my hands clean, too, also
the floor and the bedpans and the rest. But otherwise I'm an
ignoramus. Is there a medicine, for instance, perhaps even a
pill that you could mail, that can cure diarrhea? I've tried
to find raspberry syrup, but there is no apothecary in
Ysyakh, and raspberries, of course, do not grow in the ice.

I know these illnesses are due to the cold and the bad food
and the general conditions that I won't waste your time
describing. I know also that the only real cure for these
people is off in the hopeful future somewhere while they
suffer right now and right here, and—I calling myself a
revolutionary—am here with them. It must take many
years of study to understand medicine as you do, Dr. Blum,
but if there's a book I can read—I read Russian, Ukrainian,
and Yiddish—or if you can write to me some basic rules? I
want to help.

My second question is harder to ask. I need some money.
I come to you instead of to my father because, first, he hasn't
got, and, second, I don't want him worrying about me, nor
do I want to give him the chance ever to betray me again,
even by accident. Enough said. I need about 100 rubles, or
even more. It is not for a dowry, Dr. Blum. I hope I don't
have to explain more and I hope you're feeling generous.

My third question is also medical. Can you please tell me
what is the normal age for a girl to first have her menstruation? Is there an illness that would interfere with it? One
woman here says that many drop from their cycle as soon
as they enter prison life, but, you'll excuse my saying, I see
plenty of rags hanging on the clothesline in the corner of
the barracks (we have no privacy here, no way to be modest
about these things). Also, I remember that when my sister
Ruchel first came running to my mother, she got a good

slap on both cheeks that made her cry even more than the sight of blood. Now, was this also for health reasons? Another girl in the camp, younger than me, has been asking these kinds of questions, and she's very worried about herself. Please do give us some real information.

I have to stop now. You can write to me care of Anna Oleynikov, as it is written on the envelope. She is the daughter of a priest in Ysyakh and a saving grace in my life.

Please think kindly of me, even if you don't write.

Respectfully,
Buzie Kharlofsky

To build takes time, to knock down takes an instant. This lesson of patience and endurance shaped Buzie's days in the infirmary and tempered her fiber as weather does to wood. It was a lesson starkly illustrated in her work: To nurse someone back to health with only her devotion for medicine took days of persistence, while to lose someone to the Angel of Death took only a convulsion, an exhalation, a stilled heart.

Buzie became attuned to signs of progress in her patients: a heightened shine in the eye, an improvement in reflexes, an increase in appetite. She became professional in her discipline, matching her temperament to the slow pace of human recuperation, learning patience. Surrounded by men who, aside from Kuvalda, were too weak to intimidate or embarrass her, she began to realistically gauge her distrust of them and gained real confidence to match her wit, while the self-consciousness of her body that their attention made acute was replaced by physical pride, work pride, as she applied herself successfully to a thousand tasks.

Of all this she was aware, of every new skill, every virtue, every trace of maturity, almost to the point of vanity. She was her own parent, swelling with pride over her own achievement, and learning: To progress takes time; to destroy, only a moment. Nonetheless, when the crude escape plan that she had been slowly creating from scraps—from *dreydls*, letters, and dreams— was shredded one March morning, her spirit plummeted like a fledgling.

It began with a letter from her mother that listed, as Raisl did every month, the most recent emigrants from Mogilev-Podolsk.

This was delivered by Anna Oleynikov and read by Buzie as they sat together in the covered sleigh, only yards from the prison gate, with a deerskin drawn across their laps.

"I think the whole world is going into exile," Buzie mused, noting each name: Feivl and Yankel Kaminsky, gone to America, with Ruchel and the children to follow; Pesakh Dropsky, Moishe the butcher, Tsil's eldest brother, Motl, and scores more of the poor of the town, also gone. Others, like poor Shmulke and Avram the splinter and old Rabbi Mandelstam, gone to claim their rest in *Olam Habo*, blessings to their memory, wrote Raisl. And there were hints, too, that Yeshua and Herschel had successfully reached England.

"My town will be left for the ghosts. Ghosts, plus my momma's goat. I guess I won't go there again."

Anna giggled. "Are you planning a vacation, silly?"

Buzie paused from reading and gazed searchingly into Anna's eyes.

"Oh, darling, take me to the Black Sea!" cried Anna in a falsetto voice, swaying with laughter as Buzie shoved her. Sasha, the pony, snorted nervously at the commotion. Anna patted the animal's rump. "How about it, Sasha girl? A little outing?"

A surge of wind sprayed snow into their faces. Anna chucked the reins and set her pony to walking alongside the prison wall. Buzie rested her cheek against the rough canvas side of the sleigh. "You must have figured it out," she said quietly, "if you read my letter to Dr. Blum . . ."

"Figured what? You think I'm some kind of snoop?"

"No, no!" Buzie protested, kissing her cheek. "No, I think you're wonderful, Anna, the best friend I ever had—and when you get my letters from America, you *will* read them."

Anna reined in Sasha. "America?"

Buzie nodded, her eyes gleaming. "Just as soon as Dr. Blum sends money for my escape. Shh," she cautioned, impressed by her own use of the word.

"Escape?"

"Shh."

"To America? How?"

"I don't know yet. With the money." She spread her letter on her lap. "I'll need your help, too, Anna. But wait, let me read the rest—"

"My help? And who's going to dry my eyes when you're

gone? I'm coming with you!" Her voice dropped. "But, Buzie—the nearest train is eight hundred miles away. You know, you walked it. Eight hundred miles, with wolves and everything!"

"I'll get a map," muttered Buzie, bent over her letter. She felt a hollow tickling in her stomach, for the name Blum had appeared:

"*. . . after more than 25 years of service to us all. He said he wanted to die a free man in Germany. . . .*"

Anna was impatient for Buzie's undivided attention. "Look, why don't you quit that crummy infirmary and visit with us for a while? Here, look at what my father sent you." She held out a wooden crucifix, fulfilling Buzie's month-old request. "If you kiss it, you get good luck."

"*. . . Your father is heartbroken at Dr. Blum's departure. There's hardly an intelligent Jew left in town and there are none who can afford to buy those melons that your father loves. To eat and debate, this was your father's joy!*"

"Mpwah." Anna pressed her lips to the cross. "Lots of money for you, Buzie. Mpwah! America for you."

"*. . . a free man in Germany. Your father is heartbroken. . . .*"

Buzie cursed her mother's pinched handwriting and crumpled the letter in her fist, then pulled her hair before her face and bawled.

"My dear!" cried Anna, taking Buzie into her little arms. "What is it? What is it?"

Buzie wept herself dry in seconds, then felt stiff in Anna's embrace. She sat up to untie the knots in her chest. "I imagined it," she muttered. "I imagined it so hard, so much . . ."

"Yes, I've done that!" Anna agreed, anxious to console her. "And you're so sure it will come true!"

"Enough." Buzie lifted the reins from Anna's lap. "Here."

"And it *will* come true! It will all come true, Buzie!"

"Please, Anna . . . Now take me to the infirmary before Kuvalda misses me."

Inside, Buzie stoked the wood stove and set a pot of kasha to cooking on top. Patient after patient demanded her immediate attention, to loosen bandages, spoon-feed those too weak to lift their heads, wash bedpans in the snow. She had no time to grieve the loss of her plans, yet her body told the story as she trudged around like a slave at sunset.

Sitting down to her own bowl of kasha, she heard feet crunching in the snow outside and felt the sinking sensation that Kuvalda's presence always provoked. Two swallows more and she pushed the bowl aside and went for a broom to be able, as usual, to override his harassments with sheer activity.

Kuvalda summoned her as soon as he had the door pushed open. He had, leaning on his shoulder, Red Beard—named by Babushka as Jacob Smulevitch—who was wincing from pain. "This fool," announced the guard, "has bashed his own foot with his pickax."

"It should have been your head," muttered Buzie, quite audibly. "Take off those chains—where's he going to go when he's wounded? Whoa, he looks faint!" They eased the giant onto the cot nearest the stove. Kuvalda relieved him of the ball and chain, then headed to the guards' hut for handcuffs with which to manacle him to the bedframe.

"The doctor won't be here until the end of the week, and he's a butcher at that, so let me have a look at you. Maybe we can stop an infection from making off with one of your toes." She moved and spoke brusquely to hide the intimidation she felt. Jacob Smulevitch, she had learned from Babushka, was a revolutionary fighter whose name would someday be known throughout Russia. A close associate of George V. Plekhanov, he had helped to organize the 1898 Minsk Conference at which the Social Democratic party was born. In 1905, along with Leon Trotsky, he had been one of the few of either the Menshevik or Bolshevik factions to return to Russia from Western Europe during the ferment that followed Bloody Sunday. In Petrograd he had helped organize the workers' council, the *soviet*, that ran the general strike for several weeks; in Murmansk he had run a gun-smuggling operation for the revolutionary movement until the time of his arrest.

He had a reputation as an expert practitioner of devices to baffle the police: codes, disappearing inks, disguises, and forged documents. Apparently he could disguise pain, too, for he showed no sign of it as Buzie peeled off his boot and probed beneath his filthy foot wraps. Instead he rattled off probing questions about Buzie's own political past. . . .

But there was no wound! Smulevitch intercepted her startled glance with a cautionary gesture and said, "I heal very quickly. Now, a bandage, please, before our friend returns."

That evening Babushka led Buzie to the dank outhouse behind the barracks and plied her with questions about Smulevitch's welfare. "And your guard? He suspects nothing?"

"I told him that the pickax probably smashed the bones of his foot and the doctor will have to look."

"Good. Your tongue has its own imagination, my daughter. Now, listen carefully." She bent close to Buzie's ear. "The doctor who comes this week will not be that murderer from Yakutsk. He's going to be too sick himself to make the trip. Instead we get a real doctor, a miracle worker. Your job is to get the manacles off our man—we didn't count on them, you understand? You'll get rid of them. And you must keep your sweetheart and any other busybodies—"

"What sweetheart?" Buzie protested. "Kuvalda makes me sick."

"Shh . . . Even if it means pretending to be his sweetheart, you must keep him busy enough for Jacob to crawl into our doctor's little black bag. Do you understand, Buzie? We'll provide plenty of distraction for the rest of the guards, elsewhere in the camp."

Buzie stomped the icy ground to more securely feel her own presence in the stinking dark. "It's a better plan than the barrel of sauerkraut. But where does he go after Yakutsk?"

Stiffening, Babushka swatted Buzie to silence and listened carefully to the darkness. "Never mind, we'll talk later." She lifted her skirt and squatted to pee.

Buzie pushed through the rotted wooden door, then jumped with fright as a cloud of hair lightly brushed her face. "Who is it?" she rasped, staring to make out the nearby figure.

"Who is it yourself?" grumbled the other. Gena the pickpocket! Buzie cursed her by name for the fright she'd given, then walked a few feet and decided to wait for Babushka to come out. Standing shivering, tired and worn as a dry leaf, she wondered where she could find the strength and alertness to really aid Smulevitch. Of course she would try—she would sneak, steal, and sacrifice for him: The imperative was clear, her own foolish distractions had dispersed like dreams and the prebattle tension in her gut was a familiar, almost enjoyable feeling. But beneath her nerves she felt hollow, passionless, as shapeless as the smoke on the night wind even as her feet merged in numbness with the snow.

The outhouse door groaned and slammed. Babushka found Buzie in the darkness and led her inside to their blankets.

Dear Father Oleynikov—

Last year you saved me from a verdict and sentence by telling the magistrate in Yakutsk about my immortal soul. You said you saw in me the chance to save a soul for the Mother Church if only my heart were not hardened by mistreatment. Since then, I've had many prayers said for me, I've said a few myself; I've had nice hot baths in your house and finished all levels of study at your school. I've enjoyed the friendship of your wonderful daughter and I've had many privileges. But I think that my heart has hardened anyway. It feels like a dull lump in my chest. So I must ask you now to let them try me and be done with it. I'm weary of the fits and starts, the little hopes that melt faster than a snowflake. I need to know what will be—soon I'll be seventeen.

You should have no hope about my becoming a Christian or even a believer anymore, father. It is as impossible as a return to childhood. Beliefs are like clothing, I think: They may get worn yet still be repaired; but once they're outgrown, they don't fit again.

I have very little time to write. The sun has just come up and soon my day in the infirmary will begin. I think this is like the story of how Jesus said to Peter that, before the rooster crowed, Peter would deny knowing him. Here I am, waiting for the rooster. I deny your Jesus Christ. How could one man, even a god, die for all of humanity's sins? Our sins are piling up every day, we would need an army of saviors. And how can the sins of the czar be the same as the man or woman who cheats or steals or even takes a life in order to save herself and her children from poverty and starvation? You might say they are spiritually the same, these sins, but I say that one is gold and one is mud and they can't be weighed on the same scale. The world is too complicated, with too many superstitions and too many tears, to be cleaned by just a few drops of your holy water, father.

I want to surrender myself to Siberia now, to see which

is stronger, it or my mind. If your tales of miracles are true, then, who knows, perhaps I'll be vindicated, found innocent as I truly am, and be allowed to return to the world of the living. But I won't dare hope for that, because I know that "sins" are not defined in heaven, not by your god or my father's god, but by the cruel gods of the earth. By their standards I am a sinner, for I rebelled against their cruelty the first time I witnessed it.

I also know that sins like mine won't be absolved by one man or one messiah or by myself alone, but by the uprising of the whole people. Only by this floodtide of history will my soul be washed and restored to me.

A long life to you and your daughter.

Very sincerely yours,
Buzie Kharlofsky

Buzie folded the letter into her boot, then gently woke Babushka, who drew the blankets over both their heads. Her body smell was pungently sweet; Buzie held a fistful of blanket to her nostrils as Babushka told her the details of the plan to spring Smulevitch.

The initial action would occur outside the prison walls, eight miles away in Yakutsk, where Dr. Brezhno would be waylaid and beaten the night before his scheduled visit to Ysyakh. A Social Democratic "doctor," coincidentally passing through town, would tend to Brezhno (poisoning him if the beating were not enough) and volunteer to take over his rounds for a day or two pending his recovery. Brezhno's written approval would gain him access to the camp; Buzie's task, then, would be to help Smulevitch sneak out of camp in the doctor's wagon with money and minimal provisions. A row in the mess hall would provide the chief distraction for the guards. "And you," said Babushka, petting the girl's cheek, "must provide the same for Kuvalda."

"I should start a fight?"

"No, my little rebel. There are safer if less satisfying ways to keep a man occupied."

Buzie felt her insides grow cold.

Babushka kissed her brow and went on. Smulevitch would head south by dogsled on the frozen Lena River from Yakutsk and try to reach Irkutsk on the gigantic Lake Baikal by early spring, there to be coordinator for underground aid to exiles in the southern regions of Siberia. "He'll send tickets for the rest of us," Babushka said, chuckling.

If the gendarmes' pursuit was slack, however—unlikely, considering his status as a revolutionary—Jacob might elect to blend in with the scant population of Yakutsk or find sanctuary with native reindeer herders until summer, when he could pay passage on the first freighter headed north on the thawed Lena to the Laptevykh Sea.

For either contingency, the movement had supplied Smulevitch with four hundred rubles for provisions, hiring guides, and passing bribes. "This is the package he passed to Olga in the tunnel," Babushka explained. "It was a clumsy operation, but it had to be—they searched all his things the next day. They watch him so closely—they haven't learned yet that women can be just as dangerous. We'll teach them, eh?"

"Wake up, Buzie!" Fanya suddenly peeled off their blankets, then clasped her mouth shut as she saw that she had disturbed the venerable Breshkovskya, too.

"What do you want?" snapped Buzie, rising to her feet. Fanya held out her palm, in which lay the *dreydl*, snapped off at its stem. The sight stung Buzie. "What do I care? It's yours, isn't it? You think I can fix it with my spit?"

Gena rushed to her daughter at the sound of Buzie's irritable voice. "Get away before they pull you under their filthy blankets!" The *dreydl* popped from Fanya's hand as her mother pulled her roughly. Buzie had to exert herself not to retrieve it.

She remembered the letter hidden in her boot and her need to see Anna Oleynikov again, and tailed Fanya and Gena across the barracks. "Look, you see this?" Buzie dangled her new crucifix. "Another toy for you, Fanya. Rub it and it brings luck. It answers all your wishes. And the chain is gold," she said to Gena, "so you can steal it from your daughter."

"Woman-loving little bitch!" she snarled.

Buzie nodded sagely at Fanya. "If you want it, you do like the last time."

"Get away with your trash, now!" Gena screamed, kicking Buzie in the shin.

Quick as a cat, Buzie caught and twisted the offending foot, which sent the woman tumbling to the earth, even as Manya and two others rushed forward to rescue Buzie from a scuffle.

"Filthy communards!" the despised woman screeched without rising from the dirt. "You and your schemes will be suffocated under the very blankets that conceal you! And when they whip the skin off your backs, I'll be the one to laugh! I'll be the one!"

Manya spat on her head. "Blister of a woman! Be silent!"

Gena swallowed her curses at the sight of Manya's fists and rose, grumbling, to rage instead at her passive daughter.

Babushka continued to stare across the room as intently as an owl. "Avoid these two," she advised Buzie. "These are the *lumpen* of the barracks."

Buzie shrugged. "I could kill her, I could ignore her."

(I could. I could kill someone today. As easily as I lance a blister. . . .)

Such detachment governed her behavior with Kuvalda for the rest of the week, but he was no more able to see the mechanical quality of her flirting ways than a duck can discern a hunter's decoy. He was without reservation in his delight at seeing Buzie dressed for the first time in the Ukrainian blouse; he was charmed by the sudden slackening of her bitter wit; he was thrilled, intrigued no end when his grasping hands were allowed to roam, for scant seconds, over her arms, her waist, even her breasts, before she would wordlessly push him away. All this he took as evidence of her submission; a more sensitive or shrewd man might have wondered at so sudden a triumph, noticed her expression as he touched her—her face turned as if smarting from a slap—and glimpsed the wooden crucifix, peeking up from the yoke of her blouse and filed to a sharp point.

Smulevitch's escape was slated for Sunday. Buzie rose before the sun, before either the camp's breakfast gong or the silver church bell in Ysyakh had sounded. Her scalp was tingling from weird, anxious dreams and her mind was juggling the details of the plan from the moment she opened her eyes:

Four hundred rubles wrapped in newspaper, stowed inside the prison wall, twentieth brick over from the chink from the misfired cannonball, sixteenth row down from the barbed wire and you'd better hope the loose brick hasn't been frozen shut again. Now, the doctor comes at lunchtime, you've got to get the manacles off Smulevitch before breakfast ("Otherwise, Kuvalda, it's _your_ turn to spoon-feed and clean him!") and only pretend to refasten them, or else fetch the keys from Kuvalda's trousers, somehow. (God save me from fetching something else from his trousers! Ugh, what does he want from me? To soil, rip, gnaw, drool, gobble me up! Oh, Babushka, let it not come to that, I don't think I could bear it! I'd rather distract him with murder, I'd rather shove my crucifix down his throat, please, I'd rather be scarred by whips than by Kuvalda's touch.)

Crouched by the drafty wall at a distance from the huddled, snoring women, Buzie slipped out of her overcoat to don the blouse and crucifix. The blessed thought occurred to her that Anna Oleynikov would likely make a point of coming to camp early this morning, perhaps in as little as an hour's time, to invite her to church service. Dear, dear Anna. But she would have to decline, deny herself again the precious few comforts of Ysyakh just as she had nearly denied her soul's own dignity with Kuvalda to serve Smulevitch and the revolutionary movement. Ah, but later the reckoning will come, Buzie thought, grimacing as she pulled on her coat again. Sooner than soon, your friend Anna and her father will tire of you and your troubles, and then you can hug Siberia to your little bosom, _gonifte_. You'll be tried and convicted and frozen in Siberia's hold like that prehistoric elephant Kuvalda always talks about, that they dug up from the ice and fed to the pack dogs. . . .

Shh, what? Buzie froze all motion, shut her eyes to give full concentration to . . . There! A man's voice, through the wall, guttural and unintelligible . . . and a woman, replying in short bursts of speech. Buzie thought with certainty it was Fanya's mother; she could not articulate the alarm it triggered in her but instinctively snatched up her red shawl and shook Babushka. "Shh!" she whispered as the woman bolted upright. "Something's going on outside."

"What is it?"

"Guards. I don't know. Wake up, now! I'm going out."

As soon as Babushka, cursing, had thrown off her blankets, Buzie headed for the door and stepped out into the unearthly blue twilight. Cold vapors swirled across the landscape. In the stillness she heard a pack of men marching through the tunnel toward her, obviously guards by their steady, unfettered footfalls. Quickly Buzie climbed the tunnel embankment, scraping raw her knuckles and palms, then lay behind the trellis with her heart pounding against the unfeeling earth. Moments later a score of fur hats filed past her eyes. The door to the women's barracks was kicked open and a shout rose up. Sergeant Misevich hollered orders to his men as behind him Fanya's renegade mother yapped incitements and accusations. As the clamor worsened, Buzie realized how quickly daylight was breaking upon her. Crawling backward from the trellis, she doffed her bright shawl from her head, tied it about her waist inside her coat, looked around for straggling guards, then made a dash across the ice, circling behind the guards' hut itself to reach the infirmary.

Kuvalda was standing in his sheepskin coat before the open door, slapping his arms for warmth. Buzie broke her stride and labored at calming her breathing, her panic subsiding as her mind began to scheme. Obviously her comrades were in big trouble, a bunch of netted fish, but was she counted among them? How many of the half-crazy woman's denunciations were based on real knowledge of the escape plan?

Kuvalda caught sight of Buzie atop the tunnel embankment. He smoothed his moustache and squared his shoulders. Buzie likewise prepared herself, casting about for beguiling words as she climbed down, but the descent itself, with her hands already bleeding, required her full concentration.

Kuvalda shut the infirmary door as she neared. "What, were you trying to freeze everybody out of there?" she said, with only tentative arrogance.

"Only you," the young guard replied, pleased at being able to conjure a retort. He stretched his arm across the doorway, level with her nose. Smiling nervously, Buzie tried to duck under his sleeve, but he grabbed her collar and, as soon as she stopped wriggling, took a painful grip around her neck. "You're not going in there today. There's someone else for you to treat today, my sweet."

"Let go, you're hurting me!" Buzie cried, twisting free, but then stood still, assuming herself found out and captive. Moans, shrieks, and curses arising from the men's barracks behind them turned both their heads. Buzie wondered if she mightn't be safer running back to Babushka than fending with Kuvalda's tense, unpredictable ways.

"Sounds like the whole camp's got a bellyache!" He rocked back and forth on his heels, glowering at her. "Lucky the doctor is coming from Yakutsk, eh, my sweet? The doctor!"

They knew everything! All demons would be loosed on her comrades' heads! Again she felt the wind in her chest, her heart thumping like a military drum. Kuvalda saw her body tighten and shoved her back from the infirmary door. "Start walking, my anxious dove. Let me see how pretty you look today."

He prodded her steps through the snow tunnel by patting her behind as if she were a heifer. The pathway kept rising, the tunnel becoming shallower until it merged with the level ground. Here stood the punishment cell, a building constructed like a goat shed, where prisoners were chained day and night to the walls, fed from a common, splintery trough, and denied the most basic necessities and amenities. Buzie had never been inside the place but knew and feared it as a torture pit: Here Vera Figner had been burned with cigarettes until her body was a purple scab and the stones of the prison wall were worn by her screams; here strong men were reduced to rats who gnawed at their own hands to be rid of their manacles.

The stench that leaked from the door was like fingers stuffed down her throat. Buzie turned pleadingly to Kuvalda and murmured his name, then saw his face, twisted with violent urges, a gargoyle with glass eyes. He sensed her recoil and rammed her against the door, pinning her there while he undid the padlock. He heaved her into the darkness and she landed on her knees, bowed over and gagged. The place smelled as if a dead man had been rotting there for weeks, despite the natural refrigeration. Kuvalda stalked in behind her, muttering words of disgust for both her and the putrid room, then grabbed her by the hair and yanked her into a gloomy stall strewn with rotten hay. "Here, you can join your friend Smulevitch. He'll be lucky enough if he crawls out of this place!"

Smulevitch was curled up in the shadows, chained wrist to wrist and by his neck to the wall. He wore threadbare clothes and only one boot. His other foot was darkly discolored and his flaming beard was ripped to tatters and encrusted with blood and ice. The sight of the wretched man crashed through Buzie's body and dragged her heart to the ground.

"For this devil you cry!" Kuvalda raged, clenching his fists.

"And for *him* you've been dressing up, showing yourself off like a slut, and making a fool out of me! Two scheming, filthy Jews!" He pinched and slapped her cheek. Buzie sprawled out of his striking distance and twice patted her rib cage to know that the filed crucifix, her only weapon, still hung on its fragile chain. "Now you can feel your heart beating, I bet!" Kuvalda cried. "Now your little whore heart is breaking in half!" He flung her on her belly alongside Smulevitch, whom he restored to consciousness with a kick to the ribs. "Wake up, scum! Wake up and see how I handle your little whore!"

Glimpsing her comrade's eye-light, Buzie rose to her knees and reached to him like a child to a father, but Kuvalda intercepted her gesture and knocked her over with a rough slap, then straddled her and began stripping off her coat, shouting obscenities and cuffing her face at leisure to excite himself. She heaved against his weight, then fell back into a tangle of overwhelmingly vile sensations, her stored strength crinkling to ash.

The rattling of Smulevitch's chains roused her from this near-faint. His voice was constricted, hardly human: "Fight . . . fight . . ."

"Shut up with your babble or I'll rip the tongue from your head!"

Buzie snapped her cross from its chain, puny thing in her palm as she lay very still, calling together her frantic energies. Then Jacob's voice trailed off into a wheeze and again Kuvalda's hands were at her, under her skirt, poking, tearing, penetrating. Her muscles hardened like cement. Her mind was tearing loose. Her eyes snapped open and she saw him gaping from above, a vulture, with his belt open, his hands at his zipper. "No!" she shrieked in desperation, suddenly arching her back and violently flexing her hips. Kuvalda was hardly thrown, but before he could square his weight again she flew up at him, howling, and stabbed his face with her tiny weapon. The blow deflected off his cheekbone into his eye. He fell over backward, hands rushing up. Buzie scrambled away on her hands and knees, screaming to Smulevitch for help.

The giant loomed like a mountain behind the wounded guard and throttled his throat with a snap of his thick wrist chain. Kuvalda began to thrash around horribly, clawing at the chain and at Smulevitch's face, his tongue darting from his frothing mouth as if to escape on its own. "Hold him!" Smulevitch croaked. "Hold him, help me!"

Panting in a corner of the stall, watching the life ooze from her oppressor's mouth, Buzie ducked her head and threw herself across Kuvalda's knees. There she hung with her arms wrapped around his legs like a rider on the neck of a bucking horse. Smulevitch grunted and tightened his stranglehold. After an eternity of heaving and rolling, Kuvalda went limp.

"Sonofabitch," growled his killer, slamming the chain against Kuvalda's skull, and again, and again! The stinking air resonated with violence and with the sound of Buzie's sobs. Muffled voices from within and outside the punishment cell swarmed back after a deathly pause. Smulevitch rolled the corpse off his lap, causing Buzie to jump back with a shudder. "Sonofabitch," he repeated, regarding the face that lay like a dented melon in the dirt. "Same color as my foot. Look at his ugly face!"

Buzie wept violently.

Smulevitch reached along the length of chain that was attached to his collar and hauled himself over to the wall. Leaning back, he said, "That's enough. Come here now."

Buzie crawled to his side, overwhelmed by his pain, her hands aching to touch and heal him. "I'll find keys for you," she stammered, and set to searching Kuvalda's sheepskin, keeping her eyes closed.

"The prison wall," he rasped. "They told me . . . you're a revolutionary."

"Someday," she vowed, rising to her knees, "I'll be like you!"

"Revolutionaries don't live with dead men."

"You're not dead! Just your foot! In the infirmary I can—"

He clasped her mouth with his huge, chained hand. "Be still. No time for dreaming—I'm as dead as a calf bound for slaughter."

"No, no." She kissed his palm and showered his hand with tears.

A gunshot outside jerked her, trembling, to her feet. "Get out!" Smulevitch roared. "Find our doctor in Yakutsk! Use the money . . . for yourself . . . people suffered . . . Be strong. . . ."

Another gunshot shattered her nerve, yet she lingered to peel the sheepskin from Kuvalda's stiffening corpse and lay it reverently across Smulevitch's crippled legs. Pressing her lips to his temples, she murmured in her old language: "You're a Jew, Jacob? Is it true?"

"I'm a communist," he moaned in Yiddish, slumping against the wall.

Buzie slipped out the door into the clean, stinging air, her every nerve vibrating like the wings of a hovering insect. She had a summit view of the camp, broken-down trellises linking battered buildings, all the desolation of her life, gunpowder perfuming the stillness, a voice barking in a tunnel somewhere. Her red shawl lay in the snow at her feet, her fallen flag, all the dead and the dying: Old Babushka, how cruelly they would treat her, the strongest, the best. Buzie recalled the words Babushka had said and repeated as a drill during their short summer walking tours of the compound: *Animals are hunted, not human beings. When the gendarmes hunt you, run like an animal.*

She ran behind the punishment cell, prodded by the whines and groans of the prisoners inside who were clamoring for their share of the camp-wide upheaval. The guards would come and whip them silent, she thought: Be gone, Buzie, be gone! Little fool, you left your coat in Kuvalda's clutches, and they'll find it. And Smulevitch will be butchered, strangled with his own guts. . . . *Forget the dead, the wounded, forget them when you're running. Live to remember them! Animals know no past.* An arctic fox, dashing across the ice toward the prison wall. *There is no past, only the present and, each time you take a breath, the future.* The future, standing before her: a brick wall of dizzying height, topped by a haze of barbed wire and swept by stiff winds. Images of execution, of a stonecutting volley of bullets or a head-crushing brick, kept pricking her spine, pushing her toward panic. *But death happens only once! Keep living and you can't die! You can't die! You can't die!*

Babushka!

Buzie spotted the cannonball lodged low in the wall near the prison gate, counted twenty rows over, sixteen down, and saw the protruding stone, the money rock. She ran to it, scratched the icy mortar, gritting her teeth, digging with her fingernails until her fingers were bloodless. Finally the stone wobbled. She panted, dug in again, tugged with her nails, tugged . . .

It tumbled quietly into the snow.

She reached up and drew out the soggy bundle of newspaper. Passed hand to hand by a long chain of trampled souls. More than money: a mission. Oh, rich men of Russia, we'll place pennies on your eyes! I promise! I promise!

Then the air trembled with voices. Buzie threw herself, sniveling, onto the ice. A pack of guards, three on horseback and two in a sleigh, were riding from the stables toward the gate. Buzie rolled closer to the wall to exploit whatever camouflage the red stones offered, pumping her mind for strategy, but only memories gushed; minutes later she found herself still lying, half-frozen, on a mound of ice.

"Hey, get up now." She clutched the money package to her belly. "Where did you go?"

Where *will* you go? She snickered as she stood, then staggered sideways and scraped her arm against the stone. The cold was penetrating to her bones and organs, closing in fast on her ability to think. Her time sense spun and danced. She heard tinkling bells: The wind was singing. The ground was rolling. She fell again. The snow felt warm.

The bells jingled again, bright and loud, rousing her to a vision: Anna Oleynikov, driving through the prison gate, drawing up her pony, looking in every direction. Buzie struggled to her feet and screamed her friend's name, an echoless sound on the flat terrain. The vision trotted toward her, bells tinkling sweetly.

In a moment Buzie was grasping the side of the sleigh. Anna looked impossibly serene, bundled in a parka and mittens. "Where's your coat?"

"Take me out!" Buzie gasped, groping for her shoulder.

The girl drew her onto the sleigh and wrapped her in a horse-hair blanket. Buzie began to shiver uncontrollably as Anna begged her for information. "In the whole camp—there's no one even at the gate?"

"Roundup! . . . Kuvalda's dead. Please! They'll return."

"My God, Buzie! Are you—is this an escape?"

Buzie felt a raging desire to throw the sweet child into the snow and make off with the horse and sleigh. "Anna, drive!" she shouted, stomping the floor and rocking from side to side. "Drive! Drive!"

Sasha the pony snorted and turned her head to gaze warily

at the frenzied girl. Her milk-white eye silenced Buzie, reminding her of a thousand horrors. "Drive," she repeated, and nearly passed out against Anna's shoulder.

The sleigh lurched. Buzie heard the bells on Sasha's reins, saw her tail swishing, her great behind pumping, crystals of snow spraying out from the skids, the prison wall looming closer, closer, overhead. . . .

Chapter Nine / 1911

"The last time I took a New York subway to go someplace was eight years ago, when I was eighty years. Where was I going? To a meeting, where else? Fact of the matter is I was handing in my resignation to the Communist party after being a member for more than fifty years, can you imagine? It was like burying a child that you raised a whole life. But this child was in a coma, y'see, so there was relief, too.

"I was determined to make that trip myself, with no help from anyone. I took the bus and then the F train, which is the best one, air-conditioned—it goes to places like Rockefeller Center, y'see—they don't send good trains to Harlem! But it was difficult for me despite, mostly 'cause of the stairs. I can't climb into the bathtub no more, never mind stairs. And the worst part was the frustration, same like I always felt, that here you had all the working people of the city, old and young, women and men, you had blacks, whites, the Puerto Ricans, every kind of a color, all with nothing to do but stare at each other—and nobody calls a meeting! You may laugh, but, believe me, when the revolution comes to America, the subway will be one of the most important places to do your organizing. Who isn't ready for a revolution after a ride in the rush hour?

"Y'see, leaving the Party didn't mean I was leaving my ideas. It meant that I was leaving dogmatism, that's all. But still I got my dreams, still I wish I would be alive to see the payoff: a socialist America, where the subways will be a joy to ride. You'll have entertainers, and plenty of room to sit, and instead of the advertisements you'll have beautiful artwork, posters with wisdom, and hanging plants, and pictures of great people that people should be inspired: leaders like Martin Luther King, and Lenin, and Eugene Victor Debs—all kind of a good people that they lived the way they saw the truth to be.

"Yeah, in my dreams I go traveling! But in real life I can't go anywhere now, excepting if my daughter or my grandson take me out, if I'm feeling good enough to go. Or once in a while our community organization hires a bus to take us to the country for a day. But this is the way of life, y'see, and I'm not lonely. I did enough good work in my life to make an impression—people know where to find me. It's when you don't follow what your mind tells you, maybe you get scared or you lose confidence, so you do what someone else says, that's when you get lost and you end up lonely. Self-respect is what lasts the longest in this life, I think.

"Now, I have friends, even ten years younger than me, and they complain about the subways, how it's dirty and they don't like the blacks to sit next to them and it's too slow, too fast— they don't know what they want! Me, I wish I could take the subway again. To see all the faces, all the immigrants, it's like reliving my past.

"Anyone that immigrated to the United States, or anyone that they're the son or the daughter of an immigrant, if they got prejudice against different kinds of people, well, they haven't learned a thing from their whole rotten life. I know how these people think, y'see: They're scared. But if they would think instead, when they see, f'rinstance, a Puerto Rican, if they would just say to themselves, 'There goes an immigrant,' instead of 'Here comes a mugger,' they would have their eyes opened up! What difference is there between the Jewish pushcart peddler when I was young and the men in the African clothing who sell jewelry and clothing on the street today? You think the Jew was less obnoxious with what he said or maybe that he took up less of the sidewalk? You think herring on a hot day smelled better than that smelly stuff they burn?

"What else does it really mean to be Jewish in this day and age than to feel this kind of a solidarity—what's the word? Empathy. Yeah, to feel empathy with the poor, the oppressed, based on your own understanding as a Jew. To be honest with you, the rest of what people say makes them Jewish is a lot of kreplach. Mostly it's nostalgic, romantic foolishness.

"You take my grandson—excepting I won't let you, he's mine! But I'm giving you a f'rinstance. He doesn't speak Yiddish. Maybe he understands a word here and there if I say it with the right tone of voice, but for him as a Jew there's no language, no shul, no ghetto. To Israel he can't afford to go. And there's no real persecution for him as a Jew, at least not that he can see it right in front of his face. But he's a progressive guy, y'see. I can tell from how he talks. His Jewish identity means a different set of values, a different way of life, from what our crazy government and the television set and the whole system by itself gives him. Capitalism says he should make a success of himself and keep a policeman between his door and the people. But Jewish life says he should keep the door open for Elijah to come and eat.

"Now, I was talking about this with my neighbor, a black woman, Mrs. Parker. I said how when I escaped from Siberia it was exactly like the Underground Railroad for Negro slaves. So I have a special appreciation of that, y'see. It's true, every step of the way there were people that they took risks to help me. I don't even know who was in the movement and who was not, but I got passed from one hand to another, and never, not once, was a finger raised against me.

"First, Anna. She gave me identification papers, her own papers, and a big kiss. And then we drove to Yakutsk to find out what happened to our 'doctor' from the Social Democratic party. Anna even visited with Dr. Brezhno—remember, he was supposed to get poisoned? And from his house she brought me down some hot rolls and tea. Then she said I should take from her the pony and the sleigh and she would tell the police I stole them and she would send them in the other direction. Now, why did she do this for me, a Catholic girl with no knowledge of the world? I don't know. One berry is sweet, one berry is bitter, both in the same backyard. Marxism says a lot about why people behave the way they do, but ideology is more than just your economic class, y'see.

"The problem was I didn't know how to drive a horse and I was really very, very sick. So Anna found a fur trapper to take me to Oleminsk—that's about three hundred miles. I paid him thirty rubles and he didn't touch me, he was a kind man. All I remember was he looked like an Eskimo. And he shot a wolf during our trip. And he gave me a coat to wear, a fur that was worth more than the thirty rubles.

"That's how it started. I was amazed that all through Siberia there should be revolutionary people. You think they had a telephone to tell one another that I'm coming? It wasn't Babushka that spread the word—she had her hands full in Ysyakh.

"But she survived, you know. Oh, yes. She was tough, like rubber, like the rubber-band balls I used to make for my children and for my grandson after that. You build rubber-bands around a core of paper, and it bounces wonderful. And on the paper I used to write something, a slogan or a little poem I made up. And I would tell my children, 'Either you take the ball apart now to find out the wisdom, or you use it until it's worn out— but first you might lose it and never read the message.' It's a real something to ponder!

"The kids always played first, looked later, and usually they lost it. What do a few words of wisdom mean to a child? But once, just once, my son decided to read the message. He took the ball apart. He was always taking things apart and putting them back together—including me, excepting sometimes he forgot to put me back together. Anyway, he took it apart, and I remember what it said in his ball. 'Jacob'—he was named for Jacob Smulevitch, my son; it's too bad he didn't live up to it— 'Jacob, your heart gives you life, so do like it says, you'll find a nice wife, you'll always think "red" '—something like that, some foolish poetry that I wrote in Yiddish and in English and I wrapped inside it a little piece of candy. He ate the candy and then he stole his sister's ball, my son.

"The thing is, y'see, whenever I made this kind of a ball, I would start to think about Babushka Breshkovskya. She lived to see the revolution in Russia, but her party, the Socialist Revolutionaries, they had a split and a lot of them came out against

Lenin. So I don't know if Babushka got lost, like my kids would lose their ball, or if the message inside actually got changed. Fact of the matter is she became a social democrat.

"Now I'm confusing you, so let me explain. Lenin's party was the Social Democrats, with two groups, the *Mensheviki* and the *Bolsheviki*, but after the revolution we were the Communists, y'see, and the term social democrat came to mean, like, social fascist, a real reactionary. Today, f'rinstance, the Social Democrat party in America has people like Senator Moniham, whatever his name is, and also the president of the teachers' union, who's such a right-winger they shouldn't allow him to be near children!

"Anyway, it doesn't matter the name, 'cause you can't tell who's what by their name. The Nazis were socialists, too— National Socialists. Anyone can wear any kind of a uniform, y'see. I learned that the only way to know is to look at their shoes and where they put their feet. Do they take a stand with you or against you?

"But you want to get out of Siberia, already, yes? So here's how you do it. You stand on a train platform in Irkutsk and a man will ask you, 'Nice day, isn't it?' And you're supposed to say, 'Yes, and tomorrow will be even nicer.' And when you say that, he gives you a ticket and new identification papers.

"The train goes from Irkutsk all the way to Warsaw. It has just one passenger car, the rest are filled with coal, so the train moves very, very slow. But you don't talk to anyone. You just sleep, and you try to wake up calm from your dreams.

"In Poland there are not so many comrades, but you have money to pay your way and a cross to make you kosher. In a week's time you're on a boat leaving from Belgium. Now you're not a fugitive with a hundred people helping you, you're an immigrant with a hundred people crowding you! That's how it is in steerage, it's like the basement of the boat. All those that they can't afford first class or second class are there. Half of them are seasick. The other half are praying. The only way to get away from the noise and the bad air is to spend your time on deck.

"So there you are, looking at the water, and suddenly you're liable to scream, because what do you see? Siberia! We were surrounded by icebergs. The way they reflect the sun, they could make you blind. I suppose this is exactly what happened to the

captain, 'cause the next minute—bang!—we smack into an iceberg and the whole boat tips over. I had to hold on to a beam
so as not to go sliding off into the ocean. Then the SOS goes
out and a boat from England comes to save us. To England they
took us for safekeeping. And there I met Alexander Berkman,
the famous anarchist.

"I'm going too fast? This is so you can feel like I felt. My
whole body was with pins and needles. My mind was like a
book that the wind blows loose the pages. I was not a sophisti-
cate like some of the revolutionaries of Russia that they came
every so often to the United States to raise money for their
cause—like Babushka, she did this, and Trotsky, and Haim
Zhitlovsky. They were celebrities already, they had been to
Europe and all over. But I was still like a peasant girl in my
thinking, and in many ways I was still like I'm twelve years,
y'see, 'cause in Siberia life wasn't real, it was too monotonous
to grow. So to me, everything that happened from the moment
I escaped was like a revelation. If I had believed in God, I would
really be a fanatic.

"Now, Berkman was a boyfriend to Emma Goldman. His
nickname was Sasha, and he was a very intelligent man and very
good-looking. Berkman tried to assassinate the head of Carnegie
Steel, Frick, during a strike in Pittsburgh—this was in the 1890s—
and for a long time he was in jail. I was with him in England
only a couple of days before another boat came to take us, but
he thought I was the real article 'cause I came from Siberia, so
he took me under his wing. He prepared me a little for what I
would find in America.

"It's not like we believed that the streets had gold on them
like you have birdseed on the grass. The year I came was 1910,
remember, and by then nearly every Jew in Russia had at least
one relative or someone from his town in America. The pogroms
and the bad living conditions made more than a million Jews
to emigrate between the turn of the century and the First World
War, so we all had someone to write letters saying how it goes
in America. But a certain reputation for being a place where
you can make a living it had, you couldn't avoid this impression. First of all, in New York there was the garment industry,
the needle trades, and manufacturing clothing for women on a
mass scale was getting a start. So a good tailor, that in Russia he
couldn't make *bubkes* and had to work day and night, in America

he could make twenty, maybe twenty-five dollars a week. He had to work fifty, sixty hours, but that was the working life back then, you had no time for rest.

"But that was just for the tailors, all skilled workers, all men. For a girl or for the unskilled, it was a different story. You worked piecework and you came home with three dollars at the end of the week. Piecework means you get paid by the piece—like if your job is to roll cigars, you get paid a few pennies per dozen. So you never stop working if you want to make a living—you take cigars to bed with you and you roll them in your sleep.

"Now, if you think my age is showing, that what I tell you is ancient history, then go ask some of the modern immigrants, and especially the ones without papers—what do they call them? Aliens, yeah, like they come from the moon! You go ask them how they make a living. You'll hear plenty about sweatshops and piecework and taking work home, right here in New York City. And this tells you something about reform, y'see. You win a reform and you just manage to push the boulder that it's crushing you, you push it off your chest and it rolls onto someone else! What we want to do, *kinderlakh*, is to turn that boulder into powder, into matzoh meal.

"So Berkman filled my ears with stories about sweatshops and tenements, just like I'm telling you. He gave me an understanding of why we came to America—not to be loved, but to be exploited. It might be better than Russia, but—I'll never forget how he said it—if we eat grass, it's better than eating dirt, but we must never begin to think of ourselves as cattle.

"I figured out right there that I should get some kind of a job that if a depression came, you know . . . something that could maybe keep me out of the sweatshops. A job that I could keep it even in hard times. Well, I went through the hardest times in Siberia, and there I kept a job right until the end, so I made up to become a nurse in America, a real nurse. This became my ambition.

"Berkman also showed me a copy of the *Forvetz*, the Yiddish paper from New York. It says that my boat has gone under. So I write a letter to the editor saying that I'm alive and headed for America, and they should please inform 'Mrs. Markish of the Bronx' that soon I'll arrive. What a joy to write a letter without having guards to look over my shoulder!

"You know, when I think back about Berkman and all the insight he gave, I start to think that maybe a lot of people don't like those that we're political 'cause we're always criticizing the ideas—the myths—about America. But a leader must not only criticize. Ideas are precious to people; sometimes it's all they have to make them feel like they belong to some kind of a group or a community. Under capitalism our lives get divided up in such bits and pieces, like a car on an assembly line—we're kept from each other, we got to compete instead that we should cooperate, we're too busy worrying about the way we smell. And under these kind of a circumstances, ideas become ideology, and people get fanatical, 'cause they want desperately to hold on to something, some belief that makes them part of the club, if you know what I mean. And a radical must understand this; she's got to be very creative to develop new ideas, new feelings, and ways to have community—a new way of life.

"I'll never forget how my grandson—this was fun!—he saw on television an advertisement for a certain kind of a hot cereal. 'I want this.' 'No,' I tell him, 'it's no good.' Then he starts getting mad and he starts to nag, so finally I give in. I buy, I cook, he eats, it's rotten, and then he starts to cry! He could not believe that the television would lie to him! He believed in the television, y'see. So first I explained to him about the advertisements, and then I taught him to cook oatmeal for himself. And from this he learned.

"People like Berkman and Emma Goldman were not so good at this. They did not take the people as they were and move them a little further. Instead they ran way ahead and said, 'Catch up to us now.' F'rinstance, Emma Goldman refused to be married, she talked about 'free love.' Now, I as a working woman may have too many children and work like a slave a whole day, but I'm not ready to reject the whole thing 'cause this is what I know of life, y'see. This is my security! Maybe I can work for better jobs, better schools, or today you have abortion as an issue, f'rinstance, but I'm not going to throw out the baby with the bath water or the husband with his whiskey bottle just 'cause you say so. Morality, working-class morality, it's like an anchor on a boat. It keeps us from moving ahead, but it also prevents us from getting washed up on some rocks and getting wrecked.

"But let's not race ahead! These are the kind of questions that got debated for years in the radical movement. We had all kind of a splits in the movement. Right now I want to talk about Ellis Island—give myself a chance to feel young again.

"So we go back into steerage. The trip from England takes about ten days. Mostly on board we got Russian Jews, also some Italians—real peasants—and English in first class. Me, I was still thinking like I'm a fugitive and I keep to myself until the boat reaches the harbor of New York City. There we put down anchor outside the harbor, near where you now have the Verrazano Bridge. Comes to us a tugboat with doctors from the Immigration Service, and they give a look at the passengers in first and second class.

"We down in steerage have got to stay downstairs, but we know what's going on and we start to talk about our fears. We know that those that they got money, unless they're very sick with tuberculosis or another contagious disease, they're permitted to go straight to the docks and goodbye! But those of us in steerage, we got to go to the Island of Tears—that's what they called Ellis Island, 'cause if we don't pass the inspection, we can get sent all the way home. Even a child of ten could get sent home without her parents if there's a disease in her. This didn't happen so often, really—they needed workers in America! Also, the steamship company had to pay your fare going back, so they gave you an examination before you could even buy your ticket to come. Still, we had our fears, and naturally everybody's an authority on what the rules are, so you hear enough opinions to drive you crazy.

"One young fellow gets to talking to me, a baker from Lithuania—this was a poor-paying trade, even in America—and he was worried 'cause he had only a teensy bit of money. You need twenty-five dollars or they won't let you in. So we get to talking, and all of a sudden he's pinching me and saying that I should marry him. I pinched him right back! 'I'll be your banker,' I told him, 'but not your wife.' And I said he should stay close— hey, but not too close!—so if he has trouble, I can slip him a little something.

"We all come on a barge that takes us to Ellis Island. But first, of course, we see the Statue of Liberty, and, for everything that Sasha warned me about America, I was still very, very impressed with—how do you say it? The image of America. It was a hazy kind of a day, the month was June, already it was like summer. The statue stood all green with her arm in the

air, and the words of a Jewish woman, Emma Lazarus, they're
written on the inside of the pedestal, and there's gulls and boats
everywhere, and tall buildings. Here you're used to little huts
and pushcarts and wide-open fields of wheat—or snow, nothing
but snow—and now these buildings, so huge, you can't quite
believe what you see. In fact, the whole thing feels like you're
in a dream, excepting on Ellis Island they push and pinch you
plenty so you know you're not sleeping!

"You feel your feet on the island and you wonder if it's
going to maybe float out from the harbor. Then you smell the
grass, only a little bit of a smell but more comforting than the
salty air, more like home. So we come in groups of thirty into a
red building, an enormous building with green copper roofs and
ivy all over and with statues hanging over the doorway—an
eagle, a bunch of grapes, I don't remember what else. They
give us a number, a tag that they put around your neck. All
around there's people with their bundles, talking all kind of a
language and trying to behave and look nice even though they
got all the grime from steerage.

"We climb a big staircase where the inspectors stand to give
a look—maybe you're a cripple or you can't catch your breath
after you climb? If they think there's anything wrong, they
mark you on the back with a piece of chalk and you get what
they call 'detained' for an examination. Otherwise you come
into a great big hall—they could park an ocean liner in there!
All the walls are made of white tile like you have today in a
bathroom. Every room was like this so they could wash and
disinfect quickly, y'see. And they have what they call a 'cattle
run,' like, chains to keep you in line for inspection.

"The noise is unbelievable. You think you got rocks rolling
in your skull. There's hundreds and thousands of immigrants
waiting, yelling at their children, praying, who knows what?
And there's signs hanging in every kind of a language—Yiddish,
Polish, Russian, Romanian, Italian. Then all of a sudden you
got an inspector standing in front of you asking questions: What's
your name, how much money you got, where you're from, how
you make a living, are you an anarchist—questions like these.
And you try to answer with some intelligence.

"You think my baker friend had trouble? Turns out he's got
a sponsor, an uncle with a job waiting for him, so he doesn't
need to have money. Me, I'm the one with trouble. Why, with

an innocent face like mine? 'Cause I'm a young woman with no husband, and the kind of thinking that rules this world says I must be a prostitute, y'see, so unless I make a marriage right there on Ellis Island—and this happened more than once: Complete strangers got married on the spot just to get to New York—either this or I must have a relative come to get me.

" 'Eh,' says my Litvak, 'you let a good one get away.'

" 'Feh,' I says, 'I'd rather burn my own biscuits, thank you.'

"But all my possessions went down with the iceberg, so I lost the paper saying the address of my sister, I can just remember the name of the street—St. Anne's Avenue in the Bronx—it makes me think of Anna Oleynikov, y'see. So I tell the Immigration to send a cable to the *Forvetz* telling them to contact Mrs. Markish. I figure if Leah read my first notice in the *Forvetz*, then maybe she's got a subscription or she gave them her address and we're in business.

"Off it goes while I go into some kind of a cage that they have there. I sit with a little bag that Berkman gave me and with my red shawl on my head and it feels like prison all over again. But somehow, I don't know why, I felt wonderful. Sure I worried: Maybe Mrs. Markish won't come, maybe there's no one to take care of her child, or she doesn't even know I'm here, or we won't recognize each other, or she won't accept me. But the idea that I should have to go back to Russia was impossible. Impossible. I felt really free from Siberia for the first time, y'see. It's like you sleep late sometime, you wake up to the sunlight and then you stretch your arms and yawn and you think, Boy, I got a whole day to live!

"Me, I had a whole day to wait. For seven hours I sat. So something else happened, and I still blush like a tomato to tell it. All this time in Siberia I waited to get my menstruation—I had plenty of time, right? Now I'm trying to remain neat so that my sister shouldn't think I'm some kind of a *shnorer*, and what happens? I start my period, for the very first time. It's only a little bit of a nothing, but I felt it, and I didn't know what to do with myself. When Mrs. Markish finally came, she first gives me a big hug, then she's slapping my cheeks for me! 'Cause she knew, y'see, somehow she knew, hardly before we got the chance to talk. Then we hug again—and we still don't know what to do with ourselves!

"It had been eight years, you know, but I recognized her

immediately. She was always a beauty, and she wore her hair piled on top with a ribbon in front and long earrings. Always she wore that ribbon, coming from around the back of her head like you would expect to see on a gypsy, on a fortune-teller. She was a religious woman, oh, yes, but in America she never wore a wig—this was her liberation, I suppose. And she was built, my sister, a full woman, not a short little stinker like me.

"Leah was nearly twelve years older than me, and the rest of her life she spent with me like a mother. But right from the start we had trouble. Not the slap in the face—this was a joke. But when a woman menstruates, y'see, she's *treyf*, according to the orthodox. She can't so much as hand a spoon to her husband or he'll get contaminated. So when I met Mr. Markish—Lester was his name—I wasn't even supposed to shake hands with him. All right, this I can tolerate—I didn't really know him yet and I was dirty besides. But then when Yeshua walks into the apartment, and when Herschel walks into the apartment, I climbed all over them! Surprise! And Mrs. Markish got upset by this kind of a behavior. But everyone just laughed at her, she was so foolish, even her husband laughed, and by now she was used to getting her religion watered down. In America, this was the way. My father used to say—and this is why he never came to America—that the people of the Book here just become bookkeepers.

"Talk about bookkeeping! This reminds me of another *meise*. On the ship from England, I had left in my pocket maybe fifty American dollars—some I had left from the original money that I changed to dollars at the steamship office, and some Berkman gave me. So I handed my money to the captain to keep it safe, but I didn't speak English, y'see, and he had an interpreter, and I told him I got a hundred rubles, which is fifty dollars, actually. But the captain wrote down one hundred dollars, so I came off the boat with a big profit! I didn't even know how much I had until I showed my family, and then right away Yeshua wants to take and give to an anarchist newspaper, *Di Frei Arbiter Shtimmer—Free Worker's Voice*. It was a good paper, but I never even heard of it! Anyway, Mrs. Markish wouldn't let him take even a penny. 'This is her good luck,' she says. 'It's a sign that Buzie will marry a millionaire.' Yeah, a million dollars worth of *tsuris*, with such a crazy family!

"I rested a couple of days, and Mrs. Markish took me shopping for clothing that I shouldn't look like such a greenhorn. She always thought the clerks in the stores were flirting with me, I remember—she would chase them all behind their counters. Most likely they were flirting with her—she was such a goodlooker, so stately! But she took my braids and stacked them on my head so I should look like I'm twelve years.

"And I got to talking with my brothers about their activities, and they showed me newspapers and taught me my first English words—'strike' and 'picket.' And I think they really felt mixed up about me. Here I just escaped from Siberia where I was suffering for their activities—I mean, I didn't feel this way about it, but this is how it could appear. And when I told them about Babushka Breshkovskya and Jacob Smulevitch and the others, as much as I could stand to talk about it before I would cry . . . So they gained from this a new kind of respect for me. But I was still their baby sister! And a greenhorn on top of it!

"And Ruchel? Hoo, boy, if ever there was an aristocrat born in the poor part of town, this was Ruchel. She could not see past my dirty face. But I liked her kid, Nat, so this made a kind of a bond between me and her—as long as I would baby-sit!

"No one had much time for me, anyway, not to be nice or nasty. I had a family again, that's all, and this was a wonderful feeling. But mostly I slept and I rested and I ate and I relaxed for the first time in years. And in a few days I was working.

"Lester Markish at this time had a little bit of a laundry business that he stayed there a whole day with Leah and with Belle-Brokha, that's their daughter. But the rest of us—never mind Ruchel, she never worked a day in her life, but Herschel and Yeshua and me—we all worked in the same umbrella factory where Leah and Lester made their start. This was owned by Lester's cousin, Israel—Izzy, he called himself. He was a great one for making up names. Before you came to work for him, you had to accept from him your American name—he wouldn't let you fill in your card with your Russian or a Hebrew name. But everyone wanted to be American as fast as they could, so they all thought this was wonderful. Our name became Charles. Yeshua was Julius. Herschel was Harry, excepting everyone still called him Herschel. And me, I became Bessie. Bessie Charles. Eh, it sounded all right.

"Now Ruchel, you remember, was a Kaminsky, married to Feivl, who worked in a die-cutting factory, and with two children, Elaine and Nat. Nat was a baby still. And Leah had Belle-Brokha—she was eight years when I arrived. Believe me, if they would have let him, this cousin Izzy would have taken these children with their mothers and put them to work on his machines. There were lots of bosses like this, y'see, that they own a factory no bigger than a closet, so the only way they can make a living is to make merchandise that's no good, which loses customers, or else to keep the workers' wages very, very low. So what they do is they hire relatives or *landsmen*, you know, people from the same town in Russia or Poland, and they pay for the passage—a steerage ticket doesn't cost so much if you're getting yourself a slave in the bargain, hmm? 'Cause that person has to pay off the ticket by working in your shop. And meanwhile you're lending him money to get by, so he never stops owing.

"And in this kind of a shop, your class interest as a worker is not very obvious. The boss may be your uncle and often he works at the machine right next to you. But after a few months maybe you start to realize that his clothes are getting better while yours are getting holes. Still, the average workman dreams more about owning his own little shop than about forming a union. He actually admires the boss, just like the boss admires Rockefeller. Look, it didn't take much to start out in your own business. You hire a room somewhere, you rent a couple of machines, and you walk down to the docks to find a couple of greenhorns that they would work just for the smile you give them. With my hundred dollars, I could have become a capitalist.

"Instead I was a striker, a real troublemaker. Every boss called me that name, troublemaker, before he fired me. Only with Izzy I quit first. My job was to put the cloth of the umbrella onto the frame—a 'tipper,' I was called. I got paid by the piece, but I was a fast worker, y'see, so at the end of the first week I made six dollars. Then Izzy starts to think, Six dollars is a lot of money—why should a young girl make so much? So he puts me on salary instead, three dollars a week. Fine, I make exactly half the number of umbrellas that I made the week before and for the rest of the time I read a book and talk to my brothers. When Izzy says, 'What happened to your work?' I say, 'What happened to my three dollars?' And I quit, right there.

"My first year I went from job to job. I had nimble fingers and I was a good worker, but stubborn like a mule about my rights. Of course, this was a time when the whole Jewish working class was stubborn—we didn't take any nonsense from these little parvenu pigs. First we had the butchers on strike. They were getting paid only eighteen dollars a month, and the boss gave them where to live. Big deal. After the strike, they got eighteen dollars a *week* and they lived where they wanted. This was a real victory. And then the Jewish bakers made themselves a union, with a strike and a boycott, and they won, too. I even got to see my Litvak on the picket line, so he wasn't a bad guy, after all. But the most important strikes were in the garment industry. And this is where I worked mostly before I became a nurse. Before I even came to America, f'rinstance, there was the ladies' shirtwaist-makers' strike, twenty thousand women and girls that they fought with the police and the scabs to hold their picket line together. Some nerve they had, not even to wait for me!

"But I can't tell you about every single strike. They happened all the time—we went on the picket line like a child goes to the sandbox. We had to—this was a struggle for our lives. Why should making a living deprive us of our youth, our families, anything?

"I remember once I met Morris Rosenfeld on a picket line. Probably it was in 1912 during the cloakmakers' strike, but I'm not sure. I'm sorry, my head gets a little rusty. All I remember is seeing him, I recognized him from his picture. He was already a famous poet; he wrote '*Ikh Hob a Kleiner Yingle*,' about how a father can't get to see his son 'cause of the long hours in the shop. I had put to memory a lot of his verses, he was my favorite. So I strayed close to him so maybe I could meet him, and eventually we struck up a conversation. He asked me what I'm doing there, 'cause I looked so young, very skinny and small and with my braids stacked up. It came out that I was in Siberia, and this was my passport, we got into a really good conversation.

"But a couple of days later, the police broke our picket line to let the scabs come into the shop. In this particular instance, we lost. So Morris Rosenfeld says to me, 'Well, do you still want to fight?' And I said to him, 'If you lose, that doesn't mean you lost your feeling or you lost your desire. We lost the fight? Let's start a new one!'

"And I still feel this way, to this very minute."

❄

Herschel was acting crazy since he'd begun to date Rose Lifschitz. His moods swung like the March weather from nasty
cold to light cheer, blown either way by the winds of Rose's
own temperament. Everyone said that the two were headed for
marriage, but Buzie thought these were just words meant to
flatter the couple into proving them true. Still, she would have
enjoyed her lovesick brother's foolishness, except that his sweet
moods seemed briefer than the daylight in winter and always
gave way to dark, foul periods during which he was less lovable
than a shortchanging peddler. Buzie had suggested to Herschel
that he had all the makings of a boss: selfishness, an exploitative
kind of charm, everything but the capital and the courage. Yet
she had not freed herself of his influence—of her loneliness,
really—any more than she had yet freed herself of piecework in
the sweatshops.

As a result she found herself on this lone, precious day of rest
in the famous "Coney Island," seated along the Iron Pier that
stretched out from the beach over the scummy ocean waves,
slumped down between Rose Lifschitz's bundles and tethered to
the spot by Herschel's vague assurance that he and Rose would
be back soon. Not that she wanted to go gallivanting around
with them, Buzie grumbled to herself. She did not like Rose,
with her fancy horsehair slips, her ivory combs, and dainty,
scalloped collars, but considered her a vain and utterly stylized
woman and saw Herschel at his fawning worst in her presence.
Nor would Buzie admit to herself any feeling of disappointment
that the amusements were all shut down, the pier deserted but
for a fisherman, a hot-potato vendor, and a pair of pedestrians in
winter overcoats. For all that she had heard about the wonders
of Coney Island, she had judged it already as a breeding ground
for stupidity and docility. A tourist brochure that Herschel had
translated for her had confirmed this judgment, with its boasts
of spectacles that seemed to Buzie as decadent as the goings-on
in the czar's palace.

All through the hour-and-a-half journey by elevated train
through Manhattan and open-air trolley through Brooklyn, Buzie
had lectured self-righteously about the effects of such circuses
as Coney Island upon working-class consciousness and morale.
"Ahh, you're like the daughter of a Hasid," scolded Rose as
they set foot on Surf Avenue, a street lined with gargantuan toys
and tinsel palaces. And you, Buzie had thought in retort, are

the daughter of a hatmaker—and with an ostrich feather for a brain! But her reply had been simply to renew her lecture. After a quick survey of Surf Avenue had revealed that the three major amusement parks—Luna, Dreamland, and Steeplechase— were closed down with locks and boards, Herschel and Rose had abandoned the priggish girl to the bench on the Iron Pier and had gone off to discover Coney Island without a moral overseer.

Ignoramus of a brother! At Herschel's suggestion, Buzie had dressed for springtime and for comfort amid a vast crowd: a thin black skirt and a shirtwaist without even a shawl. Contrarily, the sunlight held a bold sparkle but little heat, and the only crowded feeling she had was from goose bumps up her back. Buzie resented Herschel so bitterly that the beach's natural attractions were lost on her, until eventually her anger caved in to complete boredom. At this point she heard music—a mandolin and an accordion, she guessed—and the inclination of the potato vendor's stocking cap pointed toward its source. Buzie left Rose's bundles on the bench without a backward glance.

She found the music makers along Bowery, the main promenade. With mandolin, accordion, a single-string washtub bass, and harmonica, they were playing a clumsy polka while the accordion player, a big-nosed, bald man with jowls like a rodent, sang in Yiddish:

> Oh, girl, won't you dance with me?
> I must be happy when I have the opportunity!

They stood before a peeling billboard portraying a monstrously fat woman alongside a tiny girl with a woman's face. Of the screaming English letters, Buzie could decipher only the numerals showing the woman's weight, 685 pounds, and the midget's height, 34 inches. But the contrast between the singer's love song and the atrocious figures behind him brought an impulsive smile to her lips—though she concluded after a moment's consideration that the poster was highly offensive to womankind!—and her smile was a signal that drew a prancing young man toward her from the nest of male listeners, his arms outstretched, his feet alive with polka rhythms. Without hesitation, Buzie lifted her skirt, swooped into step, and for a full five minutes felt more at ease than she had since becoming a New Yorker.

As the music waned, they whirled to a breathless stop. The harmonica player, a tall, bespectacled fellow who was vaguely familiar to Buzie, looked down the block, waved to someone, and began to pipe out a well-known Yiddish ditty, to which Buzie's dancing partner alertly sang:

> Sunday potatoes, Monday potatoes,
> Tuesday and Wednesday, potatoes,
> Thursday and Friday, potatoes,
> Sabbath it's a special treat—potato pudding!
> Sunday, again, potatoes.

The hot-potato vendor had arrived with his cart. They all hollered greetings and jokes to him while he forked his wares off the hot coals and collected their two cents. Buzie lingered and was offered a "free sample," but insisted on paying. Leaning against a fence some feet from the cluster of men, she ate and wondered about the fate of Rose Lifschitz's bundles.

Her dance partner weaned himself from the men's chatter and crouched on the sidewalk near Buzie, his jacket wide open to the cool breeze. "Still out of breath?" she asked after swallowing too large a mouthful of her spud.

"Not really." He stood to protect his honor. "I had a touch of tuberculosis a few years ago."

"And you live here by the ocean? You should be where it's dry."

He laughed. "I caught the damned thing in Colorado." Buzie had never heard of the place and kept silent. He raised his chin inquisitively. "And how do you know where I live?"

Buzie made short shrift of her potato and wished for another, just to hold for its warmth. "You fit in with the locals," she observed, licking her fingers. "Besides, nobody else comes to Coney Island this early in the year."

"And you?" He evaded too obvious a show of interest by dropping the volume of his voice. "You live in Coney Island, or Brighton?"

"I live in the Bronx," she replied with a giggle. "But I am the exception that proves the rule—in plain language, a fool." She explained with renewed aggravation about her brother.

"If I were Herschel," the young man ventured, "I might want to be alone with this Rose, too."

"Fine! So who wanted to come with them? Rose's parents are orthodox and say she's got to have a chaperon, so I get stuck! I don't even like this place. The workers who come think they're at a circus, but it's they who are the clowns!"

He arched and dropped his eyebrows. "I'll tell you what Maxim Gorky wrote about Coney Island," he said with a decisive smack of his lips. "You know who he is?"

"Of course!"

"Well, here's what he wrote in an American magazine, four years ago. The article was entitled 'Boredom.' This is an exact quote," he boasted, tapping his temple like a talmudic sage. " 'Life is made for the people to work six days a week, sin on the seventh, and pay for their sins, confess their sins, and pay for the confession.' "

"That's exactly right," snapped Buzie. "And it goes for Jews, too, not just Catholics!"

The man shrugged. "Eh, I think he's a little too serious."

"Hey, Levovsky!" called the accordion player. The band was cranking out a tune about Black Sunday of 1905. Levovsky smiled apologetically to Buzie and joined in singing as he drifted back.

Their revolutionary tune stirred Buzie to feelings that had no outlet on the garish promenade and tickled her curiosity about Levovsky's political interests. A curious little guy! His face was pale with the passion of his song and very appealing to her: a proud shock of black hair sweeping up from an elegantly wide brow, cheekbones resembling that of the Indian on American nickels, nose rather like on the busts she'd seen of the Russian poet Pushkin, whose mother was a Negro; but his skin was fair, his eyelids edged with tiny veins. He sang with his fists clenched at the waist, feet set solidly apart, his body a short, compact bundle. Buzie judged him to be about twenty-five years old. She found herself wishing that the band would strike up another polka, then scolded herself—Hey now, you're following him around like a puppy dog!—and remained near the fence, distracting herself by examining the faces of the other swaying musicians. That harmonica player again seemed familiar, though she could hardly trust her excited impressions. . . . Still, the way he gnawed his instrument and dipped his knees left and right in rhythm with the string bass . . . Buzie plumbed her memory, but only when she managed to catch the fellow's eye did recognition come. "Pesach the Lip?" She cocked her head.

He stopped playing and pushed his spectacles up on his nose. That was the incongruity that had stalled her—the glasses! "From Mogilev-Podolsk," she said, drawing herself upright for his scrutiny.

His face lit. He raised an arm to hush the others. "My dear friends! This charming listener—my God, how she has grown!— a *landsman* of mine, and more, a comrade!" With sudden caution he peered closely at her again. "You're the daughter of . . . Yes, yes, of course! The youngest one, aha!"

Buzie felt happy but clumsy in his embrace. For all the enthusiasm of such a surprise meeting, she remembered that she had not known Pesach Dropsky all that well and felt embarrassed by the kibitzing of his cronies: "Pesach the Lip? How do you earn such a nickname?" "If you're going to do all the squeezing, Dropsky, at least tell us her name!"

Buzie separated from his bear hug. "He knows me as Buzie Kharlofsky," she announced, "if he remembers at all. I was just a girl," she explained, glancing at Levovsky. "I thought my sister Ruchel might marry him—it would have done her some good, too."

Dropsky's grin showed off his gums as the men hooted at him.

"But to all of you outstanding American citizens," Buzie went on, "I am Bessie Charles!"

"Now there's a name!" cried Dropsky. "And I'm Paul, here, Coney Island Paul."

"Paltry, maybe," said the bass man, showing off his wittiest word of English.

Their banter was overshadowed for Buzie by the approach of Levovsky, who took her hand. "Yasha Levovsky," he said, "and I'm very pleased to meet you, Bessie."

"Hey!" Dropsky shouted behind them. "You remember this tune, Buzie? I played it at every wedding in Mogilev-Podolsk!" He curled his lips around his instrument. The band hastily found the beat of a Russian two-step. Yasha drew Buzie into dancing posture and asked permission with his eyes. She nodded, then shyly looked down to watch her feet step into the rhythm. But he summoned her gaze back, once, twice, by asking questions, which she answered at length to keep herself from yelping for joy.

By the dance's end, his voice and accent had breathed life

into her American name. Bessie Charles. Bessie Charles. Not "Bessie Charles, how many umbrellas did you tip today?" Instead: Oh, dear Bessie, Bessie my love!

She was Bessie now, "my love" maybe tomorrow, but no question remained in her mind of returning to safeguard Rose's silly bundles. "Maybe the waves," she suggested to Yasha, "will steal Rose's bundles away to Europe."

"More likely they'll appear next season as prizes in some arcade here."

"Prizes! That's a good one! You know what she's got in her bundles, my fancy lady? Deposit bottles. Can you believe it? She shlepped them all the way from the Bronx—my brother shlepped them, actually—just to keep them all together with the ones she finds here. She's a thrifty woman, like Herschel says. Thrifty with her brains!"

"So we'll let Rose do her own shlepping?" said Yasha.

Bessie nodded and called to the band for another polka.

Later, Paul Dropsky brought them to a coffee shop along Brighton Avenue. His enthusiasm for reminiscence was much keener than Bessie's, she only minutes away from her old name and old wounds, and concerned, besides, not to exclude Yasha from the conversation. But the few painless memories that she and Paul did swap about Mogilev-Podolsk actually helped speed her acquaintance with the young man, for Paul, with a matchmaker's intuition, boasted about Bessie's arrest and exile, which prompted Yasha, in turn, to display his own political plumage.

He was a man of the IWW, the Industrial Workers of the World, he said, and a veteran of more than one of their "free speech" campaigns, in which hundreds of Wobblies, arriving in a town by boxcar, would agitate among the workers until the local authorities attempted to suppress their activities. Whichever sort of ordinance was enforced to silence the Wobblies would then be violated en masse until the town's jail was bursting with IWW sympathizers. "And this," Yasha said, grinning handsomely behind the rim of his coffee cup, "usually forces the bigwigs to back down."

Like most Wobblies, Yasha claimed to be a migrant worker of no particular trade, now a night watchman for Dreamland Park, and was full of tales about travel and trouble. Bessie suspected that, similar to her brother Julius, he was some kind of déclassé intellectual, for he spoke a cultured Yiddish as well as fluent English—fluent, at least, to an ear that was still making sense only of monosyllabic words—and had a sympathetic cast of mind to match his clean-shaven face that she did not usually expect from lumpenproletariat. He was an animated storyteller, too, excited by his own thoughts, but he liked to listen and seemed able to abandon his preoccupations to participate almost gratefully in hers. Their conversation ambled along with all traces of shyness erased by their obvious enjoyment of one another.

Paul Dropsky, on the other hand, with his interest firmly anchored in Old World nostalgia, became bored as his sentimental feelings about seeing "the *rov's* daughter" ebbed. He lasted through a second cup of coffee, then announced, "Well, tomorrow is a working day, even for a single man. Musicians may be great souls, but they're lousy breadwinners!" He squinted at Bessie over his glasses. "It's not that I'm lazy. I could play twelve, fifteen hours a day if I would just get a penny for each song. I'd never again holler for the ten-hour day!"

Yasha explained that Paul peddled housewares, and played harmonica only as an enticement to customers. Paul positively beamed as Yasha complimented his artistry. Then Bessie stood to give her *landsman* a proper kiss farewell. They exchanged addresses—his a rooming house in Greenpoint, Brooklyn—and in a final outburst of nostalgia, Paul peppered her with questions about her family.

Her replies were filled with sad hesitations that testified to the gap in her life caused by the years of exile. When Paul at last took off, she was greatly relieved to sit, to return to the present. But her coffee cup was empty—yes, Levovsky's as well—like a notice of eviction from their booth. Clearing his throat nervously, Yasha asked if he could pay her share of the check.

"No, thank you," she replied. "I pay my own way, I go my own way."

"Please, you won't leave so soon?"

Her knees swayed excitedly under the table. "That's not what I meant."

Their first argument ensued, but ended at the cash register, where they discovered that Dropsky had paid for them both. Warmed up to controversy, Bessie began to comment on the

politics of the IWW as Yasha navigated them toward Surf
Avenue. She had heard of his organization from Berkman in
England, she said, but was suspicious of its reputation for flam-
boyance. The Wobblies might be known for their songs and
stickers and rowdy defiance of authority, "but you're also known
as fakers who abandon strikes just as quickly as you begin them.
So the workers end up singing themselves right onto a blacklist."

Yasha mulled over the criticism with his eyes to the ground.
"And you, you're unaffiliated? Are you waiting for the movement to come courting?"

Bessie planted her hands on her hips. "When I find in America
a real workers' organization, I'll join! Oh, it's easy for you,
maybe," she went on, incited by Yasha's handsome, superior
smile. "You've got no family, you speak good English, you can
travel and go wherever you like with just the clothes on your
back! Show me how you suffer—from blisters on your feet? But
show me any working girl who's managed to be strong enough
to join the movement and I'll show you a real revolutionary! A
woman knows what oppression means—it's in the air she breathes!
You men, you wear your affiliations like some kind of a badge."

With this last word, her voice cracked and she became immediately self-conscious about her volume and shrillness. She
was cold and with a headache swelling behind her ears, but such
excuses for her rudeness would only sound like complaints. Yasha,
no longer smiling, had drawn a cigarette from the pocket of
his jacket and was puffing at it with a distant look in his eyes,
his frame drawn up very straight as if he were resisting—or con-
templating—an insult.

"Maybe if you had consumption you shouldn't smoke," said
Bessie miserably, pitching for a reprieve from his scorn.

"We radical men all smoke, especially at meetings. We're
unhealthy creatures, as I'm sure you've noticed."

"Well, you less than the others," she said, nervously scratching her wrist beneath the ribbon cuff of her shirtwaist. "You
didn't have a single cigarette in the coffee shop."

"I was romancing you then," he said frankly, holding his lapel.
"Now I'm debating you. Anyway, it's time for me to get back
on the job. I smoke so as not to get bored."

"Hey! You can't say I'm boring you!"

"Not you, silly," he said, grinding his cigarette underfoot.
"My job. If you listened . . ." He took hold of her elbow and

turned her about-face, then took from his jacket pocket a huge ring of keys. "There, that's where I work."

They were directly across the street from the entrance to Dreamland Park: a cavernous archway crisscrossed halfway up by telephone wires that cheapened its imitative European grandeur. At the left wall stood a forty-foot statue of a female nude that Yasha identified, with laughter behind his voice, as "The Creation."

"The creation of a million dollars for your boss," said Bessie, offended by the figure's vulgar mystique.

"She's like you," Yasha said, "shivering from the cold. If you come on a tour, I'll fetch a shawl for you from my cabin. C'mon, Bessie. Even Maxim Gorky looked before he criticized."

Bessie took his proffered arm, thinking that a silent interlude might greatly benefit their friendship.

Inside the empty, block-square amusement park, their familiarity became to Bessie a precious thing, made rare by contrast to the bare promenades and silent exhibits. Without a milling crowd to animate the grounds, it all seemed grotesque, flimsily constructed, a panorama of unmasked lies: palaces studded with a hundred thousand dead light bulbs, airplanes shrouded in canvas, submarines trussed up and hanging like hooked fish above great vats of water, signs shouting at other signs about the wonders of the world. "We come here like a child comes to the zoo," Bessie reflected aloud, "to gain affection for a wild, dangerous beast."

"Would you not bring your own child to learn what the beast looks like?"

Their feet marked time along the rolling blacktop paths. Yasha at first felt obliged to perform as a barker at each amusement:

"The Village of Lilliput, where three hundred live midgets are waiting to make your acquaintance, young lady. Don't let them get fresh with you! ...

"Shoot the Chutes, down you go into the briny deep. Catch a herring in your mouth and you might get a prize. At least you can bring the herring home to mother!"

But Bessie's laughter became shallower each time as the silence of the abandoned park provoked terrible memories of another silence—the deathly silence of the Ysyakh prison on the morning of her escape. She could not shoo the memory away; each time it washed back, redoubled, like a swelling tide. As she fell behind Yasha's long gait and grew noticeably mum, he stood still, took hold of her hand, and questioned her with his eyes.

"Some girls wear another man's ring," she said, deeply touched by his awareness of her shifted mood. "But I wear another man's ball and chain." Then she told him about Jacob Smulevitch.

Her exile was a fact that she often mentioned but rarely described. With her brothers, the two people most likely to be interested, she always felt accusatory and without comfort when the pain of her memories flared up. With others, she found herself quieted quickly by their pity or squeamishness. But Yasha listened without letting go of her hand and with an expression of intense involvement.

". . . . I was dragged into the punishment cell . . . Smulevitch was chained by his neck. It smelled like a sewer. . . . And then the guard was on top of me. . . ."

"Let's walk," Yasha suggested, touching her back.

At the eastern fence of the park, they came upon a six-story tenement building with charred windows and cornices, an anomaly amid the glittering spirals and bright advertisements surrounding it. Bessie paused in her outpouring to ask who lived there.

It was set aflame ten times daily with low-heat combustion, Yasha explained without editorializing. Hired hands played the part of firemen who would battle the blaze while other actors and actresses leaped from the window into safety nets. Spectators paid to watch the calamity in progress and, if they wished, to help man the water pumps. During the upcoming season, the spectacle would be performed at night under newfangled klieg lights. "At the height of the season, there are hundreds of people working for this exhibit alone. They make three dollars a week, literally to risk their lives."

"And what worker does not risk her life?" Bessie said. "You have fires in the sweatshops a dozen times a week."

"Maybe we should be organizing a union," Yasha said. "They have another exhibit like this one in Luna . . . But the job is so seasonal, all the workers are temporary. . . . But, Bessie, return to your history, please."

Bessie had her eye on a rat that was climbing across the rubble at the base of the building. "Ohh, I hate these millionaire bastards!" she muttered, and spat toward the amusement, then turned to Yasha, hoping he would understand, but impatient already for fear that he would not. "They treat us exactly like dogs! What kind of mockery is this, that we should pay to watch people burn? For what did all my comrades suffer and give their lives, Yasha? Was it just a sideshow? Should I have stood there smiling like a fool at the atrocities?"

Yasha clasped her shoulder. Her body was an iron rod. A restrained smile again crept across his face, enraging her. "Here!" she cried, wrenching out of his hands. "You want to know what Siberia is like? *You* live there! *You* work there!"

"I've been there," he said. "I was on Sakhalin Island for two years."

Bessie snapped her head upright and pressed her hands to her breast.

"I know the difference between Dreamland and a nightmare," he continued, running his hand lightly across her pinned hair. "But you, I think, have got to escape from exile a second time."

"Sakhalin," she whispered, shivering. "They threatened us with that name. I want to hear!"

"And you will," Yasha agreed. "We're going to be good friends, Bessie Charles. Hey, but you're trembling, you've been trembling for an hour. Stay here a minute. Let me get you a shawl. My cabin is right in the direction you spat. And then, if you don't mind—"

(Please, not home, not yet!)

"—I'm going to teach you some Wobbly songs."

"Yasha, wait." He'd already sprinted halfway across the grounds. "Wait, I—I feel so foolish. . . . Listen, dear, I want to see your cabin, not to make you feel bad—but—please, I have to ask: What are you doing with a lady's shawl?"

"Is that all?" he snorted. "You want to know the truth? I like to crochet! Shoo!" He stamped his foot and sent a rat scurrying into the ground-floor window of the tenement. Then he held out his hand to Bessie.

Chapter Ten

Mrs. Markish sang praises of Yasha Levovsky for the entire week, in the wee hours as Bessie girded herself for ten hours in the shirtwaist factory and at dusk when Lester, Bessie, Belle-Brokha, and she sat down to her kosher meals.

"Mrs. Markish, how can you be so enthusiastic already?"

"Anyone with a nose would take one sniff and know there's a flower in the backyard."

"What backyard, the Bronx? St. Mary's Park? What?"

"Never mind, Mr. Markish. You know very well that I'm talking about Coney Island, may God bless everyone who lives there. I can smell the flower of Coney Island all the way from here, so why not Buzie?"

"Who says not Buzie? And my name is Bessie!"

Yasha had impressed the entire family on Sunday night, converting their anger and concern about "Buzie the wandering Jew" into delight that she had met such an erudite, polite, and sympathetic young man. True, he had kept her out late without the permission or foreknowledge of anyone, causing the whole family to gather at the Markishes' for a hand-wringing vigil, but hadn't he compensated by traveling over three hours round-trip —a complete stranger!—to properly escort her home? And to Ruchel's scolding and idle talk he had listened for a good half-hour without a trace of restlessness and with sleepy Nat bouncing on his knee.

"If he's not a direct descendant of King David, I'm not a kosher woman."

"Phooey. If a cossack could recite a bit of Talmud, you'd call him a good Jew."

Herschel alone was unimpressed, soured by Buzie's reckless abandonment of his girlfriend's bundles. Even after retrieving them, he complained, they had lost an afternoon of consummate joy as they were forced to hike across the breadth of Coney Island in search of her. "While you, you go play merry-go-round with this 'direct descendant' of Rasputin!"

"Go stick a hatpin in your ear."

Bessie could disregard her brother's opinions and slough off the loss of his goodwill simply because Yasha was amply filling her loneliness, with visits on Tuesday and Wednesday to St. Anne's Avenue and on Thursday to her factory at the close of the workday. By Friday morning, her feelings for the young man extended well beyond Mrs. Markish's glowing assessment. "You'd think I was more important than his job, the way he comes around!"

"When a man finds gold, he no longer cares for copper. It's good for him to spend time with us—better than you becoming a fixture in his amusement park."

Wherever they met, Yasha lent the place a party atmosphere. As if he were an old-time friend, he had an intuitive feel for coaxing her away from her unhappy memories and narrow moods. She became like a hungry person sniffing the stew on the stove; she could glimpse, for the first time, an American life of promise for herself.

To every ambition she expressed, he joined his practical knowledge:

"Twice now you've told me that you want to become a nurse. So? Is there some disease that prevents you? I have a cousin who's just now gotten her license as a practical nurse, and she was no better off than you when she began and has a lot less brains! She got her license from the Beth Israel school on Henry Street—write this down, Bessie! With your education, you could probably graduate in a week! And you might even meet a rich doctor, who knows? . . .

"What do you mean, they made you read children's books in night school? You mean you'd rather suck your thumb when the people around you speak English? You must reregister at once, Bessie! Never mind the school, it's your pride that's so childish!"

Throughout the week, Bessie was making plans and resolutions that Yasha would applaud and embellish with some of his own. She would train to be a nurse; he would solicit backing from certain musician friends and try to break into the music-publishing field. She would attend a few IWW meetings; he would begin reading her preferred newspapers and give particular attention to Morris Winchevsky, Moishe Nadir, and several others of her favorite writers. She would learn English and study American history; he would stop downplaying his Jewish origins among his American socialist friends, "like some uptown Jew or some rotten assimilationist of the *Forvetz* line," she said.

Eventually they would move together to the Lower East Side to be closer to the heartthrob of the Jewish socialist scene, the politicking of the Ninth Congressional District, the lecture halls and cafés, the *landsmanshaftn*, fraternal orders, mutual-aid societies, newspaper offices, and countless other institutions of the congested ghetto. Bessie would initiate a women's reading circle and support group for impoverished progressive writers; Yasha, a center where young musicians and lyricists could meet to collaborate. Such agreements were always sealed with a kiss, a kiss for which Bessie closed her eyes, a kiss that sparked a hundred more resolutions for the sake of their rewards as it sent her soul gliding through her body. . . .

Sadie Weinstein had lips shaped like a trumpet, but kept her voice muted on the job. "Be careful, Bessie. It's not like the guy's proposed to you already. Be careful what you do for him. Hey, don't look at me like a bee just flew up your skirt! You virgins, you think the rest of the world thinks about sex as much as you? I'm talking about your job! If you let your boyfriend go to your head, you'll be out of work in no time!"

Both women were pinning up their hair in the ninth-floor dressing room of the Triangle Shirtwaist Company, which occupied the top three floors of the Asch Building on Washington and Greene Streets near the fashionable houses on Washington Square Park. Sadie was a three-year veteran at the factory who sewed at the machine adjacent to Bessie's. Twenty-eight years old, divorced and without children, she had an easy, almost crass way of talking about intimate matters and liked to act the confidante. Throughout the week, Bessie's second at the Triangle, Bessie had been feeding Sadie details about her budding relationship. This morning, as they rode the elevator together, she had also announced her intention to confront their head man, Mr. Solomon, about the twenty-five cents he'd docked from her first paycheck the week before.

Sadie had hushed her until they reached the dressing room, then explained that every one of the company's five hundred-odd workers were dunned on a weekly basis for some part of his or her wages to pay the inside contractors. Bessie had been subject to this system at several of the tenement sweatshops in which she had labored on and off during the winter, but its enforcement at so huge and profitable an enterprise as the Triangle infuriated her.

"To hell with it. I should pay him to stand over me? I should pay so he can molest you every day when you leave—as if he's going to find a stolen needle in your slip! I'll pay him with my spit, that's how I'll pay!"

"Oh, be quiet," Sadie scoffed. "Your boyfriend's not here to be impressed."

Several of their coworkers were fleeing their vicinity, hurrying out to the floor. Talk like Bessie's could get a whole slew of them bounced. The Triangle management had the most effective antiunion policies and spying system in the business. In fact, it had been a lockout of union sympathizers at the Triangle two years earlier that had helped spark the industry-wide "Uprising of the 20,000" that had breathed life into the fledgling International Ladies Garment Workers Union. A high percentage of the bosses had recognized the union and agreed to contracts following a winter of violent confrontation between the picketing workers, most of them Jewish and Italian immigrant women and girls with some wealthy uptown supporters, and the thugs, whores, and police hired and controlled by the Employers' Mutual Protection Association. But at the strike's end, the Triangle Shirtwaist Company remained nonunion and with all the same condemnable conditions that had caused the struggle: overcrowded floors, locked fire exits, dim lighting, lack of ventilation, floors slippery with oil leaked from the sewing machines, and typically overlong, underpaid terms of labor.

It was nothing like the Cousin Izzy sweatshops that Bessie had quit as readily as she blew her nose when it tickled. There was no confusion of loyalties or class identity at the Triangle; the bosses never even appeared on the shop floor except for a brief word with one of the inside contractors, whose teams of "girls"

churned out hundreds of shirtwaists daily. Outrage such as Bessie
was feeling was a luxury, a surfeit of emotion that would be
worn down by ten or more hours of work at the machine.

The busy season had begun in the garment industry. Bessie's
holiday in Coney Island would likely be her last day off for six
weeks and her ten daily hours would swell like a blister to
thirteen or more. Already the sign was posted over the entrance
to the dressing room: IF YOU DON'T COME IN SUNDAY, DON'T COME
IN MONDAY. Even the fourteen-year-olds, whose phony papers
were never challenged by employers or by government inspectors except to weed out "troublemakers," were looking haggard
and drawn first thing in the morning. At least one of them, Sadie
had predicted, "some quiet greenhorn of a girl," would be a
suicide by May. "And you'll be a bride."

"A nurse."

"Even better. We'll all be sick by then!"

"Not me, Sadie. I don't care if I have this job or not, but I
do care about getting my twenty-five cents from that crook."

"Well, it's been nice knowing you, honey."

But the staccato hum of the sewing machines, in rows of
fifteen, two hundred and forty to the floor, steadily eroded
Bessie's clarity and sense of purpose. The smells of sweat and
machine oil clogged her senses. Her back, bottom, and legs lost
feeling as her fingers danced along yards of fabric and her eyes
narrowed to pinpoints of strain. Yasha Levovsky became a paper
doll, a fictional hero fallen back into the pages of his book, as
the reality of broken needles, snapped threads, snagged fabric,
scratches, and punctures took command and her finished pieces
piled up in the basket on the floor.

Bessie recited poetry to herself to keep her mind nimble
despite the numbing routine. Her favorite selections, long memorized, were by Morris Rosenfeld:

> The clock in the workshop, it rests not a moment;
> It points on, and ticks on: Eternity—Time.
> And once someone told me the clock has a meaning—
> Its pointing and ticking has reason and rhyme.
> And this too he told me—or was I then dreaming?
> The clock wakens life in us, forces unseen;
> And something besides . . . I forget what; oh, ask not!
> I know not, I know not, I am a machine!

The words merged like echoes with her own thoughts as she rocked back and forth in her chair, sewing in rhythm with the meter. Every ten minutes or so, Mr. Solomon's clipped footsteps and hacking cough would pass up the aisle behind her as he patrolled his work area exhorting them to work faster. "Let's break some records today, girls. Speed up those machines. . . . For God's sake, Sadie, how many needles are you gonna break today? These things cost money—I could probably buy *you* for less, and with your sister in the bargain! . . . C'mon, girls, I treat you fair, all I'm asking for is a little work. . . . Gina, keep those pieces clean, will you? Damn, I bet even the pope wouldn't trust an Italian to do his laundry. Listen, who knows wop talk? Tell this girl she's the last goddamn wop I'm gonna hire if she doesn't break some records this week. . . . Hey, cut the gabbing, girls, we don't pay for gab. . . ."

Every word a slap in the face! His patter was in English and in Yiddish, and the tone was insulting throughout. Sadie glanced anxiously at Bessie each time he passed down their aisle.

> I gaze on the battlefield; wrath flames inside me,
> And Vengeance and Pain stir their fires in me.
> The clock—how I hear it aright!—It is crying:
> "An end to the bondage! Arise, and be free!"
> It quickens my feeling, it quickens my reason;
> It points to the sweet, precious moments that fly.
> Oh, worthless am I if I longer am silent,
> And lost am I, lost! if in silence I die.

With the wary instincts of a predator, Mr. Solomon said nothing directly to Bessie for the entire morning. Meanwhile her resolution about the quarter wore down to a thin, brittle bit of anger. A quarter instead of a job? Ho, Miss Millionaire! From where will the money for tuition for nursing school, and for books, come—from poor Mr. Markish's soapsuds? So you'll spend your savings, the only savings the entire family has, and Julius will never speak to you again because you're a bourgeois, and nobody will get to taste so much as a sweet roll from your hundred stingy dollars! And Yasha? He may be as seasonal as his job, like Sadie said: a big first impression, a quick last impression, a dent in your pillow! Oh, be careful, Buzie!

Solomon at last blew the noontime whistle, then slapped Bessie on the hip with his clipboard as she shambled toward the dressing room. "Listen, girlie, you better eat a good lunch, 'cause you look hungry, y'understand? And hungry girls don't work here, not for me. Don't we pay you enough to feed yourself? Hey, *vos iz*, you don't speak English?"

He was baiting her, this much she knew. She looked at his shrewd, stubbled face and felt her tongue souring. Sadie hooked arms with her and tugged. Solomon turned back to his clipboard.

"You watch out!" Sadie hissed as they passed through the draped entranceway to the dressing room. "There are spies in your underwear around this place! That man knows everything you're thinking, Bessie, he's been around. What is he, just a cutter who's made good! He's been in your shoes, for God's sake, you can't play with him!"

Bessie looked sadly into the redhead's fleshy face. "How can you stand it, Sadie? For three years and without so much as a union . . ."

Sadie shrugged and reached for her shawl. "It's better than the street, sweetie. You go down to the docks and see what happens to girls who can't find work. Feh, what does a virgin know! Don't get me into trouble now, you better go have lunch yourself." She hurried to the elevator.

Bessie carried her bag lunch into a coffee shop diagonally across from the factory and from there rang up Yasha, whose Coney Island cabin was equipped with a telephone. His voice was tinny and pitifully distant, but nonetheless familiar and soothing to hear. Bessie flushed with relief to feel her doubts and fears dissolving.

"Yasha, I've been sewing my own heart to the fabric all day. Say something to me, dear, something just for me."

"It takes a little while to grow eloquent," he apologized, "especially when I'm talking to a box on the wall and not to you. I just woke up."

"Oh, I'm sorry!"

"Never mind. I can sleep on the job tonight—it'll be an improvement over my performance for the rest of the week."

"Please, Yasha, we can't *both* be fired. It would be a scandal!"

"Your complaints remind me of a wonderful dream I had— just woke up from it, in fact."

"Dear God, what kind of a boyfriend—"

"I dreamed that you quit that hellhole factory and met me this very afternoon at the Garden Cafeteria on East Broadway— wait, I'm not finished!—and, since you just quit your job, you let me pay for the check. And then—well, the next part I have to whisper or the operator will become embarrassed and cut us off."

Bessie squeezed her thighs together and nearly kissed the mouthpiece. "The dream is worthy of Daniel, if you don't mind my getting religious. And you yourself are a miracle, Yasha."

"You're not so bad yourself."

"But the Garden Cafeteria is right next to the *Forvetz* building, which you know would give me indigestion! Even your dreams have faulty politics, Yasha—you haven't been reading Winchevsky. I can tell. And for me to trust you after one week! I must be a fool, like Sadie says, I must be completely crazy. . . ."

"Why do you say that? When you were a child, how long did it take you to make friends with another child? Ten minutes?"

"We're not children, Yasha."

"No, Miss Seventeen-Going-on-Seventy-Five, we're not. But we are revolutionaries, affiliated or no, and every revolutionary must be as free as a child in his mind. Like a child, we must animate the inanimate. Like a child, we must make something out of nothing—"

"Enough!" Bessie interrupted. "In another minute I'll be singing your Wobbly songs right here in the restaurant." Already the cashier was frowning at her for hogging the phone and munching on a sandwich from her bag. Bessie turned her back to him, but moments later a tall Irish waiter tapped her shoulder. "Boss says there'll be no eatin' food from the outside in 'ere, young lady."

Bessie signaled her incomprehension of his English and dragged the waiter to the telephone so that Yasha could translate. By the same system she placed an order for sour cream—"No, Yasha, no blintzes, just the sour cream, to go." By the time the waiter returned with her order, she was waiting by the revolving door. "T'enk you," she said, curtseyed and paid.

Half an hour later, Bessie was sitting with Yasha in Seward Park on Essex Street, finishing her bag lunch, chiding him for the fancy straw hat he'd bought, and chattering a mile a minute. Back at the Triangle Shirtwaist Company, Mr. Solomon was cursing as he wiped flecks of sour cream off his chin and collar, and Sadie was bent over her sewing machine again.

By the time Bessie arrived at St. Anne's Avenue that evening, Mrs. Markish's *shabbas* rituals were complete and her delicious foods were pouring out of the kitchen. Herschel was off enduring a similarly orthodox *shabbas* meal with the Lifschitz family, but the rest of the Kharlofsky brood had come, and apparently even Julius had endured Mrs. Markish's piety without complaint, for a rare spirit of cheer reigned at the table, which Bessie's late-coming and unkempt appearance did not upset. Ruchel nevertheless felt constrained to upbraid her younger sister: "Bad enough that you work on *shabbas*. You can't find even one evening for the Almighty?"

"Let him make an appointment," Bessie huffed, drawing a reprimand from Mrs. Markish, who was carrying a soup tureen to the table.

Bessie washed, brushed her hair, and joined the family. She deliberately occupied herself throughout the meal with Belle-Brokha and with Ruchel's Elaine, cutting their potted beef into bite-size pieces, catching runaway peas, teasing them into finishing what was on their plates. Talk of her job loss would be *treyf* at the sabbath table as far as Mrs. Markish was concerned, and talk of her romantic preoccupations was completely out of the question in mixed company. Mostly chitchat prevailed, while the children, especially one-and-a-half-year-old Nat, provided ongoing distraction and interruption. But as soon as the dishes were cleared from the table, Ruchel, with a flair for the dramatic, pulled from her bosom a just-arrived letter from their father. "Be quiet now, children," she commanded, including Bessie in the sweep of her gaze, then proceeded to read in an animated style that had obviously been rehearsed.

The letter asked far more questions than it gave information about conditions in Mogilev-Podolsk, which Laib had summarized in a sentence: "As always, poverty; not so many weddings; as always, funerals; not so many births." He also revealed an ambivalent attitude in his questions: curiosity and wonder about America's reputed miracles mixed with caution and platitudinous disapproval of its secularized Jewish life—"where the minyan," he wrote, "must meet in the basement while the shop is set up in the best room of the house."

Julius at once bemoaned his father's silence about political affairs and with bravado began to reminisce about the Jewish Labor Bund and other left-wing formations in the Dniester River basin. None at the table besides Bessie was interested in or comfortable with such conversation, and she was in no mood to bull her way into it. Julius, however, managed to catch Feivl's eye and arrest him as a listener by preying on his good-natured politeness.

"You know, the revolutionaries are just as backward as everything else in Russia. You can't build socialism from feudalism, you need more of a foundation. Any Marxist will tell you. But in America we've got that foundation. There are no peasants here, just workers. And look at the inventions that have improved life in America, all built by simple American workingmen—not a count or a nobleman among them. Now, you take the airplane, for instance—"

"As if the elevated trains aren't enough of a misery!" moaned Mrs. Markish. "Soot and noise! Noise and soot!"

"More miserable than a horse-drawn cart with no springs?" Julius retorted. "Nowhere is it written, Leah, that men should not be able to fly. Believe me, these same machines that our dear poppa says are corrupting our faith—like the airplane, built by a couple of bicycle mechanics, can you imagine, Feivl?—these machines will someday free the American workingman from all forms of manual labor! And then he can study holy books if he's foolish enough, or just stay home and play with his children for a change. He'll be able to do whatever he damn well pleases!"

Mr. Markish cleared his throat to signal his protest of Julius's profanity. Mrs. Markish, assuming there to be bitterness in Julius's heart whenever the subject of their father arose, tried to derail the conversation altogether by bringing out coffee and babka and making the details of her table service preeminent. But this provoked objections from the husbands, who felt compelled by the "brainy" nature of their brother-in-law's topic to pursue it. Finally, like orthodox men of the old country, they convened apart from the women in the bedroom at the back of the railroad apartment.

Bessie curbed her curiosity and joined her sisters to wash

dishes—a task less *treyf*, according to Mrs. Markish's religious ethic, than the cockroaches that would invade if the dishes were left sitting in the sink. "They're the only one of God's creatures that the Almighty should have shut out of the ark," Mrs. Markish said. "This would be a Second Covenant with his children in the Bronx."

"And what about human cockroaches?" said Bessie, trying to broach the subject of her job loss. But Ruchel became squeamish and commandeered the conversation, steering it to family topics: husbands and children. Bessie's announcement kept rising to her lips and receding as Ruchel addressed only Mrs. Markish. When the girls tumbled in, clamoring for cake, Ruchel snapped at Bessie: "Can't you keep them occupied? Leah and I have things to discuss!"

Apologetically, Mrs. Markish, too, dismissed Bessie by asking her to serve dessert to the men in the bedroom. Bessie shuffled from the kitchen with a loaded tray.

Finally alone in her room, a cubicle between the dining room and Belle-Brokha's playroom, Bessie sat at the windowsill, staring out at the gas lamps and busy, dark treetops of St. Mary's Park, which fronted their street and extended several blocks east. How fine it would be to stroll there with Julius and discuss his modern ideas as equal comrades! She could tell him about the fancy gadgets in Dreamland Park and quote to him from Maxim Gorky. Oh, yes, she could hold her own with him!

As if a machine alone will do anything, Julius, anything more than manufacturing fancier shackles for the workers to wear!

The men's voices leaked into her earshot, Julius's very sharp and animated. Bessie ached to know what he was saying, what plans . . . Then baby Nat toddled, unsupervised, through her room. "Hi, Nat! Where are you going, to see your poppa?" The boy pitched forward, excited by the very feat of walking. He made it past his cousin Belle-Brokha, who was demonstrating to Elaine the game of jacks on the floor of her room; but as he reached the doorway of the back room, he slipped on the braided rug and began to howl. Bessie rushed to him before Feivl could even stand. By cradling the baby to stillness in the doorway, she earned a full minute of listening time. Julius was wound up in words:

"The field is restricted, I know. Even in America, Jews are all but legally barred. But I've applied nonetheless to the University of Chicago, and when I graduate, I swear by the hair on my old man's chin, I'll find a job as an engineer! I'll find an open door or I'll open one for myself. I won't be deterred!"

The excitement and admiration that Julius's rhetorical style stirred in her was undiminished from her girlhood. Bessie left the room recalling the days when she had followed her brothers into the woods and into the revolutionary movement itself. They had scolded and rejected her, exploited and ultimately incriminated her; yet by comparison with the attention and solidarity she'd received in those days, she felt now like a scullery maid. "What do you think, Nat?" she said, playfully hoisting the boy from her hip onto his back on the floor. "Do you think I ought to be changing your diaper every Friday night just because I'm unemployed?"

Unemployed. Unaffiliated. Unmarried. A greenhorn. A girl. Julius would go to Chicago and become the Jewish Thomas A. Edison and bring a revolution—he thinks!—by turning a few nuts and bolts, while she could only eavesdrop on his glory and punch the clock at one sweatshop after another and endure the insults of greedy bosses—and of Ruchel, too?

Her appreciation for Yasha blossomed, sweetening her breath. So go, she told herself, take him to the Lower East Side, you with your hundred dollars. Take him, make a business, and leave the sweatshops like you left Siberia. Why doubt anymore the promises that life has made to you?

Nat slipped under her arm in a creep toward the kitchen. Bessie walked straddling him until he noticed her feet and, giggling, tried to stand. "Here," she said, "you be my talking dummy." She crouched and seated him on her knee in imitation of a ventriloquist's poster that she'd seen in Coney Island. "Now, tell your momma: Aunt Bessie threw sour cream at the boss today, and she's gonna throw something at Rucheleh, too. . . ."

She could see into the kitchen where her sisters were conversing. Nat glimpsed his mother's back and reached for her, but Buzie held him tight and shushed his whining as she listened closely to what Mrs. Markish was saying:

". . . . If you tell Feivl, and then *he* can tell Mr. Markish. Especially that he shouldn't worry. If he does, our baby will be born with colic. Colicky babies for worried parents. I'll work until the day arrives, and I'm sure Buzie will help even more than she already does. . . ."

"The little anarchist might start a strike against you."

Nat squirmed at the sound of Ruchel's voice, then with a grunt and a fart made a bowel movement in his diaper. The stink rose to Bessie's nostrils as Mrs. Markish said, "Rucheleh, you don't understand our Buzie. She's a sincere person, God bless her, and when she hears that I'm in a family way . . ."

Bessie stood Nat on his feet. "Go, take your mess to Ruchel." The kitchen conversation froze.

She was like a drunkard recovering from a binge all the next day: depressed, resigned to sobriety, but still tingling with the ideas and impulses that all week had possessed her. She spent her morning on the Lower East Side, pacing the streets between Canal and Delancey, canvassing stores and factories for employment. But her effort was halfhearted; she was more attracted by the room-for-rent signs wired to the fire escapes of a dozen tenements and to the window of a storefront on Rivington Street that would have been the perfect site for the kind of café or reading circle about which she had daydreamed with Yasha.

The street held warnings, too, to offset such temptations. Prostitutes loitered in front of the cold-water flats on Ludlow Street, heckling men and lifting their dresses to show off naked legs and bellies as casually as a merchant one block over on Orchard Street would unfold a bolt of fabric. On Howard Street an evicted woman was bleeding from the forehead and cursing the ancestors of two burly men who were standing on the stoop of her building with their arms folded across their chests. On Suffolk Street a wobbly, drunken man kept reaching down to the curb to pick up the shadows of domesticated pigeons that were flying in broad arcs overhead. Soon he fell over.

These were the potholes in the streets of gold. The pushcart peddlers steered clear of them; the factory workers rushed past; the housewives looked away and shushed their youngest children, who gaped and asked questions. Bessie felt truly like a greenhorn, a young shoot growing through a crack in the corner pavement and quaking amid the clamor of buggies and pushcarts, the arguments of peddlers and customers, the cries for attention. She recalled by contrast the customs of charity and respect that ruled the streets, of Mogilev-Podolsk. There the stakes were less high, people's ambitions were less inflated, and the misery was better distributed, she thought. Yet this was the fruit of that vine, this Lower East Side, bloomed from the hot incubation of steerage: the burst pollen pod of Jewish poverty and persistence. And someday it would be her garden. . . .

But first she had to tend Mrs. Markish's garden. Let the baby come, Bessie thought, and let the work of my hands clothe and feed her just as Leah has done for me. Let my money pay for Leah's freedom, not my fun; without her, I'd still be caged on Ellis Island. Without her devotion, I'd be a blotch on this sidewalk, not a tourist, surely not a human being. Patience, Buzie, patience. You spent four years in Ysyakh. The Bronx is surely no worse.

(Not if Ruchel keeps her distance, no . . .)

By 4:30 she arrived at Washington Square Park, late for a rendezvous with Yasha. She found him on the eastern perimeter of the park, wearing his silly straw hat and watching with pleasure the children who ran up and down the path before him. Horse carts lined Washington Place at his back, parked before factory lofts that blocked the sun from the streets. Bessie leaned against a fat, bare maple to watch the man as a stranger, but in a moment he spotted and hailed her.

She was weary, restored to the Spartan state of mind with which she had toured Coney Island the week before. In a businesslike manner, she sat next to Yasha and explained her predicament, speaking dispassionately to lessen the value of what had been lost. "Everything we've spoken about will have to be postponed, of course."

"Of course." Yasha doffed his hat and balanced it on his knee.

"It makes more sense. Really, we're still almost strangers."

"If your lips were kissing me now instead of lecturing," Yasha said, "you wouldn't feel that way."

"If my lips hadn't been kissing you all week," she retorted, "I might have eaten that sour cream and kept my job!"

"Excuse me for poisoning your mind."

"You're making fun of me, Yasha."

"Oh, Bessie!" he sighed. "You're seventeen years old! You were made to be teased!"

She realized the choice he was presenting: to be angry, insulted, and melodramatic, or to swallow the medicine and carry on. She lowered her cheek to his shoulder, relieved to sheathe her belligerence. "Will you wait for me, Yasha?"

"Does a farmer wait for his crops to ripen? I'll wait, I'll wait for you and for the revolution."

"Can't you be a little serious?"

"I am very serious." He squeezed her hand. His eyes embraced her.

"I have to find a new job," she declared, sitting up primly. "Mrs. Markish doesn't even know that I quit the Triangle. But tonight, when I have no pay envelope to give her . . ."

"I'll get you a job at Coney Island," he suggested. "You can jump out of the tenement window ten times a day. A window all your own."

"Oh, you!"

"Right into my arms. You'll be the darling of Dreamland."

"All your jokes and promises!"

"What promises? Look here, I saved your youth and good-looks yesterday, Miss Charles. That factory was wearing you down."

A horse at the curb whinnied, a suspended sound that reached Bessie from the city din and distracted her with a strange, utterly brief memory of the Mogilev-Podolsk pogrom: the bridge, the road, the shul, the gunshots . . . She shifted uncomfortably on the hard bench and began to speak. Yasha was kneeling now, looking back on Washington Place. More of the parked horses were fretting and snorting. Pigeons rushed from a tree and soared west across the park. "It's a fire," muttered Yasha.

Bessie saw a puff of smoke hovering at a high window of the Asch Building on the far corner.

"It's your factory! There's a fire!"

"No, no, that's not my . . ." First second third fourth fifth . . .

A dark bale of fabric sailed from an upper window of the building. It opened like a handkerchief and became a human figure. A cry, audible from a block away, went up from the crowd that was gathering on the corner.

Yasha hopped over the back of the bench. Bessie climbed after him, then was struck still on the grass by the sight of two more falling, fiery bodies. As she reached the curb, a team of three muscular horses pulling a red pump engine rounded the corner, tearing up the cobblestone only yards from her nose.

She ran up the block, tailing Yasha, thinking about the factory's interior, the sweating wall, the flammable piles of fabric, just yesterday! And another body hit the pavement. Yasha leaped up in recoil. A mob of terrified women was spilling onto the street through the Asch Building doorway. A dozen were standing and hanging from window ledges on the eighth and ninth floors, screaming and weeping as blades of fire slashed at them.

"Don't jump! Don't jump!" Bessie screamed with a score more spectators.

The fire escape, packed like a sardine can with helpless women, tore from the building in a slow-motion agony of metal and rust. Yasha turned to Bessie, his face contorted with grief, his arms outstretched. She touched his chest and pushed past him to search for Sadie Weinstein. Smoke had filled the narrow corridor of buildings. The firemen were at last spreading their first life net. Three girls jumped from the dangling fire escape in a huddle, struck the net simultaneously, and tore the men off their feet. Bessie began to shout Sadie's name just to blot out the constant thudding of bodies on the pavement.

Chapter Eleven / 1917

"You never get so acquainted with death that you're not surprised when it touches your life. But I've been close to dead a few times, so at an early age I came to see myself as a survivor— one that she should be dead but I'm not, y'see, so I started to negotiate for life, to earn my life. Every day I would think, I'm alive! And then I would go and prove it.

"Death always let me through, but never left me alone. Like it was fattening me up. Like in the Bible when God makes signs to frighten the Jews that they shouldn't misbehave. The first lesson for me was Jacob Smulevitch. My life wasn't worth one of his fingers. When I think now how as a girl I got angry 'cause they were planning for his escape instead of mine, I still feel ashamed. So when I came to America, I felt like I had to make it up. There had to be a reason why I should be alive and not Smulevitch.

"Then I met Yasha, and I changed. His love and his admiration gave me reasons enough that I should live. But at the beginning, y'see, I was up in the clouds. Love is a very powerful thing when you first taste it. I began to think maybe if I just hold Yasha's hand, everything will get better. Then death touched me again. It's the cure for idealism.

"The Triangle fire affected me deeply. Such a terrible, terrible day. Nearly one hundred and fifty workers got killed. Many burned—Sadie Weinstein burned—or else they jumped, two and three together, hugging each other like children so that the nets tore like they would be tissue paper. I felt like—like what? That the people, the people's movement, the reality of class struggle . . . it took my ugly little face out of the clouds and shoved my nose into the sidewalk, into the pools of blood from these girls, and it said, 'This blood is yours. Next time it will be you.'

"Two years later, Joe Hill said like I felt. He was an IWW man, a songwriter, and they framed him for murder. He said before he died: 'Don't mourn—organize.'

"So I found for myself a place in the struggle. I made a new commitment. Also to my family: Mrs. Markish didn't know I quit the Triangle factory, y'see, and she was visiting with a friend when the news came about the fire. She fainted right in this woman's kitchen. And she was in a family way, remember. A policeman had to come and take my sister home. So when I got there, she gives such a cry and she takes me around like I should be her own daughter—ohh, she was a precious human being, my sister Leah.

"Anyway—first thing I did was relief work for the victims and their families. The Italians, especially; they had less organization than the Jews, so they needed more help. You had families, Italian and Jewish, with two, maybe three different relatives lying in the morgue, and some lost all their savings in the fire. Their daughters and wives had the money sewn into their stockings and it just burned up—they didn't know from banks, y'see.

"For the survivors we paid rent, food, medical, everything. Many were in a state of shock, so we tried to send them for a rest in the country. I gave a little from my savings, but I didn't have to give much, y'see, 'cause it was not so hard to raise money—the rich will gladly give for relief. The owners of the Triangle gave, too. Sure. They'll always pay for handkerchiefs and wheelchairs and bandages, so maybe we'll forget who caused our misery in the first place. Maybe we'll think it was—how do you say it? An act of God—yeah, an act of God. He should drop dead for such acts.

"There's a story that says that a rich man died and came to the pearly gates and says to Saint Peter, 'Here I am! Let me in!' And Saint Peter says, 'First you got to tell three good deeds that you did in your life.' And the rich man says, 'What, good deeds? I was a businessman. I made lots of money and I gave work to many people.' But Saint Peter insists.

"So then the guy remembers: 'Once I was on Delancey Street in my limousine,' he says. 'I was going to my favorite restaurant. And I saw standing in the cold an old man. His pants were torn, his toes came sticking out from his shoes, his teeth were chattering, and he was picking food from garbage cans. I felt like that man should be my own father, I don't know why! So I told my driver to go and give the guy a dollar.'

"Peter asks Gabriel if this is true. Gabriel checks the book of life and says, 'Yes, it's written there.'

"Then the rich man remembers something else. 'Once I went to the opera and I saw there an old woman selling flowers. It was a pitiful bunch of flowers, like weeds, actually. But I felt like that old lady should be my own mother. So I told my driver to give her a dollar.'

" 'Is it true?' Peter asks Gabriel. Gabriel checks the book and 'Uh-huh, it's true.'

" 'So what else?' Saint Peter says to the rich man. 'Just one more.' And the rich man thinks and he thinks, and there's a long line waiting behind him to get into the pearly gates. . . . '*Nu?*' says Saint Peter. And finally the rich man gives up.

" 'So what should we do with this guy?' Saint Peter says to Gabriel.

"And Gabriel says, 'Give him back his two dollars and he can go to hell.' And he closes the book.

"So there you have it. We did not forget who it was that made our misery. For a whole week the city mourned and protested. I gave out flyers with the YPSL—the Young People's

Socialist League; this was the youth group of the Socialist party. We had a funeral march in the pouring rain, all the unions, the whole progressive movement, over one hundred thousand workers. Then at Cooper Union we had a protest meeting—I heard there for the first time Morris Hillquit of the Socialist party. He was very radical that night, a very good speaker. Within a month I became a YPSL. Then later I saw that Hillquit had two faces, and I didn't recognize him for a leader no more.

"But that's already something else, and it's enough already about the Triangle fire. It's been on television already. People think by now it's just a *bubbe meise.* You can't find a shirtwaist even in an antique store no more. All the clothes you get today are made in Hong Kong. Isn't this how you think? But you're wrong. Our system has a hundred Band-aids put on it—we got unions, we got social security, workmen's compensation, welfare —and don't forget, people died to win these things! But still the system bleeds and cracks and grows blisters and it'll never heal. Sure we got sweatshops today, in Hong Kong but also in the Bronx. Like I said, the new immigrants, especially those that they got no papers, they're in the same boat as the Jews and the Italians and the rest in 1911, only today it's more hidden. America has learned how to wear makeup, y'see. No sooner do you have one mask ripped away, there's another mask to take its place, some other piece of propaganda to justify what's happening. And oftentimes the radical movement itself starts to believe in the propaganda, and from this it takes many years to recover.

"World War One, f'rinstance. They told us it was the war to end war. Actually it was a war so that the big capitalist powers could divide up the world. No worker—American, German, Russian—no worker anywhere would benefit from such a bloody war. But the radical movement split about whether we should support what they call the 'war effort.' Yeah, an effort. I'll tell you who makes the effort: the workers. No strikes, speedup in the shop, service in the army, killing, that's a war effort. The only effort the ruling class makes is to try to disguise their profits.

"Now, I was in YPSL at this time, but I never got too active with them. From the beginning I thought they were only luke-warm revolutionaries. Those that they were leaders in the Socialist party, too many of them supported the World War, and I couldn't go along with this. All right, it's not so bad to be un-affiliated. We did plenty on our own. One thing we did, f'rinstance, we started a group called 'The Shnorers.' This means, like, a beggar, in Yiddish. It was a group that we should support young poets and writers so that they should be able to write. We had a storefront on East Fourth Street and Second Avenue, we used it for a café, and there would come progressive speakers and all kind of a personalities. The Shnorers got a good reputation; even the uptown Jews would come for a visit. We raised enough money to keep going, and also to give a couple of scholarships and to publish two books of poetry ourselves. And we lasted more than fifteen years in the same place!

"Then there was the Little White House. This was a house on Staten Island that we made there a shelter for women who were pregnant with no husband or else they were trying to break away from prostitution. We would sometimes go to the docks and compete with the *gonifs* and the pimps that they tried to take hold on young girls who just came off the boat. This was relief work more than political work, if you know what I mean, but it made me a lot of friends and even some recruits for my ideas. And it saved lives. What could be more important? Even my religious sister, Mrs. Markish, she would raise money in her congregation for the Little White House. Me, I called it the Sadie Weinstein House, and I gave half my savings to help get it started.

"Both the Shnorers and the Little White House had mostly Jewish people involved, but during this time I also began to get acquainted with American-born socialists and to broaden my ideas about who makes up the class struggle. First there was the Paterson Silk Ribbon strike, 1913. Yasha and I would go sometimes to picket. It was a very long, difficult strike led by the Wobblies. I met there in New Jersey a woman named Elizabeth Gurley Flynn. Turns out she was an important leader in the strike. From an Irish background, and most of the workers in Paterson were Italian and German. But it didn't matter, she could talk to anyone.

"Gurley Flynn was just a few years older than me, and a good-looker—the newspapers always talked about how good-looking she was, like it was this and not her mind that made her an important fighter. She had long black hair that she usually wore in a bun, and she had eyes that looked sad 'cause they were slanted down, like a hound, you know? She could look pathetic or angry or very beautiful with those eyes. In all the photographs, she always cocked her head to one side like she was asking a question of the entire world. And one eye strayed a little, especially if she was tired. So she had a very deep expression. But she was right down-to-earth and a fighter in the truest sense of the word, never giving up, always helping others to keep it up. For years she went with the IWW, but later she rejected anarchy and joined the Communist Party; and still later, during McCarthy, they nearly drove her off a cliff with their investigations, the bastards in the government. But she stuck with us until she died. We were close friends—we were neighbors in the Bronx.

"You know, I'm starting to feel now like a young girl that she talks about her movie idols. It's ridiculous for a woman my age to feel like this, but I can't help it. I'm not talking so you should think I'm a celebrity, y'see. I'm talking so you should understand. You are my family, *kinderlakh*, and the only wealth I have to leave you is the experience, the people that I sat to dinner with them, and most of all my belief that together we can build a better world. Not so many people believe this anymore.

"These men and women that they're my heroes, you don't learn about them in school, y'see. You don't see them in movies. You hardly even see them for a statue in the park. All you have is an old woman's stories. And look at my competition! All the papers and the magazines and the television that says I'm senile, I'm miserable, I'm old, and there's nothing worse than being old, yeah? Just like we look at a cripple and we see only the deformity, that's how we look at old people, like age is a deformity. Oh, there's lots of deformities, everyone's got them: the way we smell, the color of our hair—everything that doesn't come out of a bottle is a deformity in America.

"Listen, I watch television plenty, I like to keep it on just for company. Such company! You see black and white and policemen all eating from the same table and dancing in the same room. You see all the working people happy. It's enough to make you sick. I can't believe for a second that the masses of people in America actually believe what they see on the television. But still, it makes them feel that something is wrong with them that they're not so happy like the good-looking young people drinking Coca-Cola on the television. All this crazy fantasy so that you should go out and spend your money on nonsense. Television is a hundred times worse for America than vodka was for the Russian peasant.

"But someday we'll have a show on the television that talks about real life, about radical people. And the unions and the progressive organizations can be the advertisers, they can talk about their activities and get people involved. What do you think? Johnny Carson would go for it? Maybe he could act as Yasha Levovsky in a movie—or he can play me if he just puts on a wig.

"Ach, the whole thing gives me a headache. You'll excuse me, my *kepeleh* doesn't work so good anymore. But I'll tell you about how I became a nurse, and then maybe the headache will get scared and go away. Being a nurse was a very important decision in my life, y'see. It meant I always had a good trade and my family had what to eat. And I could be active 'cause I didn't have to go looking for work, the work found me. I would come to meetings all the time in my uniform—they began to call me the Red Nurse.

"But it was hard. We worked twelve hours a day for fifty cents an hour—nineteen cents while you train—and then you had first to take care on your family. Most of my life I slept on the installment plan. But it was a good living: You help people, you touch their lives in a most basic kind of a way. And you feel confident that you can take care on yourself and your comrades.

"I went to nursing school in 1913. By that time Yasha and I made up that we should live together. But when I had to do my training in Montefiore Hospital in the Bronx, it was such a long trip, so we made up instead that I should take a room that they had for students in the hospital and then, when my training was finished, we would live together. Yasha was working as a piano tuner at the time; Dreamland Park was already burned to the ground in 1911. So he made a decent living and he took an apartment on Hester Street, and he made it nice so I should want to come live with him.

"I was a good nurse, if you don't mind my saying. I had a feeling always for people that suffer. I'll give you a f'rinstance: At Montefiore Hospital they had what they call today 'retarded' children. They lived there in a special wing, with a big porch for them to sit. One day while I'm still in training they put me there as a substitute. The regular nurse was sick. And I knew from seeing how that nurse treated these children that she didn't care. She was like a robot. She put their food on the table and some could not even reach their hands to eat. Or she would feed one, but for the rest the food gets cold. She didn't care, that's all.

"Me, I took the children in their wheelchairs and I made one great big circle. I put blankets on their shoulders that they should be warm and I ran from one child to another with a spoon and I fed them all this way while I sang to them. You could really see the life coming into their eyes, like if they could talk they would really have something to say.

"Now, Jacob Schiff, he was on the board of directors at the hospital, and he had an office there, and I guess I was making a ruckus with my singing, 'cause Jacob Schiff comes to the porch and asks me what I'm doing. He talked to me in English and he was surprised to hear my accent, 'cause with my light hair he thought I was a *shikse*. Well, Jacob Schiff was a nice guy even though he was a millionaire. He asked me some questions about what I'm doing, and I show him it's just common sense. I said how I learned from these retarded children, the way they would sit and one that she could talk a little bit would teach the other; they had unity, we didn't.

"In the end, Jacob Schiff paid for me to go to school to improve my English. To the Ideal Preparatory School I went, for six months. The first day he sent me in his car! And for my birthday I got a pin, solid gold, and with a little chain. 'To Bessie Charles, with warm regards, Jacob Schiff.' It was engraved on the pin. This pin eventually saved my life. I'm pretty good at exchanging little things to save my skin, y'see.

"Also I was a nurse to Sholem Aleichem, in 1916 just before he died. He was the honorary president of the hospital where I worked, Beth David, so when he got sick, they asked for nurses to be volunteers, and I was one of them. I came to his apartment, and I wore a new uniform, 'cause here I was gonna meet the great Yiddish writer. And 'cause of my blond hair, he called me the *Yiddishe Shikse*. And he says, 'Come here.' I went over. He says, 'It's a new uniform you got?' I tell him yeah, excepting I washed it once. Then he says, 'I'll tell you a little story. A fellow was very much in love with a girl but she didn't like him so much. So one day he comes for a visit with a new pair of shoes on and she's wearing a new blouse. So he says, "This is a new blouse?" And she says yeah, and he says, "Wear it in good health." Then she looks down at his shoes and she says, "This is a new pair of shoes?" He says yeah, and she says, "Go in good health." '

"Then he touched my hand. 'You know,' he says, 'not only are you a good nurse, but I like the way you laugh.' Hey, you think I'm not going to laugh when Sholem Aleichem tells me a joke, me personally? Believe me, it's worth it to learn Yiddish just to read Sholem Aleichem; his words are like honey in your mouth.

"I worked nights. And the next afternoon I received a call that I shouldn't come again. Sholem Aleichem is dead.

"*Oi,* when I think back to all this . . . life was good to me, y'see. Like it should always be for the young. I had a job, I had where to live, and a boyfriend that he thinks like I think, and all my political activity—we felt so important. And compared to how they had it in Europe—ach, God, they were dying by the thousands. By the millions. Twelve million Russian peasants got dragged from their plows to the trenches to fight with Germany. In the Russian cities there was no food and no coal. The Russian peasants used to eat from one huge bowl and in their shack was usually a great big stove that they slept on top and took steam baths inside—but the stove was cold now and the bowl was just as empty if you had one person than if you had six. The war meant starvation for Russia. The system was falling apart, just like the rotten thing it was.

"From my father we used to get letters that they sounded like he was in an earthquake. We got one saying how it was getting in the Ukraine that the convicts—this is how he thought of the revolutionaries from Siberia—he says that the convicts are getting more respect than the rabbis, the chief of police, or anyone. So from this we could tell that the Revolution is coming to Russia.

"We watched it very close in the newspapers, we that came originally from Russia but also everybody that's interested in socialism. It looked like it was really going to happen, y'see. Then in March of 1917 the czar abdicated. And the whole world was glad. It was like one of the biggest countries in the world should be run by a monkey, so that nobody who calls himself a human being can stand it.

"So they set up a provisional government with Kerenski at the head. This was a bourgeois government. What I mean to say is it gave more political freedom than the czar gave, but it

represented only the capitalists and the landowners and the
professional class. Not the workers. The proof of this came when
Kerenski didn't make peace with Germany. He continued the
killing so maybe the Russian peasants wouldn't have the strength
to make more revolution against him!

"You had a country let's say with a hundred and fifty million
people, and a hundred and forty-nine million haven't got what
to eat and they can't read and they stumble through their lives
like a blind person. Now the Revolution has come, and the war's
still going on, so everything is crazy—it's like you have a great
big pot of water that boils, and you need the kind of leadership
that can keep the heat under the pot but control it so the whole
thing doesn't spill out or turn to steam. And this is what Lenin
did. He took a nation, a whole nation, and he shaped it with
his hands, with his mind. Not by sitting on some throne, no. He
lived like a criminal, like a dog. It's like you should take Albert
Einstein and put him in a basement so he can't see the stars, this
is how the Kerenski government did to Lenin. But in the basement, y'see, that's where you find the foundation for the house,
and the plumbing, and the electricity. Lenin understood Russia
like he built it himself.

"Now, in addition to Kerenski, we had the *soviets*. These
were committees, congresses, of workers. In all the big cities you
had them, and also the sailors on their ships and the workers in
their factories. Lenin's party, the Bolsheviks, they recognized
that these *soviets* were the start of a real workers' government,
y'see, so they supported them and gained influence.

"So right from the start you have two governments, the
soviets and the provisional government, and it's like a tug-of-war
between them. Plus the war with Germany was still going on,
and Japan says they're going to invade Siberia. And into the
middle of this comes who do you think? That's right! Bessie
Charles! With a whole lot more people from America—how
do you say it? Expatriates, yeah. Kerenski invited us and says
he'll pay our passage; all those that we suffered from the czar,
we should come back now and help build Russia. He meant to
help build his government, but many among us were sympathetic
instead to the Bolshevik cause. Instead that we should help
Kerenski, we helped get rid of him.

"Boy-oh-boy, we were so innocent! We knew it would not
be exactly a picnic, but if you asked us, you would think we

were a religious bunch going up to heaven. So much enthusiasm
we had! We had no idea that we would be fighting the counter-
revolutionaries, fighting for our lives, actually, for three years.
We had no idea what socialist revolution would bring—Russia
was the first in the world, remember. And when an entire nation
has a drastic kind of a change that everything's gonna get organized different, every person will be looking with new eyes,
everyone will be growing in new ways—well, this is history,
y'see, something that no person can guess or even understand
completely.

"We left in March. My family didn't like what I was doing,
but they knew they couldn't stop me. I had to go to Russia,
even if I had to go alone. It called to me, it was like a child that
she should be sick; you want to go heal her, you want to feed
her, you're ready to give your blood. In my mind, Russia was
still my homeland. There I grew, there I suffered. And by going
back to make revolution, y'see, I would be paying back all those
that they gave their lives for me, for the movement. I kept
thinking how I'm going to go to Ysyakh and build there a hospital, I'll name it Beth Jacob for Jacob Smulevitch.

"But I kept telling Yasha that I'm only taking him to introduce him to my parents! This was our joke. But it did feel like
we were going home. Only we had to come in through the
back door. From New York, we took the train to San Francisco.
Among our group was Leon Trotsky—later he became the
leader of the entire Red Army. He was a brilliant man—I heard
him speak more than once in the New Star Casino in Manhattan;
at that time he lived in New York and he wrote for the Russian
paper, *Novi Mir*—the *New World*. I used to sometimes sell this
paper. But I didn't like Trotsky, and I don't know who did. He
was a big wheel, but he had too great an opinion of himself. He
couldn't be warm with people like Gurley Flynn or like Berkman. When he spoke to you, f'rinstance, he would sit and everybody's supposed to stand in a circle around him. What kind of
a revolutionary is this that he speaks to you like a king on his
throne?

"From San Francisco, Trotsky took the first boat. They kept
him four weeks in Australia until Kerenski said that the British
should let him go. Trotsky wasn't yet a committed Bolshevik,
y'see. Boy, Kerenski must've kicked himself in the pants later
on! So we got on the second boat, me and Yasha. In our group

was Fanny Kaplan, the woman that she later on shot Lenin. If I knew this, I would throw her to the sharks!

"In Hawaii they held us five weeks. While we were waiting, Yasha and I got married. We were beginning to understand that it was not so easy to go and make a revolution, y'see. But we knew the Salvation and the Red Cross had already come to Russia, so I figured maybe with my nursing certificate we might be able to pass as Red Cross if there came trouble, and we should be married—it's easier to protect each other. Actually, with all the groups you had fighting in Russia, it was really like the whole World War was happening there; and with all that, you could have a wallet full of identification papers and a handful of wedding rings and it wouldn't do you any good.

"From Hawaii we went to Japan and to China, only we barely got off the boat at these places, and finally we came to Vladivostok. This is a Siberian town just above Korea, and with very tall hills so it looks like San Francisco. So Yasha kibitzes me, he says we're back in San Francisco, our honeymoon is over, did I have a good time? And right there I started to cry. I don't even know why. Everyone was cheering and I cried. I held on to Yasha and I kissed his face all over. It was like we were at the very center of life. We had our lives in our own hands, and the regular problems that keep you busy every day were completely gone. You feel clear, so sure about what you're doing. Every breath you take is, like, conscious, aware, you know that you're breathing. This is what making history feels like.

"But history is not made so fast. They say that a Jewish man once upon a time came to God and he said, 'To you a thousand years is just a minute, and a million dollars is just a penny. So please, God, give me a penny.'

"And God said, 'Wait a minute.' "

❁

The port waters were green-gray beneath clouds stretching in a dark, broad sheet to the horizon, as though the harbor had blanched itself of sunlight and summer color in order not to stir the guns of the American and British warships brooding under listless flags at its mouth. Crowded on the deck of a Russian freighter, Bessie's comrades quieted at the sight of the hulking ships. Captain Biletzky, a self-proclaimed Menshevik and supposedly a friend to Aleksandr Kerenski, had forewarned many of the leftists on board to take their red banners down from display. "Vladivostok is no revolutionary stronghold, my friends. It's a port—of entry and exit—and nobody's saying yet who's staying and who's leaving. You'll be too green to tell your friends from your enemies!"

"Red, not green! Red! We know who our friends are!" cried Molly Malinow, a YPSL comrade of Bessie's from New York, raising high a red flag.

With a curse for the Bolsheviks who were polluting his ship and crew, the captain lowered his bullhorn, leaving it to the foreign battleships to drive home his point.

Yasha rubbed his shoulder as if Bessie's grip had left him sore. She laughed through her tears and kissed his cheek, then asked, apprehensive as she regarded the distant wharf: "Where to from here, Levovsky?" He reminded her of their first scheduled gathering at the Hall of the Soviet of Workingmen's Deputies along the town's main road. But she was speaking more generally. "It's like we never left Russia, like I never got away from the gendarmes in Ysyakh. . . . So how did you come to be here with me, Levovsky? Which is the dream, you or this?"

"We should follow the leadership of that bunch." He nodded in the direction of Meyer Lazansky, the aging editor of the *Novi Mir* in New York and a longtime associate of Leon Trotsky. Lazansky was standing at the railing with a group of his close chums, scrutinizing the receding battleships. "I've been talking to one of them, Hank Slotnik—"

"More women than men on this ship," Bessie hooted, "and you say the men should lead."

Yasha shrugged. "So perhaps you'd like to lead us?"

"Ha! See if you can keep up with me!"

He frowned at her abrasiveness. She squeezed his hand apologetically. "And what about you, my sweet Wobbly? Do you feel at home?"

"Like a Zionist in Jerusalem. It's familiar, Bessie, all of it. . . . Sakhalin Island is not far out to sea from here."

Bessie rubbed his shoulder. "There'll be no more Sakhalin anything for us, Yasha. We're going to be housed in the czar's palace this time."

"We'll go where we're needed," he said grimly, and knelt to secure the straps on their duffel bag.

The steamer's engine rattled shut. The sensation of slow drift through the warm wind and the slapping, sloshing waters quickened Bessie's pulse as she surveyed the whitecapped seascape. Her heart was racing, prodded to sudden misgivings by the sight of the city's massive hilltop fortresses, the cannon of which had been shipped months earlier to Russia's western front, leaving Vladivostok a naked jewel on the ocean's shelf. Bessie huddled against the forecastle wall and drew a purse from her underwear. From it she fetched a five-dollar bill, half of what was left of the hundred dollars with which she'd arrived seven years earlier at Ellis Island. Strange how she remembered that time: The frozen Lena River, the steam from the pony's nostrils, the smoke from the steamer's stacks, the icebergs, the Litvak baker, merged together as in a dream, but clearer in her mind than events just two or three years past. . . .

And look at you there, my pirate, my Coney Island *luftmensch*. How will I hold on to you while everything changes around us?

She pressed the money into Yasha's hand. "My dowry. In case we're separated, for a day, for a night, who knows?"

He protested, of course, with an impatient look: She was the woman, more vulnerable. . . . "But you should have learned, Yasha, from our first day together," she insisted. "We split the bill, no matter how much it is."

He drew her close. She sobbed and, with embarrassment, hid her face in his chest. Their bodies stretched and stirred. Suddenly a boat horn blasted on the port side. A tugboat had arrived to guide the steamer into port.

The crewmen were obviously Bolshevik, crying "Comrade!" to anyone on deck who waved. Following a perfunctory consultation with the imperious Captain Biletzky, they escorted Meyer Lazansky and his friends aboard the tug for a round of salutes and embraces. "Looks like somebody's expecting us," Bessie said as the leftists on board again broke out their banners. The tugboat revved its motor, and Molly Malinow began to sing:

> Hold the fort, for we are coming!
> Union men, be strong!
> Side by side, we'll battle onward!
> Victory will come!

But Captain Biletzky had been correct in his appraisal of the city's political climate. The wharves held people more various than the cargoes. Emigrating noblemen and ladies, unnerved by the fall of the czar and unconfident of the loyalties of the Kerenski government, had flooded the port and could be seen supervising the handling of their overstuffed trunks and haggling with ship stewards over weight limitations as they prepared to depart for the drawing rooms of Western Europe. Lurking around them, hoping to secure a cast-off cloak or pair of shoes, were transients of all kinds: army deserters, disabled veterans, camp followers, orphaned children, outnumbering and more rotted than the mooring posts along the docks. Shipping agents wrote figures into ledgers propped against their sweaty waistbands; representatives from foreign companies consulted with ship captains and other polished men; tough, independent traders of many nationalities hovered among the longshoremen and sailors to see what sorts of black-market goods could be siphoned. Among these and others, Bessie's comrades moved like a bright red patch on a torn tapestry.

As they approached a steep hill of cobblestone and tar, Bessie helped one of the repatriates from her ship coax her four children along with their baggage. Yasha was leading a few steps ahead, conversing with that Hank Slotnik fellow. Bessie took heart at the sight of their conversation; the revolution, she had begun to fear, began and ended in their own ranks; she even fancied hearing marching orders and parade rhythms floating on the air like a lariat to bind her band together. . . .

Looking to the hilltop, she saw it was true, and cried out to the children to look: A company of sailors was entering the intersection, purifying the disordered atmosphere with their crisp, cohesive steps. They wore red neckerchiefs and carried ten-foot banners painted with Bolshevik slogans: "Factories to the Workers! Land to the Peasants!" "Down with War! Peace to the World!" "All Power to the Soviets!" But at the sight of them, the woman at Bessie's side gave a shriek and herded her children toward a doorway, instinctively fearful that so militant a procession as this could only fetch cossacks or a hail of bullets.

But these were no pitchfork-toting peasants or ragged strikers on the march; these were seasoned, disciplined sailors who hailed the straggling Americans by marking time in place and singing a song of devotion to the Red flag. Not a word of love for the czar father! Not an anti-Semitic innuendo! Bessie shuttled back and forth in their ranks, smiling and clapping and joining their song, remembering, in dark flashes, the secret meetings, the smuggled sentences, the endless anxieties and quick outbursts of vengeance that had been the texture of her childhood. Now, to be marching with sailors under the open summer sky as a Russian revolutionary . . . ! The pride of the moment swept her away. She raised a fist into the air and remained in the sailors' ranks as they saluted and advanced.

Fortunately, their destination was her own: the Hall of the Soviet of Workingmen's Deputies, located in an armory that had long been depleted of weaponry. It was a palatial building draped inside with banners representing the many factions whose deputies were assembled to conduct the business of merging the sailors' and the workers' *soviets*. Dozens of men were drifting in and out of the building, but Yasha managed to spot Bessie and yank her from the procession of sailors as they flowed into the hall through studded oak doors.

"Where have you been?"

"Oh! In heaven!" She gasped for breath.

"How can you go to heaven without your husband?"

She slipped her hand under his folded arms. "So now I'm in double heaven."

"If you behave," he said, "you can be my footstool in heaven."

"If you don't behave," she replied, "I'll give you a splinter—and not in your foot, either." She pinched his backside. He let out a yelp that turned heads. "Now hush," said Bessie, victorious.

The first speaker, Constantin Sukhanov, president of the Vladivostok Soviet of Workingmen, had mounted the podium at the opposite end of the armory. His amplified voice caromed from wall to wall with extreme distortion. Bessie strained to make it out, to clean the sounds of their echoes. He was greeting the sailors, the Union of Miners, the Railwaymen's Association, a dozen shop leaders from factories and canneries in town, and "our comrades from America, whose solidarity and strength will inspire us all to higher levels of commitment and sacrifice for the Revolution." By way of such introductions, Sukhanov was offering a confident report about the *soviet*'s political clout in Vladivostok. It was too specific in local detail for Bessie to follow, yet she listened without budging for two hours as a series of speakers described the challenges and dangers facing the city.

Yevsny Nabokov of the Railwaymen's Association: "The life-line of our city is the Trans-Siberian. It is so poorly guarded by the provisional government that thousands, literally thousands of German and Austrian prisoners of war, supposedly in transport under armed guard, are committing acts of sabotage and terror against local populations to the north. Comrades, we can't wait for Kerenski to put an end to the disruption. His patriotism goes no deeper than his purse! We must defend ourselves and our city, brothers! *We* are the lifeline, now!"

Comrade Melnikov, Menshevik Commissar of Post and Telegraph under the provisional government: "We have word that the German army is advancing on the harbor at Riga. Under these stressful conditions, Prime Minister Kerenski has announced the appointment of General Kornilov as supreme commander of the Russian armed forces."

"Kornilov's worse than the Germans!"

"Kerenski's after the Petrograd *soviet*, that's what he wants!"

"Peace, peace, the working people want peace!"

Peter Zebetsev, secretary of Bolshevik party affairs: "Comrades. I come to announce that membership in our glorious party has reached two hundred and forty thousand this month! Comrades! Only six months ago we had but twenty thousand! There is no doubt that our party will soon hold the majority in the *soviet* of every major city in the West!".

"What about in Vladivostok?"

"Not as long as the warships stand in the harbor! Snakes at the crib! Snakes at the crib!"

"The war is a rich men's folly! Stop the war! To hell with the Allied ships!"

Bessie felt like a rudely transplanted stalk in a ferocious downpour. Her shins ached from standing in one place and her head ached from the glut of details and conflict. Over the microphone Sukhanov was now introducing Meyer Lazansky, "editor of the daily *Novi Mir* and an exile in America for six years." Yasha joined the group that accompanied the elderly man to the podium, then wove his way back to his wife and slipped his arm around her waist. "I've been telling Hank Slotnik all about you."

"Feh, you must be boring him," she said.

* * *

"You're the American nurse—Comrade Levovsky's wife? Welcome, Bessie." Sukhanov stuttered before he could pronounce her American name. "I hope you've had some time to rest."

Bessie had been embarrassed by the special treatment that she and Yasha had gained by his contact with the *Novi Mir* group; while others from the boat were scattered about town in workers' houses, on shop and factory floors, in barns and elsewhere, they were housed in a clean, carpeted church, receiving continual offers of food and clothing from local admirers and sharing generally in the prestige of the revolutionary leadership. But she'd hardly had the strength to scold Yasha for currying favor before she had fallen asleep across a pew.

"I heard something about your background from your husband and I thought you and I—well, I at least, would appreciate having a word with you . . . about my father."

He was seated sideways in the first row, a wiry, tense young man, toying with bits of his sparse beard. She had woken just in time to see him approach and to see Yasha and Slotnik closing the door to a front room in which they were meeting. Momentarily she felt excluded, but then was more intrigued by Sukhanov's overtures and, lowering her tingling feet to the floor, gestured for him to sit closer.

"The subject is my father. Name, Victor Sukhanov. Position, magistrate—a hatchet man for the czar. He sent more revolutionaries to prison than he has toes and fingers. In the past, when I was a student, my father—"—he caught his voice rising and cleared his throat—"my father arrested both me and my sisters. . . . You must meet them, by the way, before you leave our city."

Bessie smiled uncomfortably. Why had Yasha disclosed so much of her past to this man?

"I have not arrested Victor Sukhanov," he continued, making a cage of his slim fingers, "but I have more than enough evidence to do so. Even the bourgeois parties want to prosecute. Hell!" He thrust his hands into his trouser pockets as he leaped to his feet. "They'd like nothing better. The Cadets, the SRs, even the Mensheviks, they're all screaming for his blood!"

"I'm sorry," Bessie said at last, "but I'm a greenhorn here. How can I advise someone like you, in your kind of position?"

"Someone like me?" He shrugged and dropped onto the pew again. "Comrade, little children have given me good advice during these months. Superstitious old women have saved me from my own intellectual follies. Please, you've had experiences of your own in these matters...."

She held up her hand to calm him, to help him maintain his dignity, and yet found it a struggle to engage her own feelings in order to get beyond the most facile level of sympathy. "I don't know what my husband told you," she said, glancing at the doorway into which Yasha had disappeared. "Usually he brings me away from the past, instead of this."

"Your husband simply told me—"

"I haven't had time to hate or forgive my father," she blurted. "Who knows, maybe I should thank him for the education! He's been out of my life for years, comrade. I get a letter once in a while, I send a little money. . . . *Oi*, please, my father's just an old rabbi who couldn't stand that he might see his wife or his daughters get raped by cossacks. What do you know of this kind of thing? He thought he could convince the government not to make pogroms. Like a peasant convinces the river not to make a flood! Magic."

They shared a grim silence, staring at the rack of prayer books in front of them.

"My father's not an evil man," Sukhanov quietly affirmed. "I know what he thinks. He's deeply religious. He believes he was serving God. He took no bribes."

"Yeah, yeah, mine, too," said Bessie. "But mine was reaching to yours—yours probably blamed the Jews for doing the devil's work, no?" She stared resentfully at Sukhanov, wondering how so young and fretful a man had come to stand so centrally in the events of the day. She recalled her first impressions of others, too: of Lazansky and Trotsky in New York, where they had been indistinguishable from any other poor, disgruntled intellectuals of the Lower East Side. How could these rabbits have become lions overnight? Or would this revolution of theirs prove to be the same as Yeshua's desperate band of arsonists in Mogilev-Podolsk? The memory of those harried days shriveled her spirit. She shook her head. "That song the sailors sang as they came into the armory today—I sang with them, but now I can't recall ..."

Sukhanov recited the lyric with elegant diction:

Remember the blood in Siberian snow,
Remember the tears that salted the sea,
It will make the earth warm,
It will make the seas calm,
But first, revolution!
Liberty's storm!
It will make our earth warm,
It will make our sea calm,
But first we must make ourselves free!

"I must memorize that," Bessie said. "Let it be my little piece of Torah." She looked sidelong at Sukhanov and smiled. "Did my husband tell you of Ysyakh, Siberia? I was the youngest in the camp for much of the time. In my family I'm the youngest, too. I'm not used to having people come to me for advice."

"When it comes to making revolution, we are all wearing diapers," he said.

"Don't ask me to change diapers, comrade," Bessie warned. "Put a woman on the council of the *soviet* if it's a woman's point of view you want. I hardly saw a woman in the entire hall today!"

Sukhanov stood, stiff with annoyance and ready to bow out. "Your modesty does not become you, comrade."

"Neither do your diapers fit, comrade!" she retorted. "Your problem is political, not personal. If you'd try to think not as your father's little boy but as the president of the Workingmen's Soviet, you might find an answer. Obviously your father deserves punishment—he should be hung up by his toes! But first you must ask yourself: Why do the bourgeois parties want your father's head? Do they really care about his crimes? Or do they plan to simply repeat them?" She tilted her head back as though she had a nosebleed. "If you were Jewish, you'd understand, you'd feel it in your bones. Don't you know the word 'scapegoat'? They'd rather guard your father than guard the Trans-Siberian. They'd rather make a spectacle than make a revolution."

And I, Bessie thought, would rather be with Yasha than with my bitter memories. She wanted him, to gorge herself on his warmth. Even when Sukhanov broke his long, reflective silence to praise her insight, she recoiled, flinching with memories of every martyr she'd had the misfortune to know and every word of praise with which she'd been shackled to struggle, relentless struggle. A sage today, a nurse tomorrow, shot dead the next day, who knows? "Do you want to do me a favor?" she interrupted the young man. "Get my husband for me. . . . You seem to have found some answers," she assured him.

Yasha found her singing the sailors' anthem quietly to herself. "Is something wrong?"

"Something's wrong," she agreed. "I have not seen you for hours and we're in Russia. Come with me."

As they strolled uphill from the church, Yasha began to fill her in on all that he'd learned about the struggle for Vladivostok and for revolution across the land. She listened gladly, earnestly, letting his voice bind up her confidence, nodding often. The harbor lay steaming five hundred feet below, its ships distant enough to be more of a tourist spectacle than a threat, while in all other directions rolled the green and yellow hills beneath a cloud cover that had begun to break up into fat wedges. Soon Bessie was feeling comfortably anonymous, reasonably private again. "I'm glad someone here knows what they're doing," she cheered Yasha's report. "I've been feeling like the revolution is just an idea that I got in a dream."

"My love," he said, taking her hand, his face vibrantly colored. "The real leaders of this movement are just arriving today, tomorrow, right now, from exile. You and I haven't begun to grasp the kind of effort that men like Sukhanov and Nabokov and the others have put into their organizing. It's on such a scale! A true Wobbly couldn't conceive of it! For months the Bolsheviks were nothing but criminals, hunted like dogs, Bessie. And now a cossack with a cannon would not dare arrest them! They've won the working people to their side—they're the only party in Russia that truly champions the working people's cause! Factories to the workers! Land to the peasants!"

"Husbands to the wives!" she sang, leading him off the road onto a steep mud-and-grass slope.

He held back, tugging her hand. "Listen to me, *bubeleh*. Whoa." She turned to him with a rapturous glow in her eyes. "Hey, you really like the things I'm telling you?" he asked.

"Whatever, Yasha. Yes. Everything." She rushed to embrace him, but he only petted her cheek and lowered himself to a dry patch of grass.

"Let me tell you—they're very interested in your nursing

background. And the fact that you carry American papers. They say you might be very useful. . . ."

Her face hardened. She shifted her weight but remained standing on the incline. "Useful for what, Yasha?"

"For transporting certain people—important people—into Russia, or from place to place."

"In a barrel of sauerkraut, I suppose!" She unclenched her fists and smiled ruefully. "*Oi yoi yoi*, what did I expect, a honeymoon?" The damp earth soaked her knees as she dropped to his side. "We move slower as lovers than we do as fighters, you know that? And everyone's got more of a use for me than I have for myself—except you!" She toyed with his suspender straps, then gripped the waistband of his pants, pressing her knuckles into his warm belly. "Oh, love, we're going to be separated by all this, aren't we? This revolution feels like—I don't know what." She shook her head. "All the pressure—it's like before you even came into my life."

"Shh." He pulled her head to his chest and caressed her hair. She closed her eyes and kissed the soft center of his palm. "We have a train ride together," he said, "across the breadth of Russia. Together, you hear? And we have your parents to visit. Don't worry so much, Bessie."

She breathed deeply to ventilate her fear. "I am thinking too much," she confessed. "All the time. It's no good. But you see, there was never before in my life someone like you!" Again she grasped his hand and held it in her lap. "You're the only choice I ever made, Yasha. To love you, to live with you . . ."

"In a better world. A decent world. We have no choice."

"You're my better world!" She pulled his hand to her thigh, her belly, her small breast. "My love, you gave me my name, my warmth."

Yasha glanced self-consciously toward the road. Bessie rocked on her knees with laughter. "About revolution, you're confident! About love, you worry!" She lifted her skirt above her belly and threw the hem over his head, pulling his lips to her navel. "Only God will see, darling. And he'll like it."

Yasha squeezed her knees and stroked her lean thighs. "God will tell your father. Let's move further off the road."

"No. Take off your pants. Oh, my *luftmensch*, let me hold you, let me have you!"

Chapter Twelve

Oh, Yasha, we've kept secrets from each other and now they feel like holes in my heart. Every little secret swells up when you're separated. Like it could actually kill the one you love over a great distance. It's the mistake you made that costs—the bad judgment, the blood you drip when the cossacks are hunting you. But at least I'm going to think about you every minute, Yasha. If I could only write these thoughts and not just think, think, think. But I am, I'm going to keep you as close to me as this baby in my belly.

Oh, why didn't I tell you? I didn't know for sure, Yasha. I feared it more than I hoped for it in a place like Petrograd, with the cossacks in town. . . .

"There's the train, you hear?" said Melnikov, the elder and scrawny one of the two comrades at the front of the wagon. He turned and gave a curt nod to Bessie. "Better get ready, girl. You too, Georgi."

Georgi, a powerfully built fellow, drew a shiny rifle from the flour sack on his back and held it, muzzle down, between his knees. Bessie wrapped herself in her red lace shawl and climbed down from the wagon, reviewing procedures in her mind. . . .

And if I were arrested now, I'd have no information, nothing to give but my tongue. But soon I'll know your secret, my husband, just who it is I'm meeting here and why I've been treated like royalty by our comrades in every place from Vladivostok to Petrograd. And soon you'll hear my secret, as soon as we're reunited—oh, my love! I only hope our revolution has room enough to treat a baby with some gentleness.

*Okay, I'm closing my eyes now and if the train comes to a
stop before I count to ten, then we're going to have a girl. . . .*

"What are you doing, praying?" Melnikov scolded her.

The station was in the town of Svetogorsk, just south of the
Finnish border above Petrograd. It consisted of no more than the
station signs, a slab of concrete, and a broken bench. The tracks
were overgrown with weeds and ferns on land hemmed in by
marsh and swamp. In the clear light of the late afternoon, Bessie
saw no one else awaiting the train or approaching along the
muddy road from the south.

The train lumbered in, slowly, slowly, and halted with a great
squeal and slamming sound. A blond head poked out the rear
doorway of the second car. Bessie bustled over.

"Hello," the young man hailed her. "How are the mosquitoes
on Lake Ladoga?"

"Very light at this time of the year," she replied, shouting
over the steam hiss of the idling train. "They prefer the Russian
climate."

He hopped onto the platform and glanced left and right. No
other figures had disembarked. "But if the mosquitoes bite?"

"I've got salve," Bessie said. "And we can always go indoors."

"Good—comrade."

Satisfied of her identity, he vaulted back aboard and in a
moment appeared with two others. One was a young string bean
with a stocking cap on his head. The other—obviously her man,
judging from his calm reliance upon the others as his body-
guards—looked like a middle-aged Finnish railway worker, wearing the black jacket of his trade with a black cap tucked into
his breast pocket. Tied around his jaw was a white toothache
bandage that fell in floppy rabbit ears across his bald pate.
Bessie assumed it was a fake. "Oh, dear, does it hurt very much?"

The trainman was clanging his bell. The stranger had barely
time to shake the hands of his young escorts, who looked primed
for an embrace or to go on their knees for a blessing. When the
train lurched into motion, they had to run to get aboard.

Bessie strolled toward the wagon arm in arm with the
stranger. "I'm your nurse," she said. "My name is Bessie
Levovsky."

He nodded but did not take the opportunity to identify himself. A short, solidly built man, he moved with solemn grace, an

air of both deep absorption and alertness, and seemed relaxed despite the ordeal that she imagined he'd endured in escaping the mass arrests in Petrograd. He had a large-domed head that he kept inclined slightly forward as he walked, and, like Yasha, a round, smooth-shaven face with nearly Asiatic features: high cheeks, a snub nose, eyes pinched with crow's feet. Bessie felt simultaneously drawn to and intimidated by his sobriety, and so related on professional terms.

"Is your toothache genuine?"

"Unfortunately."

"It's not the most inconspicuous hat," she agreed. "But I have some mint oil in my bag in the wagon. I'll make you a nice liniment when we—" She stopped in midsentence, for she had yet to be informed of their destination. "Or else," she added hastily, "Georgi, one of the comrades, has a bottle of vodka in his sack."

"No," said the stranger, meeting her gaze for the first time, "I'll try the mint."

So I'm an escape artist! And you're my publicist. Bessie Kharlofsky Levovsky Houdini. Remember Houdini? Mrs. Markish took us for my birthday, remember? First he was naked and handcuffed, then they hung him in a trunk and wrapped it with more chains—and two minutes later he's outside the curtain in a tuxedo, sniffing a rose. Now, that kind of entertainment I like! Not locks and not chains could keep him from the people, hmm? Even if he had a secret helper behind the curtain. So I've got a secret helper in my belly! I feel that way, I do—she makes me bulletproof, at least until I've given her—or him—a name.

A name, a name. I'm ashamed to ask this guy's name—probably I should know just by looking at him, hmm? Actually, I think only Melnikov knows—he's the older of the two comrades—and he's so irritable, nobody can talk to him.

Bessie's arm ached from fanning the mosquitoes away from her patient's face as he slept to be rid of his toothache pain.

"Right turn at the willow," said Georgi.

"By God, if this road gets any muddier, we might as well swim!" groaned Melnikov as his horse whinnied from the effort of dragging the cart across a particularly swampy stretch of road.

"I don't swim," Bessie said.

"Never mind, little comrade," said Georgi. "I would let you walk across my beard before I'd allow a single toe of yours to get wet!" A mosquito put an end to his chivalry with a bite on his sweaty neck. "Damn beggar!"

"I've got some pine tar," Bessie offered. "But only a little."

"Ha! You're more of a woodsman than me!"

Carrying this man to freedom, even while I carry our baby into the world . . . oh, I like this work, Yasha. I'll never forget how it was done for me, my exodus from Ysyakh. Now I'm repaying the movement. And at last my memories give me strength instead of pain. I've got my nerve back. I felt it returning to me, actually, like blood in my veins, when those escaped prisoners boarded our train at Belogorsk. Oh, I'm glad you were with me then, my darling! At first I cringed like some bourgeois woman—seeing their bonfires out the window, and the manacle on the foot of one, and everything about them—their smell, their shaved heads, the way they sucked at their cigarettes . . . it began to remind me, it brought it all back, it filled me with anger, such a terrible anger, the kind you can hold in your hand like a gun, you can spit it out like a bullet. Oh, when I see the poor, poor peasants of this country, and the wretched of Siberia, and the factory workers in Petrograd, I really start to think that the revolution is the most merciful end that the ruling class could hope for. Quick. Not too bloody.

You, Mr. Sakhalin Island, you felt at home with those scarecrows, hmm? And no, no matter how many times we sing the "Internationale" in our communist lives, even when we teach it to our baby in a Soviet Russia, it will never be more stirring than how you sang it with those prisoners, those wretched but liberated men. You knew it, you knew it was their song.

I love you so much, my darling. . . .

"Hoo, I'd like to wring the neck of whoever made this map. I can barely read the damned thing."

"And since when do you know how to read, Georgi?" said Melnikov.

Georgi ignored his teasing tone. "Since I found something worth reading," he replied, turning to Bessie and the stranger, who was curled on his side atop an army blanket. "What I mean is, since I joined the Bolshevik party. They taught me how to make sense out of the squiggles."

"What do you read, comrade?" asked the stranger, despite his swollen mouth.

"Everything!" Georgi declared. "I'm no illiterate. I read wall posters, flyers, newspapers, whatever I can get my hands on. My favorite was *Iskra*, until the Mensheviks took it over. Ah, they ruin everything they touch—just look at what they've done to Petrograd, the dirty sellouts."

"You liked *Iskra*?" said the stranger.

"It was my primer."

"Were you in the Party that long ago?"

"Thirteen years," Georgi said. "I joined thirteen years ago, just when the split came with the Mensheviks."

"And what do you think of *Pravda*?" He propped himself up against the back of the cart and rubbed his jaw.

"Good paper," Georgi said, "but you can't keep up with it—they've had to change their name so often to fool the police."

"So do we," sighed Melnikov. "My own wife doesn't know what to call me on any given day."

Bessie leaned between them. "Is that because you're undergrounders or because you're bigamists?"

Melnikov humorlessly slapped the reins against the horse's back, but Georgi was sputtering with laughter. "Oh, very good, comrade, very good!"

The stranger asked what kind of work Georgi did.

"Me?" He wiped his hands on his knees and put the map aside, then swiveled around completely on his seat. "I cut trees, trees as big around as this wagon, with these hands." He extended them for Bessie to see and feel his thickly callused palms, then closed a fist around her fingers and laughed. "If I'd been the Lord Jesus they couldn't have driven the nails through, huh?"

"Yes, yes! Let go!"

He wagged a finger at his questioner. "And the editors at *Pravda* had better not forget the men who are responsible for the paper they print on. Unless they'd like to try goatskin for a while! You know, with Kamenev as editor, I thought the paper was actually going to go for the Menshevik position on this war! Telling *me* to go get shot so *they* can be called Russian patriots! But that's been corrected by this man Lenin, the same comrade who founded *Iskra* with George Plekhanov, am I right, Ivan Melnikov?"

Melnikov fished the map from the wagon bottom again. "See how far to Lappeenranta, Georgi."

"Lappeenranta—it used to be my swimming hole! Don't worry, I know every tree on this road without that useless map. Now," Georgi resumed his discourse, "this man Lenin has my respect. He's a worker's intellectual, no parlor revolutionary. I'd give my right arm to meet him."

"I'm with you," Bessie piped up. "I want Lenin, no other, to sign my Party card."

"Listen to her!" Melnikov hooted. "She agrees with everything, from Christ-killing to the two-line struggle, hmm? Pretty soon there won't be a Bolshevik leader left to sign your little card, Comrade Levovsky!"

Bessie concealed her blushing face. She had spoken only from vanity, to hide her ignorance of these names and internal Bolshevik affairs and to please Georgi by agreeing with his opinions. Now even the ducks winging overhead seemed to be laughing at her before they set down in the wetlands with a splash.

Georgi touched her shoulder. "With a red shawl like this one," he said, "the leaders will fall all over each other trying to sign your Party card. Don't worry, little comrade."

"But you," said the stranger, holding up a finger to Georgi, "if you give up your arm, how will you then cut trees for the revolution? To meet one man? It's not one man or one newspaper that counts, comrade. It's the correctness of one's political line. This is what makes history!"

"Shh," cautioned Bessie, trying to feel less useless, "you really shouldn't be talking so much with your tooth."

He slumped down and drew his coarse blanket up to his chin. "The morning after I left Petrograd, the *Pravda* offices were raided and smashed. But there are enough cadre in the city who grasp our political line, you see, so now we have a living newspaper! Even with the leadership dispersed to the four corners, the struggle goes on."

This was the closest to a shred of personal testimony he had offered them. Georgi, struck dumb with uncertainty as to the protocol of their mission, looked to Melnikov for guidance, but he just kept his shoulders hunched, his eyes lowered before the sun that was sinking into the thick marsh air straight ahead on the road.

Bessie looked with exasperation from man to man. "Isn't it time that we—spoke? Who's going to hear, the mosquitoes?"

"Lappeenranta," murmured Melnikov. "We'll have some good Finnish herring and cheese there."

The stranger patted Bessie's arm. "Everything will become clear to you when we reach Helsingfors. The *soviet* there is very sympathetic."

"Vladimir!" Melnikov snapped. "If you have a toothache, this kind of loose talk will infect it."

"I'm talking to my nurse, man."

"She may not even accompany us to Helsingfors. She's not even a card carrier!"

"We'll rectify that soon enough."

"Vladimir, you did enough talking in Petrograd!"

"Ivan Melnikov," he replied, "it was not the disaster you think it was in Petrograd. But you've had to handle the stray sheep, so you think the pen is empty! How long do you suppose the cossacks can hold a working-class city like Petrograd? Long enough to reveal their masters, the Mensheviks, as the poisonous snakes that they are, that's all! But our Party could not remain neutral, Ivan Melnikov. The sailors of Kronstadt, the machine-gun regiment, our most trusted allies who were also the most exploited by the war, they simply lost patience and went for their guns. They want to end the stupid slaughter! How could we have remained neutral? Better to suffer defeat with the masses." He finished with a chopping gesture.

Georgi was standing, peering and pointing westward. "There —you see a lake, Ivan? Damn, the marsh looks all the same— but I think . . ." Then a gunshot broke flatly across the marsh, igniting the grasses as scores of nesting fowl took to the air.

"That's the place!" Melnikov cried, flogging his horse and instructing Georgi to fire his rifle twice into the air.

The wagon's bumps and bounces brought a wince of pain to the stranger's face. Bessie located a tattered sheepskin at the bottom of the wagon and slid it beneath his head. "Stay low," she warned. "The breeze is chilly. Don't touch. Leave your tooth alone."

The mosquitoes swarmed heavily about their heads in the re-maining shafts of sunlight. Bessie was applying her last dabs of pine tar to the stranger's forehead when he asked in low tones: "Levovsky, it's a Jewish name?"

She nodded, and tipped his chin to get at his neck.

"Tell me, do you think Comrade Melnikov is an anti-Semite?" he said.

Georgi was shouting more observations about the lake. Bessie saw only a tumbledown fisherman's shack propped on stilts in the marsh. She watched Melnikov rein his horse and wondered, with a flushed feeling, about his irritability. "It didn't occur to me," she said. "I was more worried about my own ignorance. . . ."

"There's a difference between comradely criticism and viciousness. And there is backward consciousness even among our veterans."

The wagon rolled to a halt. Three men approached through the marsh in thigh-high boots, scattering birds in their wake. The stranger calmly waved to them while continuing to talk to Bessie, as he would do, she realized, even on the barricades; intelligence and acuity were second nature to this man. "The Jewish people," he was saying, "will more and more be joining our movement as they realize the consequences of counter-revolution. A defeat for the working class now would mean terrible slaughter for your people. In the meantime, we in the Party cannot tolerate anti-Jewish sentiment that plays right into the hands of the enemy. When we get inside, perhaps they've a copy of my pamphlet on the national minorities question."

The three were close enough for Bessie to hear their boots sloshing in the algae-green water. "Comrade Lenin!" cried one, waving. "Yoo, Comrade Lenin!"

"What's he saying?" Georgi wondered aloud, standing tall on his seat.

"My name," said the stranger.

Chapter Thirteen / 1919

"That Lenin should recruit me, should actually give me his
signature on my card, this was like the pope should give it to a
Catholic! I took care of Lenin in that swampy place for three
days, until he went deeper into Finland. I didn't go with him
then 'cause I was in a family way and starting to feel sick from
it, y'see, so I thought I would be a burden.

"Now, you want to know if I still got the card and for how
much I would like to sell it, yeah? Sure, I saved it, but we had
the kind of a life that you couldn't hold on to nothing, y'see,
not even a little piece of cardboard. You couldn't even hold on
to your friends—one minute you're standing talking and the
next minute he's lying there dead and you can't do nothing, you
step over him and go help those that they're still alive. . . .

"Sometimes I sit alone and I think, How did I go through all
that stuff? All the killing, the turmoil. And I have to go and
give a look at the little bit of the red lace, the tablecloth from
my father's house, so I should be reminded, Yes, it happened; yes,
you survived. I think the only reason that this bit of material did
survive is 'cause it's made of lace, y'see—all the bullets and
the blood can pass through without ripping the fabric to shreds.
But, no, I got no piece of paper with Lenin's name to prove
what I'm telling you.

"But I would like to talk to Lenin *now* for three days. I know
more than I did back then. I would ask Lenin why we still have
anti-Semitism in the Soviet Union even though you have there
socialism—at least *they* call it socialism. What would he say to me?
I don't know. Maybe he'd say that it's not his fault—like he

said to the lumberjack in our wagon, 'One man alone does not make history.'

"But Lenin had a progressive view of the Jewish question and of national minorities in general. It's true that he believed in assimilation—he thought that socialism, real socialism, it would end the differences among working people, including the religious and the ethnic and the prejudices that keep us divided. Maybe he was right, excepting I'm not going to wait around for some kind of a pure socialism before I protect myself and demand my rights as a Jew. But the thing is, Lenin was against any kind of a *forced* assimilation, that you should deprive a people of their culture or their history or their right to self-determination. So, in practice, the Jews under Lenin had these rights: We had a flourishing culture, supported by the Soviet government. We had newspapers in Yiddish, and schools in Yiddish, and theater, books, everything. We had Jewish collective farms. And anti-Semitism was against the law! Y'see, Lenin understood that anti-Semitism is reactionary, it's counter-revolutionary, it makes the Russian peasant to shoot into the shul instead that he should shoot into the palace.

"To have a progressive understanding about the national question in 1917 required a great deal of wisdom, y'see, 'cause national chauvinism at that time played a very strong role in Russia. You had Kerenski saying that the war with Germany should continue, it's a patriotic war. Lenin said no, it's a war only for the rich so the working people shouldn't fight. This was called 'revolutionary defeatism,' but it was hard even for the Bolshevik leaders to accept it. I suppose when your country is being attacked, it's hard not to get chauvinistic.

"But Lenin was right, y'see, 'cause after Germany got defeated and the Allied countries saw that Russia is now a workers' state, you think they had respect for the self-determination of the Soviet Union? They did not! They kept their armies there and they made counterrevolution. This came after the October Revolution, when the *soviets* took power from Kerenski and the Bolsheviks became the leading party in the Soviet Union. We weren't the only party, not even the largest party, but the leading party. The largest, f'rinstance, were the SRs—Socialist Revolutionaries—if you count the left wing and the right wing as one party. More splits, yeah—if the parties of the left were made of glass, the glazier would get rich! So the SR was the peasants' party, and there were lots of peasants in Russia. But the Bolsheviks controlled, like, the nerve of the revolution, the workers and the sailors and most of the army.

"So after the *soviets* take power and establish what we call 'the dictatorship of the proletariat'—this is where the working class supposedly is the dictator over the rich instead of the other way around—and suddenly the Ukrainians declare themselves an independent republic under Simon Petlyura, and the Georgians say they're independent under someone else, and they all make war on the new Soviet Union. And on the Jews. *Oi*, you had pogroms at this time worse than ever before. Petlyura killed thousands and thousands of Jews in the Ukraine. And all the old czarist generals came back into uniform—you got Denikin and Petlyura and Kolchak and Semënov and all the rest, the White Guard, we called them. And these reactionaries are supported by the French and by the English and by the Americans and all the rest that they don't want socialism in Russia. So for three years we had a civil war, a bloody war between the Reds and the Whites. The Vladivostok *soviet* was one of the first to fall to counterrevolution. And the Allied battleships blockaded the ports, and people began to starve all over the country.

"The worst fighting was in the Ukraine where I lived and where I had my child, my daughter Hannah. I had to bandage many Red Army men and I saw many others that they needed shrouds, not bandages.

"Now I bet you a nickel that you don't even know about this history, am I right? 'Cause in the schools in America they don't teach about socialism and revolution, they act like the American Revolution was the last one on earth and it solved everything 'cause now we got television.

"Hey, I'm not knocking the American Revolution! I'm just trying to continue it! The right-wingers say I should go back to Russia—yeah, after sixty years in the United States and doing more good work than they ever did, I should go back. If I go anyplace, it's gonna be the grave! And then who's going to explain to you about the past? So that when whatever *gonif*'s living in the White House tells you about how the Soviet Union's trying to take over California, you can tell him right back about the time when the United States tried to take over the Ukraine!

"It's a dangerous thing to be ignorant of history. Now, I heard last week a young man, a Jew, giving a lecture about Israel to my club, a Jewish-culture club. And all we heard from him was Palestinian, Palestinian. He was radical, yeah, but he was born in maybe 1954, y'see, and he didn't even read newspapers until when—when do you start to read newspapers? So all he knows is maybe since 1973, with Israel occupying the West Bank and denying the Arabs their national rights.

"Now, I support the Palestinians, I do. They got to have a homeland for themselves just like the Jews needed a homeland after what Hitler did to us and the whole world didn't raise a finger. But the way this young man was talking, you know, Zionism is the worst thing in the world excepting maybe cancer! He didn't even know what the Arab nations, all of them, what they did to Israel to make the Israeli people so scared and belligerent. He doesn't understand anti-Semitism; even though he's a Jew himself, he still makes jokes about Jews and uses the word 'genocide' like it should describe a bad haircut. He was a good guy, actually, I knew that. He meant well, and he fights for socialism. But he was so ignorant of history! He was so ignorant of history!

"So for him, y'see, and for people like him, I start to bargain with the guy upstairs that he should give me some more years that I can struggle and educate the young radicals. But I don't have good credit with the guy upstairs, so I moved fast: I had this young man to my house for coffee and we talked, we talked for three hours until I thought my teeth would fall out, I was so tired! And I told him to come visit me again—he's the nephew of a man in my club, so he comes sometimes to the neighborhood, y'see. So even if he didn't like my ideas, he liked the cookies I gave him and he learned that the *alte khalyeras* that he's lecturing to are not all senile and that there are other progressive ways to think than his own.

"How can I express this thing so I won't have to say it again? I know you want me to talk about Yasha and the revolution and our daughter. I'm like the *balebusteh* that she's still setting the table after everyone is finished eating. But do me a favor, be polite and listen. 'Cause history, y'see, it's a living thing, and if you don't feed it, if you don't listen and repeat the stories, if you don't keep it growing, then it dies and it disappears.

"Even today with the Holocaust, all those that they actually survived the camps are dying off, they're old. So what's going to happen in twenty years when there's nobody left to show you the tattooed numbers on their arm and to tell you, 'I was there, I saw it all'? Already you got this reactionary bunch of right-wingers, Nazis, actually, that they're saying the gas chambers never happened, the six million Jews didn't really die, it's all just a lie to get sympathy for Israel. Isn't it unbelievable, that even this genocide, that it's like an enormous bleeding wound on the face of the human race, and people still don't even know about it? It's only now in the past number of years that Jews all around the world are realizing that we got to, we got to come out of the closet, we got to wave our bloody flag and shout, 'Never again!'

"Same thing for the Soviet Union, in a certain kind of a way. You might not like Stalin, I might not like Stalin, we both might not like the kind of a place that the Soviet Union is today, but we should understand how it began, how the entire capitalist world tried to strangle the revolution in the crib—so this affects how the country's gonna act as an adult, y'see. The whole country had this blockade by the foreign ships, like I told you, and the whole country was close to starvation. We had socialism that it didn't yet know how to crawl and already it had to walk and run and jump and push and pull in order to survive!

"It survived, yeah, but with many bruises. Many bruises that never healed. The Soviet Union was like a blade of grass that it grows through the crack in the sidewalk—a miracle of survival. You know, a famous Jew, I think it was Ben-Gurion, he said that a Jew that doesn't believe in miracles is not a realist. I would say the same thing for a socialist. Every socialist revolution has been a miracle of survival. Cuba, they had to survive the Bay of Pigs, remember? And Vietnam, they had to survive all the napalm and the killing for so many years. . . .

"All right, now, stories! What do you want first, the good news or the bad news? I got plenty of both, y'see. There was not a day to go by that was just a day to go by during the revolution. We were busy, busy just for our survival. It was not a game, it was not like you talk politics with a friend 'cause it's raining outside. The people of Russia knew nothing but work and slavery and sickness and religion. They could never feel their feelings or know their minds; they were drunk with hardship, actually. Now suddenly the Revolution gives them back their lives, it gives them power. From this their minds caught fire! Everywhere you go there's people talking politics, people growing opinions like a boy should grow hair on his face or a girl should grow a woman's figure. For all of us, everything we did became for one purpose: to be sure that we would win against the White Guard.

"And in the middle of all this, I had my baby. And with a whole regiment of soldiers to take care of besides! Maybe it wasn't such a good idea, but listen, I didn't sit and plan it this way. I knew about birth control, sure, but after two months on the boat . . . Vladivostok was not exactly a shopping center that you get whatever you want! Anyway, mind your business. I had a girl. This was not my daughter Janet, no, this was my first, Hannah. We named her for Yasha's mother that she died from consumption in New York. So maybe this was a mistake, to name our child for such an unlucky person? I still play these superstitious kind of a games—f'rinstance, at night, when I look out the window, if I see in the next apartment building three windows that they're in a row and they got lights on, then that means my grandson is smiling, wherever he is. Anyway, we named the girl Hannah, and if that was a mistake, I didn't learn, 'cause I named my next one Janet, after Yasha, 'cause I loved him like I can't begin to tell you.

"After my own father or mother I wouldn't name a child, y'see. I didn't hate them, but there was no understanding between us. Yasha and I came to visit them just at the time of the October Revolution, and there's all kind of a things going on in Mogilev-Podolsk. They had a *soviet* of their own, everything. But to be in my father's house, you'd think it was a *shtetl* maybe a hundred years ago. It's not that my father was senile. He wasn't so old and his mind was good. But he withdrew from all the excitement; with the same stubbornness that he once had as a fighter, now he withdrew. He blocked out everything excepting religion. Can you believe, for a whole month Yasha and I stayed in their house and not once did my father mention what happened with my brothers and with me in Siberia? There was just one time—I went down and I found him in the cellar; he was looking for something, a candle, I don't know. And when he saw me on the stairs he got very nervous and said, 'Shoo, you'll fall and you'll lose your baby.' Then for the rest of the day he sat in his room and when you went in there the air tasted like ashes. But this was the only time he showed his memories, his fear. Otherwise he was a clock with the arms stuck.

"But he liked Yasha, 'cause Yasha knew about books and about travel, which my father liked to hear. And Yasha knew how to make nice to people. It wasn't a compulsion, but he knew how to be charming, if you know what I mean. So they got along good, and I kept my distance.

"My mother and I got close, about things for women, you know. I was grown and in a family way and I knew how to cook and to do things with my hands, so she liked to have me for a daughter, I suppose. There was a familiar feeling between us, more than I had with my father. I remember she kept calling me Leah by mistake—I was all her daughters in one. So we had familiarity, but also I had this feeling that I'm with someone that's blind or crippled and they get along all right but you always feel sorry. This is how she was. She gave her whole life over to her husband and to the traditional way of the Jewish woman, and now it was too late. She knew it, she wished maybe it could be different, but she was resigned to her life. She sighed all the time and gave out blessings like a dying woman.

"I guess every generation looks back and feels sorry for the one before. Not just 'cause they're old, but 'cause they're finished, if you know what I mean. The bread is baked and it's a little stale already, but they got no time to bake another. With my parents, especially, history just passed them by. Their whole way of life came to an end in Russia with the revolution. The orthodox way was attacked from all sides. You had the pogroms by the White Guard. You had new ideas to compete and rules to restrict from the Bolsheviks. You had industry that made the Jews into workers, into a proletarian people, both in America and in Russia. All these things, they broke down the walls of the *shtetl* for good. I guess you could say that my brothers won their struggle with my father after all.

"But it's strange when you see that your parents no more have power over your life. They become like plain people, you see them in a more personal kind of a way, maybe, but always they look sad. Like a king that lost his crown. But with parents, y'see, unless they've been very cruel to you, it's not like a revolution against the king. You don't feel the satisfaction or the liberation. Instead you feel almost like, yeah sure, you took your life from their hands and into your own, but you also took some of *their* life, 'cause you are part of them, part of their flesh and blood.

"All right already. Who do you think I am, Dr. Spock? These are things that everybody knows, each in her own way. This is the book of life. Especially I understood these things 'cause I was pregnant myself, with dreams for my child in a new society. And it's such a thing—you give birth with so much pain, and you raise your children by giving so much of yourself. A mother always has pain—something that feeds on her, all her life, some kind of a desire that you want to be fulfilled by your child, you want to eat her up. And you never know really how to separate from her; she's a part of your *body*.

"My parents never saw their grandchildren. They died in 1921, my father first, then my mother. It had to be; they had nothing to say to the world anymore, only to God, so God took them. Even their children were strangers to them, and Hannah, Hannah was just a bulge in my belly. That's all they saw, my belly and the blanket that Yasha was crocheting for her, for him—we didn't know, of course, so the blanket was white.

"That's right! My husband knew how to crochet. He was a *luftmensch*, in a nice kind of a way. In English, word for word this means 'air man,' and that's exactly what Yasha was: He's got nothing and he knows everything, he goes everyplace and he stays nowhere. He sparkles, he rains, he laughs, he cries, and he brings you the sun, every day. . . .

"Now that's enough talking. I want a cup of coffee. I make it special—European coffee, I call it. You put one spoon chicory for four spoons coffee. My daughter, my Janet, she brings me chicory. She takes care of her old lady."

❁

"Look at that moon. Right over your shoulder. They won't even need a sharpshooter. Bessie!"

She turned into the shadows of the night, away from the torchlit infirmary tent. Slotnik took a step and caught her arm. "Let go!" she snarled, yanking free. "Go look at my daughter before you talk. She's turning blue, Hank, she can't breathe!"

"If you get shot, it won't help Hannah."

"Why should they shoot? We're a hospital camp. They'll see that I'm a woman, I've got no gun. . . ." Oh, damn him for making her hesitate!

"You're wearing trousers, Bess. Your hair's falling out. The way you look, they'll shoot just to put you out of your misery."

"Oh, go shit in the ocean." Again she stalked away, but Slotnik persisted, tailing her to a grove of trees that sheltered the wagons and horses of the ambulance corps. The animals, tethered to a long rope tied between two trunks, stirred and snorted at their approach.

"Your husband said I should make jokes to you if you get all crazy," Hank said. "I'm sorry, Bess."

"Yeah, I'm sorry, too. I'm sorry our goddamn doctor got shot and I'm sorry Denikin was ever born. Now I've got to make the Americans sorry, too."

"All you need is one fool with a rifle—"

"And all I have is one daughter!" She ducked under the rope, slapped two of the huge animals aside, and ran from the grove, expertly dodging the moonlight.

Slotnik intercepted her a hundred yards down the road when a creaking wagon drawn by a fast-trotting team of horses forced them both into the shallow trench beside the sandbag barricades. Bessie was relieved to see the wagon empty; there were no new wounded, as yet, to torture her conscience and beg her back to the infirmary with their moans. Breathless, she laid her head against the sandbags and peered up at the stars, dusty in the moon-washed sky above the dark mountain ridges. Hank stood watchfully, not daring to advance or touch her. "Bessie . . ."

"Help me now, darling," she said, turning her face to him, resting her cheek against the rough bags. "Watch out for me. If any of our crazy cossacks think I'm surrendering or betraying them . . . you'll explain before they shoot, yeah? In the back—I couldn't stand to get it in the back."

"Stay here and rest," he said. "You're nervous, you've seen too much, too much suffering."

She looked uphill at the cluster of flimsy pup tents in which some two dozen cossacks, the remains of a whole cavalry regiment, lay recuperating or dying. "Lucky for the Revolution these few became Bolsheviks," she said. "They're like oxen—you pour whiskey on their open wounds and they lie there grinning at you. 'Yes, comrade,' I tell them, 'in the new Russia there'll be life for you, even with one leg.' I feel like a priest promising heaven for them. I wish they would scream sometimes, scream so the mountains would crack. Scream like babies!" Her knees buckled as she broke into tears. "Oh, my baby! My Hannah! She can't even cry to me! I can't stand it, to watch her drown!"

"Shh, Bessie, she's going to be all right."

"No, she's gonna be dead! Oh, God, let go!" She broke away and threw herself upon the sandbags. Slotnik at once grabbed her jacket. They froze like cats on the edge of violence.

"Hank Slotnik," she said at last in a controlled voice, keeping her back to him, "you can't do this to me. I don't give in, Hank. You'll have to be my enemy if this is the friendship you give. I'll beat you senseless while you sleep, Hank. Don't you see?" she cried, whirling around and breaking his hold. "It's not for Hannah only! None of us can take a breath. In a day, maybe in two, Denikin will come over the mountains and we'll all be on the barricades. You know it's true. Novorossisk has already closed its doors to us. The poor people, they want food, not politics, and they'll get it from anyone they can, anyone they think is going to win! Hank, you know it, our only route out of here is the sea. The Americans have got to stand aside."

"Stand aside!" he sneered. "Are you kidding? International politics will just stand aside! President Wilson's lackeys will just stand aside! On your say-so! You're Moses, aren't you? You're going to part the Black Sea down there—"

"I'm a survivor, that's what I am! And they're human beings, whatever President Wilson thinks. They're tired of war, they want to go home. If I can just let them see Hannah, in their minds—"

"You speak rotten English," he grumbled.

"And they're fighting a rotten war! But they are workers, Hank."

"Like hell. They're strikebreakers! Tell me, in America, did you ever *convince* some lousy scab not to break your picket line? You have to do it with your fists!"

A patrolling sentry, one of their own, was hollering from a distance for them to stand and identify themselves.

"Go talk to him, Hank. Please."

"Ahh, you're a fool. You've got marbles in your head instead of brains." He touched her cheek with two fingers. "Keep your head low, at least. You hear? I don't want to have to break any kind of bad news to Yasha if—the next time we see him. When he comes back . . ." He backed away from her. "Stay low."

Then he turned and ran, waving his arms and yelling to the sentry.

Bessie leaned back, trembling, against the barricades. Hank's clumsy words about Yasha, whose survival and return from another combat zone in the West was no more assured than anything in the blockaded, information-starved Ukraine, had untied the knot in her nerve. She tried to concentrate on Hank's conversation with the guard, audible in the chill, quiet air, but this only inflamed her tension; she could feel and hear her blood pressure mounting, hissing in her skull. Dropping to her heels, she hugged her stomach and rocked back and forth, back and forth, peopling the trench with ghosts—Smulevitch, Sadie Weinstein, little Tsil the cobbler's daughter, corpses along her path of survival—to beg their blessings and assure them that she needed only to rest, to prepare her thoughts, blow a kiss to Yasha, make a wish for Hannah . . .

And move her bowels. Her intestines were turning over like dead fish in a pool. "*Oi*, these bodies, what they put us through," she muttered, lowering her khaki trousers and underpants. At once she let loose a hot explosion that left her insides empty and groaning, then found a bloody bit of bandage in her jacket with which to wipe herself. There's my white flag for the *Amerikaners*, she thought. To show them how human we all are in the worst ways. The best and the bravest, they got no perfumed linens, y'see, no clean uniforms. I'll show them every wound, every glob of pus. Like their own Valley Forge, where their great-grandfathers froze with George Washington. Now, you've got your speech. Should have worn your red shawl, you'd look like a lady in the moving pictures.

She was climbing, hammering her toes in between the bags, glancing down at the white shroud covering her mess on the ground, saying to herself, Don't fall into *that*. In a moment her head and shoulders were over the top, her hands gripping the front edge of the bags as her feet probed for a secure hold. A salt breeze from the Black Sea, a diamond-crusted pool of darkness across the plain, bathed her face and filled her lungs.

"American sailors! Hello, American sailors! I come on the wall to talk to you."

Lanterns burned boldly in the windows of the boathouses that the Americans had seized from the fishermen of Novorossisk. Rotted timbers from the wharves were stacked as a sparse barricade across the field, little more than a stone's throw from the sandbags. The proximity of the Americans startled Bessie as it had each morning for two sleepless weeks when she would emerge from the infirmary tent, heavy-limbed and preoccupied with Hannah's suffering, to see an American sailor waving at her from across the raw stretch of earth.

"Hello! Who is from New York? I live six years in New York. Listen, I got no bomb, okay? No gun. I make work as a nurse. We are hospital here."

One of the boathouse doors creaked and slammed. Lanterns waved and flickered in the distance.

"I say to my comrade, you will not shoot me. If you want shoot, you got boat, hah?" The deck lights of the American cruiser, the *Black Eagle*, shone like a constellation in the harbor. "Big guns. You can shoot plenty. But I know, you wait for Denikin, hah? . . . Please. My English is no good. Six years I live in New York. The Bronx. Work at Montefiore Hospital. I was a nurse. I learn English in Ideal Preparatory School. Learn American history. George Washington. American Revolution, seventeen seventy-six. Now Russian Revolution, nineteen seventeen."

A brilliant beam of light poured across the field, silent, on target, daggers in her eyes. Bessie shriveled like a raisin and almost lost her toehold. An American voice, rude and heckling, called out to her. "Please!" she cried, her head bowed, but climbing higher as though the searchlight were a holy beam. "My daughter is very sick. A baby. She cannot breathe. Please. We need a doctor! You got a doctor? My baby needs doctor!"

She lifted one leg over the top of the barricade. A shot rang out and a bullet thudded into the sandbags some feet below. "No!" she shrieked, clenching her fists and lying like an infant on her belly in the blazing circle of light. "Don't shoot! I got no bomb, nothing! Don't shoot!"

She heard more voices calling back and forth from the boathouses to the barricade. Swallowing the knot in her throat, she hollered, "Please! We want like you got—bread, freedom. Free Russia! No more war!" But again that raspy voice catcalled across the field, spitting in her face. She shuddered and lay low, and then the air cracked into pieces.

The bullet tore open her right foot, pain clawing at the muscles of her leg and buttocks. She grunted and rolled off the sandbags headfirst into the swift rush of shadow and earth.

* * *

Bessie passed in and out of consciousness all night, her sleep bloated with dreams that ran, tripped, and broke into pain and discomfort: her foot stinging under bandages, her daughter burning at her side, every memory a snare, every thought dreadful. She would try to duck back under to sleep—better the chaotic nightmares, to fight, to scream, to run, to have Yasha running toward her or Babushka Breshkovskya's fat form to lie behind, better this than to lie like a sausage with eyes, waiting for Denikin. But then Hannah's labored, mucusy breathing would pour into her ears.

"I need alcohol," she muttered into the darkness, clogged with groans and snores. "Alcohol and a sponge . . . she's on fire. . . . Who's there?"

A nurse was gliding past her head. "We have alcohol only for wounds," she said.

"Give me some," Bessie demanded drunkenly, then cursed the woman until her breath gave out.

The tent walls trembled. Bessie reached over to rub her baby's chest. Her own hand felt detached, a plucked flower without nectar or scent, wilting on the hot, hot skin. "Sleep, baby. Sleep."

> Your poppa has gone to town,
> To bring you a dancing bear
> And ribbons for your hair.
>
> Sleep, baby, sleep.
> Poppa has gone to town.
> He'll bring you a little lamb,
> And bracelets for your hand.
>
> Sleep, baby, sleep.
> Poppa has gone to town.
> He'll bring you a little brother,
> And chocolates for your mother. . . .

Hannah died without a whimper late in the night, her life evaporating so gently that Bessie, in her stupor of depression and dreams, did not notice until the body began to cool and stiffen beneath her hand.

She recoiled, and then the realization stabbed her, cracked her open. Sprawling on the ground, gripping Hannah to her breast as though her own heartbeat could inspire a revival of life, she wailed, sucked in her breath, and wailed louder, in protest, in helplessness. Her comrades came running, and surrounded her, faceless in the dark.

For an hour she bled at their feet, her arms molded around Hannah, her fears and memories dissolving into mucus. They knelt beside her, offered consolation, made promises. But Hannah died again and again in her arms, growing cold like the ground, and Bessie whined, and whined, and screamed out her misery a dozen times.

Finally she dozed, a squeezed sponge in her comrades' arms.

When she awoke, she was back on her cot, tucked beneath a blanket. The eastern wall of the tent was aglow with morning sunlight. Her head was leaden, aching. . . .

And Hannah was gone—her corpse, her blankets, her diapers, snatched away. Bessie swung off her cot and hobbled, then hopped ferociously across the stubbled ground. Two nurses, Molly Malinow and another, caught her in her clumsy, headlong rush toward the exit flaps.

"Molly, what are you doing?" Bessie cried, helpless to struggle against the big woman's restraint. "You think we're so different, you think we're so alive?"

The other nurse laid a hand on her shoulder. "It's only the procedure, darling."

"Shit on procedures, you! I want my daughter! Oh, Molly!" Her lip trembled. She looped her arms around Molly's shoulder and laid her cheek against her arm. "Don't you see? They'll do the same to us, Molly. They'll break our struggle, call it a bad dream, then dump our bodies in the Black Sea."

Molly reached across with her free hand to smooth back Bessie's thin hair. She cupped her chin and looked into her brimming eyes as though searching for a reflection of her own. "I'll bring you—don't cry anymore, Buzie."

"No more," Bessie whimpered.

"We'll say goodbye?"

Bessie nodded, her tears darkening the dirt.

The tent flaps parted in front of them, pinching their eyes with a flood of daylight. In filed a group of six men, ushered by Hank Slotnik, who was speaking in a rising voice about food provisions. Flanking him were two bedraggled comrades and, standing tall and attentive, scanning the disorderly tent with a grim set to his mouth, a square-shouldered man in a clean white U.S. naval uniform, attended by two American sailors in pea coats.

"Hello, Bessie," said Hank, his head bowed before the sight of the haggard women.

"Let me sit," she pleaded, leaning heavily on Molly's shoulder.

The American officer removed his hat. The two Russians in the group fetched, at Molly's direction, Bessie's own cot. Hank helped her sit, then kissed her hand. "You," he whispered in Yiddish, "are the bravest woman alive. Your next child will grow up in paradise! You hear? We're all going to live—because of you. Because of you!" Turning to his guests, he brushed the dust from his knees. "Now, English. This is the girl. Captain Owen—from the ship—this is Bessie Levovsky."

From close up, the captain's uniform, despite the rows of silk and bronze across his chest, was not all that elegant, with a button missing, the cuffs frayed, the seams yellowed from pressing. His cap-in-hand stance seemed folksy, awkward in a workingman's way, but with his big shoulders and belligerent, deeply lined face, clean-shaven with a stiff inch of silvery hair on top, he looked perfectly capable of exerting authority and a shrewd brand of the haughtiness common to his class. In all, Bessie felt as though confronted by an alert but friendly police dog. She quickly collected her wits, putting up the calm mask of her nursing profession.

"You're the girl on the barricades?" Owen said in a deep voice, an English not of New York City.

Too exhausted to translate, Bessie looked to Hank and Molly for help. Molly managed to figure out the meaning of "barricades" first, and Hank in turn assured the captain that Bessie was the girl.

"Well, I'm sorry about her foot," Owen replied. "Your foot." He pointed down at her bandages.

"Is okay," Bessie murmured.

The captain beckoned one of his aides. "Tell this young lady that the man who shot her is in the brig for disobeying my orders."

The sailor translated into crude Russian. Bessie shrugged at the news.

"Well, she sure had more to say last night, didn't she? Now listen, honey." He leaned into her view as one might do with a sulking child. "I heard about your little girl. By God, I'm even sorrier than that. I lost a little girl myself, years ago—polio disease."

Bessie absorbed little of his meaning as she turned over in her mind the news of the imprisoned sailor. Such democrats, these imperialists! she thought. A single herring gets netted while all the sharks get away with a mouthful. "I got a question." Her voice cracked from disuse, but she cleared her throat and went on. "You send to jail the man who shoots—but you help Denikin. Is the same thing! I . . . ." Frustrated by her ineptness with the nearly forgotten language, she rattled off a speech in Russian to the translating seaman. Hank Slotnik groaned at her words and slapped his forehead.

"Sir, she says we should all be disobeying orders, sir."

"Go on, Mr. Coburn."

"She says our orders are to assist—what's his name, sir? I can't translate what's she's calling him, I don't know the swear words. . . ."

"General Denikin," said Owen, as though he were suppressing a belch.

"Denikin!" Bessie shouted. "You help Denikin! And he comes—"

"*Sha shtil*, Bessie!" warned Slotnik. "They brought us food this morning. And shovels—to bury your Hannah!"

"What's he saying?" Owen asked his aide.

"Don't know, sir, that's Jewish they're talking."

"Sounds like German to me."

"Yes, sir."

"I used to hear that when I was shipping out of New York—the swabbies used to call it 'Jew York.' But I don't cotton to that kind of prejudice, mister. . . ."

Bessie was weeping again, facedown on the cot, following her give-and-take with Hank. To her comrades' amazement, the captain crouched in his whites alongside her and stroked her hair. "Listen, honey, I know how you feel. When my little gal died, it was a terrible day. Mr. Coburn, come over here. Tell this little New Yorker—aww, Jesus, look at this! Her hair's falling out." He stood and drew a wide handkerchief from his jacket. "Probably got the typhus and God knows what else.

This is one hell of a war." He blew his nose while glancing appraisingly around the infirmary. "Let's get out of here. We'll send in the doc to have a look. Washington can't complain—as far as the rest of the world's concerned, there's not an American ship in Russia south of the fifty-fifth parallel. We are below the fifty-fifth parallel now, aren't we?"

"Yessir, captain."

"How many of these paupers you think there are in this camp? Enough to invade Alaska? You think we have to worry about Alaska?"

"I wouldn't know, sir."

"Well, if you wouldn't know, Mr. Coburn, and you're standing right here, then how do you suppose Secretary Baker of the War Department can make a decision back in D.C.? I'd say he'll just have to rely on our word for it, wouldn't you? Now, find out who their commanding officer is. Whoever sent that gal on the barricades last night is one devil of a C.O."

The translator queried Hank in Russian. Hank raised his eyebrows at Molly, at Bessie in her lap, and at his own emaciated girth. "Tell him it's Karl Marx," said Molly in their private language.

"It's anybody who's still alive," he told her. "We'll have to call a meeting." He explained to the Americans.

"Fine," said Captain Owen. "We'll see you for lunch, then. More of the same that you're having for breakfast, okay?"

Oh, my stiff little girl, my little dead bug, shall I bring you to show the Americans? Shall I bring them here to your new house, to meet your new friends, the dead cossack, the dead peasant, the dead milkmaid? Each one I knew by name, by their pain, and each I watched die. You I slept through. Forgive me, my love. And not even a decent rag to cover your sweet face. Oh, my baby, we got nothing to give you. No funeral, no prayer, no God.

"We have shovels now. We can bury them."

"No time, Buzie," said Molly, holding her under the arm.

"No time? Why, Molly, you really think we have something to rush for?"

"I don't know, Buzie. We're between two worlds. You jump over a crack in the earth and you don't know until you land."

Bessie turned away from the charnel house. "Well, we got lunch coming. This is something." She sat on the muddy ground to spare her foot the agony of her weight. The sunlight blinked and a chill passed through her. "The idea that we could still have a future . . ." She raised her knees to her chest and looked at Molly over her shoulder. "It gives me strength, Molly. If this foot weren't torn to pieces, I could work so hard."

Molly stepped away from the fetid hut and sat by her side. Bessie had her lips pressed to her own bare forearm. "You were smart to take her away in the night," she confessed. "Now I can't even bear to pick her up. . . ."

Molly listened and searched her face like a lover.

"I thought I would cry until my eyes fell out. I thought my skull would burst—like the quicksilver in our thermometers, how it breaks into little pieces?" She frowned at the image, then sobbed again. "And now I don't even want to look at her! Oooh, the smell here is rotten, Molly, it's like Siberia. We had a punishment cell . . . God, we had nothing, just foolish ideas to keep us warm. If Hannah could have seen me in that place, she would have known to find a better mother. . . . That was the problem, Molly: I had two children, all along, two infants—Hannah and Russia. Hannah I barely knew. Once, I remember, I counted her fingers, her toes, every one. I kissed each toe. Once."

Molly touched her knee. "You had no time for sweetness, my dear. Too many worries."

"With Yasha always coming and going," Bessie agreed, her eyes large with tears. "Russia got *all* of his time."

"And Russia is still alive," Molly said. "You'll see, as soon as we get a newspaper—this little camp is not the Bolshevik government."

"Yeah, sure. . . . Oh, Molly, I'm not a human being anymore!" Bessie moaned with her face close to the earth, giving Hannah her due, until the breeze made her shiver and she had to confess to herself, yes, she was hungry.

A meeting of the forty-three intact comrades in camp, including nurses, drivers, and soldiers, elected a committee of five to negotiate with the Americans. Hank Slotnik and Bessie were among them, Bessie the lone woman and on crutches. They rendezvoused with Captain Owen's expanded party in the muddy no-man's-land between the camps, where the Americans had set up chairs and a long table set with biscuits, dried beef, and coffee.

There were introductions to endure, pretensions of respect and due process, but the chill in the air from the sea, and the occasional distant rumble of cannon from the mountains to the north and east, prodded all the participants—the Bolsheviks with fierce tension, the Americans with businesslike sobriety—to speak as directly as the tedium of translation allowed.

Captain Owen had with him a flat green ledger—his captain's log, he explained to the Russians through Mr. Coburn. "I have recorded here from October twenty-seventh—what's that, four days gone?"

"Yes, sir."

"We have in our possession four fishing vessels belonging to the locals. Mr. Taylor?"

"Sir?"

"How many human beings you suppose you could fit onto one of those boats?"

Mr. Taylor estimated thirty to thirty-five adults, which elicited a soft whistle from Captain Owen. "They're liable to have water up to their belly buttons!"

"I think the boats would still be seaworthy, sir." Taylor defended his idea as the Russians all leaned forward like novice lip-readers to make out their argument. "They pull two, three thousand pounds of fish into one of those things."

"Fine," said Owen with a frown, "I just don't mean to be picking these folks out of the Black Sea. So we're talking now about one hundred and twenty people, and they have over two hundred in this place. Mr. Coburn, please explain to our friends here the concept of *triage*."

Instead, Coburn slammed down his coffee cup and kicked back his chair as an ambulance wagon drawn by a sweaty team clattered to a halt on the road behind the sandbags.

"More wounded," said Slotnik, and to the Americans, in English: "No trouble. Peace."

"More wounded," remarked Coburn. "That's more to leave behind." His eyes were still pegged to the barricades, atop of which three comrades had mounted and were waving for attention. Mirroring them were American sailors, at the ready with rifles among the timbers strewn at the edge of their camp.

"Go ahead," Bessie told Hank in Yiddish, "before we get holes in our heads."

A fence of tension ringed the table as Hank trotted off. Bessie threw herself against it head-on. "Back to business now. What do you mean," she asked Coburn, "that we leave people behind?"

She understood at once and cut short his reply, looking directly at Captain Owen. "We leave, they die. No. We all go."

"You all sink," Owen retorted, but his use of "sink" as a verb confounded her.

Slotnik came back breathless. "Denikin's retreating! The comrades brought word from the front. He's retreating!"

Mr. Coburn quietly translated for the captain while the Russions whooped and slapped one another.

"But of course he's in retreat!" Owen hollered at last. "By God, what kind of communications do these Reds use, smoke signals? Tell them, would you, Mr. Coburn, that General Denikin has been retreating *toward* Novorossisk for more than a week now! I imagine he's going to need the same treatment that we're giving these folks—boats and the works. Off to Turkey like a whupped dog."

Still the news thrilled Bessie, even as her comrades blushed and slumped before the Americans' clearly superior knowledge and systems. The fact of the White retreat vastly increased the prospect that Yasha was still alive! He leaped into her thoughts like a peerless ballet dancer.

The negotiations went on until the coffee in the pot was as cold as seawater. Made reckless by the poverty of their options, Bessie abandoned tact and womanly complaisance as she insisted, in a dozen different arguments, that Owen provide transport for the entire hospital camp, not just for the healthy and mobile.

Owen in reply dropped the pretensions of his rank and cursed her as a cowboy would a rebellious horse. He boasted of his humanistic values and the risks he'd taken in the past for the sake of principle, even as he iced over her appeals. His final word was that he would confine his men to the boathouses from ten to midnight—"In other words, we won't watch"—and leave four boats docked in the inner waters off the beach. There would be provisions, including some lifejackets, for one hundred and twenty people.

* * *

The boathouses hummed with voices, sounding to Captain Owen like human beehives. The men would loosen up with their captain gone, he thought: gamble for higher stakes, pull out the hidden flasks, stoke those potbellies until they're almost too hot to sit by. Smart move, he complimented himself, not to keep the men on board ship these weeks. Here they get to stretch their legs, and the civilian population doesn't have to suffer with any kind of "shore leave."

Owen pulled up the hood of his parka and stared at the cold moon. He was not an unconfident or fretful man, yet had been reevaluating all evening his decision to let the Reds through his blockade. They were harmless enough, but such considerations would not show up on the damning memos at the War Department, nor would the scrappy little Jew girl be there to shame the brass into forgiveness. . . . The mountains were quiet, no cannon fire now, quieter than the rolling waves. Owen wondered about the fate of those who would be left behind. Slaughtered by Mr. Denikin, no doubt, unless I really garrison the port. Haven't even got the manpower for that, never mind the permission. I guess it depends on whether Denikin comes in strutting or crawling. But I wish those Reds would put their wounded out of their misery. I could shell the place to dust then, cover their tracks. . . .

A hundred and twenty of 'em. My good man, that's a lot to let through and still call yourself a neutral.

What's it all about, this civil war? I wonder. What in God's name besides slavery could rip a country in half? Or bring back a gal like that, all the way from New York City and with an infant in her arms, poor kid . . .

Oh, now, Owen, don't you go thinking about your own miseries. My God, you're a soft touch, you are. Fact of the matter is, it's about time you retired, captain, and gave Millie a full-time husband for a change. Yessir. How many years you think you got left on this earth?

10:38. Nice old watch . . . dear old Millie . . .

10:45. Slotnik's battered timepiece ticked like a bomb in Bessie's hand. Almost time to go, Buzeleh. We go early 'cause it's gonna be a fight, 'cause that man has lifeboats on his ship and someday we might be friends and laugh about it 'cause he's a good human being, but, damn it, I'm going to put a gun to his *pipik* and hold him for ransom if he won't let us take every half-dead comrade in this camp! Now, goddamn you, foot, heal! Stop it with your stinging and your pain! Who are you the spokesman for? I need reminders of my misery?

She was the flagbearer, the policymaker, the inventory-taker, the spokeswoman with a wounded foot to prove her courage and a debilitating word of scorn for any who disagreed with her. So they worked, some with the energy of hope, others from the habit of following orders, all with mindless persistence; they worked at dragging themselves and each other or at lifting, hand and foot, those too weak to move. They carried themselves across wooden planks spanning the trench, through a torn-down section of the sandbag wall, across no-man's-land, through the timbers, past the tents and lockers of the Americans, past the noisy boathouses onto the pebbly beach. Bessie swung back and forth on her crutches among them, egging them on, addressing personal words to every man whose face, or hat, or particular way of limping she managed to recognize.

Her first declaration, repeated a dozen times: "We're going to live. Do you hear me? Your body doesn't know it yet, but we're going to live. All of us!"

"Hold together. Never mind the pain. It's just proof that you're alive! Come on now, you don't have to smile, it's enough to walk, just keep walking. Soon we'll be marching again!"

"We're going to cross the water, comrades. All of us. Don't worry about Denikin—Denikin is a lie, a fool, the ocean will swallow him. We're going to glide across the water, yes, my cossack friend, like your good Lord Jesus did. Come on. We're going to live. All of us."

"Carry him, carry him, don't let go. You're an animal with three heads, the three of you, together. One animal."

"We've escaped before, all of us, how often? Escaped to fight again. Escaped from Siberia, escaped from believing in the czar father, escaped from his goddamn gendarmes and his goddamn lies and the goddamn Germans and now the goddamn White Guard. But this is the last time! No more running. Keep going, my comrades, be strong!"

"This is a strike, comrades. All for one and one for all. We'll sit down on the beach, every soul that we have, and we won't move until we win. Solidarity, comrades! Solidarity!"

"Sing with me, my brothers and sisters. Sing with me! Let's drown out Denikin's cannons!"

Arise, ye prisoners of starvation.
Arise, ye wretched of the earth.
For justice thunders condemnation,
A better world's in birth!
No more tradition's chains shall bind us
Arise ye slaves no more in thrall.
The earth shall rise on new foundations,
We have been naught, we shall be all!
'Tis the final conflagration,
Let each stand in his place!
The international working class
Shall be the human race!

11:46. Summoned by his officers from a walk along the shore, Captain Owen beheld the macabre assemblage of Russians on the beach and knew at once that the Jewish witch had outfoxed him—had reached into his uniform, plucked his heart, and would not return it until he earned it. She came charging at him across the sand on her crutches. "You got boats, little boats, on the ship," she cried in that rough and blunt English of hers. "All my comrades, we all go!"

In the presence of his officers, there would have to be an argument; he almost winked at her. Yeah, go on, Owen, tell her about regulations, about your superior command back home, tell her about American neutrality. Then ask her for her secret, by God. Ask about her version of the Bible, ask her to visit you back home in Nebraska. Tell her to have another baby, tell her to live a long, happy life. . . .

Fifteen minutes later he dropped the charade of refusal and issued an order for his men to fetch three of the *Black Eagle*'s ten lifeboats. "Without the life preservers, Mr. O'Hara. If they sink, why, the little lady could probably make them fly over the goddamn ocean."

1:06. Bessie lay numb and exhausted in the fish-stink hull of one of the fishing boats, listening to the droning motor, fighting nausea, regretting the lack of a spare blanket with which she might have covered and dignified the body of her dead child. Suddenly an explosion tore through her loneliness. Her fear was that other warships in the harbor, maybe the British or the French, whom the American captain had steadfastly refused to contact on the gadget he called his "radio," were firing upon her makeshift convoy. Dragging herself topside, she and a score of comrades looked back to the coast to see their hospital camp in flames, under small-artillery bombardment from the beach.

Chapter Fourteen

Bessie leaned on the dresser, her lame foot raised, as she stared into the mirror like a painter before a canvas. "This is me?"

"You'll have to take off the shift before I can swear to it," said Yasha, a tawny elf on the bed behind her.

"Don't believe it," she replied. "My behind lost weight, too." She was ninety-two pounds and gaining, her arms and legs all bone and tendon, her belly hanging. Her hair was cropped short and growing back as it had fallen out, in patches, but brown, no longer the curly blond mop that had prompted Mr. Sholem Aleichem himself to call her the *Yiddishe shikse.* "Look at me— I've got Jewish hair now," she mused. "Even while I was nursing cossacks and not even calling myself a Jew—no, me, I was an American! But my *shikse* hair was falling out. It takes just one pogrom to convert the assimilationists!"

"Why don't you put on sackcloth and sprinkle ashes on your head?"

"Don't make fun, Yasha."

"I'm not! You're like your father, did you ever think? When

it comes to these pogroms, you're obsessed, you're morbid. So go, put on sackcloth."

"No, you," she said. "You put something on. Aren't you cold like that?"

"No, my love, I'm warm in this room. But you, you're not really even *in* this room, are you?"

"Yes, I am, Yasha. Yes." But she kept staring into the glass, afraid of his embrace, unable to reconcile this exquisitely private moment with the chaos and strife surrounding them. Two hundred thousand Jews had been slaughtered in less than a year by the White Guard and Petlyura's Ukrainian nationalist movement. Two hundred thousand Jews, trampled into the dust and cobblestone of a thousand villages. This had been the portion of news that Yasha had served at their reunion—that their baby daughter now shared a mass grave with her people that ran the length and breadth of the Ukraine. How could he relax and cast off his mourning, now, like some whore in widow's clothing?

He reached to the floor to search his crumpled trousers for cigarettes. "I know where you are," he said. "You're back in Siberia. Back in Siberia without even your time of the month flowing. You're shutting down like a machine." In the mirror he could see tears glistening on her cheeks. "Good for you," he muttered, striking a match.

"Why good?" She hobbled about-face. "I haven't cried enough for you? You want more?"

He drew a blanket across his hips. "No, dear. Even a statue cries when the rain falls. I've got news to tell you: It's laughter that makes a human being."

"But I'm not a human being," she moaned. "I feel dead, inside and out."

"So let me in!" he entreated her. "Let me in. I've got life." He reached out his arms. "Come here, my hard-liner, my poor momma. You know that you're a better Bolshevik than I, a great woman, you are."

She could bring herself no closer than the bedpole.

"Bessie, it's not sex I'm talking about, just sex . . ."

"I'm so ugly, Yasha."

"I want your ugliness. I want to warm you. I want to heal you. I want to kiss your scabs, do you understand?" He snuffed his cigarette in an ashtray to gain control of his own welling emotions. "I want to be family with you, Bessie, even without our baby."

She clasped his hand and knelt carefully on the mattress, her eyes wet and shut tight. "Oh, my *luftmensch*. All week long, on the street, limping around with all the other sick, used-up women from all over . . . waiting for the next wave of invaders. They wait for customers, I wait for you. To find you."

"Here I am," he said simply.

"Yes, you are. I sigh, you come. On the air currents. Sometimes, you know, I think of you as an angel."

"By all means do. But we knew about your boats. We knew where to find you. It simply means that we're winning, Bessie, at last we're winning! We're not an underground movement anymore, not even in the Ukraine. We're winning."

She lowered her cheek to his broad, flat chest. "You are an angel. My angel."

He rubbed her neck. "And you are a great woman. My great woman."

"Mmm, you are warm, like a bed of coals."

He rested a hand between her buttocks to comfort her. She crawled deeper into his embrace until she could feel their hearts beating together. "Do we have time to get under the blankets?"

"Unless General Wrangel enters Alushta tonight, which would mean that I'm one hell of a cockeyed spy! This town is neutral as far as I can tell. And you and me, we're paid up in advance for a whole night."

"What does the landlord think of a—a Young—"

"Young Men's Christian Association. Try to get it straight."

"An American missionary who goes with a prostitute," Bessie remarked.

"Why not? You have a soul to save as much as anyone." He kissed her ear. "Either he knows I'm no missionary, or he knows you're no prostitute, or he thinks this is how Americans practice religion and he wants to convert!"

Laughing, they resettled beneath the covers, where Yasha's body heat mounted, melting her to sleep.

He lay wide-eyed into the night, pressing his thigh to hers, adoring her nearness and blessing every corner of the room—the walls and drapery, the floor and bolted door—for protecting them from exposure this one night. A night for the guts to relax. Even if we're only hiding our eyes, Yasha thought, sometimes

that's better to do. If I were to end up before a firing squad, I
might very well ask for the blindfold. Who knows? Never
mind that.

He felt like an animal in its lair, kept company by his own
breathing. He wiggled his toes, cracked his joints, felt for a pulse
along his inner thigh. He had not been without clothes for
weeks; the soft vulnerability of his skin and the diligent functioning of his heart and lungs enthralled him. Such monkeys we
all are, he thought. Simple monkeys! We kiss our wives, feed our
babies, rest our feet . . . "revolution," we call it, but really it's
just bananas that we want. Like Father Peretz's poor Bontsye
the Silent: Offered all the treasures of heaven, and all the poor
monkey can think to do is ask for a hot roll with butter each
morning. The angels wept for Bontsye Shwieg. Why not the
bourgeoisie? They've got hair on their knuckles beneath those
fancy gold rings, they're monkeys like the rest of us. Bastards.
For our roll and butter they would kill us. And for what, what
is worth killing for in this monkey life? Such unimaginative men,
with their glutted brains and bellies—if they would just give
out the hot rolls, they could know paradise in their own time!
Ahh, bastards, to hell with your blindfold. I'll stare you full in
the face, you devil's men.

But listen to yourself, Levovsky. The fact is you might die,
is that so? By firing squad, no less! But Hannah used to shield
you from all that. Your life was too precious to be measured,
then.

He lay his palm on Bessie's belly, regretting the sex drive,
still lingering as a current through his flesh, that had driven
her off to sleep. He wanted to engage her now beyond the
repartee that so often filled their time together, to enter that
hollow where her soul was hiding and coax her out, as always, as
ever. This hide-and-seek is our ritual, he thought, turning restlessly onto his belly. It was I who hung the mourning dress that
she wore after the Triangle fire and fitted her out for nurse's
whites. It was I who thawed her blood from the deep freeze
and turned her into a *mensch*. Now again, my love: no more
crying, no more squatting in your mudholes. This one safe night
that we have, I can't let you sleep as a stranger to me through
this one safe, silky night. . . .

Stirred in her sleep by Yasha's caresses, Bessie reached for
her baby, who throughout infancy had slept between them,

whether on a bed or pallet or plain ground, enlivening their
slumber with sweet stinks and sounds. Her hand clutched and
twisted the linens. She moaned as the sound of Hannah's strangled
breathing smeared across her consciousness and the pain from her
wounded foot tied her calf muscle in a knot.

"I'm sorry," Yasha stammered as her back stiffened to his
touch. He was kneeling behind her on the mattress, swaying
like some great bird in a courtship ritual.

"Don't be sorry," she managed to mutter through dry lips.

"I just need to be with you," he said urgently. "It's the one
night . . ." He tugged her hip and mushed his bristly face into
her belly. "Oh, God, I want to be with you! It's why I'm here,
to make you feel better, it's why I'm on this earth!" He crawled
clumsily over her knees and then rose straight-backed at the foot
of the bed. She could feel his excitement swelling, his seams
bursting. His hands slid under her backside; his bushy hair
brushed her thighs. Moaning, swaying, he cried, "I love you,
Bessie! I want another baby, now. I want to squeeze it from this
body!"

She reached down and found his cheek, his ear. "Please, my
luftmensch—get me some water."

Yasha froze, then drew back from her like some dark, brooding snake. Bessie grabbed for his hand. "I just want to be able
to kiss you," she whispered hoarsely. "I'm so dry."

In the morning they sat at the curtained window, inspecting
Bessie's few belongings in the daylight. Yasha was still in his
underwear, relaxed and purring with good humor.

He would bring her to the building of the International Red
Cross, he explained. He would introduce her there as a refugee:
an American-taught private nurse to an elderly American businessman who had been killed, say, by a band of thieves near
Novorossisk. Because of their personnel shortage, the Red Cross
was sure to welcome her, he said, first as a patient, later as a
nurse, particularly upon his recommendation as "Mr. Lemhoff
of the YMCA. Mr. Lemhoff is German-born, which is why he
speaks English like a kike."

Bessie could feel her spirit crawling back to her as Yasha
relieved her for the first time in months of responsibility for the
future. Beyond that sense of relief, however, she was unfeeling.

Every uncontrolled meditation seemed to bottom out in misery or foreboding, so she curtailed them, concentrating instead on her husband's instructions and encouragements.

"The Jacob Schiff pin!" he hurrahed. "You've still got it. Oh, I'm telling you, the fates are on our side!" The gold pin from her Montefiore Hospital benefactor had earned the status of a true charm by turning up time and time again throughout the war after days or even weeks of neglect, usually at the brink of loss in a torn pocket or worn-out satchel. "It's a perfect calling card," Yasha went on. "You couldn't be more convincing if you carried a tongue depressor in your brassiere!"

Next he examined her red shawl, full of holes and pulled threads. "Wear it, it's elegant. You're supposed to look like a refugee."

"Supposed to?"

"Wait, what's this?" He had found her Party card, the one bearing Lenin's signature, among a string-bound batch of papers. "Oh, God, Bessie, if you were caught with this . . ."

"You said *we* would enter Alushta, not Wrangel!" she argued.

"*Nudnik*, there are two armies fighting. How can I predict whose cannon will fire better?"

"Ours will!" She snatched the soft-worn cardboard from his fingers.

Yasha cocked his head as though listening for her thoughts. She returned his gaze with pleading intensity. He patted her knee. "It's been your fig leaf, I bet."

"More," she said. "Much more. It's the only thing that makes me different, even with the typhus, even with the haircut, even on the street. I'm a Bolshevik. I met Lenin!"

"Shh, give me the card." He stretched out his hand. "I'll hold it, and you hold me. I can always call it a souvenir that I picked up somewhere. Obviously my name is not Bessie Levovsky."

Sniffling, she raised her head and handed him the precious card.

"My name is now Frederick Lemhoff." He was suddenly speaking English in a voice flushed of warmth. "I work with the Young Men's Christian Association. You will call me Mr. Lemhoff, do you understand? Good. Then you understand, too, that I can do nothing for you now but hold your hand like a father and quote to you from the Scriptures."

"In your underwear?" She giggled, but regretted her joke

as he began to dress, removing himself from their intimacy garment by garment.

"You'll visit me," she begged him. "When you can . . ."

He held her hand. "My love, *you* are my Party assignment now. I'm here to make you better, as well as to find out who's who in town. Who will sympathize with us if we return to Alushta? And we will return, believe me. The Whites are falling apart; they're made of shoddy stuff. It's just that the seacoast towns have to contend with all the garbage as it streams out of Russia forever." He glanced about slowly at the rumpled bed, the dresser mirror, the streaky window. "Collect everything, even your shadows. I'll meet you at the blacksmith's barn in fifteen minutes."

"The way I limp around, I need more time."

Yasha nodded and waved her out the door.

While stranded on the streets, Bessie had been able to shun her memories and plow under her fears, chanting slogans to herself, labeling hardship as necessity, suffering as sacrifice, homelessness as internationalism. There had been no letup, moreover, in the demands made on her by the scores of survivors of the sea voyage from Novorossisk who were strewn like crabs throughout the ramshackle fishing village.

Then Yasha's regiment had swept through, collecting the healthy, supplying food and blankets to the sick and unfit and organizing them into mutual-aid teams. Departed within hours of their arrival to confront Wrangel's renegades in the North, they had left behind tranquil streets. Bessie's walk to the blacksmith's barn was torturously peaceful but for the pain in her lame foot, which seemed to magnify as she fretted about the possibility of infection

No infection, they declared at the Red Cross following her admittance, then bathed her with sponges and tucked her between sheets in a warm but airy room of honey-colored wood. Four other women, indistinguishable lumps beneath their blankets, were asleep despite the blaze of daylight from the windows. Their slow breathing and snuffling, and her own empty, watchful mood—missing Yasha, feeling helpless again—it was Novorossisk all over, that misshapen evening-into-dawn of Hannah's death. Bessie lay in her crinkly bed, shuddering as her memories rolled across her face, memories like molten metal from the caldron of war in which she had boiled for more than two and a half years, memories like shrapnel exploding across her bed . . .

"Here's music to make the gefilte fish dance!" cries Pesach the Lip, mouthing his harmonica as momma carries the appetizer to the sabbath table. Poppa is sullen, ready to smash his fist to the table and shout for silence while Yasha vaults to his feet and performs a solo polka around the room. Bessie's insides are twisted. How can she eat, feeling this way?

Poppa watches her, tests her, postpones his outburst. Why won't Yasha stop so they can sit and eat? But now Pesach's playing revolutionary songs, gasping for breath between bars, and Yasha is whirling, grinning, stomping his feet on every step, singing: "With hearts heavy and sad we bring our dead/Who shed their blood in the fight for freedom."

And look at the gefilte fish, bouncing on the platter! Smash! goes poppa's fist. Bessie bolts from the table, her head throbbing. Yasha shimmies toward her, arms outstretched. "No!" She ducks under his advance.

Running, aching. Cornhusk dolls are strewn in a row from the side door of the house to the well in the backyard. Bessie hurries, gathering them up to bring to the children at the hospital, then dumps them in a heap as she hears Hannah's weeping voice, far away. Down in the well? On tiptoe, Bessie peers into the dank, drafty shaft. She sees water glistening, dark shapes bobbing, clustered around the water pail, reaching up the rope.

Now she cranks the pulley, fetching the pail foot by foot into daylight. It steams and stinks in the air, filled to the brim with brown slime. Bessie shuts her eyes and dumps the mess over the railing of the Iron Pier, and the ocean swallows the stain and sweeps back.

There she is, there's Hannah on the bench, kicking her naked legs, waiting to be diapered. Bessie rushes to her, feels her smooth behind, and gazes deeply into her eyes: beady little slits, the face strangely cherubic, cheeks like hard apples, lips swollen, cherry-red, pouting. "You're not my Hannah . . ."

The creature spits an acrid stream of blood and rises up with sprouted wings to lunge at Bessie's eyes. Bessie screams and flings it over the railing. . . .

She convulsed awake. The dream slithered, still breathing, beneath the bed. Bessie filled her lungs with air and was relieved to see the daylight, yet lay still so as not to lose memory of the dream....

There was time, now, to think. Time at last to sew up the holes in her life so that the future would not pass through it like loose change from a torn pocket. Bessie doubled up her pillow and leaned back against it, calling to her ghosts, those in the well: Before you catch cold, my dears. Come, visiting hours are in session at the Red Cross. I'm as far from the war now as a cloud in heaven. Come, your death will not be contagious.

Oh, sweet Smulevitch, you first. With chains around your neck and death in your eyes, you found words to give me freedom and life. I lie here now, and I'm like you, Jacob. I told you I would be, no? You're my dybbuk, Red Beard, I am possessed. Even in the warmest rooms, even in my husband's embrace, I feel your cold chains dragging across my mind and I remember what love really means and what freedom really costs. And then I rise, rise! Because I'm going to build a hospital in your name, Jacob. I am. In my new Soviet Union. And can we give it a Jewish name? Beth Jacob. What would you say now if I asked, Are you a Jew? So many thousands of our people killed this one infamous year, Jacob. Can we mourn them in any language but the *mameloshn?* Can we avenge them with any act but revolution?

Honor to your memory, comrade.

Hi, Tsil. Hi, dear. Do you remember the games we played? Of course you do—you never lived long enough to forget them. Do you remember how we made up nicknames for all the good citizens of Mogilev-Podolsk? Thinking we saw animal spirits in their faces, their postures, their occupations: Itche the groundhog and Nakhum the sea gull, Ruchel the pheasant, and Tsil the goat. But did you have a second name of your own? I don't remember, I remember only Tsil. What did they write on your tombstone? Here Lies Tsil—Who Played with Hobnails, Who Collected Pebbles, Who Loved Buzie. So it went; every day brought us a new name for a new game. This was revolutionary! To be named for our deeds, our deeds only.

But with that, my Hannah goes nameless. My tiny jewel in the sand. You were not of this earth long enough to do deeds or even to inherit the pet names my mother left to me. Oh, dear, be kind. Leave my dreams now, leave. We have no accounts to settle; you were too young to keep accounts. The failure's all mine: I built the nest too shallow, and your sister pushed you out, as she did to me, out of childhood, out of motherhood. But I hovered, I flew, while you fell like a stone. . . .

A rustle of linens disturbed Bessie's séance. She leaned up on her elbows, light-headed but alert, and saw a group of three— two nurses and a stout, white-jacketed man—entering the room to make rounds. The man immediately arrested her attention: Evidently a doctor, greeted warmly by the patients whose examinations he supervised, he held an attraction for Bessie reaching deeper than her need for medical care. Whereas all else in the room stood starkly apart from her dreams and memories, arousing her to be cautious, he seemed not so foreign or threatening. A comrade? she wondered fancifully, gaping at him, searching her impressions for an answer, becoming so engrossed as he neared her bed that his first words, in English, evaded her altogether.

Suddenly his meaty hand encircled her throat, as though in the span of her daydream some awful decision had been reached.

"Relax, my dear."

He was simply probing for her glands, with a gentle touch. Bessie sat passively on the mattress edge for the remainder of the examination, which included some painful prodding of her wounded foot. Throughout, the doctor plied her with questions, distracting her from her pain far more than he could have realized as she sweated to comprehend enough of his English to both reinforce her masquerade and give information, crucial to her well-being, about her bout with typhus, her weight loss, her wound.

"I understand you're a nurse," said the doctor, "with a rather expensive recommendation from Jacob Schiff."

The philanthropist's name needed no translation. Bessie hazarded a reply: "I know him at Montefiore Hospital. I work as a nurse."

"I've never been there," said the doctor, letting down her blouse, then folding up his stethoscope. "But Schiff was not the businessman who brought you here to the Soviet Union."

She noted with interest his use of Russia's new and revolutionary name and stole another peek at his exceedingly familiar, silver and gray, square-cut beard. Who was he? Her fists were curled around the answer. Then Yasha bounded into the room, heels clicking on the hardwood floor, a Bible tucked into his armpit. He seemed to falter as the doctor turned his way, but never broke stride. "Hello, Miss Charles," he hailed Bessie in English. "I came to see how you're getting along."

"Thank you, Mr. Lemhoff. I like to see you." Very, very much! She nearly bobbed up to kiss him as he came toward her bedside with a private grin on his face. She wanted to scold him for dancing through her dreams, trick him into speaking Yiddish, pull him into bed . . . Oh, for the day when the Red Army would take the town!

Yasha swiveled toward the doctor and offered his hand. "Lemhoff of the YMCA. You must be Dr. Blum."

Bessie's recognition exploded from her lips, startling everyone. At the mention of his name, Gideon Blum's face and manner had become preciously familiar to her, like some flitting bird suddenly stock-still upon a windowsill. "Dr. Blum! I can't believe it! It's as though the whole world were built upon my very own life!"

Blum squinted at her, comprehending her Yiddish but maintaining silence.

"Don't you know who I am?"

"Really, I treat so many," he demurred in the mother tongue, but with a self-conscious glance at the nurse still in attendance. "Let me see . . . Charles . . . Charles . . ."

"Charles-shmarles!" she squealed. "*Ich bin* Buzie Kharlofsky! Kharlofsky!"

Blum's hand sailed across his scalp.

"There!" Bessie cried, triumphant. "And you, here! If I had thought . . . I would guess that you're still in Germany, like when I wrote to you from Ysyakh. . . ." The words fell from her tongue before she could catch them. Embarrassment at once made her eyes drop. That girlish letter, as she recalled it, was full of whining concern about menstruation!

Blum scrutinized her face to cement his memories, but in a somber, stiff manner that made Bessie feel more exposed than comforted by their prior relationship. She had expected and invited with her enthusiasm a hug, or a handshake, or at least a flurry of nostalgic inquiries. Instead, she was under investigation, and regretted dredging up her political past as their first topic of conversation.

When at last he asked, "What are you doing in Alushta?," she lied neatly:

"It's as Mr. Lemhoff said when he brought me here. I was a

businessman's nurse. I had been living in New York with Leah—hey, you remember her, my oldest sister?"

"Leah, of course." The memory fetched a smile from him, but Yasha's nervous entry into the conversation—"You know one another, do you?"—erased it.

"So it seems," Blum replied. "I understand, Mr. Lemhoff, that you are of German extraction, is that right?" Blum switched abruptly into German to inquire into Yasha's background. Bessie managed to decipher much of it with her Yiddish as a tool.

Yasha acquitted himself decently, she thought. "But I have been an American citizen for many years," he concluded, maneuvering the conversation back into English, with which both men were more or less equally skilled.

"Not so many, I think," the doctor said. "You're a young man—not much older than she. So. Buzie Kharlofsky. It is good to see you alive and healthy. When you're up and around, let's have a chat. But first, get well."

She bowed her head as though receiving a blessing. Blum uttered some phrase of instruction to the nurse, bowed curtly to Yasha, and strode from the room.

Yasha's brow was plainly etched with concern. "Tell me, how do you know each other?"

"Oh, don't you remember? He's the one who—"

His nostrils flared wide. "Excuse me, Miss Charles. Unlike Dr. Blum, I am very bad with Yiddish."

"Oh . . . yes." She slumped back onto her pillow. "Is too long for me, this story, in English. You got time for a long story?"

The nurse came between them with a thermometer.

Dr. Blum and Bessie had their chat three weeks later, on Christmas Day, by which time she was functioning as a nurse and hardly limping as she made her rounds through the baronial mansion that housed more than seventy patients—including five comrades from Novorossisk, whom she swore to secrecy regarding her identity.

She had already assisted the doctor in several surgical procedures—removing bullets from wounds and a fishhook from a local boy's throat—two births, and countless examinations, but their interaction had been of necessity confined to the business at hand; Blum was polite but aloof, treating her no more familiarly than he did any of the women on staff. Bessie interpreted his distance as a reprieve, consciously granted her as a gift, from the pressures and pricklings of his suspicion.

Pressures came her way instead from Yasha, with whom she lunched frequently and had rendezvoused three times during the month for a night together in the hotel. Yasha was on edge, strained by his prolonged masquerade and by the information gap separating him from his regiment. He was finding the people of Alushta to be less pro-Bolshevik than he'd hoped, though the opinions they expressed in the presence of an *Amerikaner,* even one with the reputedly liberal YMCA, were sure to be shaded toward conservatism, he realized. Still, frank discussions with the village notables—the priest, the constable, the owner of Alushta Cannery Works, the undertaker—as well as with workingmen, fishermen, and shopkeepers, had revealed to him a widespread, war-weary neutrality tempered by a distinct resentment of the swelling refugee problem. Worse, there were certain anti-Semitic, pro-White Guard elements who had twice scribbled on walls and windows violent slogans against Jews, Communists, and "German agents." Yasha suspected and feared that these fanatics might be organizing themselves into an armed faction. The Jewish community, in turn, was as jittery as a caged bird, small, helpless in feeling and circumstance, clinging to their shul and their pushcarts and ready to peck at anything that moved or cast a long shadow nearby.

Little of this came as news to Bessie. She had been among the comrades from Novorossisk as they had been denied friendship and assistance from all quarters, including the church. She had watched peasant women and their children, obviously neutrals in flight from the northern battle zones, digging for clams or fishing with string and safety pins in order not to starve in the face of the town's lack of charity. Her patients had told her tales of the Revolution that were full of pain and disappointment and left her gasping for want of optimism.

She was therefore less interested in Yasha's investigations than fearful for his safety. He was a skilled actor, no doubt, erudite beyond her expectation in matters of Christian faith, Russian history, German culture and geography, and other fields of likely interest to a YMCA man, yet she felt a fearful embarrassment on his behalf whenever a friendly townsperson crossed their path, as though "Mr. Lemhoff" were merely a boy shuffling in his father's shoes and fooling no one but himself.

Their nights together in the hotel were a strange, unnerving mix of pleasure and anxiety. The proprietor would barely look up to offer a civil word as they passed his desk; yet time and time again as she mounted or descended the stairs, she would catch him sneaking glances at her like some scheming rodent eyeing a piece of cheese. The window in their room was a gash in their privacy, always on the verge of shattering; the mirror gave an unbearably stark portrayal of their frailty; the door was a lean sentry; the bed was a heady, vaporous dream. She would cry to her husband, "You're my world, my everything!" and repeat it softly as she lay in the crook of his arm long after their lovemaking. With all her blunted hopes, she turned to him for repair; all her new world visions had been humbled to simpler dreams about their family-to-be and a normal, healthful life somewhere.

Migraine headaches assaulted her for the first time in years, laying her low for whole days. Loud noises jolted her into near-panic and clumsy mishaps. She threw herself into her nursing tasks with indefatigable energy, cherishing the health of her patients but never sharing the comfort that she provided them. Yet her despair remained inarticulate until Gideon Blum at last accosted her on Christmas Day.

She had just entered through the glass-paneled doors of the Red Cross mansion following a shivering stroll along the beach. Dr. Blum leaned from his office door and beckoned to her, luring her from the hubbub of the ongoing party in the lobby. Two glasses of red wine stood on the ink blotter on his desk.

"Look here what the baker gave me for Hanuka," Blum said in Yiddish as he slid open a drawer. "Fresh mandel bread! Without so much as asking if I'm a Jew. Help yourself, dear." He held out a glass to her. "I've been looking forward to this, as I hope you have. It's hard to be a Jew in this organization, even if you speak with sophistication in five languages. I think we need a Red Mogen Dovid rather than a Red Cross here in the Ukraine." He sniffed his wine as though it were a flower. "There, you see, I've become a Zionist in my old age. And you, what have you become?"

She sipped her wine to brace herself by its bitterness. "I've become a nurse," she said, to defuse his investigation, but with genuine pride. "It's the one sure way to do good in this world."

"Spoken like a true healer. I share your belief, heart and soul." Blum clicked his glass against hers. "*L'chaim*, then. To our dreams of the past. May they prevail against all nightmares of the present."

Outside the office door, the other nurses were unwrapping gifts, chatting in French, laughing at the quips of some local businessmen who had come to wish them holiday cheer. Outside the sunny window, boys were hollering and running through the street as the church let out its services. Bessie sipped from her glass again and gazed at the motes of dust swirling in the shafts of sunlight.

Blum rolled his glass between his immaculate palms, then set it down decisively. "I must tell you, I think your Mr. Lemhoff is a fraud. Do you agree? Ach, Buzie, don't flinch. Why don't you sit?"

(Hold still, stupid! You can't lie, because he already knows the truth. But you can pretend, because he's a gentleman. . . .)

"Perhaps I say it too baldly," Blum added, "but this is my diagnosis."

Bessie's voice was pitifully weak and tinny. "I did not know you were making an examination."

"I'm afraid it did not take great effort," he replied. "Obviously he's not a missionary, not even a Christian. He's a Jew. And not a German, either, but a Russian."

His pinpoint accuracy devastated her. She felt more brittle than the glass in her hand. The tiny bit of wine in her stomach soured.

"Of course, I am a Jew and a German," Blum said, watching her closely. "For the lay person, his disguise works quite well, I would say. Even the priest seems convinced. But I, I watched the two of you. I know you, Buzie. You haven't changed." He stepped aside from his desk and offered her a slice of mandel bread. She felt too nauseous to even hold the food in her hand.

"Too dry for you," he observed. "The truth sticks in your throat."

At this her hackles rose. "From the moment you saw me here, you've held my past against me!"

Blum held up a cautionary finger. "Not so. You know me better than that. I've been a progressive man always—I simply don't believe that bombs can bring a solution!" He lowered his ponderous weight to a chair across from her. "I'm a doctor, not a politician. Still, I try to please God. What about the letter you wrote to me from your exile? Were you just flattering me with the praise you heaped? About my charity toward the poor, my attempts to have you released—ohh, I remember that letter, Buzie! It was dreadfully important to me, to have my work affirmed that way, if only by a child!"

"You were a friend," she agreed, shamefaced, her head bowed.

"How could I do otherwise for a child? Bad enough that I abandoned our town and your father! Conditions became intolerable—I had another life to lead, I said to myself. But your letter tailed me—for once, the postal system was efficient!—it tailed me all the way to Berlin. My God! And I want you to know," he added, leaning closer still, "that by the time I managed to accumulate the money you requested, you'd already escaped. I heard it from your mother."

She was ready to confess. The breath was there in her lungs, the words were teetering on her lips, if he would simply squeeze her once more. They both rose to their feet, Blum returning to his place of authority behind his desk, Bessie wobbling, sick and uncertain.

"Now, I trust you to do what comes naturally to you," Blum said. "I know with whom I'm dealing, Buzie Kharlofsky. I remember the day you were arrested: In the morning, your father came and told Reb Yankel and me that you had been sneaking all over town, in contact with your brothers' gang. When he accused you, he said, you played the cutie pie. Nonetheless, you delivered his message to your brothers—to your own enduring misfortune."

"I was a child," she murmured. "Maybe I had foolish ideas."

"And now you are an adult," Blum warned, "so stop with the foolish ideas! Let's swallow our medicine before it evaporates completely, Buzie. The fact of the matter is that the Red Cross cannot remain in Alushta. The town is very close to a take-over, and if the White Guard conquers, I myself will be endangered, both as a German and as a Jew, along with others on my staff. And if the Bolsheviks come—well, my dear, the Red Cross is simply not a revolutionary organization. We cannot help further their godless cause."

His words nauseated her, as already her organs were floating upside down, all out of place. She pinched the beveled edge of his desk to steady herself and swallowed rapidly like a bullfrog to control the rising nausea.

"If you and your Mr. Lemhoff wish to come to Turkey with us," he said, "you may. I would even request that you do—there's good work to be done with us, Buzie, we are internationalists in the truest sense. But you have a few days to decide, as I know you'll need. This is your life's work, and I respect that fact. So. There's an American ship, the *Black Eagle*, a warship, headed our way from Constantinople."

Bessie laughed, then caught her breath like a paranoiac, knowing at once that Yasha would say no. Just as he had danced in her dream, he could not, would not, stop.

"My dear? You don't look well—is there something—"

Bessie gagged and fled from the room.

The *Black Eagle* again. Dull gray and motionless against the horizon. Beyond it lay Turkey, where Denikin now lived, driven out of history, ushered to oblivion by Captain Owen, his armies and his evil reduced to sea scum. And Wrangel would be next: The Red Cross radio operator had had word on his receiver days before of the White Guard's dissolution up north. If she could only brace herself now, cling to the rocks like a starfish at the turning tide. Clamp shut her clamshell and eat garbage with the rest of the refugees, long enough to survive. Or dig down, a sand crab, burrowing northward to some secure communist stronghold, way behind the battle lines, where the future was already in place.

The future lay in her womb, instead. Precious, delicate, tangible if only in the nausea she felt each morning and the food she craved all day. The world seemed inhabited by a mere dozen human beings, all returning to her now to beckon her to safety, away from the illusory "masses" and the ideals that had fallen like torn sails across the deck of her ship.

Yes, I'm pregnant, she announced to the American captain, god of the sea, who smiled down at her from the cloudbanks.

I'm pregnant! she cried to Hannah's bones in the earth. I'm pregnant, she told the waves as they spared none of the eroding beach this New Year's Day of a new decade in the new world. . . .

"Go, have the child. Take Blum's offer. I'll call for you."
"No, Yasha, we're both pregnant."
"All Russia is pregnant, mamenyu, *and at the point of delivery."*
"Then we'll stay, damn it, we'll get through! Like always. I won't worry."

So she had agreed. In the honey-colored room, with Yasha's hand pressed in hers, with a hundred refugees daily coming to plead for the opportunity to escape that Dr. Blum had reserved for her, she had agreed. To stay, to spy, to fight, to die. For Yasha, no longer for some greater cause. For him.

But I'm pregnant! she screamed at the two hundred thousand dead Ukrainian Jews whose bodies had poisoned the landscape for her.

I'm pregnant, she wept to Mrs. Markish of the Bronx, to Jacob Schiff, whose gold pin still hung on her lapel.

An arc of freezing water swept across her shoes, shocking her old wound and cramping the soles of her feet. Bessie jumped back as the water fizzled down into the gasping sand.

She gathered her duffel bag into her arms and walked. Having left the Red Cross without a flourish, unwilling to officialize her decision before seeing Yasha again, she felt now an urgency to get on with it, the two of them in his room, committing their lives to one another and stepping into the future. But there was no hurrying along the beach, where people had gathered by the wretched hundreds to worship the distant warship, scavenging fuel for their fires, trading their possessions, spreading wildly ignorant rumors. Their children squatted at play among heaps of clamshells, empty tins, fish carcasses, and sandy, sopping papers and rags. Bessie hated and resented them all for their neutrality, their single-minded instinct to leave the tormented land. . . .

"But if we stay, my luftmensch, remember: You owe your life to me. Forever. No sudden surprises, ever."

"*Such an optimist! You're the kind of woman who gives birth to a two-headed child, you know that? You can't make up your mind what to do.*"

"*Sha, sha, I'll stop thinking. I've already made up my mind for you. Hold me, Levovsky.*"

"Look!" yelled a refugee woman, sputtering potato and pointing her gaunt hand across the water. People at once rushed into the freezing sea up to their knees to wave and holler at the string of boats that had been launched by the *Black Eagle*.

Bessie pushed on to the end of the beach where the sand gave way to boulders and dead ferns, then entered a stand of white pine separating the waterfront from the town's main road. Here the ground was brittle with frosted leaves and pastry-thin pools of ice, crunching to mud beneath the boots of scores of people in exodus toward the beach. Bessie hiked her woolen skirt and lifted the duffel bag to her shoulder, wondering how Captain Owen would handle this onslaught of hundreds more than he'd handled at Novorossisk.

On the street, too, people were hurrying past her, egging on their children, clutching bundles, panting with effort, all headed in the direction opposite hers. At last she stood still, alarmed by the mass movement. They were running from something, eyes at the backs of their heads. She turned a corner and collided with a comrade from the camp in Novorossisk, still wearing the bandage she'd wrapped around his bloody brow two months earlier. His face was a sweaty ball of red and he was panting like a dog. "What is it?" she whispered, clinging to his blanket to impede his headlong flight. He gulped for air, began to stammer something, then pushed past her as she loosed her grip, her eyes rolling up the street, her feet starting to backpedal.

A mob of men, horses, and banners were gathered before the blacksmith's barn. At their head rode a cossack on an enormous white stallion that kept rearing up and pawing the air with awful grandeur. Torches blazed among them, spotty in the daylight, throwing a halo of heat distortion over their center. A second Novorossisk survivor, tailing the first, shouting into Bessie's disbelieving face: "Wrangel's murderers, a handful, and greeted like the Messiah by the scum of this town! Watch your ass—they're hunting us down!"

The report of a gun dislodged him in panic from her path.

Bessie saw the White Guard supporters stealing horses and hardware from the barn as the smithy stood beside their torches with
folded arms, helpless but defiant. Over his head, less than a
hundred yards beyond his barn, the "Rooms for Rent" sign on
Yasha's hotel quivered in the heated air like an underwater message. Bessie's mouth was chalky, her tongue a strip of parchment.
Another careless gunshot dropped her to a crouch. She hugged
her duffel bag to brace herself against the onrushing stampede of
frightened human beings. Boots and shoes clattered past, drum-
ming up her own flight instinct, but she remained rooted like
an acorn near the mother tree. . . .

*"I gave birth to our first with the sound of guns in my ears.
For this one I want to hear only birds and crickets and then her
cry of life."*

*"But you know she'll come out singing the 'Internationale,'
if she's any daughter of mine."*

"Oh, you! You'll go out singing, won't you?"

"I hope it will be so."

*"As long as you're old and senile by then, I hope, too. Now
stop, Yasha, there's no one giving prizes to revolutionaries today."*

*"Or to worry-warts. You keep nagging me not to die. I'm
sure the Angel of Death is not so good a nudge as you."*

"That's why I'm a nurse."

"And a revolutionary? Persistence is our weapon."

"Yes, that too. Always. . . ."

"You're still my Bessie, then."

Still his Bessie. She rewound her ratty red shawl around her
head. The forest of legs and skirts thinned out around her. Even
the mob up the block seemed quieter, waiting like sharks for
blood to be spilled as the blacksmith dared to argue for his
property with the mounted cossack. Fixing her eye on Yasha's
window, she rose up.

A small boy slammed into her and bounced off her chest with
a shocked expression. Bessie fell back against her duffel bag,
then took the child into her arms and fetched his cap, a dried-out
leather thing that she pressed into his chest. "Here, little comrade. Don't cry now."

She said this in Yiddish, without thinking. He wrinkled his

nose and regarded her warily, then tugged his cap on with two hands, in polished imitation of a sporting man, his elbow brushing her eyelash. She flinched but held him. "Are you hurt?" she asked, now in Russian.

A great shout went up. The barn had been torched and was belching white smoke. She held the boy at arm's length, stared into his glossy eyes, and forced herself to smile. "Don't be scared, boy. I'm a nurse. I'll take good care of you."

"Mikhail! Mikhail!" A woman was bleating from the edge of the pine woods. The boy brightened at the sound and tugged away from Bessie's hold. "Sha, be still," she insisted, "I'll carry you to her." She drew him yet closer, gathering him up, but his whine mounted like a siren and he shoved his hand into her cheek, pushing her head back, a finger gouging her nostril. She groaned as though disemboweled as he broke free and ran.

"Your cap!" She scooped it up and waved it feebly. Gunpowder hung in the air, stinging her scratched nose and eyes. Glass was shattering up and down the street. The barn fire raged, with one group fighting the flames and another fanning them with torches. Men pummeled one another and rolled in the mud. One lay dead, staring at the sun. Bessie waded through the smoky carnage like a shadow, her eye fixed on Yasha's glinting second-story window, as people ran toward the beach and clipped her left and right.

The hotel owner was standing guard before his double doors at the top of the stoop with a stewpot inverted on his head and a shotgun cradled in his arms. Bessie took a step up the stairs, but he shook his head slowly and waved her back with the barrel of his gun.

"My husband," she pleaded, "on the second floor. Please."

"Don't care if he's at the gates of heaven. Nobody comes in while this mess is going on." He gestured toward the street, then pivoted on his heels and readied the shotgun. Two men swerved from his path as though struck by lightning.

"Will you let him come out?" Bessie begged him.

"His bill's paid. In American dollars, too."

She backed up into the street, cocked her head, and screamed Yasha's name, turning her throat inside out until his face appeared in the glass. "Oh, Yasha," she murmured, a hallelujah to herself, then jumped up and down, waving her arms and shouting, "Come down! Hurry!"

The hotel man shouted. Thunder broke at her back and blew her headlong to the ground. It was the cossack rogue, galloping up the street, dragging the blacksmith by a rope tied around his ankles and flanked by two more horsemen, who were shooting their rifles indiscriminately at people, buildings, the clouds, the sun. Bessie was spattered with blood, glass, and filth as the horses' hooves pounded past her skull.

Her ears were clogged with terror, her nostrils with smoke from the dying barn. She opened a single eye and saw a shard of glass stuck upright in the dirt just inches from her face. It fell flat as the earth shuddered once more beneath her cheek. She rolled her head and saw the proprietor sprawled bloody across his staircase. She tried to raise herself, but her trembling arms gave out beneath her weight.

A wall of the barn peeled off, casting fiery chunks at her feet, driving her, coughing and on her knees, through the mud. Up the block, through the haze of smoke, she saw the white horse rearing, stomping the ground. At the base of the hotel wall, a man with hair like Yasha's lay like a bent spoon. Her heart rattled violently against her rib cage. She looked up at the "Rooms for Rent" sign, skeletal in the smoke, and at Yasha's window, obscured, then revealed, obscured, then she screamed. It was an empty, splintered frame.

"Please, don't make me talk on this. It's enough to make a person senile. It's ridiculous—he's dead how long, sixty years? And still I can feel it, that after all our struggle and all my fear, and the times we got separated and the times we got together, and the vision that we shared, after all this that should make us—how do you say it?—indestructible. Then all it takes is a little stinking piece of metal that if you found it on the street you wouldn't even put it in your pocket, and this took the life of my man.

"I wanted to stop the clock. I lost my mind. If I had been old like I am now, or even just sixty-five, I would become senile from the grief. This happened once to a friend of mine, exactly like I'm telling you. Her name is Jessie Rothman. She was a wealthy woman, not with servants, but well protected, if you

know what I mean, even though she was a comrade. Then—
bam—her son Robert dies from cancer, he's all of forty-two.
And a month later her husband dies, natural, but dead is dead.
Then the hammer blow, the third one that drives in the nail—
her daughter, Ruth, she got killed in an automobile crash. Boom,
boom, boom, she had herself a little holocaust, all in one summer. Each funeral, always the same cemetery, I held her up by
the arm, and by the third time she's not even trying to stand
on her own two feet no more. She wanted the earth to take her.
Her body kept going, but her mind stopped. *Oi,* these healthy
ones like Jessie, when they become senile it's a terrible thing.
You almost wish they'd be crippled. 'Cause when they move
around, they find trouble—you find them maybe in a closet,
or at an open window. I know—for years I worked in nursing
homes.

"Jessie is in a nursing home now. Not like that rabbi—what's
his name? Berman, Bergman—you know, I don't remember
names for those that I hate. He builds a sewer, this rabbi, and
calls it a kosher home. But Jessie's in a good home, we got some
other *khaveyrim* living there, excepting she herself is too far
gone to be involved in anything political now. But when she
walks around, she still carries the *Freiheit* under her arm. That's
our *Yiddishe* newspaper, the *Morgn Freiheit*—a better paper
there never was, and I helped begin it in 1922. So Jessie, my
Jessie Rothman, when she carries the *Freiheit*, it gives her life,
y'see. She carries it around like it should be her teddy bear.

"Now the other day, oh, about three years ago, when Jessie
first had her trouble, I found her in her apartment—she lived
here, in the same building as me, only fancier—I found her in
her closet. A mess she was—she didn't bathe, her hair was all
crazy like one of the mops hanging there—yeah, a broom closet.
'What are you doing here, Jessie?' I said. And she says this is
her coffin and she's going to die.

"No, I won't let her die. I believe in life—life is the bottom
line unless you got great physical agony, but for the spirit
there's always hope—I learned this many times. So after I bathe
her and I give her some tea and some crackers, and then she gets
an appetite, and she gets happy like a baby—sure, happy to see
me, to see a human being. So I'm making for her a kugel, and I
stand over the stove 'cause she's lying down, it's okay to leave
her, and I watch the *lukshen* get hot, and I think about what

it is to be senile, what it is to be so unhappy that your mind begins to crumble, your mind goes to sleep. And do you believe it, I burned the noodle pudding? I never burn kugel! But this time I got carried away with dreaming, remembering . . . how when Yasha died, how I lay next to him in the mud, not pretending to be dead, no—I *wanted* to be dead. I wanted the cossack to come back and shoot me between the eyes like a sick horse. It was the first and the only time in my life that I gave up. Even knowing that there was a child in me, it felt like . . . Please, how much do you want to hear about such a miserable kind of a thing?

"Dr. Blum actually came looking and he found me. I almost had my wish, y'see; a bunch of hooligans came and saw me lying with Yasha and they said, 'Aha, she's a Bolshevik.' But Blum defends me; he says, 'No, she's a nurse, and this is her job, to find out if the man is dead.' Some nurse! I looked dead myself. But then Blum shows them the gold pin from Jacob Schiff that it shows I'm from America. Yeah, he actually knelt down and took it from my collar while they stood with guns stuck in his belly. And finally they said okay, and they kept my pin but they let us go.

"Then I had to be led like a girl that she's half-asleep, away from Yasha, away from Russia. We went on the *Black Eagle* to Turkey, Constantinople, and finally to America. The Bolsheviks finally won the civil war, y'see, but then they closed the borders of the Soviet Union for a few years to keep out the counter-revolutionaries that they shouldn't come and start trouble. Now, don't you go thinking, Aha, you see? They close the borders so no one can get out, 'cause they got there a terrible dictatorship. This is easy for you to say, but, tell me, are you going to not lock the door on your apartment after you get rid of a murderer, or a robber? Are you going to let him come back and rob you again?

"But I couldn't go back, either—and to tell you the truth, I didn't want to go back. It's like you wake up suddenly from a dream and you can't go back to it, not even if you fall right back to sleep. So finally you get out of bed and go have a nice breakfast with your family and you tell them about your dreams. What did I have left in Russia, my land of dreams? A few friends—Molly Malinow, Hank Slotnik, a few others that they came to Alushta to mop up the White Guard. Y'see, the reactionaries weren't taking over the town, they couldn't. They were just having a party, a little pogrom, the dirty bastards. But friends, friends when your heart is hanging out of your mouth? Friends are not enough. I was glad to go back to America, I wanted to have my baby in America. Captain Owen brought me on his ship, of course. What a sweet man he was! If all the military men in the world thought like him, they'd play pinochle instead of throwing bombs. I knew him for years after, until World War Two, when he died.

"So I came back. And again Mrs. Markish took me in. She and Lester now lived in Greenpoint, Brooklyn, which was better than the Bronx. They had a house there instead of an apartment, and closer to the Lower East Side, which was to us, like, the cultural center of the world. It was Paul Dropsky, the harmonica man from Mogilev-Podolsk, you remember, he was the one who introduced them to Greenpoint. He lived there, even though he took the name Coney Island Paul. And he was in love with my sister Ruchel—she was a real good-looker if nothing else. So he became a great friend of the family in order that he should be close to her. It used to make Feivl very jealous, and Ruchel would use this as a weapon against her husband: that if he doesn't treat her good or do exactly like she says, then she's gonna go run off with Paul. Excepting that Feivl made a good living while Pesach was a *luftmensch*, and, believe me, my sister Ruchel was not going to follow the call of the wild unless she heard it on a very fancy Gramophone!

"Yeah, sure, we had Gramophones then, and the radio— listen, everyone who was anyone saved up for a radio, what do you think? And you had airplanes flying and automobiles taking over the street. Henry Ford, I remember, he was the big *makher* of the automobile industry and he used to print vicious anti-Semitic articles in his newspaper. It was called the *Dearborn Independent*—independent of brains, I think. And the articles were not in the least subtle. So we got a boycott going on his cars, and it was very successful, y'see, 'cause the boycott is a wonderful thing. The worker has two hands, one that makes and one that buys. If he keeps them both in his pocket, then boy! The boss comes right up and wants to shake hands on a new deal.

"Now, all of these things came to improve life in America, right? Just like I came to improve life in America. It's true. I was still a revolutionary, my ideas didn't get buried with my husband. Maybe because he never got buried, he was still alive in my mind. He stayed with me, like all the other people that they died in front of my eyes, they were still a part of me. I used to talk to them. It's like I saw many times in the hospital: A man loses his arm, but he still feels it, for a long time after, he thinks it's there. But the thing I mean to ask: Isn't it something how, when the human race improves, it's always got to take a war? The Revolution came from the war, the radio came from the war, the airplane. Why is it we get creative only when it comes time to kill? Yankee ingenuity, they call it. Not me, I call it the profit motive. They take your son to Vietnam and they give you a new television to watch him get killed. You get a new toy, a new game, but the rules are the same and we all lose.

"Everyone thinks that the 1920s means gangsters, right? Italians with guns, fighting with Eliot Ness. Listen, it's true, excepting they weren't all Italians—I lived for a while in an apartment building owned by Lepke, a real killer, and a Jew! I didn't know who he was, and he wasn't a bad landlord, actually. . . . But the point is, the gangsters were also in the government, y'see, and in the corporations. There you find the real *gonifs*.

"The United States came out from the war smelling like a rose. We made lots of money—the rich did—and we gained control while the old capitalist countries started to slip. But the Bolshevik Revolution and the Soviet Union that got created, this really scared the pants off these capitalists in America. They felt it right in the *kishkas*. Just the idea that one of the biggest countries in the world should be controlled by the workers! Hoo boy!

"So here in the United States the government makes what you call a 'Red scare.' This is what I came home to. In 1920, f'rinstance, we got a new immigration law, which made it that Jews and Italians and other people from the poor parts of Europe, these people could only come many, many less than before. And then you got raids from the FBI—no, no, excuse me, it wasn't yet the FBI, excepting that what's-his-name, the biggest Hitlerite— J. Edgar Hoover, yeah, he led these raids. The Palmer raids— they named it for the attorney general, Mr. Palmer. We had almost ten thousand arrested, mostly before I even got here. Arrested for what? For being illegal aliens, for being socialists, for being unemployed, anarchists, you name it. The Constitution became a tissue paper that you could wipe your *tukhas* with, if you don't mind my saying. And this was a shameful thing.

"The worst was Sacco and Vanzetti. Them you know about, yeah? Italian anarchists, one sold fish, the other fixed shoes. They got framed for murder and boy, we put up a fight. All over the world we had demonstrations to save Sacco and Vanzetti. I remember once I spoke at the New Star Casino for Sacco and Vanzetti. By accident. I just went to listen, y'see, but then the speaker, Rose Pastor Stokes, she got arrested right there at the door. So we had no speaker. And then the chairman of the meeting, he sees me, and he says, 'Now Bessie is gonna speak.' To hundreds of people he says this. And I'm supposed to talk in English! I nearly dropped dead. But my comrade, Shula Kaplan, she's with me and she says, 'Bessie, you know how when we shmooze over coffee and you tell me your ideas? So pretend now you're just talking to me. Just shmoozing. Go slow.'

"Well, I don't remember what I said, but it was good 'cause I got tremendous applause. After that, they wanted me for a speaker all the time. But it didn't help Sacco and Vanzetti. They got murdered for their ideas. There was no good evidence.

"Now, I said they were the worst case, but really, the worst is what happened to the blacks, the Negro people, that they would take a young black man and accuse him of something, usually of raping someone, y'see, and they would take him and hang him without a trial. Or a trial with twelve Ku Klux Klan on the jury. Now, you talk about mugging, you talk about being scared to go out at night, so can you imagine what it is to know you can get lynched for doing nothing, just for being a human being with brown skin and two legs to stand on?

"The Ku Klux Klan, they had over four million members at this time. Four million! They could make a city from their members. And they did, you know, they actually controlled the governments in places like Texas and Louisiana—even California. Four million members! This is so, so, so much more than the Communist party ever, ever had. But tell me, in school, did you ever learn about the Ku Klux Klan? Did you ever have a lesson about racism, about anti-Semitism, about all this kind of a hatred?

"This is one of the problems in America, y'see: They act like 'racism' is a dirty word, and it is a dirty word, but you can't go cleaning up your mind by brushing your teeth. The whole idea that we can solve something by not talking about it—this is a very *goyishe* kind of a thing, in my opinion, and it's crazy. What people don't understand is that racism is dirty but it's a natural dirt, natural to our way of life under capitalism, natural to America since the time we had slavery, from the very beginning. So anybody who lives in America and is not in some kind of a way racist, that person is either a liar or he's deaf, dumb, and blind like Helen Keller—heh, not so dumb, she was a real progressive, I met her once. Anyway, maybe that person is the Messiah, and then we can all sit back and relax.

"*Oi*, listen to me, I better calm down a minute. I get too excited when I talk about these fascists like the Ku Klux Klan. I get a headache, always with the headaches. But if the time comes when we talk about the fascists and I *don't* get a headache, then you better ask, 'What's the matter, Bessie, are you sick?'

"This is all very personal to me, y'see. Not just 'cause I saw pogroms. But I got a neighbor, f'rinstance, Mrs. Parker, a black woman. Her son, you shouldn't tell anybody, he's in jail. I don't know why, I don't ask. He's upstate in New York, so Viola's got to travel there three, four hours each week to see him. It's making her into an old woman. But the thing is, there are guards in the jail, right here in New York, there are guards that they're Ku Klux Klan. Can you imagine, an ignoramus like that, so full of hatred and sickness, and he's in charge, with a gun and a club, he's in charge of the life of a black man? Of lots of black men! Many of those that they're in jail in America are Negro, y'see—just like we had in Siberia, in most of the prison camps nearly half the prisoners were Jews.

"Anyway, this is how I began to learn about the struggle of the black people. We had in 1931 the Scottsboro boys. These were nine black men, young men, in Alabama, and they were accused of making a rape on two girls. White girls. It was a frame just like you should have around a picture.

"But I'm getting tired of talking about this stuff. I feel like some kind of a dusty old book, if you know what I mean. Now, if you don't know about the Scottsboro boys, just wait, it'll happen again, something just like it, and then you'll learn. 'Cause if I do all the complaining, if I tell you about Sacco and Vanzetti, about the Palmer raids, about Henry Ford and his filthy ideas—he actually gave money to help Hitler get started, did I tell you? But then you're gonna say, 'She's a Communist, she loves Russia, we shouldn't listen.'

"They say this kind of a thing all the time about Jews: We're not loyal, we're not patriotic, we can't be trusted. It almost makes me laugh! I think of Henry Ford, the true-blooded American, and he gives money to Hitler! I think of all the corporations today that they control the earth and they make of a nation a toy, a playground, a garbage dump. You think the imperialists are patriotic for any one country?

"Let me tell you how I think. I may be a Communist, y'see, but you may be dead if you don't listen and learn.

"First of all, my name is Bessie. I'm a woman, a human being. I got a family. Second, I'm a Jew. I've eaten Jewish food a whole life, I read a Yiddish newspaper a whole life, I was discriminated against a whole life. However much I thought of myself in other ways, as a worker, a nurse, a revolutionary, an internationalist, however many layers of clothing I wore to keep warm, it was the Jewish part that was like the handkerchief next to your heart. Not a flag, no. A handkerchief.

"This doesn't mean I'm a Zionist, even though I'll defend the Zionists against those that call them fascists. Sure, there are fascists in the Zionist movement—there are fascists in every movement, including socialists, including in the Soviet Union. This I learned. So I defend the Zionists, 'cause too many times I hear an anti-Semite saying 'Zionist' instead of 'Jew' and then he can get away with it. But I'm not a Zionist myself 'cause I don't believe that Israel is my homeland. America is my home— I live here, I fought here a whole life, my children are here, it's as simple as that. And Jewish oppression, y'see, it's always a part of something bigger. F'rinstance, I read in the *Freiheit* about Argentina. They're persecuting the Jews—you got a fascist bunch there in power, and they're doing terrible things. But what's happening to Jews, y'see, it's a part of what's going on with the whole progressive movement in Argentina. The fascists are out to get us all.

"But this is a big subject. My point is just that Jews can't solve the problem of anti-Semitism by being separate from other nations. We got to have our own nation, sure, 'cause when Hitler made a genocide against us there was nobody to help. And it's a foolish thing to feed your neighbor if you got no food for yourself. But the point is, your food will run out, too, unless you take your neighbor and you plant a little garden together.

" 'Cause we all live together on this little world, so many of us, and we got nowhere else to go. I know, I've been—I traveled all over, on the way to Russia and on the way back. It's not like you have in the Bible when Abraham says to Lot, You and me, our nations, we don't get along so good, so you go over on that side and I'll stay on this side and then we'll have enough room to be happy. Where in the world is a person going to go now, to the moon? I don't want to go there, you got Nixon's name up there! Yeah, you forgot, didn't you? He's got, like, a little plaque with his name on it. I'm sure he lies at night and he's thinking, Oh, boy, I'm the only man with his name on the moon. And I wish I could go there myself just to take his name and kick it into the sun. Already we got pollution on the moon!

"Talk about the moon, my grandson came the other day for a visit and he told me he figured something out: that if you take all the hamburgers that they sold already at McDonald's, if you take these and pile them on top of each other, they would go to the moon and back. There's your monument to Richard Nixon, he should drop dead already. I remember, McDonald's gave him lots of money to get elected, and then he kept the minimum wage low so that the youngsters that they work at McDonald's don't get paid a decent wage. He was one crook, that Nixon.

"I see the moon out my window—if it's there, I see it—and I don't think of hamburgers, y'see, but I look out on all these apartment buildings and I think, What if all the people they should light a candle in their windows all at the same time, and gather their families to have a look? It would be lovely—even the moon would come closer to have a look! And then I think, What if all the people in the whole wide world should for a second put aside what they're doing and hold hands? In a great big circle around the world, and across the ocean we would stand on ships, everywhere we hold hands. In the hospitals, in the caves, people getting born, people dying . . .

"It's impossible, of course. Just the organizing—our lives are always moving and changing; this is the way of the world. But imagine for a second that we could do it. Every soul holding hands. What do you think would happen? This will tell if you're a religious person or not! You think the earth would glow brighter? I'll tell you one thing, and you don't have to be a rabbi to know it: People would never be the same. We would remember this thing and celebrate for a thousand years.

"Now forget holding hands. Here's something we could all do, actually. We could all at the same time stop what we're doing, just stop, and be quiet. *Sha shtil.* Turn off the television, park the car, turn off the oven, finish combing your hair, let the fish swim without catching them, let the children play without teaching them, let the books sit on the shelf, let the money sit in your wallet, and stop. Breathe.

"The ocean, the sky, the earth, you'd see, it would all talk to us. It would say, 'Where have you been?' like you might say to a child. And it would hug us, like a mother hugs the child. If we would just stand still long enough.

"I think maybe the old can better understand what I mean than the young. 'Cause some old people, they can see how foolish it is, all the rushing around. Still, they're scared, the old people, they're scared that the earth will do more than hug them, if you know what I mean. And they're sad, actually, 'cause they can't rush, they can't drive, they got no hair left to comb. Listen, getting old doesn't make you wise—that's a lot of nonsense. If a whole life you wear a mask, then when it gets wrinkled it's still just a mask, and your eyes don't see any better and your heart gets weaker all the time and you get rotten, not ripe. So I'm just talking for myself—maybe I'm just talking *to* myself, who knows? I just know that I'm not afraid to live, not afraid to dance and sing, not afraid that I should feel something deep, something that moves me, maybe even makes me cry, like an old Yiddish song. I'm not afraid of these things—I haven't got like some old people got, arthritis of the heart. After all I lived through, what have I got to be scared of?

"Now, we got a lunch program for the senior citizens here where I live. I helped organize it—we had to fight for seven years to get the city to give it, just that we should have a hot lunch every day for a hundred and fifty senior citizens, for fifty cents. Seven years! Can you imagine if we asked for supper? But when I go there to the community center and I see some of these *alte khalyeras*, how they gotta be the first in line, and they push, and they eat like horses, I lose my appetite, it depresses me, 'cause these people are so pitiful. This is the system we live with, y'see. You take, you don't give. And if you never saw for yourself a revolution, and you have no idea, excepting maybe in your dreams, you have no idea it could be another way—not even at the lunch table . . .

"I'm not saying it so good. I'm not a poet—I wish I was. But when I talk about holding hands, y'see, to me this is socialism. And when I talk about hamburgers to the moon, to me this is disgusting and it's capitalism—how else can you call it?

"The thing is, we got to get along, and have peace, and have respect for each other, and no more genocide. And we got to make a plan together. So never mind holding hands—but nobody should be so rich, so high and mighty, that to him we all look like cockroaches that he can step on us. Socialism means you can walk on the street and feel good about what you see in the windows, on the signs, in the other people's faces. And you can look everybody in the eye.

"Listen, you want to do what we used to call in Workers' School a 'class analysis'? You want to see how America works? Go stand on a street corner, maybe on Wall Street, and watch the people's eyes. The man looks at the woman until her eyes fall. The young stare at the old until the eyes fall. The rich look at the poor, same thing. Whoever got to look down or walk so they always got their eyes on the ground, or those that they take drugs so they can always have their eyes closed— these are the ones that they need revolution the most. Everybody knows this. Everybody plays games of power with their eyes. This is why when they would lynch a black man in the South, you would maybe hear for a reason: 'He looked at me funny.' Funny? He looked at you like a human being, that's all, an honest human being, and he could see right through you.

"Blum said to me, before I left him in Turkey, he said, 'Look at me, Buzie.' And I looked. And I saw there in his eyes all the ghosts. I saw myself to be a child, just a girl in a big, scary world, and I cried. I let it out for the first time, that Yasha was dead, and Hannah was dead, and I had no one to love me, and I could cry all I want 'cause there's no reason not to— nobody is suffering more than me. And then Blum said, 'Good, it's good you should cry. Just like your baby's gonna cry when he comes into the world. You cried, now you can live.'

"It wasn't a boy, my baby, but she sure did cry! The nurses had to wear earplugs! And she looked at me, this baby, she looked and looked and looked into my eyes like she could see all the people living inside me. I'll never forget this. Janet, I named her. This is like Yasha in English, for a girl. Janet Charles —it was too much, already, to keep the name Levovsky. I would have cried every time I looked at her.

"I was living with Mrs. Markish, resting, recuperating. Not just from giving birth. From everything. I was still with pain in my foot from getting shot. My stomach and my gums were bad from typhus. I was a mess. And I couldn't stand to work as a nurse—I didn't want to be close to all that suffering. But there was no other work, 'cause we had an economic slump after the war—first, prosperity, then a depression; it's like a drunk man that he gets a hangover, this is how it goes in America. So eventually I went back to work for my cousin Izzy Markish. He had a great big umbrella factory. A real bourgeois, he became. And he said I could work part-time for as long as I'm not a troublemaker!

"So Mrs. Markish took care of Janet, along with Belle-Brokha —she was already fourteen, maybe older—plus there was Leah's second one, Max—and I went to work. It was good for me, to talk to people again, talk a little politics. . . . I even liked to make the umbrellas. It's good for your mind when your hands are working. And I became politically active very soon. . . . But you've had enough with politics, I think. I'll tell you something better. I met there a man, and he was going to be my second husband.

"Daniel Sainer. Isn't it a nice name? He worked in the factory to make repairs—the machines, the electricity, whatever needed fixing. Then I came along, and Sainer, he had an eye for broken things.

"He was very kind, very intelligent, very progressive, and handsome, too—not like an actor, if you know what I mean, but because he was gentle and intelligent, so he had the kind of a face you can get close to. Very thin hair and a handsome Jewish nose, small blue eyes. Okay? And a kind of a shrewd look, like there was something always going on in his mind.

"I like the kind of a man like Sainer who looks you in the eye. Men have so many kind of a ways to, like, control you. They can talk, they can be very intellectual, especially the radical men, and they can beat you if they gotta, so it's very easy for them to make the rules. But if they look you in the eye, first of all, they see that you're a human being. That's all you need to begin.

"Sainer had lost a wife and had two grown children, and we began to talk on all kind of a things. Then one day he said to me, after a few times that he drove me across the Williamsburg Bridge to Greenpoint—he had a great big car with, how do you call it? Like the gangsters used to have . . . Running boards, yeah. So he says, 'Listen to me, Bessie. You've got a baby girl, and you had a hard life, and a hard life ahead of you. And me—'

" 'No, Sainer,' I said, 'I can't listen to you now.' I knew what he was going to say, y'see. But I tried to say it in such a way that he understood, he wasn't personally insulted. He was always a sensitive man, like not too many men that I know—that quiet way of understanding. So I really didn't have to worry. 'Cause the next day he comes to work and he gives me a key, and he says, 'This key opens the door to a little cabin in Camp Nishtgedeiget'—this means 'Don't Worry'—Camp Don't Worry. It was a new place that it belonged to the radical movement, near Beacon, New York. And Sainer said, 'I already paid that you should have food for a week and wood for the stove. So go, rest with your baby in the country. When you come back, maybe then we'll have a talk, if you feel like it.'

"Ohh, goodbye, Cousin Izzy! I remember, it was the beginning of October. There was nobody there but a caretaker and a couple of writers. And every night there were shooting stars. So I counted them, I made wishes, I played all kind of a games, I shivered and wrapped myself in blankets and watched the stars. And I fed my baby. From the Milky Way, yeah. From the Milky Way."

PART TWO

Chapter Fifteen / 1934

"My favorite smell, that I will take with me to the grave, is the way the earth and the trees smell before the rain. Even here on the seventh floor, I can smell it from the park down there, and when it rains I open the window and I breathe. If someone should see me, they think, She's crazy, what does she want, pneumonia? But it's such a thing to smell the earth's perfume— I don't care if it brings pneumonia.

"The sidewalk starts to steam from the humidity and you know it's gonna rain, any second . . . and when I smell this, I remember Camp Nishtgedeiget. There you had it—the smell of life. Every day with my Janet, and she was so happy, so good, and I felt glad that I lived through the revolution to have this baby, to smell this rain, to keep going on with the fight.

"I ended up staying there three weeks, and then two more for my honeymoon. You know when I got a vacation like that again? Now! Excepting when you're an *alte khalyera* like me and you think about your health so much, it's not exactly a vacation. But I'm not complaining! Listen, I intend to hold in my arms my great-granddaughter, so don't worry, I got time.

"Every year Sainer sent me to Camp Nishtgedeiget for a vacation. And in a certain kind of a way, he himself was my vacation. It's not like he was so rich or something that I didn't have to work—I worked plenty, as a nurse, mostly at night. And from this I learned to crochet and do that kind of a work with my hands, 'cause there's not so much to do at night in the hospital, not all the time, 'cause the people are sleeping, which is the best medicine of all. So one day, a long time after I came to feel like myself again, I brought out my red shawl that to me it was like a prayer shawl, and I decided to fix it up nice. I wanted to make a little jacket—I thought it was too old-fashioned to wear a shawl. I learned from another nurse how to work with lace, y'see. . . . This just now reminds me of a Yiddish song that we used to sing in the Jewish People's Fraternal Chorus. It says, 'From the coat, I made a jacket, almost new. From the jacket, I made a vest, almost new. From the vest, a cap; from the cap, a pocket; from the pocket, a button; from the button— a song!'

"So I worked, sure, but Sainer was my vacation from being crazy, from running all the time, from worrying. I had with him a home and a man that he would be there, not going here and there like a Wobbly on the freight trains. Sainer was older than me, maybe ten years, y'see, and he wanted a home.

"I was a full-grown woman and enjoying myself. Listen, I could even vote—1920 was the year that the government admitted that I'm a human being even though I'm a woman, yeah? Excepting here, y'see, I was too radical, 'cause I used to say, 'What's a vote when you got a snake running against a vulture?' The radical movement saw women's issues only as a part of the class struggle, and the suffragettes had lots of rich women in their movement, so we were extremists, we made fun.

"Later on I learned different—I did what you call 'women's work' in the Communist party. I don't mean I typed, I mean I organized women for the Party, and we demonstrated against home relief and against evictions and against the high cost of living, and then I came to understand the woman question in a broader kind of a way. I came to love my sisters with a political feeling, y'see—they were the ones that I could really have a conversation with and we would understand each other. Just to become active, we had to figure out what to do with our kids, how to get supper on the table before you go to the meeting, how to gain a little confidence so you should be able to talk to a meeting . . . so we had a very deep and natural kind of a solidarity. And I came to feel this, especially when I myself had trouble in the Party for being an independent woman with a big mouth. The men didn't want me for a leader, I can tell you that.

"But Sainer was my *khaver*, a real comrade. And soon we

had a son, Jacob. I began to feel like a great big tree that it's blooming all over—excepting I never grew past five feet!

"Sainer and I were both members in the Communist party as soon as it formed—we were charter members. This came from a split in the Socialist party. I already told you how the Socialists had a left wing and a right wing, and some like Hillquit that they talk from both sides of their mouth. But the right-wingers were in the leadership. Comes the Red scare, and some, like Gompers of the AF of L—he was one of the worst, a real union boss. I remember he saw me once to a meeting and he wanted me to sign up to work for him as a speaker. But I said, 'No, you can't put a ring through my nose, not even if it's gold.'

"Y'see, Gompers and the other union bosses—that's what I call them, bosses, 'cause they smoke their cigars so much that you can't see through the smelly smoke—they tried to make nice with the capitalists, y'see. Here you got workers getting deported for no reason, and plenty of unemployment, and all kind of a *tsuris*, and yellow-dog contracts that say a worker can't belong to a union—and Gompers comes out with a line that you would expect from the boss's nephew: against bolshevism, against immigration. He swallows the idea that it's not the system that's sick, it's us, the critics, the radicals. And so they quarantine us and start to throw us out from the unions. The AF of L is losing members like seltzer loses the sparkle!

"Meanwhile, the radicals are getting kicked out of the Socialist party. Hillquit and the social democrats outlawed whole chapters and broke up what you call the 'language federations'— these are for Socialists of one particular nationality, that they can work together in their own community. Sainer, f'rinstance, was in the Jewish Federation, and when he left, boy, he took many friends with him. This is one of the saddest things about the split, y'see: In many kind of a ways, it slowed down the movement in America 'cause it separated those that they're foreign-born from those like Debs that they're American-born. So the Communist party—we organized it immediately—it had mostly immigrants for membership, and it took many years before our party learned to speak to the American worker, to be an American party.

"Now, if you know a little history from this time, and you yourself are not a Communist, you're gonna say, 'Bessie Sainer, how come you and your *khaveyrim* never got along with nobody but yourself?' Or you're gonna hear some Social Democrat talk—even if he's an old man, he's still got the grudge—and he'll tell you that the Communists take orders from Moscow, we don't care about America. So now I'm gonna answer these charges, okay? You don't have to be a detective with me, this is not gonna be like Nixon with his Watergate. I thought plenty about the mistakes we made in the Party.

"It reminds me of a little story about an old man, my age, that he once goes to steal food in a supermarket. And since he's got no experience, he gets caught. And the judge gives him a very long time in jail, fifty years. So the old man says to the judge, 'Your Majesty, how can I serve a fifty-year sentence when already I'm eighty-eight years?' And the judge says, 'Do the best you can.'

"The thing is, you don't condemn a movement forever 'cause it makes mistakes. When we first organized the Party, we were still greenhorns. We had lots of revolution in our blood, but we didn't understand how it goes with the American worker. Until the Depression came, y'see, there wasn't much to say to the workers about socialism and revolution.

"But we said it anyway—we had big mouths! 'Cause we were very excited by the Russian Revolution—it's like your best friend should get married. We wanted a Soviet America! This became our slogan. And it's true, the Soviet Union had a great deal to be admired before Stalin came and destroyed it. Lenin warned against Stalin, you know. He wrote a note, 'Be careful of this guy Stalin, he's a chauvinist, he's not a good leader.' But Stalin took that note and kept it in his underwear, I don't know where, until by the time he showed it already he had a gun pointed at everybody's head.

"But it's not like we in America got paid by Moscow to make revolution. It's not like we were spies that we wanted for Russian soldiers to come and take over California. What I want now is that my work as a Communist should be understood in America as part of America, 'cause that's what we wanted—to be part of the American tradition, the progressive part of the tradition.

"What did we do for America? We built the CIO, that we got millions of workers into unions. We fought for the rights of the Negro people, something that nobody, but nobody, did excepting the Negro people themselves. Against lynching, against

Jim Crow, against all kind of a discrimination and racism that makes for the ugly part of the American tradition.

"Also we led the fight for home relief and for unemployment insurance. So I may not leave more than a few hundred dollars for my daughter and my grandson when I say goodbye, but I left them already their social security, their unemployment insurance, all this kind of a thing. That's not so bad.

"But I can't tell you everything we did, it takes too long. The thing is, I don't have to justify about becoming a Communist. It was a patriotic thing. And when it became ridiculous to belong, I left. Nineteen seventy-three. The Party became fanatical against Israel. You couldn't remain a Jew and a progressive and with a brain and remain in the Party.

"But I never left the progressive movement itself. The *Freiheit*, f'rinstance. I still read it and I still support it. *Freiheit* means freedom, so *Morgn Freiheit*—that's the whole name—it means morning freedom: that every morning you should wake up and feel like a free human being. We began this newspaper in 1922. We knew that the Jewish workers need a Yiddish paper and we never liked the *Forvetz*. They were wishy-washy about everything that's progressive; even their Yiddish came to you like—how do you say it? Like soft-boiled eggs, all watery, with pieces of English stuck in it.

"Eh, but who cares? I'm such a Red, I should be blushing! You listen to me, you would think I'm standing on East Broadway pointing with a rock at the *Forvetz* building. I can still feel all these feelings, y'see; it's like an old marriage that's no good, but the bickering, the arguing, it's a way of life. Like I heard once a comedian say: 'I got married to my wife sixty years ago,' he says, 'and right away I knew it was a mistake.' This is how it went between the Communists and the social democrats—a real civil war. Me and my brother Herschel, we would fight all the time. I would warm up by hollering at him with his rotten ideas, and when it came time to go on the picket line, I was ready for the bosses! And then eventually Herschel and I stopped talking for years. We weren't fooling around with this stuff.

"But I don't want you to think that the Communist party was my whole life. I never went full-time to be an organizer, though they asked me more than once. I was good with words, y'see, especially if I spoke in Yiddish. I remember way back during

the First World War, when I was a YPSL, the government had
on the platform in Herald Square Mary Pickford, the darling
of America. Everybody loved Mary Pickford like a kitten. So
they had her to sell war bonds—she would give a kiss to each
guy that came and bought. We were against the war, so I said
to one young man, 'Hey, look out—that's the kiss of death!' So
all the radical newspapers started to print this thing that I said.
And I got a reputation.

"For a couple of years I was the Party Secretary for Section
Five. Now . . . let's see if my *kepeleh* wants to work or if it'll
go on strike. . . . This district, I think it went from way downtown up to Forty-second Street, east of Second Avenue. This is
how I remember it, I may be wrong. But it was a lot, a lot of
work. And it was not a job that it paid, y'see. I saw how those
that they took Party jobs became bureaucrats—and then you lose
democracy. So I kept my Section Five very loose, very democratic.

"For a while I had trouble with the Party leadership—they
were still secret, nervous from the Palmer raids and from all
the time getting arrested. They thought it was better that just a
few people should do the work and tell everybody else what
to do. But I argued for democracy. Without democracy, you
get like with a box of strawberries: If you get one rotten one,
then the whole box spoils. And I said to my comrades, 'What's
the rush? Where are you running? It's not like the workers
in America are ready for a revolution so that all you gotta do
is give them boxing gloves and tell them who to go hit.' Yeah,
you could give the Russian peasant a bomb in one hand and a
potato in the other and he'll fight for you. But the American
people had more sophistication. So many people lost their revolutionary commitment when they came into the shadow of these
tall, tall buildings.

"So now you're gonna ask, 'Bessie Sainer, how come you're
so smart and the rest are shnooks?' But I had my experience in
Russia, y'see. When I looked back on this, I didn't remember
just the songs and speeches, I remembered the hardship. I
remember Lenin, yeah, but Lenin with a toothache! So I didn't
become idealistic about revolution like some that they think the
Messiah already came to Russia and all we got to do is pay his
passage to Ellis Island. I knew how down in the mud the Russian
people lived. They didn't dream at night about how to become a

millionaire, they were too exhausted to dream anything. So I knew that the kind of a revolution that you need for them is not the same for America.

"But when the Depression came to America, y'see, then the working people began to think, Hey, something's wrong that my children haven't got what to eat but they're dumping potatoes into the river to keep the prices high . . . something's wrong that I can't find a job after working twelve hours a day my whole life. . . . The whole system fell over on its back and was kicking its legs every which a way. And that's when we were ready to help give leadership to the movement.

"But I couldn't be so active in the 1930s, 'cause I already lost Sainer, y'see, and I had a terrible time just to feed my children. So here we go with another story. . . .

"Sainer died in 1929, after two years with cancer. It was very bad, he suffered a great deal. His lip was always bleeding from how he bit it so as not to yell. He became an old, old man like I wouldn't believe when we first got married. But after eight years that he gave me so, so much, I gave it right back.

"He went for two weeks to the hospital, but then he didn't want to go back there no more. So I took a leave of absence from my job, we lived on what we had saved, and I borrowed from my sisters. And I took care of him. It was hard. I had to keep the kids quiet all the time. This was bad—they thought I was a mean mommy, if you know what I mean. Especially Jacob, that he was only five years. You know how kids are with noise—it follows them like a shadow wherever they go. But Sainer couldn't stand it.

"A lot of the time I sent them to Mrs. Markish, only by then we called her Momma Greenpoint—this is what Janet gave her for a name when Sainer and I lived for a while in Manhattan. We would go to see Leah in Greenpoint, so to a child she became 'Momma Greenpoint'—and even when Momma Greenpoint moved back to the Bronx, she remained Momma Greenpoint. Now, during the time of Sainer's illness, Momma Greenpoint was taking care on Laibl—this is her grandson, Belle-Brokha's son, named after you know who in Mogilev-Podolsk. Janet and Laib were about the same age and they got along good, but Jacob was never happy, 'cause he was right in the middle. Elaine Kaminsky—this is Ruchel's daughter—she already had a baby—but just a baby; Jacob couldn't do nothing but look at him. And Ruchel's other one, Nat, he was already a young man, maybe twenty years. Besides, we didn't see Ruchel and her kids much 'cause I didn't get along with her, she was too high-class.

"I keep searching my mind for something to tell you that will show you what kind of a man Sainer was, 'cause I find it embarrassing, you know: Here I can tell you more stories about the Communist party than I can tell about my husband! I keep coming back to his car, a great big car that he would fix it on the weekend. To drive in this car to Camp Nishtgedeiget, or anywhere, anywhere, this was our great pleasure. Whenever I think of Sainer, I see him . . . well, either he's about to die—his face was all white stubbles and wasted to the bone—or else I see him driving the car, like from a profile I see him: He's got wire-rim glasses, and a quiet kind of a smile, 'cause he likes to drive, y'see, it was a great passion for us.

"We did not have passion like I had with Yasha. This was different. Sainer was more a friend, someone that he's very familiar and a great comfort. I suppose if we had more time, more years to be together, then this feeling would become love, it would become something precious. It's like an old foolish *tchatchke* that you keep it on your shelf, year after year, without even noticing. Then one day you clean house, and you pick up this thing, and you love it with all your heart, just 'cause it's been there so, so long. But we didn't get to this point, we were always so busy with making a living and our activities—him working days, me working nights, meetings all the time. In a certain kind of a way we were both married to the movement, for all that I tried that we should have a life of our own. I'm afraid that this is how it goes if you try to be a revolutionary. Instead that you can change the world, the world gobbles you up.

"I was forty years when Daniel Sainer died . . . such a long time dying . . . and I never again lived for a man. I took boarders, yeah, but they never got fresh with me. And I had one guy, Paul Vogel, that we sort of lived together for a while, but it turned out he was a sick man, and I said, 'No, this far and no farther.' For three husbands to die on you, you start feeling like maybe there's something wrong with your cooking!

"I had to give up on that stuff. Maybe if I knew I was going to live another fifty years, I would have bought a new dress and some perfume. But I had to be careful—I had to be, like, hard, 'cause there were men in the movement, like there's men every- where, they see a woman that she's independent and they try to make a date with her so they can humiliate her. I'd rather have it that they should be scared of me! Too scared to complain about their wives 'cause they know that, before they even try to kiss me, I'm gonna criticize them for being a lousy husband.

"It's not like I slept all the time by myself, all right? Hey, what do you want that you should talk like this to a woman that she's eighty-eight years! That's enough. You know what Sainer would say to you? Like he said every day to the kids: He'd come home from work and he'd say, 'Now, who's been bad? Tell me now so I can beat you before I wash my hands.' Every day. And the kids would come running for a great big 'beating.' Them he'd hug, even with his hands all greasy and dirty from the machines that he fixed, 'cause he said that kids and dirt go together, just like tomatoes in the garden. But me he wouldn't touch until he washed his hands. This was his idea, not mine! This I'll always remember: following him to the bathroom, watching him rub his hands with soap under the water, and I would give him a towel, and he would clean his glasses, and I would stand there against the wall, waiting. Then he'd put on the glasses and take a look at me.

"I burned many suppers this way, believe you me."

❁

"There's nothing for you to approve, Leah. I'm not trying to organize *you*. I just want you to take the kids tonight." Bessie rinsed her tea glass under the faucet and glanced at the clock, round and shiny on the windowsill amid Momma Greenpoint's swarm of plant cuttings: 5:10. Not much time to negotiate . . .

But Momma Greenpoint had already agreed. "Tonight or any night. Your children always have a home here."

"*Oi*, Leah, you make me feel so guilty. But you understand: The idea that these fascist bastards should be—"

Momma Greenpoint winced as though pricked by a pin.

"But they *are* bastards!" Bessie reiterated. "And the idea that they can rally, with radio and with newspapers watching, spread- ing their poison . . . and there's nobody even to hold up a sign denouncing them? I can't allow this."

"She can't allow it," Momma Greenpoint muttered, fetching an apron from its hook on the wall. The loop slid cleanly over her stacked braids. "So, you're not going to work tonight?" The unspoken accusation flashed in her big eyes: *For this you miss work; for the sabbath, never.*

"I am going to work," Bessie said. "After the demonstration. In fact, I've got to go iron my uniform." The Red Nurse, her comrades called her. They would greet her on the picket line tonight, outside Madison Square Garden, amid the blue cops and the gray Nazis and the drabs of the unemployed who congregated there to beg from the crowds, her whites arriving like a dove on the hot pavement: *Aha, here comes the Red Nurse. Now we got bandages against the scabs!*

Momma Greenpoint pointed a spatula at her. "Maybe you should go look in the mirror. You'll see there a forty-year-old widow."

"A widow! For how many years does the Talmud say I'm to be called a 'widow'? You always see me in terms of a man, Leah! Who do I have for company? Is he married? What does he look like? What does he do for a living?"

"So? What's so terrible? You, you see everything in terms of fighting!"

Bessie threw up her palms, then waved them before her bowed face as though to erase the conversation. "No fighting with you. You have your sabbath, I have my demonstration. This is life in America."

"So go get the kids or you'll be late," Leah replied, quick to restore civility to her tone, adding, with a wave of her spatula: "I don't want you getting criticized by your cronies."

Bessie gave a paltry smile and left for home, less than two blocks away. All would be well with Leah, she hoped, in the morning when she came for the kids. They would be playing on the floor, chattering in English; Lester would kibitz his orthodox wife out of her mood, and the *shabbas* peace would be established to her satisfaction, if not set in stone.

These hopes were overturned, however, when Janet came into her mother's bedroom to remind her that the Young Pioneers group to which the girl belonged was leafleting a supermarket near Hunt's Point in the early morning. The storeowner had committed a variety of offenses: refusing to hire Negroes, even

as porters or stock boys; refusing to distribute day-old bread
to the Unemployed Council of the neighborhood; and gouging
customers with variable prices. "And the other day a man got
caught stealing, you know? An unemployed worker?"

"Are you asking or telling?"

"And you know what they did to him, mom? They knocked
out his teeth!" She looked injured, too, indignantly tossing a
thick wisp of hair from her eyes.

"Who?"

"Who do you think? The guy who owns the place. He's
got goons. He's a real fascist!"

Bessie sat on her bed, the only place to sit in the room, to
roll on her orthopedic cotton stockings. "*Ziskayt*, you got something to learn about fascists. Y'see, there's a difference between
a *gonif* and a fascist, just like you got . . ." How to translate
into English the distinction between a philanderer and a rapist?
Bessie was shy to talk about such things with her daughter and
lamely said, "Like you got matzoh balls and kreplach."

Janet clung to her idea. "Clara Shwartzman says that fascism
is a petty-bourgeois ideology, so even Jews aren't immune to it."

Bessie retreated into Yiddish before this verbose display. "If
you don't mind telling your stupid mother, what does it mean,
'immune'?"

"It's when you can't get sick," she replied charitably in her
mother's tongue. "Then you're immune."

Bessie reached down the front of her uniform to tug at her
brassiere. "So the man who owns the supermarket is a Jew?
And Jewish people shop there? So why do we do our picketing
on *shabbas*? This is how we're going to organize Jews?"

"Oh, God, everybody shops on Saturday, ma!" Janet switched
nimbly into English to press her advantage. "The stores are
closed Sunday. Anyway, *you're* going to a rally tonight and it's
already *shabbas*."

"Yeah," Bessie confessed, "but I don't like it. Not for the sake
of religion, Janet—you know we don't go along with that kind
of a foolishness. Momma Greenpoint makes you light the candles, but not me."

"That's okay, mom, I like spending time with Aunt Leah."

"I know you do," Bessie said gratefully, kissing the girl's
forehead, sweet as cream. "Laib is coming, too."

"Oh, good!"

Bessie sat again on her squeaking bed to put on her white shoes. "So where's your brother now? Tell him to go get ready. And watch out," she hollered as the girl skipped toward the door, "that he packs good."

What pack? She glanced down the front of the uniform again. You with your girdle and brassiere—you're better packed than anyone! Both undergarments were required by the Mt. Sinai Hospital dress code, but Bessie wondered whether she wouldn't be happier with the girdle tucked into her pocketbook, along with . . . what? Something heavy for self-defense . . .

Jacob knocked on the half-open door, a single, reluctant rap. "What is it, Jacob? Don't come in, I'm getting dressed."

His voice was as mournful as a wound-down Victrola. "I don't want to go to Momma Greenpoint's."

"You gotta. Momma's got a rally and then I got to go to work. No discussion."

"I want to go to Aunt Ruchel's!"

"I said, no discussion!"

She always became taciturn en route to demonstrations, as though entering a combat zone. Tonight she was traveling with seven comrades from the Bronx—all, besides Albert Bronstein, a good ten years younger than she. As they argued, joked, and sweated beneath the slow-turning subway fans, Bessie kept her face to the window and watched the yellow tunnel lights streak past. Beneath the rumble and vibration of the train, she found her ghosts, and abided with them, and thought about the cruelties in the world that had cost them their lives.

Bronstein, too jittery to sit, grabbed a straphang and dropped a bundle of thin *Daily Workers*, the English-language Party newspaper, on Bessie's lap. "We've got to sell these."

DARROW REPORT: NRA HELPS MONOPOLIES

Washington, July 16 . . . Progressive trial lawyer Clarence Darrow today called Pres. Roosevelt's National Industrial Recovery Act a "boon to conglomerates and monopolies." A report released by the National Recovery Review Board, of which Mr. Darrow . . .

"We've got to sell these," Bronstein repeated. Bessie nodded but failed to stir. "What's the matter, *khaverteh*, you're not feeling good?"

"The whole country's not feeling good," Bessie replied.

The train brakes screeched as they lumbered into the 145th Street station in Harlem. Bronstein impatiently tapped his bony finger atop his stack of newspapers, still on Bessie's lap, as he waited for the noise to subside.

COUGHLIN CENSURED BY A.F.L. BOARD

Detroit, July 16 . . . Demagogic radio priest Father Coughlin was censured today by the executive board of the American Federation of Labor for his use of non-union printing shops for his weekly publication, the so-called *Social Justice.*

Coughlin's estimated listening audience has swelled to 10 million, according to the bourgeois magazine, *Fortune.* . . .

Bessie listlessly scanned the *Daily Worker* as Bronstein lectured to her in his viscous Yiddish accent. "Heh, don't worry, the fascists will give themselves away soon enough. American workers aren't blind. You get close to fascists, you can see for yourself what they are. . . ."

AMERICAN JEWISH COMMITTEE CONDEMNS NAZI BOOKBURN-ING. *In a strongly worded statement, the AJC today condemned recent bookburning campaigns in Hitler's Germany, but typically linked the condemnation to an outrageous attack on the Soviet Union. . . .*

"Besides, Roosevelt's not about to let the right-wingers . . ."

LEWIS THREATENS WALKOUT. *United Mineworkers Union Pres. John L. Lewis threatened to pull his union out of the A.F.L. if the labor federation does not abide by its convention decision to pursue organizing drives in mass-production industries. . . .*

The train was hurtling down the long express corridor from Harlem to Columbus Circle, rattling the rails so loudly that

Bronstein's voice was reduced to a sheep's bleat. Bessie watched her other comrades, divided by the noise and bench arrangements into three couples: Milton and Sonya, sitting hip to hip on the straw seat, smiling at Bessie as her eyes brushed theirs; Rose and Shirley by the door, sharing a giddy moment, standing with their ankles crossed below midcalf skirts; George haranguing Sylvia with some point of doctrine, plunging his finger toward the dirt-encrusted floor. They were all so full of verve and spirit, looking cool in the heat like well-preened birds in a shady tree. To befriend them, she would have to be drunk, to somehow loosen her hold on the precious dignity that kept her buoyant even through the blackest of moods. . . .

"Tonight we got these Friends of New Germany to deal with. Real hooligans." Bronstein's sounds reassembled into words as the train shot into the Columbus Circle station. "They actually spy for Hitler. Don't ask me how I know—I know. Listen, I'm a regular fortune-teller. I used to run a booth in Coney Island, did I tell you?"

Bessie actually looked at the scrawny man for the first time. His mouse eyes shone with excitement through his scratched wireframes. "I guessed for customers their age, their weight, their height, even sometimes their profession. You know what was hardest? Height. They would wear lifts in their shoes to fool me! What you got to do," he advised in a low voice, "is look at their arms, how low they hang."

Half-interested and half-amused, she was totally doubtful that this bookish guy had ever known Yasha, or Paul Dropsky, or any of the spunky old Coney Island crowd. Bronstein was working his tongue like a taffy twist to hold her attention, but there was no competing with Yasha Levovsky, emerged now from behind her memories, dancing toward her open-armed, eyes full of sky. . . .

"What do you say, Bessie?"

"What? . . . Oh, we're here!"

He shadowed her as she fled the car. "What do you say? You want to go for coffee after?"

The little *shtunk!* Bessie whirled around furiously as though he'd pinched her. "I work nights, Bronstein," she snapped, and found no more to say, but waved to the others, keeping her chin high above his fallen gaze, wondering: Was her reek of loneliness that strong?

Their group coalesced with some Lower East Siders, including a squad of strong-armed men carrying canes. "What do you have in your bag of tricks, sister nurse?" asked Freddie Nelson, an IWO man.

Bessie drew from her pocketbook a fist-size statuette made of marble. "It's the head of Bartolomeo Vanzetti."

"Nicola Sacco," argued George, the maven, taking the bust into his hands. "Yikes, it weighs a ton!"

"I'm sticking with the Red Nurse tonight, folks," announced Freddie, who stood head and shoulders above her. "She came prepared."

"Phooey, prepared," Bessie scoffed. "By accident I got this. I forgot to exchange pocketbooks. And what about you, trouble-maker? Since when do you limp?"

Freddie tossed his cane from one hand to another like a soft-shoe artist. "It's nothing but a peppermint stick."

"So some of us carry candy, and some carry sculpture. Now mind your business."

Smiling demurely, she found herself staring into the eyes of a flat-faced, slovenly woman standing with two men at the perimeter of the group. Bessie closed her mouth as the three scrutinized her, her statuette, her white uniform and shoes, like tailors taking measurements. One of the men leaned close to the woman and said something in Yiddish—or was it German? She tipped back her greasy head and laughed, then turned to buy penny gum from a vending machine.

Bessie looked to big Freddie for comfort, but saw behind him a more frightening sight: a wedge of men in swastika arm-bands clumping double-time up the stairs. "Like pigs to a trough," Freddie said. "Look at them go."

"Book burners!" Bronstein hissed, quaking at Bessie's elbow. "Their idea of the world makes hell look good."

"Here, let's save our voices for the demonstration," advised Freddie, motioning for them all to go.

Upstairs, the air was yellow and sultry, sagging into evening. Police with their barricades ringed the concrete coliseum, dividing the pavement between rallygoers and spectators. Bessie scanned their meaty faces while walking toward the corner of Fiftieth and Ninth Avenue, site of the Communist protest, with the militant miners' song *Which side are you on, which side are you on?* running like a radio jingle through her mind. As she paused to breathe in a pleasant manure scent that had drifted over from three mounted police at the curb, she was bumped by Shirley Wasserman. "Jesus! Excuse me! I'm looking everywhere but ahead!"

"Don't worry." Bessie bent to rub her scuffed shoe.

"I can't believe how many there are." Shirley was staring at the double line of German-Americans filing into Madison Square Garden, among them cadres of the Friends of New Germany carrying printed placards: HANDS OFF GERMANY . . . LOYALTY MEANS NEUTRALITY . . . IMPEACH COMMUNIST ROOSEVELT . . . ANDOVER, N.J. SALUTES ADOLF HITLER. She looked as jittery and vulnerable as a sparrow in a covey of pigeons, dressed as for a date in a pink blouse with a floppy bow tie. Bessie decided to deliver her into Freddie Nelson's protective custody as soon as possible.

"There we are." Bessie pointed across the avenue, where their own signs hovered behind another row of police barricades: STOP FASCIST TERROR! . . . RAISE WAGES, NOT PRICES . . . HOME RELIEF NOW. But the sidewalk was barely passable, cut in two by police and littered with vendors, hawkers, and unemployed men, the hardcore jobless, without even homes to return to at dusk. Shirley gripped Bessie's arm as they advanced.

The men were drawn to them like fish to dangling worms: first, a slender young fellow in a banged-up fedora, who asked urgently, "You got a dime?" Bessie sized him up with a glance. He was dirty, but neither stinking nor so begrimed as to be an alcoholic or professional tramp. She asked what he planned to do with the dime. "What's it to you?" he retorted. "Your name Eleanor Roosevelt?" He turned away with his fists clenched.

"Wait, I don't mean to be a wise guy." Bessie opened her bag. The man removed his hat and eyed her hungrily. "I can't give you any more than a dime."

"That's all I asked for."

"Yeah, you and the rest," she said. "We got a regular lineup here. Plenty of unemployment for everyone in America. Look, you better read this if you know what's good for you." She drew a leaflet from her bag and handed it over with the coin. "It's about a meeting—Unemployed Councils. You should come and get organized, if you're smart."

He turned away without a smile or thank-you, but was examining the literature. "You know, Shirley, my father used to say, 'If you give someone a fish, they eat today; but if you teach them how to catch fish, they eat for the rest of their life.' This, he said, was in the Talmud."

"My father's a fanatic, too," Shirley complained. "Full of that kind of stuff."

Bessie squinted up at her, surprised at their miscommunication. "How old are you, Shirley?"

"Twenty."

"You speak Yiddish?" she asked in Yiddish.

"Excuse me?"

Oi, never mind. "Come, let's give these out."

They distributed the leaflets to men along the block until a gray-haired cop stopped them near the corner. "None of that," he commanded, eyeing Shirley's tall slenderness.

"What's the matter," Bessie said, "it's not a free country no more?"

"Go on, get across the street." He prodded her girdled rump with his nightstick.

She dumped Shirley at Freddie Nelson's side—"She's a real greenhorn, so make nice"—then penetrated to the center of the crowd. Sid Frankel of the Executive Committee was leading the rally with a bullhorn to his lips: "Bad enough for the working people of America to have this misery of a Depression on their backs! Bad enough to have a president whose so-called reforms mean saving corporate profits!" His voice sawed the air. "Bad enough to have a government that takes nearly two decades to recognize the Soviet Union—the only workers' democracy on the face of the earth! Why did it take so many years to admit the Soviet Union to the League of Nations? Because imperialism needed the time to carve up the world for its own table, isn't that right, my friends?"

"YES!" shouted handfuls of people.

"Are we going to let Adolf Hitler destroy the only workers' state on the face of the earth?"

"NO!" Bessie answered with the rest.

"Are we going to let the fascists take over in America, in any part of America?"

"NO!"

"Two, four, six, eight, help us build a workers' state! Two, four, six, eight—"

"HELP US BUILD A WORKERS' STATE!"

The group numbered about two hundred. Following her initial burst of vigor, Bessie wearied of the chanting, which seemed impotent as thousands of Nazi sympathizers filed into Madison Square Garden before her eyes. "At least we should try to sell newspapers up and down the block," she commented to a sister at her side.

"Shh, listen. We're going in now," the woman predicted. Frankel had lowered his bullhorn and summoned a hush upon the ranks. The darkness of evening deepened and the street noise rose as Bessie strained to make out his voice.

"We can't hear!"

"Louder!"

People standing closer to Frankel passed word back to the others. "We're going inside now. Leave your signs. No signs."

"What do I do with my *Freiheits*?"

"What, we're going inside?"

"You didn't know?"

"You did?"

"Groups of ten, he says. Buddy system. Everybody should take a buddy. You want to be my buddy?"

"What should I do with my *Freiheits*? A whole bundle . . ."

"Where's the nearest hospital? This he should announce—someone tell him to announce it."

"Please, comrades," said Frankel through his bullhorn, "a little discipline. Quiet, please! Everything will be explained."

As he broke off again to confer with his lieutenants, James Walker, a Harlem organizer, took the bullhorn and initiated another round of chants, which faded quickly as people prepared to move out. The few black comrades in attendance, whose skin color would invite instant violence were they to enter the Garden, circulated through the crowd collecting picket signs, newspapers, and whatever valuables people wished to leave behind. Bessie held on to her weighted pocketbook with a polite "No thank you" to the comrade who offered to hold it for her.

Bronstein sidled up to her after turning over his bundle of *Daily Workers*. "What's the matter, Bessie, you don't trust him?"

"What's the matter with you?" she replied. "You think I discriminate? Only against fools, Bronstein." She hooked arms with Sonya and Milton. "Two things I got to get rid of, Bronstein and my girdle."

The door to the ladies' room squealed and slammed on Shirley's plea that Bessie hurry out. They were all anxious not to linger in a bunch amid the steady stream of spectators, particularly not while uniformed Nazis were ostentatiously patrolling the corridors. "God, I wish we didn't look so Jewish!" Shirley had lamented after passing a security squad.

"They didn't see your horns," Bessie had replied, her hand on Freddie's arm as he limped past the brutish men.

The concrete bathroom was damp, sour, and nearly soundproof. Bessie waddled toward the toilet stalls, her rubber soles sucking against the tile floor.

"Listen, I think they're starting!"

Bessie's pulse quickened as she saw the greasy blond from the subway platform standing by the sinks, tugging her girlfriend's arm—"Never mind your lipstick, come on!" The woman's beady eyes widened at the sight of Bessie's white uniform in the mirror, and she swung around like a loaded cannon.

Bessie cursed her rotten luck and, whistling without sound, locked herself into the nearest stall, then nearly panicked in the enclosure, banging the wall with her elbows and knees as she tried to get at her girdle with a minimum of undressing.

"What's she trying to do in there, lick her pussy?" The voice echoed off the high ceiling and drenched Bessie with self-consciousness. She coached herself: Scream for help if you've got to, darling—your friends are right outside. Quick but calm, now, just get done what you've got to get done.

"Can you smell it, Irene? Jewish women give off such a smell, it's a zoo!"

Bessie plopped onto the toilet seat and pulled her girdle past her shoes, then braced her feet against the door and rolled her stockings to just above the knee, breathing quietly, carefully . . . but every seam would appear in place, unruffled by their terrorism, every seam . . .

"We better report it to management, Irene. Communist infiltration of the bathrooms! She'll probably collect our shit and send it off to Moscow!"

Bessie could smell her own sweat as she stuffed the hated girdle into her bag—done, finished, good riddance. She flushed the bowl for camouflage, took a firm grip on the bag's handles, gingerly unbolted the door . . . gulped air in case she needed to scream . . . Go!

They were still by the sinks, glaring at her. Bessie slowed immediately to a dignified walk, then bolted as soon as they moved toward her. Thank God her comrades had waited! She burst upon them and beelined for Freddie Nelson with an urgency that put everyone on alert. "We got trouble. Two women in the bathroom . . ."

"I see." Nelson nodded toward the two as they pitched out of the bathroom and, seeing Bessie among allies, hurried off hand in hand to seek friends of their own in the now lightly trafficked corridor. "We divide up," Nelson said decisively. "Milton, Bessie, you, you and Bronstein. The rest with me. We're going in, okay? Shirley, ready? George? Everybody? Fine. Separate ramps." There was a sharp whistle around the bend. "Let's get the lead out, people!" Nelson hollered.

Bessie's five moved down the ramp in a tight pack like fish into the open sea: an immense sea of light and sound, with fifteen thousand seats filled across the main floor and first mezzanine. The distant stage was backdropped by an American flag, each star man-size. From the balconies on all sides hung swastikas and homemade messages. Already exhausted and wet with perspiration, Bessie clutched a back panel of Milton's shirt as they sidled between rows, between knees, between mutterings and complaints, searching for empty seats, her lungs aching for a pause, her eyes dodging contact with the turning heads.

Back at the rampway, a Nazi squad stood peering, pointing.

Bronstein waved and bounced up and down, caught Milton's attention, and dropped like a dead man into the nest of chairs he'd found. Mercifully the houselights blacked out as the speaker onstage thumped the podium for his final time and fetched a boom of feedback from his microphone. Bessie collapsed into a chair, panting hard as applause surged through the hall. In the partial darkness, her uniform seemed luminescent.

Milton touched her wrist and whispered with his chin on his chest: "There's a police station near exits twelve and thirteen, under the mezzanine. Pass it down: In case real trouble breaks out . . ."

Better Mayor LaGuardia's boys than Hitler's own, she agreed, though doubtful that the cops would exert themselves to protect

"Commies." In a nervous whisper, she passed on the information to Sonya. Bronstein, several seats removed, remained uninformed. But minutes passed and no one arrived to roust them, nor did sounds of scuffling arise from the general hubbub. Bessie soon began to surrender her acute sense of alarm, for the sounds and lights, the banners and rigmarole, were pleasurably familiar, similar to those at Communist mass rallies....

"*Communist, Nazi—you're all the same! Anti-Semites! So you speak Yiddish, so you write a Yiddish newspaper, so? The cossacks spoke some Yiddish, too!*"
    "*Don't be so smart, Leah. I saw pogroms, not you! You were safe already in America!*"
    "*Yes, and I bless America for that safety! Not like you!*"

Could it have been just one short year ago? Yes—the day after Hitler's ascent, Bessie remembered: She'd had a bloody shouting match with Momma Greenpoint, who'd dared to compare that German butcher to Comrade Stalin. With the kids whining on the floor and the walls about to shatter . . .

"*You haven't got Jewish hearts, none of you! Why do your friends all change their names if they're not ashamed?*"
    "*Oh, Leah, this is America! Our brother Julius changed his name, no?*"
    "*Yeshua had to! The way they discriminate . . .*"
    "*Against Jews but not against Communists? Are you kidding, Leah?*"

A boys' choir had assembled on the stage with rehearsed precision. Spotlights hit them and the audience hushed. The conductor gestured and high-voiced harmonies billowed into the arena. Bessie squinted across the distance at the blur of young faces, the flapping pink lips and dark mouths, until she found it—there, the optical shift and illusion, like a strange shadow cast by a familiar object. The chorus had become a creature, a single life form with two dozen blinking eyes. Bird or buffalo? An insect with the conductor's arms for antennae? All of these and more: a creature of great sentience and greater yearning. Bessie had shown Sainer this vision of hers—how to squint just so to make one life of the dozens—at concerts they used to attend of the Jewish People's Philharmonic Chorus, before she'd joined the chorus herself, to lose her loneliness.

"Little mother, if only all the world could sit with us in the balcony, holding hands, sharing these sweet songs."
"If only, yeah. If only we could've sold enough tickets to fill this hall tonight!"

Bessie chuckled at the memory as an enthusiastic round of applause filled the arena. Well, *khaveyrim,* do we applaud, too? These Nazis and these Nazi-lovers, how is it they can raise such sweet-throated children as these, hardly older than my Jacob? And how is it their faces look human when their minds are so poisoned? How is it, when their lips should be blistered, their eyes burning, their ears growing like cauliflower, and their bellies bulging?

And there it was again: the chorus creature. Who were these people? she wondered. Where did they fit into the Party's definition of fascism? She had memorized it in her first class in Workers' School: "The open terrorist dictatorship of the most predatory sectors of the capitalist class, with mass support from the impoverished middle class and demoralized sectors of the working class." But how do the words become reality? How does the misery of the people get molded into fascist rage, the blind anger, the self-annihilation?

"If we would stop fighting with the social democrats on Essex Street, we would sell tickets like hot cakes. Does it matter whose newspaper wraps the herring, theirs or ours? Feh, it all smells of fish!"
"Never mind, Sainer. They smell like skunk."
"Shh. All right, Bessie, let's listen."

As the choir finished its performance on a resounding high note, the air split open with applause and cheers. Bessie shuddered, feeling each clap as a whiplash, punishment for all sectarian errors of the past. Every worker here is the signal of our failure, *khaveyrim!* And now? We're going to erase our mistakes by bloodying noses?

The applause finally waned. "What's going on now?" she whispered in Yiddish to Sonya, who was tall enough to see the stage.

"Shh. Speak English." Sonya smoothed her skirt. "It's their führer, Heinz Spanknoebel. Now," she added with a nasal sigh, "the fun begins."

"No, we should just listen," Bessie pleaded in a loud voice, as though she were speaking not only to Sonya but to Sainer's hovering ghost. "We listen, then after we can talk, and figure out about this movement, and make some kind of a plan—"

"Shh!" Brushing Bessie's words aside, Sonya lifted her bright eyes to Spanknoebel at the distant podium.

"My dear Friends of the New Germany . . ."

The phrase by itself won shouts of endorsement from the floor; but as Spanknoebel summoned silence with an upraised hand, the scattered teams of Communists began to heckle him, most heavily from the mezzanine. Bessie felt the keen frustration of awareness that has come too late as her hands curled for combat and her heart enlarged in her chest. At her side in the darkness, Milton coughed and edged forward on his seat. Shouts of dissent flooded every pause in Spanknoebel's rhetoric, yet he seemed oblivious, speaking with a thick accent and with amplification so loud that every phrase needed silent repetition to be distilled and understood. "*New York Times* . . . German-American patriots must learn what the Jewish bourgeoisie . . . the fatherland . . . usual lies, of course . . . National Socialist party . . . of unemployment to the most low . . ."

The applause he received was to Bessie a welcome camouflage for her comrades' heckling; but when, following a moment's lull, Milton jumped up and shouted, "Down with Nazi slave labor! Power to the German working class!" in a grand, bassy voice, there remained only darkness in which to hide. Nazi security men were wading through the seats with flashlights beaming. Men were glancing at Milton and perking up for a fight by giving orders to their wives and children and grumbling to one another.

Bessie felt Sonya rising from her seat and caught her by the elbow. "Please don't. I'm not in the mood for a beating tonight."

Sonya wrenched herself loose, but her confidence was so

jarred that her declaration—"Jobs for all in the Soviet Union!"—came out short-breathed and diminutive against Spanknoebel's persistent drone. But Milton and Bronstein took up her words as a chant: "Jobs for all in the Soviet Union! Jobs for all in the Soviet Union!"

"Shmucks, who are you organizing?" Bessie grumbled as, feeling more blind than safe in her seat, she stood and looked for an escape route—the aisle, the balcony, the sky-high gridded ceiling blazing with spotlights and resounding with Spanknoebel's voice—wanting out, out! of the tangle and buzz and darkness. Before you got to eat Momma Greenpoint's *tsholent* without any teeth in your head!

"Jobs for all in the Soviet Union! Jobs for all—" Sonya cried out as she was pelted from behind with a half-peeled, half-sucked orange that fell wet against Bessie's arm. Milton swung around to search out the offender and froze in the glare of a flashlight. Bessie could see the guard approaching, a shadow behind his swirl of light, shoving chairs aside, apologizing to those few Germans who were still seated, and she saw Bronstein in his path, sloganeering and gesticulating like a matador with his back to the charging bull.

"Bronstein, shut up!" She folded her chair and let it clatter to the floor. "Yoo, Bronstein, come on, we're going!"

Sonya cursed her with a panicky sideward glance. "Go, go you little social fascist!"

"You *momzer*," Bessie shot back, "I should beat you myself." But the thud of the German's truncheon against Bronstein's chest and the little man's squeal of pain broke them apart. Bessie slipped her bag from her shoulder as she sidled up the row—"Excuse me, mister, lady, excuse me"—imagining as she felt its heft that she would strike out like a slapstick artist, clunking her enemies cold and catching her comrades on the backswing! Fifteen thousand slain by a single handbag! "Sorry, excuse me, there's trouble, I'm a nurse. Look out!"

Damn it, damn it! Bronstein was already sprawled across toppled chairs, still being kicked by that sonofabitch Nazi. Bessie swung her bag on a downward arc and lost her grip on the handles as it struck the guard squarely on the back of his head and flattened him while bursting open in a shower of keys, coins, girdle, and stone. She hauled Bronstein to his feet and shoved him to the aisle while he moaned about his cracked spectacles and bloody nose. "Now we can go for coffee, Bronstein." She looped arms with him and dragged him up the carpeted incline.

Chapter Sixteen

Bessie's wit and confidence drained off all at once when her supervisor, Mrs. Malincott, finding her in the nursing station applying cold compresses to Bronstein's swollen face, ordered her to find a clean uniform—"Yours is an absolute mess, Mrs. Sainer! I'm surprised at you!"—or to go home without pay for the night. Though Malincott charitably said nothing of the impropriety of Bronstein's receiving treatment behind the desk, the curtness of her reprimand and its threat of banishment to a long, idle night overwhelmed Bessie with an acute feeling of wretchedness and wrongdoing. She tried to carry on by reaching for a fresh cotton swab, but then Bronstein groaned again, as he had been doing for an hour to console himself, and her hand shriveled, remorse and loathing sweeping away her strength. She had hardly the goodwill left to bandage his nose and direct him to the nearest subway.

By elevator she reached the basement, and entered the laundry room. The dry, astringent air stung her nostrils as she wandered among the laundry bins looking for Mary Jane, a Negro laundress whom she alone among the all-white professional staff respectfully addressed as Mrs. Gittins. Mrs. Gittins was a fat woman of paradoxically quick gestures, with a doubtful, jowly face and gray hair stiffly shaped like a *sheytl*. Bessie had been attracted upon meeting her by the forthrightness of the woman, so unlike many Negroes who, she found, diminished and belittled themselves among whites.

Mrs. Gittins was at her pressing table, running an endless supply of laundered pillowcases through her presser. "Ooh, my," she said at a glance, "who you been cleaning up after, Mrs. Sainer? Ain't you just beginning your shift?"

Bessie was too choked up to speak. She began unbuttoning her uniform and, as Mrs. Gittins came near, raised her arms overhead like a child waiting to be undressed.

No girdle. Belly flesh, panties, sagging nylons. Her bag, her money, keys, wallet, I.D., now in the hands of some Nazi hoodlum! Bessie gave in to her tears, which fell in enormous drops on Mrs. Gittins's broad brown arms.

"I don't mind, I don't mind getting rained on," she said, easing the uniform over Bessie's head.

"You got such wonderful hands," Bessie said, though her lips were parched. "You should be a nurse yourself."

"Uh-huh," she grunted. "But it would take a whole *bathful* of cold cream to make these hands soft—and white." She snorted and threw a cautious glance at Bessie. "So what happened to you, Mrs. Sainer? Some man gone and done something?"

"No . . . no. You got a little water?"

Mrs. Gittins brought a cupful of some sugary iced tea and a fresh, warm sheet for Bessie to wear. "I don't mean no insult asking 'bout your problems, y'understand."

"I know, sweetheart. I know."

Mrs. Gittins spread Bessie's uniform across her table and sprayed bleach and hot water directly on the stains. "See, where I come from, Mrs. Sainer, if I see a nigger girl looking mussed and bawling like you—don't mean no insult, now—but I got to figure that's either a man or the Klan that's got a hold on her. Man or the Klan. Them white men go dressing up in sheets like you got on now, and they making a devil of a noise, lynching niggers and everything. You know 'bout that, Mrs. Sainer, I know you do."

"Why do you call yourself this name? Why?"

"What's that, 'niggers'?" Her iron hissed against the uniform. "Don't matter so much what you call people, 's my opinion,

Mrs. Sainer. It's what's inside your head that makes things happen, good and bad."

"But other people," Bessie argued, "when they hear you talk like this . . ."

"Other people, I might say other things." Mrs. Gittins ceased working and laid her palms on the table. "Mrs. Sainer, I know how *you* think. You treat colored folk with respect."

"I do, why not? You're a human being, aren't you?"

"Well, I thank you for that, I do," she said pridefully. "But let me tell you something, Mrs. Sainer: You and your kind, you're the only ones, the *only* ones that think like that. I read that paper you gave me, time you asked if I could read?"

Bessie nodded. They were inching closer and closer to intimacy, to dealing. Bessie was beyond tears and alert now, political antennae trembling. It was always a risk, propagandizing on the job, but this woman had shown such intelligence, such feeling for her own opinions! She was Party material, for reasons beyond her skin color, Bessie thought: genuinely proletarian, caring about others, a *mensch.*

"Well, that was a fine paper to read," Mrs. Gittins said.

Bessie agreed, with relief. "I knew you would like it. So whenever you want the *Daily Worker,* you come to me. It's your newspaper, y'see."

"I thank you, Mrs. Sainer. I'll do that." She picked up her iron again. "But I got a question for you, Mrs. Sainer. They had something in that paper, something 'bout the Klan, 'bout how they go lynching niggers and it got to stop and all. Question is, how you plan to stop them? Ku Klux Klan is the devil's own child, Mrs. Sainer, they ain't nice men. And the damned government ain't going to help do nothing for no colored folk, not unless you elect Mary Jane Gittins for president!"

Bessie smiled. "Good, I'll be your assistant."

"Seriously, Mrs. Sainer. What are you-all going to do? You can't go beating them with your own fists—there's usually more of them than there is of us."

"No," Bessie replied, clenching her fists and rising from her stool, rallied by Mrs. Gittins's words. "There's more of *us,* y'see. You said it exactly right, Mrs. Gittins. We got to do something, and we can't just beat them with our fists. And the answer is we got to organize, plain and simple, better than they're organized! We got to make sure there's more of us than they got!"

Mrs. Gittins thumped the table. "Ain't you the prophet in your underwear! Get on board, children!" Still guffawing, she peeled up Bessie's uniform for inspection. "There, that looks fine to me, Mrs. Sainer. But if it ain't clean enough for your superviser or somebody, you just bring it on back and we'll put it through the wash, that's all. I got plenty of work, but I know *you* must've got dirty for a good reason."

Trudging up Prospect Avenue from the elevated station, Bessie received both shy and eager greetings from several of the twoscore persons, mostly Young Communist Leaguers, who were gathered at the corner of 169th Street to make and listen to speeches. Even Joel Goldberg up on the soapbox, midstream in a declaration about unemployment, paused to wave at her, so she reciprocated, standing still to listen. (His delivery's not bad—the passion's not phony, and his face and his hands I like, they talk . . . but he ought to go slow, give it time for the words to sink in. And he's got to look at faces and read them, let *us* guide his talk.)

George Korman came from around the ring of listeners to wish Bessie a good morning and supply her with weekend *Freiheits*. He was the youngest Party member on staff with the Yiddish newspaper. "Tell me, Bess, what happened to you last night?"

"What do you mean, George? You were on the train with me."

He nodded like a sympathetic mourner. "Sonya Stein says she's taking you up on charges."

"She *what?*" Her voice spilled across the gathering, turning heads. Bessie's fame as a hard talker and street agitator had everyone primed for excitement.

George beckoned her for a walk and cautiously took her elbow.

"I saved Sonya's own family," she flatly declared, "that they shouldn't be evicted. I led the group that we moved all their furniture right back in while the marshals just stood there. *Nu?* Tell me already."

"It's only what I heard," George said in Yiddish. "I met Milton in the grocery."

"Milton." The name was like a mouthful of spoiled food to her.

George shrugged. "You don't have to like him . . ."

"Good."

"But you may have to answer them. They say you ran out. You had a little trouble or something, you got scared . . . ?"

She couldn't walk; another step would detonate her. "Those young snotnoses!" She bit off the rest of her curse, remembering that George was one of them, barely graduated from the YCL to the Party. She could make no claims on his loyalty, as her accusers, his peers, might.

"Sonya's got a broken nose," he reported, averting her stare.

"If she had two noses, I'd break the other one! Who the hell is she, George? Argh, to hell with it—I've got a family to go feed."

"Bessie," he called to her back, "it's not official yet."

"Oh, no! Don't you interfere, George. Let her take me up on charges! That'll be one hearing our Party won't forget!"

He winced at the sharpness of her tone. Halfway down the block behind him, the hopeful and curious were again watching Bessie at the expense of the soapbox orator. Embarrassed, angry, her emotions aswirl, she thrust her hands toward George, groped for words to exempt him from her hostility and beg his loyalty, then succumbed to rage again and turned toward Fox Street.

Momma Greenpoint's apartment was as dark and somnolent as the heavily waxed exterior corridors. As Bessie freed her swollen feet from their white casements, Lester came into the foyer, barefoot, in trousers and an undershirt. "It's like a morgue in here," she complained.

"Shh. Leah's still in bed."

"She's sick," Bessie concluded soberly.

"A little." He stepped across the kitchen threshold.

"You're hungry?"

"A little, sure." He thanked her with a smile.

"All right, but open the shades first. It's ten o'clock in the morning. Where are the kids, did they eat? Are you starving my kids?" She peered into the icebox. "*Oi*, you don't even have eggs."

"Sure we have eggs," Momma Greenpoint called from her sickbed.

"Never mind, *balebusteh*, I'll send Jacob." In an undertone to Lester: "What's the matter with her?"

"The same. She gets tired and droopy, a regular piece of cloth."

"You ought to be a husband and get her to a doctor."

"She won't go."

"Make her go. Jacob! Jacob!"

Janet came instead, treading lightly in the darkness, dressed in her blue and red Pioneers outfit. "Hi, momma. Aunt Leah's sick."

"Sweet girl, you stayed home to take care on her?"

"Mm-hm."

"That's the right thing to do. Don't let nobody in your organization tell you different. Family comes first."

Janet searched her mother's face as Lester let in daylight. "You've got a headache, mom?"

"Plenty of headaches. Listen, darling, you go do what you want to do now. You don't need two *alte khalyeras* to take care on."

"Take care *of*, ma."

"Off, on, never mind. Next year I'll go to college, now I'm too busy. Where's your brother?"

Janet shrugged and turned her face away, mumbling, "On the roof."

"*Gottenyu*, I've got a pigeon for a son. Make Mr. Markish some coffee, darling. He's an invalid, he can't do for himself—he's a man. I'll be right back." Bessie donned her sister's slippers, parked on the linoleum beneath the kitchen table, and went to fetch Jacob and a moment of solitude for herself.

The stairway to the roof was dusty and the door flaked rusty chips as she shouldered it open. The sky surrounded her at once, its brightness ripening the pain that had begun to swell behind her eyes. In a moment she saw Jacob squatting by the tar wall of the street-side cornice, looking at her. "Jakey, not so close to the edge . . . Hey! What are you . . . ?" A carton of eggs lay open at his feet. His hand darted out and replaced one in its cup. As Bessie charged, he bolted upright. She hauled him in from the edge and stung his cheek with a clean, hard slap that made him howl. "Eggs you throw! You sick in the head? I ought to throw you!" She swatted him again and he took the blow with shoulders hunched. "This is your idea of fun? People are starving and you throw eggs at them?"

Not until the third blow was delivered did she feel the hesitation and heartache that usually choked off her first impulse to hit. Jacob sensed the pause and ducked away.

"Get over here!" she hollered. "Pick up the rest of those eggs and get downstairs right now!"

Her purchase of an orange for Jacob as they walked to the elevated station somewhat patched up feelings between them. On his best behavior, Jacob even postponed peeling and devouring the fruit in order to tote the full basket of eggs that his mother had mysteriously, extravagantly purchased. But their exchanges were brief, sullen, and trivial, hemmed in by her anger and his fear of punishment. Bessie welcomed the train's clatter as cover-up for their unease.

Jacob skipped to the front window, adjacent to the motorman's closet, to watch for landmarks and glimpses of foreign neighborhoods. What am I going to do with him? Bessie wondered miserably, plucking that worry for consideration from among the many crowding her thoughts. "What am I going to do with him?" she had pressed Momma Greenpoint, lying in her sickbed, immediately after the incident on the roof, while Jacob was sulking in the bathroom. "I can't get through to him, Leah. He makes me wish I could fetch Sainer from heaven just to come and talk with his son! I can't even joke with Jacob; we always have a misunderstanding."

Momma Greenpoint was pale and red-eyed but elegantly composed with her hair ribbon in place, her sagging bosom rising and falling beneath the sheet. "It's very hard. A widow, two kids . . ."

"But it's only Jacob who makes me feel that way! Janet is a living doll! She cares, she listens, she wants to learn. But to *him* I want to say, 'Wait until poppa gets home! He'll give you such a spanking!' And I can't even say that. Sainer never used to hit—not like his lousy wife. . . ."

Momma Greenpoint's pensiveness was punctuated with little

resolute sighs. "It's *shabbas*," she had finally announced, "and you've hardly been home all week. Why don't you spend a day with your son? *Shabbas* is for people, not just for God."

A classic Momma Greenpoint platitude: uncomplicatedly practical and oddly provocative. "You," Bessie had avowed, wiping little beads of sweat from her sister's brow, "are a wise woman in spite of yourself."

Jacob stared expectantly at his mother each time the train came to a station. Finally he returned to her side, fidgety, his voice braced for rejection. "Are you going to tell me where we're going?"

"You think I should?" She regarded him with some bitterness, but looked away before she felt its bite. "Maybe."

"Before we get there?"

"Maybe."

He scowled and rolled his eyes.

"Don't be arrogant, Jacob," she warned. "You understand?"

His ears, pointed like a pixie's, reddened. "How come you made me wear my Pioneers' uniform?"

"Why, you don't like it?"

"Uh-uh, it's stupid." He trotted back to his window.

Bessie shut her eyes as the train lurched left and right. Anger, anger, go away. The boy is a sweet rose. Break off the thorns one by one, and forget it when they scratch you. Forget it. Reach . . .

. . . into the basket of eggs. She held one up to the light like a jewel and, with a glance at the boy—he was watching—fetched a laundry marker from her purse and began drawing on the face of the egg. Not until she'd directly beckoned him, however, would Jacob approach.

"We got to mark up all these eggs," she said, "with a message—like this." From her pocketbook, she fetched a piece of paper and spread it on the seat next to her. It was a wrinkled flyer—

MEETING OF THE NYC UNEMPLOYED COUNCIL
Thurs., July 31, 6 P.M.
N.Y.C. Workers' School, 140 W. 13th St.
—Soup and Sandwiches—
ORGANIZE FOR UNEMPLOYMENT INSURANCE ! ! !

Across the eggshell she printed only the date, time, and address. Jacob took it into his hands for a sober examination. "I want to draw faces."

"You can draw on the other side," Bessie agreed, "but you write the message here. I got a marker for you, too, okay? You got a nice handwriting."

He absorbed the compliment mutely, then looked up, directly into her eyes. "Where are we going?"

"Hooverville," she said, bending for another egg.

The original Hooverville had been a six-month encampment of World War I veterans and their families in Washington, D.C., where they came as the "Bonus Marchers" in December 1931 to demand of the federal government relief from Depression poverty. Named for the president, whose conservative Republican policies were the most blatant causes of the prolonged hard times, Hooverville was broken up by soldiers following Congress's summer adjournment. The two veterans left dead were the final blight on Herbert Hoover's record that helped make Roosevelt's 1932 election victory a romp.

But despite two years of the New Deal, shantytowns of the unemployed and impoverished still dotted the riverbanks and parkgrounds of major cities, including New York. Shunned by all but their residents and the Communist party, these Hoovervilles had become nerve centers for the Party-led Unemployed Councils, which counted as members hundreds of thousands of out-of-work people across the nation.

A regular part of Bessie's political work was visiting twice monthly the Lower East Side Hooverville, on the East River south of the Williamsburg Bridge, to provide some health care and first aid, particularly to the children, and to keep the flame of militancy high. There were twenty-eight shacks on the site, patchworks of corrugated cardboard, wood scrap, army blankets, and odd chunks of construction material filched from abandoned construction projects throughout Manhattan, built on muddy, gravelly landfill. Water was obtained through an elaborate makeshift of pipes leading from an underground main, and confrontation with city officials over this and other code violations had flared up frequently before Mayor LaGuardia's progressive administration had taken office in January. In fact, two bulldozers had been parked at the outskirts of the landfill as symbols of city authority, removed only when the Hooverville citizens began operating one to raise windbreaking mounds of earth and stripping the other of levers, windows, plate metal, and other useful materials.

Most people were loitering or laboring outside their hovels in the noonday sun. Bessie gathered their attention effortlessly by walking through the camp, banging a large pot, and stopping every few feet to address her audience.

"Herbert Hoover used to promise a chicken in every pot, yeah? So how come we got not even a bone?" At this point she would lower the pot over her head and strike it with her wooden spoon. "Aha!" Her head reemerged with a bright smile. "Now I got the answer! Those guys in the government, they don't know that we got empty pots! Otherwise they'd fill them with eats like they promised, right? So come on, everybody, grab your pots and let's make some noise! In case President Roosevelt's a little hard-of-hearing, he'll still get the message!"

Her patter varied and improved at each station as a growing crowd of men, women, and kids beat tin cans and cast-iron pots in unison with her. Bessie kept glancing at Jacob, trailing embarrassedly behind her, as she hoped to see his eyes opening wider, his lips spreading into a smile, his heart expanding to embrace the crowd. But he remained as aloof from the clamor as a veteran alley cat.

"Dear friends!" cried Bessie, raising her hands to still the banging. "The truth is we can yell for food, for relief, for unemployment insurance, for everything we deserve. But if we stay here in Hooverville, our noise will reach only the police station next to City Hall, and then we'll get arrested for making a riot!"

She had stepped onto a stack of industrial pallets meant to be split up for firewood. More than sixty people were gathered before her, all gaunt or overstarched, quieting themselves and their children and buoying her with eye contact and alert expressions. "Let me talk to you all a minute," she said, but her plea was unnecessary: They had no other business but to listen and crowd together. Unemployment had removed from their minds the time clock, the ambitions and vanity that deafened the average person to street agitation. Bessie found their attention startlingly strong.

"You got the misery that loves company, comrades," she said. "Unemployment. And you got plenty of company! Eleven million in America without jobs. Now, I know some guys, they lose their job and they don't want to talk to nobody. No matter how lousy the job was, they lose it, somehow they lose their dignity. But next time I meet a sourpuss like that, I'll bring him to Hooverville! 'Cause I can feel your solidarity just standing here. I can taste it. Every one of you's lost something—this is what brought you to Hooverville to begin with. But look at you now! Look at what you got! Look at each other."

People actually turned to look at their neighbors, and Bessie felt a surge of tenderness for them that carried her beyond the pale of words. Her teary gaze swept across the landscape to their battered huts, piled like garbage between the bricks and shadows of Manhattan and the sluggish river that at its mouth had no current of its own but flowed either way with the tide. Everybody into the water! she thought. They would all be baptized to socialism, and Hooverville would be their *soviet*, a community that would be impenetrable to Spanknoebel's fascists when they came crawling up the banks of the East River.

The memory of that insanity in Madison Square Garden, just hours ago, began to fray her attention. Fatigue was unstringing her muscles, tingling her skin. She tipped her head back to breathe in order to maintain a loud, level voice. The sky was a thin, sunny blue, so distant . . . distant like Jacob, squatting in the gravel to one side of the crowd, tossing pebbles in short arcs toward her rickety platform. "Jakey," she called to him, "get the eggs. And my bag!" He gladly bolted off.

Bessie squinted at the sky again. "I'm disappointed in the weather. There's no manna falling from heaven. Used to be, God gave you a few rules to live with, and if you were good you'd get freedom from the pharaoh and free eats. These days we get nothing but the rules, no eats."

"Amen," piped in a contralto voice. "No freedom, neither."

She was a black, young, bony woman with matted hair and three beanpole children encircling her like a fence. Bessie's eyes widened when she smiled down at them, and other Negro faces suddenly appeared to her in the crowd: a dusty, gray old man with a face like a raisin; a fat, walleyed woman overfilling a rusty metal chair; a brawny young man, arms folded on his chest, and his handsome wife, skin colors of butter and bran; and others, with angry mouths, intent eyes—none of that hollow, languished look that hung on certain of the more vulnerable, scarecrow whites. Bessie could almost hear Mrs. Gittins's hee-haw in the air, the bitterness that prompted it, and the courage that turned it into belly laughter. Got to recruit that woman! she promised herself, and crowed: "Look at you! Black and white, Jew and gentile. You know when's the last time I saw it? In Siberia! The less we had, the more human we had to be. Otherwise we're lost, y'see. . . . But some men, they get knocked down and they lay like worms. But you, women and men, you got arms and hands, you been selling to the bosses your power and now maybe they don't want to buy it, so to hell with them! You reach out—you reach out . . . Eh, but who needs me to talk? I don't have to tell you nothing. Hooverville, you really got something going."

"I'll give you my house if you give me yours," heckled the woman with three children.

Bessie hurled the remark back without blinking. "My neighbors wouldn't let you, lady! I know how to turn back on the electricity! I'm a star!" She patted her coiffure, show-girl-style, winning laughter from the crowd. Jacob brought the eggs with fortuitous timing, enabling Bessie to glide into her appeal. But every considered word now seemed wooden and puny compared to the feelings piled up inside her. Her lips kept opening in vowel shapes, without breath; her thoughts began to stumble over the shored-up heap of words, until silence seemed the only alternative. Perhaps the eggs could speak for themselves? She plucked one from the basket and, mindful of her audience, held it at arm's length in a grand gesture.

Jacob had drawn an awestruck, saucer-eyed little face. His own?

"Okay. I brought you all a little present. From the Communist party. Eggs. Four dozen eggs."

A smattering of her listeners clapped hands excitedly.

"These are the eggs," she went on, getting again into rhetorical stride, "that Herbert Hoover's 'chicken in every pot' forgot to hatch. They're the eggs that FDR is too chicken himself to nationalize. They come from the Communist party, and don't

you forget it, all right? Everyone who knows me knows I'm a
Communist. Anyone who doesn't, now I'm telling you! But it's
not charity, my eggs. Just like home relief is not charity, and
unemployment relief is not charity. That's what we're fighting
for—our rights! If they don't want to give us unemployment
relief, let them give us the factories we used to work in. We'll
make plenty of jobs for ourselves."

Bessie looked down at the basketful of scribbled egg faces,
then across at Jacob. "My son, Jacob Sainer," she announced,
"will give out these eggs. One for each adult. If we run out,
then you should all make one big Hooverville omelet."

Jacob pouted and threw his gaze to the dirt. Bessie pleafully
thrust her hands forward, then lifted her face to the crowd.
"Don't throw away the eggshells, whatever you do! Take a
look, there's a message written there about a meeting of the
Unemployed Council. If you want that you should have more
eggs, you got to organize. Come to the meeting, Thursday night.
If you came once already, come again, and bring somebody else.
Organizing is like eating, comrades—you got to keep doing it!"

Bessie stepped to the pallet's edge, knelt, and held her arms
out to her son. "Come, dear," she entreated him in Yiddish, then
stepped back as a Hooverville man lifted Jacob by the shoulders
and set him upright on the stage.

"One to a customer, Jacob." She demonstrated by handing the
egg she held to the strongman. "Nicely, *tatenyu*," she implored
as Jacob performed his task indifferently, holding out eggs for
any comers. "Form a line," she had to insist when four or five
people grabbed at once for the undesignated offerings. "Jacob,
please! Hand it to one person!"

He shook an egg in the face of the slow-moving Negro
oldster. "Here! Take it!"

Bessie dug frantically into her pocketbook and yanked out a
wrinkled leaf of paper. "Everybody, everybody line up, please!
I got a petition here for unemployment relief. Please, before
you take your eggs, let us have your signature...."

Bessie was well prepared to refute Sonya Stein's charges at her
hearing at Party headquarters the following Wednesday, and
lost no time in making her case. Against the charge of desertion,
she defended herself with a written statement that she'd wrangled

from Albert Bronstein after an intensive hour of struggle with the man's ego:

> To Whom It May Concern:
>   It should be known that my respected friend and comrade Bessie Sainer was personally responsible for my safe escape from Nazi hooligans at the Madison Square Garden rally of the so-called Friends of the New Germany. Sister Sainer heroically knocked to the floor a uniformed thug who had already beaten me to within an inch of my . . ."

"Bessie! When you say 'within an inch of my life,' it sounds like I was helpless!"
"You were."
"But, Bessie! I could have fought back. He got me by surprise."
"You were just lying there to gather your strength?"
"No, no! But the way you say it here . . ."
"Look, Bronstein, would you rather we should take a picture of you now, with your face like a piece of meat that the butcher pounds? We can put it on the front page of the Freiheit: *"Khaver Bronstein after fearlessly defending the honor of the Party . . ."*

> . . . life. In doing this, she busted her bag and lost all her belongings. In my opinion the Party should reimburse her.
>
>   Sincerely yours,
>   Albert Bronstein

"I got a spare set of keys," Bessie noted as New York Party head Israel Hampton set down the document with a barely concealed snicker. "But this . . ."—she presented a second slip of paper—"this is a list of what else I lost thanks to our *stupid* Party line, and this . . . this is the uniform I ruined thanks to our *stupid* Party line. There's a tear in the armpit. . . . And this is the orthopedic stocking I tore thanks to our *stupid* line. They're expensive, these stockings, and you can't buy a single—oh, and this is how I spent my *shabbas:* I got a petition here for unemployment relief, fifty names from Hooverville . . . here's a bill for four dozen eggs I bought to give out in Hooverville. Oh, and

this is a Party card for a new recruit from where I work, Mrs.
Mary Jane Gittins, a Negro woman. Hampton's got to sign it."

Hampton and Sid Frankel, who had led the Friday night
rally, contemplated the heap of material and paper that Bessie
had piled onto the conference table while Milton softly read
Bronstein's statement to Sonya, whose nose was a mound of
bandage between twin beads of bloodshot.

"Big deal!" Sonya cried shrilly at its conclusion. "And if my
boyfriend wrote a letter saying I could fly to the moon, you'd
believe it?"

"No, no," Bessie retorted, " 'cause you're *both* a couple of
fakers!"

"Let's drop the name-calling," Frankel admonished her, pounding the table.

Bessie leaped up. "Don't worry, Frankel, I've got a name for
you, too. And you," she rebuked Hampton. "Now that I'm here
on charges, thanks to these fakers, I'm gonna make charges of
my own! And you're gonna listen! . . . Now, you got to stop
treating the fascists like you can just beat them with your fists
and they'll go home! We're not children playing in the street!
We got to make a united front against the fascists, and first we
got to understand, fascism grows on the same tree as us, the
same branch as us, it's a weed in *our* garden—"

"Bessie!" hollered Hampton, arresting her by his volume.
"Bessie," he repeated as she scowled at him for interrupting.

"What, Izzy, what?"

Hampton frowned wearily and turned to the recording secretary for these proceedings. "The statement from Albert Bronstein can be taken as sufficient evidence to disprove the charges
against Bessie Sainer. The chairman instructs Comrade Sainer
to remove her junk from the conference table in five seconds
or face a new set of charges. The rest," he added, "is off the
record. Now look, Bess, why don't you join the Executive Committee again? If you've got something to say about Party policy,
that's where it should be said—not at a Nazi rally. You've had
national experience—you've had international experience, for
Christ's sake, and you're an admired and outstanding Communist.
How many years has it been since you were fully active,
Bessie? Since Daniel died, am I right?"

He had switched table settings on her. Suddenly her heap of

"evidence" was an embarrassment, for Hampton was taking her far more seriously than she'd taken herself. "Excuse me," she said quietly to Milton, "could you pour me some of that water, please?"

Milton squeezed Sonya's hand and did as Bessie asked. Bessie stood to collect her old uniform and nylons from the table. "You know my problem, Izzy," she said while working. "I got kids, a job . . . but we should talk more." She stuffed the clothing into her bag, then wagged a finger at him. "But first, the Party owes me money. So I'm leaving the bills right there on the table. I'm giving half the money to her"—she thumbed at Sonya —"to pay for her new nose. The rest I want—there's still a Depression going on, you know!"

Chapter Seventeen / 1941

"To live as a revolutionary means you got to trust yourself. 'Cause you're always gonna be persecuted—until you win. And you're gonna have a career that nobody pays for it. So you got to work a job, and it's like working two jobs, y'see, 'cause making revolution is full-time. Probably you'll be poor despite. And always with a hungry kind of a feeling, excepting it has nothing to do with food, if you know what I mean.

"You got to be crazy. You got to believe that you, a little stinker, can take to be your enemy the most powerful men in the whole world—and beat them! You got to believe you're a hero, even when in the mirror you see a bum.

"To me, *kinderlakh*, the world looks so sad. Like when you see a child with polio. The child that she should walk and run and dance, and instead she sits and suffers. Y'see, we got the potential in America that we shouldn't have to worry about things. About food, clothing, health, disease. We got so much wealth in this country! We got machines that they can make miracles, we got farmers that they can grow food faster than you can eat it. It's true, we got thrown out from the Garden of Eden a long time ago, but this new place we built for ourselves, it's not so bad! You maybe take it for granted, but I'm still looking with a peasant's eye, y'see. Every time I see an airplane fly, I still give a look, I still say, 'Oh, boy, look at what human beings can do!'

"So America should be one big Camp Nishtgedeiget. We should be working together to make life meaningful, to make it that human beings can fulfill themselves and each other. Meaningful! Aie, but the profit system is so stupid! It makes it that bombs are more important than buildings, hospitals, schools, houses. Now, I read in the *Freiheit,* it said that since World War Two the United States paid more than a million million dollars on weapons, on war. We got only five percent of the people in the world, but we spend fifty percent of what the whole world spends on bombs. Wonderful. I'm sure that the old people that they're eating dog food to stay alive, they must feel wonderful to know there's a bomb just for them to protect them from communism.

"So why doesn't it stop already? It's torture. It's like once I saw with my family when we went for a vacation to Lake George. They got there some kind of a fort from the American Revolution, and they take you for a tour and they show you the dungeon. They got these cells in the dungeon that they would put a prisoner inside, and the ceiling was too low, lower than the guy was tall, y'see, and the cell was too narrow for him to sit, so he got to stand stooped over until his whole body becomes like a pretzel. This was the most painful thing for me to see. And this is the human spirit under capitalism.

"And when you have a vision of something so much better, then it hurts even more. Sometimes I say to myself, How can Rockefeller be so blind, so dull, that he'd rather have money than *nakhes?* How much could it mean to him, another car, another airplane, another swimming pool, another young woman? I mean, they could be like the Messiah, these guys. They could give so much to the world, they could actually save the world. They could save millions from starving! They could give educa-

tion to everyone. They could get rid of the bombs. But can
you imagine, one of them stands at a cocktail party and he says,
'You know, I been thinking . . . we sure are messing up the
world, aren't we? I'm gonna stop manufacturing deodorant,
I'm gonna stop manufacturing bombs; instead I'm gonna make
sure that all the old women in the United States got what to eat.'

"The rich can't understand this idea, y'see. They see us as
little bugs, very far away. They can't so much as go to the
bathroom without a servant to come and wipe their *tukhas,* so
they can't have sympathy for what it means to be hungry, or
cold, or any of that. The rich can't be visionary; they're too
busy congratulating themselves and making out that they're
very important people, that they deserve everything they got
'cause they're so wonderful. They're too busy holding on to
what they got, to the way things are.

"And this is the revolutionary's reward, y'see. Don't let any
bastard tell you that revolutionaries are only those that they're
frustrated and without any purpose in life. I had a better time
with myself, with my life and with my soul, than any Rockefeller,
man or woman. I mean it. Why? 'Cause I could live the way I
wanted, the way I believed, knowing that with every breath
and, yes, with every sacrifice, I was going with life, with progress,
with humanity. When I went to sleep at night, I would smell
flowers, the springtime, the future, coming into my dreams.

"So never mind the rich *shtunks.* They're not gonna hear me
talking and they'd steal my teeth before I could get another word
out. But the thing is that their ideas, their cynicism, their racism,
this is everywhere. People don't need Bessie Sainer to know
that the corporations got us by the necks, they got our children
by the necks. But people don't believe that we as human beings
can do better. They don't believe that the young black boy
that he mugs could instead help old people to cross the street.
They don't believe that a woman that she's a secretary a whole
day could maybe cure cancer. They don't believe in the potential of working people, even though every day they look at the
great, tall buildings and the bridges and the everything that we
built.

"And this is why they need Bessie Sainer. But where can I
point for inspiration? To the Soviet Union? Feh, they gave up
on revolution in the Soviet Union. The people aren't free or
happy. They're not working together to make their lives good.

They're not growing. They're not, like, that the whole human race should evolve into something better. Instead they got a system with bureaucrats, and the bureaucrats are happy to call it 'socialism' so they won't have to make something better. They're cynics, just like our leaders are cynics. You know, it's amazing how a government will work so hard to change a name instead that it should change a policy. Like you got here the War Department. It became the Defense Department. You think it makes the bombs behave better? It's like they think they can fool God and get to heaven this way, like God just listens to what they say and never bothers to watch what they do.

"But *my* idea about heaven is different, y'see. And you better pay attention, 'cause I'm far ahead of you on line. It goes like this: We *all* get judged at the same time. We're *all* the chosen people. If we blow ourselves up with the nuclear bombs, we all die and we all go to hell. No personal revolution and no personal salvation. No prayers. God is a deaf-mute.

"There's a *meise* about this, about salvation. It says that a Jewish man dies and goes to heaven, and who does he meet at the gate? Not St. Peter, no, not Johnny Carson, not his rabbi, not his wife, but God. God himself. So the Jew is very honored, to say the least.

"God brings him to a little room, sets him down to a table, and puts in front of him a plate of shmaltz herring. A meal with God! So the man bows his head. But when he looks down, he can see right into the other world, y'see, and down there in hell it's a real feast—steak, lobster, all kind of eats. So the Jew says to God, 'Almighty,' he says, 'I'm very honored to have lunch with you, but please explain to me—how come down there they got a smorgasbord and up here with the Lord of the Universe I get only herring?'

" 'Feh,' God says, 'for two it doesn't pay to cook.'

"Judaism doesn't talk so much about heaven anyway, 'cause our job is here on earth—we're supposed to make everything nice and ready for the Messiah, right? At Yom Kippur, f'rinstance. If you're a good Jew, you're supposed to atone for your sins. But first you got to go make up with people, 'cause God won't listen to you before you settle your business with human beings.

"Boy, if my father could hear me talking now! A real Hasid, his daughter! But it's true, I always held on to two ideas that they're basic to the Jewish tradition. One is that the Messiah didn't come yet, so don't stop working. The other is that the Messiah is gonna come, so don't stop hoping.

"Now, twice it looked to me like the dream was coming true. I felt revolution in the air, and maybe I wasn't just a part of a little *meshugeneh* bunch. But it's a funny kind of a thing: I could never eat from the pot that I cooked. Instead I got burned holding the handle.

"The first time you know already—the Bolshevik revolution. But me, one day I'm dancing in the streets, the next day I'm crying on my daughter's grave.

"Then came the Depression. We built a very powerful movement. We made the CIO, millions and millions of workers joining new unions, and the Party gave leadership to some of them. We were very busy, and with eighty thousand members! But for me it was like sitting by myself on a big, crowded beach. You watch everybody that they're bathing and running and eating knishes and lying around smooching, and you, you get to feel like a hot little peanut. First of all, I was lonely. I had money troubles, with the kids growing up and needing things. And I had problems with my health that went back already to the bad food in Siberia and the typhus in the revolution: My gums were bleeding, my headaches came all the time, my foot where I got shot began to hurt, I had a weak stomach—and if I say anything more, you'll charge me for a prescription, yeah?

"Plus I had all kind of a disagreements with the Party. We made a terrible mistake with the Hitler-Stalin pact, y'see. This was in 1939, and Stalin had to make the pact with the Nazis so the Soviet Union shouldn't get attacked. Fine. It's true, the other countries, especially England, they were trying to push Hitler into a war with Stalin so they should knock each other out. But for us in America to suddenly drop the struggle against fascism, for us to say it doesn't matter who wins the war in Europe 'cause they're all imperialists—this was ridiculous, and it was anti-Semitic, 'cause it ignored what Hitler was doing to the Jews all over.

"I remember, before the pact, I could go to Momma Greenpoint's Hadassah women and ask them to help us send a group of Americans to fight fascism in Spain, f'rinstance—we had there the Lincoln Brigade against Franco. Many in the Brigade were Jewish, plus there was a group from Palestine also going to Spain—about four hundred Jews—so the Zionists said, 'Yeah, it must be an important struggle.' But then in 1939, 1940, when these same women came to *me* to ask for money for Bundles for Britain, to help England fight Germany, and I said, 'No, I won't give no money even if I had it, 'cause England and Germany, they're both imperialists against the Soviet Union'—well, these women were ready to tear my eyes out! I felt like a real fool, 'cause in my heart I knew we were wrong, y'see.

"The Party lost everybody's respect, especially among the Jewish people. But I was tired of arguing. So I stayed quiet. I wasn't ready to quit. The Party was like a family.

"Then Momma Greenpoint gets very sick. Turns out she's got a blood disease, like leukemia but not leukemia. All along she had it, from when she was a child, but now it was getting ripe, y'see—and now they're first learning enough to know what kind of a disease it is! So I had *tsuris* with her, I worried, I took care, I had to buy her medicine, I had to help Mr. Markish to keep up his furniture store—they had this now instead of the laundry. Janet gave up many holidays to work in that store, too. . . .

"But that's enough talk about trouble already. Like my sister Momma Greenpoint used to say, 'With people, you laugh. With God, you weep.' I don't want to waste words, not about *tsuris*, not about the Party, not about Jacob. Let *him* come and talk to you, let him come tell you what happened that he can't stand to be with his mother. You know when's the last time I saw my good son? At his uncle Herschel's funeral, ten years ago! And he didn't even give me a handkerchief to blow my nose. No, I don't want to talk about this kind of a personal nonsense. You want to be a revolutionary, it's a career, I told you. It keeps you plenty busy."

❊

Ruchel was holding court to show off a luxurious Persian rug that Feivl had purchased for their living room. Slender, pale, and attractively sedate in a reupholstered chintz armchair bought "for cheap" in the Markishes' furniture store ("I did my sister a favor when I saw it wasn't selling"), she had positioned herself at the carpet's edge, facing the foyer, where she could receive each guest's expression of admiration for the rug as a personal tribute. Her husband stood like a palace guard in the doorway, advising all to remove the April mud from their shoes before entering.

Bessie came in with Momma Greenpoint on her arm, kissed Feivl, assessed Ruchel's strategic arrangement, and made a point of loudly saluting Paul Dropsky, who was across the room sprawled on the sofa like a pampered dog. "Hey hey hey, Bessie! Hello!" He sprang up, spry for a man of sixty, and came at her with open arms. Good, she thought, let Ruchel wait for her compliment.

But Momma Greenpoint was bubbling. "Rucheleh! It looks like the Rothschilds' palace!"

Ruchel purred and held her elder sister's hand to her cheek as Momma Greenpoint extended a stockinged toe toward the plush edge. "*Gottenyu*, you could sleep on this rug! You wouldn't even need a blanket, the way it swallows you up."

"Another place for my sister to be lazy," Bessie teased, stepping up behind the armchair and regarding Ruchel's gauzy yellow hair.

"Hello, Bessie," Ruchel singsonged to her as if to a child. It was a demeaning tactic, but in Bessie's opinion it made Ruchel sound senile.

Bessie returned the greeting with a kiss to her cheek. "Mmm, your skin is still like butter," she confessed. "This is why Feivl keeps you so well."

"May he prosper through a dozen depressions," Leah unthinkingly chimed.

Bessie took her around the waist. "You can forget the Depression now, dear. Die-cutting doesn't make a living when the factories are closing down."

"True, true," Ruchel agreed, mouth set in sour memory of less pleasant times.

Bessie bristled at her affected solemnity. "Feivl's good fortune is the war in Europe," she said, "and having me for a sister-in-law so he could get to meet Captain Owen at my house last Hanuka."

"Nonsense," protested Ruchel. "One meeting with an old sea captain doesn't make a business boom!"

"Oh, no? Ask your husband where he got the idea to manufacture radio parts?"

"Common sense," she snapped. "Don't *you* think we should prepare ourselves for war?"

The question was an indictment, carried over from the last bitter family debate, Bessie versus everyone, at Momma Greenpoint's seder:

RUCHEL: How can a Jew sit there and compare Hitler to England? How?

BESSIE: They're both out to get the Soviet Union! If two gangsters start killing each other, I should worry?

HERSCHEL: You and your Party—a bunch of dirty hypocrites!

LEAH: No name-calling, please! Be nice. Why do we have to talk about things we can't agree on? Let's hear from Janet about her young man.

HERSCHEL: Another Communist draft-dodger!

JANET: Don't be an old fart! There's no draft and you know it. Even Captain Owen said he hopes there won't be one.

JACOB: I hope there is.

JANET: *You* hope for whatever will aggravate mom, you creep!

RUCHEL: Very nice how you talk, Janet! That's some manners your mother taught you!

NAT: Aww, cut it out, mother. You try to make everyone into a child.

BESSIE: You'll have to be a general in the army before your mother will call you "sir."

RUCHEL: Nat's too old to be drafted!

LEAH: Please! Nobody should join the army!

RUCHEL: Jews should be ready to fight Hitler!

BESSIE: Oh, but your son's too old? Why don't you stop your whining, Ruchel? I was fighting Hitler while you were eating chocolates all through the Depression.

HERSCHEL: But now that your bloody Uncle Stalin is ready to shake hands with Uncle Hitler—

BESSIE: Look who's talking! You were chasing widows while I fought the fascists! You and your friends, you were too sectarian even to join the popular front! So now you're a bigger hypocrite than you were during the First World War.

LEAH: They're giving numbers to the war! *Oi gevalt!*

"You want to prepare for war?" Bessie replied now to Ruchel. "There's your Nat, eating your delicious chopped liver. So leave your fancy armchair, my sister, and go dress your son to be a cannonball. Jacob you can leave alone." She stalked away.

"He's left alone enough," Ruchel retorted, stinging Bessie's heels.

Bessie hoped Momma Greenpoint would tire quickly. No one here but social democrats and ignoramuses! Ruchel's fancy-shmancy house, fancy-shmancy food—just like a czarist princess she lives....

(But listen to yourself! Momma Greenpoint should get sick so you can go and hide, hmm? How low have we sunk, *khaveyrim?* I can't be in human company anymore. I wish Hitler would attack the Soviet Union already! Anything to give us back our souls!)

She brushed glances with Herschel by the buffet table. He was dressed in a disheveled suit, eating from a paper plate, and making quips to his nephew Nat, who looked bored. Herschel, she thought, you look like a poor old *melamed*, you know that? So rumpled and wrinkled. Are you still waiting for your strumpet wife to return to you after ten years? Maybe you'd like a sister who could press your clothes, you old social-democratic bastard? I use less starch than Ruchel, I promise.

Yeah, so give me a call....

She shied away and bumped shoulders with Paul Dropsky, who had followed her. "Another one of Ruchel's gang! They're everywhere!" she cried. "So? Which bunch of anarchists are you mingling with these days?"

"Bessie, I got a new *klezmer* band," he said. "With the sweetest young clarinet player you ever heard in your life. What a lad!"

"So? Why don't you run off with him?"

"Pshh. Still with the sharp tongue. With a mouth like yours, you should have taken up an instrument."

"I did," Bessie said, "I play the thermometer. So where's your harmonica, Pesach? My sister won't let you play in the house?"

Dropsky winked. "That's the only thing she *will* let me play with."

"I told you, she won't run off with you unless her husband goes bankrupt. How can you waste your time on someone like her?"

"She's a beautiful woman."

"Yeah, yeah, so's Greta Garbo. But I got news for you, you can't have her either."

He shrugged, palms upraised. "We all have our addictions, yes?"

His, she had come to suspect, was young male musicians. Well, good for him—he'd be more sick in the head if he were actually pining away for Ruchel!

Paul patted his pockets to locate a harmonica. "So how are you, Bessie?"

"I'm nervous like a fly, to tell you the truth," she confessed, touching his arm. "Monday I find out if I got a promotion at Mt. Sinai. My supervisor's quitting—retiring."

"You got the qualifications?"

"Sure. I worked in every department but the laundry room. And even there I organized."

"So what are you nervous about? Shall I play a little lullabye for you?" He raised the shiny harp to his lips.

"Don't play yet," she said. "Come with me, I've got to find my son. He'll be listening to the radio and he'll bite your head off if you make noise."

"Noise?" said Paul. "I beg your pardon, woman!"

She shushed him again as they entered Ruchel's bedroom. Jacob was sprawled across the floor with his ear to the speaker of his aunt's new Stromberg-Carlson console radio, a hunk of dark mahogany shaped like a Holy Ark with a needlepoint rose-pattern speaker face. Bessie could feel the speaker's bass vibration through her feet.

"Jacob, say hello to Paul."

"Shh. I'm listening."

Paul knelt by him. "To what?"

" 'Fibber McGee.' "

"Any good?"

"Eh, it's all right. 'Amos 'n Andy' 's next."

Paul glanced over his shoulder at Bessie, standing with her arms crossed. "That's the one about the *shvartzes*."

"Yeah," Jacob chimed. "Kingfish . . . Madame Queen . . ."

Bessie groaned. "I wish I could plug up your ears from this kind of a nonsense! Let me ask you, my son: If Mrs. Gittins came to our house, would you play this kind of a show for her?"

He turned a scornful gaze at her. "Not on our radio. It's a piece of junk!"

"Hang me for it! If this miracle machine makes you so

smart, you can live here for all I care! Let Ruchel feed your big mouth!"

She could remember vividly his excitement as a boy when she'd brought home their table radio, bought on the installment plan for Hanuka. He had hopped around the room like a toad, played with all the dials, answered unabashedly the rhetorical questions of the kiddy-show announcers, and then—what a child!—dismantled the entire mechanism with a screwdriver when she was off to work at night. "Jacob!" she'd wept the next morning, "it'll be a whole year before we even pay for it!" "Don't worry," he'd replied, "I'll put it back together." And within two hours, with hardly a drop of sweat or a break in his concentration, he had reassembled the million-plus parts and, it seemed to her, greatly improved the radio's sound.

Paul raised a cautionary hand to soothe Bessie, then settled more comfortably next to the boy. "It's a real humdinger, this set."

"You're not kidding. It's got FM, too. They're not broadcasting much on FM, but someday they will, 'cause you get better fidelity with it."

"No kidding? So this is the Carnegie Hall of the radios."

"That's right," Jacob agreed. "And you see how the band's lit up? And the tuning is real precise."

Bessie longed to be able to imitate Paul's easygoing paternalism: his ability to kneel comfortably on the floor, understand Jacob's lingo, be genuinely interested in and knowledgeable about his subjects or at least able to ask intelligent questions. She had not known such intimacy with her son since his adolescence, but had stood apart, worried by his mean streak, intimidated by the manual competence and mechanical mind that he'd inherited from Sainer, and bruised by his increasing unfamiliarity with her. Even when their activities coincided naturally, at meals or during their few outings, she would engage him with ulterior motives: to observe and teach, to quantify and evaluate.

"You're always organizing me, ma," he had told her during a recent argument.

"You always want something from me. If I do something good, you want a share in it."

"There's something wrong about a little nakhes *once in a while?"*

"But it's the same if I do something bad. Something really rotten. It's like I'm doing it to you. I'm damaging your idea of what I should be."

"I'm a mother, Jacob."

"Ugh, these advertisements," Dropsky protested of the jingle on the air. "Can you imagine if my band played an Alka-Seltzer advertisement at every bar mitzvah we went to?"

"You *are* an advertisement. You advertise the wealth of the man who hires you." Jacob's perception came, as usual, as a passing remark, while he busied himself with the radio dials.

". . . that it's about time we gave credit where credit is due? Well, I'm glad you feel that way—now go pay that bill collector, he's been following me for weeks. No, wait, he fell into a financial hole. Well, that's a relief. Here's his address, you can send him a check. On second thought, here's *my* address. . . ."

"Hey, Groucho!" Jacob cheered, settling back on his heels.

"Jacob, please," Bessie said with a grimace, "can we go home? We've got something to talk about, no?"

Dropsky again tried to mollify her. "How can a man leave when Groucho Marx is making with the jokes?"

"I'll tell you how," she replied in a resentful burst of Yiddish. "You want to hear a joke my son told this morning? He said if I can't afford to send him to school to learn radio engineering, he's gonna learn it in the navy! Big joke, with a war coming!"

In shuffled Herschel with a big hello for everyone. "What about war? You got the news on?" he called to Jacob over Bessie's head.

Bessie was on a short leash. Herschel, too, had the knack, the male charisma, though he was a hundred times stuffier than Paul. So Momma Greenpoint would remind her again tonight that the boy needs a father! For what? she thought. Foolish boasts, big, callused hands to pat his shoulders and squeeze his knees?

"What's cooking?" Herschel said. "How's my smartest nephew?"

Bessie cut across his path and reached for the on-off dial on the console. This much I know how to do, she thought. "I'll get it," Jacob growled.

The illuminated band selector always reminded Bessie of the dashboard in Sainer's old sedan. When the light flicked off, it left her with a dead feeling. She cleared her throat and absently mumbled hello to Herschel. He returned her greeting with surprise, having expected a snub.

We spend too much time at Momma Greenpoint's, Bessie complained to herself as she and Jacob entered their apartment after delivering the elder woman to the door. "Where are we gonna sit?" she mused aloud. Jacob was at the kitchen sink, gulping water.

He carried a glassful to the table in the adjacent dining alcove. "Here at the table?" she said. "You don't think the walls in here are sick and tired of hearing us fight?"

Jacob ran his hand across the top of the table radio as if flirting with the idea of turning it on. "Tell me," Bessie said, pulling up a chair, "is it really such a terrible radio?"

"Not for what it is. It's all right."

"Am I really such a terrible mother?"

He snorted and sat back in his seat. "Don't ask stupid questions, mom."

She looked away from his glowering face. "It's not so stupid, Jakey. I'll tell you why. Y'see, I want to know, is the idea that you should join the navy really 'cause you want to learn a trade? Or is it more like running away from home?" She awaited an answer. His silence dripped on the table like an icicle. "Y'see, I got nothing against you learning a trade. I couldn't be what I am today if I wasn't first a nurse. So you like the Lone Ranger better than you like Karl Marx? Believe me, Stalin won't know the difference, one more, one less. But I will know the difference if you join the navy, Jacob. . . . Please," she urged, "you said we would talk."

"I want to learn radio engineering," he reiterated grudgingly.

"Good! It's a wonderful trade. There's even Jewish people on the radio, so maybe you won't find so much discrimination—"

"That's show biz," he said. "That's not what I want. I want to engineer."

"All right. So why don't you do like I told you and write to your uncle Julius in Chicago? He's an engineer."

"I know, I know! RCA. And I'm not going to write to him!"

"But why not?" she pleaded, despairing as her words piled up without effect. "You want *me* to ask for you?"

"No!"

"I could call him and explain—"

"We don't even have a telephone," the boy muttered.

"So? Momma Greenpoint has one. Your aunt Ruchel has one—"

"Two."

"She could have a hundred and she'd have nothing intelligent to say!" Bessie shouted, her temper flaring. "You don't want a career for yourself, Jacob! You just like to make a career of criticizing me! Nothing I do is any good."

"Nothing *I* do is any good," he retorted. "You're a goddamn dictator!"

"Oh, you'll have it much better in the navy," she sassed him, "taking orders from all kind of a fascists."

"Nuts to your fascists." He pushed away from the table. "You see fascists like a drunkard sees pink elephants. You're ready to fight them off and save the whole fucking world—"

"Don't talk to me in that kind of language!"

"—but when it comes to having a couple of lousy hundred bucks so *I* can do something with myself besides carrying one of your picket signs . . ."

"Jacob," she said, panicking, "sit down. Sit down!"

"Why should I? I'll sit down in a classroom. At a workbench. Not in your crummy Workers' School! All they teach you there is how to make your own noose. Shit! I've had it with the YCL bringing me their cheap megaphones to fix. I want to work with broadcast equipment!"

"Good, good! I want this for you!"

"Well, I don't need for you to want it," he screamed, "I need for you to pay for it! I'm not going to lie around in the Sainer family ditch, waiting for someone to piss on me so I can call them a fascist!"

"Jacob!"

"No! That's where you belong, maybe! You live in some kind of dreamworld, you and all your stupid friends. A bunch of working stiffs all day, and then at night you make believe there's actually something to your lives, like you're a bunch of Supermen—"

"Not supermen, no!" she shrieked. "This is not class consciousness! You're talking like Hitler!"

"Oh, for Christ's sake." He snorted and shook his head. "I'm talking about a comic-book character, ma. He's from another planet, the guy who flies around? He's a shlep all day and at night he performs miracles."

"Socialism is not a miracle!"

"Boy, are you a dodo. Forget it." He buried his nose in his glass of water.

Bessie slumped back, cheek to shoulder, calculating: It's only two hundred and fifty dollars. You'll get it, you'll get it, it's not worth fighting. "You don't think we need socialism, huh?" she said bitterly. "In the Soviet Union, Jacob, the schools are free."

"In the Soviet Union, they haven't got enough radios to fill a Woolworth's. Okay?" He peered through his glass, momentarily fascinated by the distorted view of familiar sights. "Anyway, the whole world's going crazy. That's why I like working with equipment."

The front door slammed and Janet shouted an innocent greeting from the foyer. "Look," Bessie hurriedly concluded, "I'm doing the best I can. Why do you think I took the test to be supervisor? But you're only seventeen years, my son."

"I know how old I am."

"And if you go to school now, or in the summer or in the fall, it's not such a difference."

"It's a difference to me," he warned. "I'm joining the navy right after high school."

"*Gai gezunterhait*. The whole world may be burning up by the summer. I should worry so much about you?" She fell silent as Janet entered the room. "Now, what do you want for supper? Will you eat kasha varnishkas?"

"Again?" Jacob groaned.

Janet patted her mother's shoulder and kissed her cheek. "I'm taking care of supper tonight, ma. What's the matter? You look terrible."

"I'm nervous," Bessie confessed with a wave of her hand. "Comes time to go to work . . ."

"But you're not working tonight."

"All right! So I can't worry in advance? What are *you* so nervous about, *mein tokhteh?*"

"I just want you home tonight. And don't worry so much about a fifteen-dollar raise, you'll worry yourself right into a hospital bed. Go lie down, ma. I'll call you when dinner's ready. Keep that low," she warned her brother as he reached for the radio dial. "Very low."

" 'Radio Debates.' WCPUSA, your Communist party station. Presenting tonight: 'American Response to the Hitler-Stalin Nonaggression Pact.'" Then he'll say, "Comrade Sainer, it is not in the interest of the American working class to get involved in an imperialist war." Then you'll say, "So how come everybody wants to? Even my son is looking to join the navy!" Then he'll say (quoting Lenin) something about false consciousness among workers, and I'll say, "Listen, comrade, I support the pact just like you, but does that mean that we in the United States must be neutral?" And he will say (quoting again from Lenin) something about the fruitlessness of opportunism, and I'll say, "What opportunism? I'm talking about life! Look at what's happening to the Jews in Poland, Austria, France—isn't that enough to show you the difference between the Germans and the British?" And he'll say, "Protecting the Soviet Union is the most important thing we can do for Jews. And I'll say, "But how does our neutrality protect the Soviet Union?"

And then Jacob will say, "C'mon, change the station to something good! I'm bored!"

And he's right, my American brat. We're boring ourselves to death with words. Are we gonna stop Hitler with our words? If we get Groucho Marx into the Party, maybe—we can kibitz our way into socialism. Hey, Mr. Rockefeller, did you hear the one about the working class that one day it organized and demanded of the ruling class good wages, control of the factories, and all that? And the ruling class said, "Why, of course, why didn't you just ask?"

Fact of the matter is, I should've stayed in the USSR. There, on the barricades . . . I could've started my hospital, maybe become a hero of the Soviet Union! I would have given birth to my daughter on Soviet soil and to hell with Jacob! So the world would have one less radio engineer and I would have one less critic!

Oh, dear world, I don't want my son in a war! Didn't I fight

enough for the whole family? Jacob, Jacob, why does every-
thing look so different to you? Why do you see only my ugli-
ness and never my beauty? Why does suffering and pain rouse
your scorn, never your humanism? Who are you, boy? Who
are you? ...

"Mom?" *Rapping lightly on the open door: Into my dreams,*
she walks. Across my tears, she wades. "Dinner's ready, mom.
Should I turn on the light?"

"What time is it, darling?"

"The radio just said six."

"The radio. America's god!"

"You still have a headache, mom?"

"Come in, *mommasheyne*, you're too far away." Bessie patted
the edge of her mattress and felt it sag as Janet sat.

Janet squeezed her hand. "Dinner's ready."

"You think I got an appetite? I got worms crawling in my
stomach."

"Come on. Forget about what Jake said. He won't do any-
thing until he finishes high school—he's too smart to be stupid.
Come." Janet stood. "I have a surprise for you." She opened
Bessie's closet and found the red lace vest.

"This is your surprise? It's older than you."

"Put it on instead of debating with me, mother."

"Hey," Bessie called after her, "who's the *balebusteh* around
here?"

A minute later she stumbled, squinting, into the brightly
illuminated kitchen. Janet was kneeling by the open oven
door, keeping her long hair from getting singed by holding it
with one hand behind her neck in a ponytail. "Tie your hair
when you cook, Janet," Bessie complained.

"You don't look fresh from the beauty parlor yourself."

Bessie spun around. Momma Greenpoint and Lester were
sitting with Jacob in the alcove, grinning behind an elaborate table setting.

"But what's the occasion?" Bessie cried as she hurried to
embrace them.

"We need a formal invitation?" Momma Greenpoint said.
"Janet says come, I come." She took Lester's hand in hers. "And
he comes with me, my shadow. Look at him—the thinner I get,
the more he fills out! He's eating me up alive!"

"Hey, what's making her into such a romantic?" Bessie asked Lester.

"Hot stuff!" Janet rushed a steaming casserole to the table as the oven door slammed. Jacob leaned toward the dish, sniffing.

"*Oi ziskayt!*" Bessie said. "What have you been doing? What are we celebrating?"

There were paper cups filled with sweet, thick wine set at each place. Janet raised one for a toast. "To your last weekend as a just plain nurse. And a *l'chaim* for your new job."

"And what else, Jannie?" Momma Greenpoint teased her. "Ho, look at her, Mr. Markish, she's a regular beauty queen when she blushes."

"There's more?" Bessie was elated.

"What, what?" Jacob demanded to know.

Janet slipped into a seat and cupped both her mother's hands. Her own looked like orchids, long and perfect. "*Nu?*" Bessie said, withdrawing her hands as Janet tried to kiss her fingertips.

"Willy asked me to marry him, mom."

"My darling!" Bessie's eyes filled with tears as she rushed around the table to embrace her daughter, whose face was a squeeze toy, saying Yes, I do, to Willy, to Bessie, to the world.

Chapter Eighteen

Janet climbed Convent Avenue against a stiff wind that ballooned her pegged pants out from the hips and swept back her hair like streamers, what Willy admiringly called her "winged victory" look, though she had protested:

"The winged victory's got no head!"

"Right you are. Nor do I when I see you sailing on the wind."

"Ooh-la-la."

"You look great today. See you at two."

Janet smiled at the fresh memory. It was a rarity for Willy to emerge with such a romantic flair from his mental labors and brooding moods. She glanced at her wristwatch: 1:50. Good, he would appreciate her punctuality.

Crossing to her side of the street at the corner, a professor, with overcoat and briefcase, gave Janet an admiring glance. She was at once aware of herself in his eyes: long legs in corduroy, old tweed jacket open to the cold, stomach flat and taut in a white button-down blouse, neck graced by a purple cravat, her mother's gift. She tossed her head to shoo a wisp of hair from her eyes, then measured her steps to overtake and pass the faculty man.

Three Negro men lounging on a brownstone step grew mum as she neared. Janet nodded in a kindly way to all three—her eyes flashing hurt and sympathy for the intrinsic pain of Negro life—then provided a lingering view of her profile by watching with exaggerated interest a fourth man on his hands and knees scraping rust from a cast-iron fence. How raw his hands must feel! Brrr ...

The professor passed her again. Well, she would not overtake him a second time. Speeding up slightly, she watched the back of his head, preparing to look away the split second after their eyes would meet. The wind rattled two garbage cans as her shoe hit a rise in the pavement. Who saw her stumble, anyone? Her eyes darted left and right to intercept and humble any smirking witnesses. But even the colored men were no longer watching.

The street was more trafficked beyond the stone arch marking the border of City College's North Campus. Students filed to and fro on the walkway to Shephard Hall, or slouched, bookbags at their feet and cigarettes burning, along the low, gray stone wall that separated the sidewalk from the dead lawn. Janet scanned for Willy's tall, hatless figure and fixed her face into a tough pout, one eye squinting slightly in concentrated scrutiny. Chin up. One hand in a pocket—no, make it both hands on your hips. Where *is* that boy? I look like a streetwalker! She lifted a heel to the lamppost behind her, regarded her watch again, caught the eye of a good-looking boy, and looked over his head indifferently.

Bessie watched her shoes on the Harlem pavement and vaguely noted the cracks, squashed bottle caps, and chewing gum on which she was stepping while Mrs. Gittins, huge and slow at her side, complained about the community:

"We got contradictions here, Bessie, make me want to cash my chips in as Party supervisor right now. But when I wake up in the morning, I'll still be living here!"

"I know what you mean. And this is exactly how I feel about the Party itself."

Mrs. Gittins stuck to her own complaint. "Now why couldn't we turn out more'n a hundred people today? These niggers know the army's going to Jim Crow them to death or get 'em shot; why they so hot to fight Hitler? When'd we ever steer them wrong? Ain't nobody but the Party fighting for black folks, 'less you going to talk about Marcus Garvey and his foolish strutting! But I can still count more niggers in front of the liquor store on my block than we had on our march!"

She was panting for breath as they stepped from the curb to cross 125th Street. Bessie noticed and slowed their pace, though she had nervous energy enough to run circles around her lumbering comrade. Hurry, daylight, drip away, she thought, glancing up the wide corridor toward the majestic metalwork of the Triboro Bridge. Let the night come already. I'm ready to climb Mt. Sinai. *Thou shalt be supervisor.*

"What's tickling you?" asked Mrs. Gittins, noticing Bessie's smile.

Bessie shook her head and reverted to their discussion. "You shouldn't feel bad about a hundred people, Mary Jane. If we were marching in a Jewish neighborhood, we wouldn't get nothing but curses. People think the hammer and sickle is no better than the swastika."

"You going to get yourself in trouble with the Party all over again you keep talking like that."

"The Party *is* my trouble. Why? You bringing me up on charges? I come to Harlem to make you look like some kind of a organizer . . ." Mrs. Gittins ducked her head and guffawed. "Next thing you know," Bessie continued, pushing to the limits of heresy, "Izzy Hampton's gonna be shaking hands with what's-his-name, the fascist hero with the airplane . . . yeah, Charles Lindbergh!"

Lindbergh was the beloved of the ultraright America First organization, which always mixed a strong dose of anti-Semitism and racial hatred with its demands for American neutrality.

"Are you kidding?" cried Mrs. Gittins, standing still to catch her breath. "They wouldn't square off with nothing less than shotguns!"

"Hey, what's the matter, you can't get your breath?"

"I'm fine, I'm fine," Mary Jane insisted, withdrawing from Bessie's touch. "You just better catch *your* breath a minute, sister!"

"All right. So let's talk about something else."

"Mm-hmm. Let's talk about getting us some lunch."

As Janet watched Willy loping toward her across the tiled cafeteria floor with a trayful of coffee and cake, a Benny Goodman tune with high, sighing vocals by Lionel Hampton drifted through her mind:

> I know why I waited.
> I know why I been so blue.
> I prayed each night for someone
> Exactly like you.

"You know you're wonderful?" she said, smiling without waiting for his endorsement. "I love watching you walk—you've got such a sense of confidence. But it's not cold like some of the phonies around here. I mean, if something happened that required your attention, you'd be there."

Willy tugged his earlobe and shrugged. There was no getting used to Janet's outbursts. "I'm not the only one. . . ."

"Are you kidding? You mean me? I have no confidence, Willy, I'm a busybody, that's all."

"In other words, you're a flirt," he teased her.

She peeled his hand off his coffee cup and raised it to her lips. "What would you do if I began singing love lyrics to you right now?

"You make me feel so grand
I want to hand the world to you.
And you seem to understand
The foolish little dreams I'm dreaming,
Schemes I'm scheming..."

"C'mon, Jan, we've got business to attend to." He patted her hand. "You've got this peculiar habit of lighting up like a spotlight!"

"I'm sorry."

"Don't be. It's good for me. I have never in my life received so much attention."

"I love you, Willy."

He gulped some coffee and winced at the noise level in the cafeteria. "Me, too, but not in public, okay? So—how many you think we've got coming today?"

"Oh, not many," Janet said. "I handed out my share of leaflets, but people are simply not taking us seriously."

"Never mind us," he said, lightly rapping the table. "This isn't just a Communist issue, it's a matter of academic and intellectual freedom."

"You don't have to convince *me*, William."

"If we let the state on campus to investigate supposed Communists, what's going to happen next? They'll start sniffing after Morris Raphael Cohen?"

"Just yesterday you were complaining what a liberal Cohen is."

"A brilliant liberal," Willy said. "I'm learning a fantastic amount in his class. He makes us use our brains, and that's what I care about. I'm not like your mother, Jan, I can't get fanatical about the—"—he lowered his voice—"—the Party line. There are larger issues."

"It's funny," Janet replied, "I was just thinking that the only other person I know with your kind of—bearing—is my mother." She reached again for his hand. "I really hope you guys get along."

He nodded, gave her a squeeze, and let go. "Then there's Bertrand Russell. I'll bet anyone on this campus that the damned state is going to prevent his appointment here next semester. Can you imagine? Here you've got working-class students about to study with one of the great progressive minds of the twentieth century, and these idiotic Red-baiters are going to ruin it!"

Janet smiled, proud of his passion. Sipping her coffee, she thought about her mother and the wedding to come. It would have to include a real tribute to Bessie—maybe we can get Mr. Wasserman or some other important *Freiheit* person to officiate? "Hey, Willy? Let's talk about our get-together for the wedding. Who are we going to invite?"

"I don't know, Jan. . . . I hate it when you change the subject like that," he grumbled.

"Aw, c'mon," she coaxed him in a childish voice. "I wanna."

He softened and stroked his lean chin in mock concentration. "Okay, let's see now . . . Bertrand Russell . . . Albert Einstein . . . W. E. B. DuBois . . . Paul Robeson . . . Joe Stalin . . ."

"No women? Is this your stag party, William?"

"Just my side of the family. From your side, who do we need? Bessie is a party in herself."

"Atta boy. She really is, isn't she?

> "I know why my mother
> Taught me to be true.
> She meant me for someone
> Exactly like you."

"So, who do you think is my competition for the supervisor job?" Bessie asked in a playful tone after Mrs. Gittins had called out their orders to the counterman.

"I dunno," the black woman said. "Won't be nobody from the laundry room. Listen here—how come you so caught up in your *career* all of a sudden?"

Bessie shrank into her corner of the booth as though Mrs. Gittins had pulled a gun. Throughout their walk, the conversation had seesawed between their old laundry-room intimacy and a new, creeping distrust that was surprising and unsettling to them both, but for Mary Jane to turn on her now seemed like a swindle. What personal aspirations could Bessie cling to and publicly defend in a pint-size coffee shop in the middle of the suffering Negro ghetto? "I need some money," she said simply.

"If money's your problem—God knows we *all* got that problem!—then you ought to be out organizing a union for them nurses 'stead of getting yourself in good with management."

"Please, Mary Jane, stop with the lectures—"

"I ain't lecturing and I ain't gonna lecture! I'm just telling you, it hurts to see you straying like you been straying, criticizing all the time and getting involved with all kind of personal junk!"

"It's not junk!" Bessie snapped back at her. "What's the matter with you, Mary Jane? You talk like I'm out buying a string of pearls for myself. I told you about Jacob. You don't think I should try to help him out for a couple of lousy dollars?"

"Not if you got to sell out the working class to do it, sister— hell, no! It's like watching my own Negro preacher making eyes at a whore."

"Oh, my God." Bessie laughed bitterly at her rhetoric, then grew fiercely silent as the counterman hustled over with their lunch platters. She watched Mrs. Gittins dig in, watched her bosom hovering over her plate, her flabby arms nearly spanning the table from end to end, sweat beading at her mouth and brow. An overnight success in the Party, Bessie mused: a big black woman, one of the genuine downtrodden—so let's make her a district leader, *khaveyrim*. Never mind if she knows anything about organizing. . . .

Bessie stared disconsolately at the wallpaper.

"C'mon, Bess, whyn't you eating? You going to have to pay for it."

Bessie nodded and held the sandwich like a gag against her teeth.

So now you're a big *makher*, huh, Mrs. Gittins? And you can wear your Party membership like a cop wears his badge. You think I don't know how much you want to get out of that lousy laundry room? You'd do anything so that the Party should put you on payroll!

The egg salad tasted sour and the white bread was a stale lump in her throat, but she could no more complain to the counterman than she could speak her feelings to Mary Jane, though the scenario of silence would be far more poisonous:

That Bessie Sainer, I tell you, ever since she become a supervisor, she think she too good to visit ol' Mary Jane in the laundry room!

Bessie pushed her plate aside and essayed a response. "You know, Mary Jane, the Party is like my child. When your child does something you don't like, or it looks like it's going to hurt the child, you yell, sure, but you don't lock him out of the house, do you?"

"Uh-uh."

"No, you agree too easily, Mary Jane. This is only—what, your sixth year in the Party? It's my twentieth. That's older than my own son. As old as Janet. And it's the people like me, that we take responsibility for the Party—we don't just go along with it 'cause we want to be bosses, bureaucrats, if you know what I mean! You got to be a mother to the Party, not a wife."

Mrs. Gittins lost her reply in a wheeze as she began to choke on her food.

"Raise your arms, raise your arms!" Bessie said. "You want a hit on the back?"

Dearly beloved, we are gathered together . . .

"No more questions, no more lies, stop the Rapp-Coudert witch trials!"

"God bless America!"

"Get the Commies off campus!"

"Draft-dodgers!"

"Why don't you go back to Russia?"

. . . in the eye of God . . .

"Two, four, six, eight, we don't want a fascist state!"

"Like hell you don't!"

"Yellow-bellies!"

"No committee on campus! No committee on campus!"

Janet's picket sign, STOP RAPP-COUDERT, caught the wind and backed her into Willy, who took her around the waist and pulled her into step. "You're not chanting," she observed. "Are you depressed? You want to keep talking about the wedding?"

Removing his cigarette from his mouth, he spat a loose speck of tobacco and sputtered "Now?" in astonishment. "Janet, you'd be ready to talk 'wedding' in the middle of an earthquake!"

"This is hardly an earthquake," she replied sullenly. Both groups, the protestors and their hecklers, were small and flagging in spirit. Janet personally knew everyone on line, eighteen faces in all, Communist party or American Student Union members without exception. She shrugged and redoubled her grasp on the sign as the wind kicked up again, tramped with Willy twice more around the circle, and said, "We're such a bunch of social rejects on campus, I would think you'd at least want to stay in good with your family, your parents. So what if we have a rabbi? I don't mind."

Willy threw his cigarette to the pavement with a curse and dropped out of line to sit, sulking, on the stone wall. Of course the hecklers turned their taunts on him—"What's the matter, big boy, Stalin's got you marching too hard?" "Wait'll Uncle Sam gets hold of you, buster!"—but they were easy enough to ignore and too outnumbered to be feared. Janet felt a tap on her shoulder. Jerry Levy, Willy's number one friend, slipped into place at her side.

"What's the matter with lover boy?"

"I don't know," she said. "He's all worked up about his parents. You know how religious they are."

"Do I ever." He whistled low.

"Well, they'd like a little tradition in our wedding. Something other than the Red flag. But when I try to talk to him about it . . ."

"Uh-oh." Jerry paused to chant with the others: "NO MORE QUESTIONS, NO MORE LIES . . . Will's more of a *mensch* than me, baby, I tell you. I try hard not to introduce my sweetie pies to my old man. His accent is enough to make 'em wonder if ol' Jerry's got anything left after his circumcision."

"Oh, God, Jerry!" She turned her face away and snickered.

"How can you understand? You've got a great mom. She's modern. In fact . . . if you give me her phone number, I'll give you these." He dangled a rabbit's-foot key chain before her nose before dropping it neatly into her jacket pocket. "Keys to my place. I was going to give them to Will, but this way it's much sexier. Go have a nice leisurely talk about religion. I won't be home till ten o'clock. Maybe you'll find your rabbi under my pillow."

"Oh, stop!"

"Go, skedaddle!" he said. "The Rapp-Coudert creeps are miles from here. They do their business in a dirty little downtown office."

"I know!"

"So they won't miss your silvery voice of protest. Go—go get laid."

"Jerry! Will you stop!"

"I'll give you just five seconds to stop blushing and then I'm gonna call your mom and ask her out on a date."

"She doesn't have a telephone. So there."

"That won't stop me, baby. She's got a fire escape. One . . . two . . . three . . ."

> Once, long ago, in the foolish town of Chelm, the rabbi was on his deathbed. And as the high holidays were approaching, and the doctor had given up all hope for the Rabbi's recovery, the important Jews of the town held a meeting to determine how to elect a new rabbi. . . .

The story rose like yeast in Bessie's mind as she walked. It would be a parable for all her feelings about bureaucracy, about Mrs. Gittins's deterioration into a Party hack. And the *Freiheit* would print it, she was sure; they were hard up for writers, since Moishe Nadir and most of the top-notchers had dropped out because of the pact, the goddamn pact! So, Bessie thought, I got a new career. Maybe I better submit it under a man's name? Ben Kharlofsky . . .

> "He must be a man of **great** stature," said the tall one.
>
> "He must have a strong, powerful voice," said another, in a strong, powerful voice.
>
> "He must have a long, devout beard," said a third, stroking his long beard.
>
> Then Nakhum the Sea Gull, the *luftmensch* of Chelm, who had been lounging on the street alongside the window of the synagogue, stuck his head into the doorway. "Don't you think you should consult the rabbi himself about who his successor is to be?"
>
> The wise men of Chelm scolded Nakhum for eavesdropping, but they all said: For once his advice is worth something. Some angel must have been careless to drop a good idea on Nakhum's head! So they went to the rabbi's house, paid their respects at his bedside, and then the oldest and wisest of the bunch said, "What kind of man shall we seek to replace you, *rebbe?*"

I got to write this story down before I lose it, it's getting long! But I got to get work before I lose *that*—it's getting late!

She had reached the northeast corner of Central Park after more than a mile of dreary tenements, cubbyhole brownstones, small stores, and countless faces, work-worn and suspicious, Negroes and increasing numbers of whites as she had ploughed southward into the German and Irish ghetto. The sudden splay of amber and brown and the generously wide, deserted western sidewalk of Fifth Avenue drew her; the traffic light at the corner blinked green at her glance as behind her a doorman's whistle pierced the air. The wealth here was as stark as the poverty of East Harlem. Fire hydrants dotted the curb and kept it clear of parked cars. Clean awnings graced the building entrances, and limousines like vaults stood here and there, waiting, shining.

The rabbi lifted his frail arm to point to his caftan, hanging on a hook across the room. "That cloth," he said with strain, "is a simple cloth—it takes a simple man to wear it."

What did the rabbi mean, "a simple man"? wondered the wise men of Chelm.

The rabbi continued: "The life of a rabbi belongs to his people and to the Most High. He must have no other occupation. Find a man whose bed is the earth and whose roof is the sky. . . ." Then he sank into his pillow, too exhausted to say more.

But the wise men of Chelm had heard enough. "The rabbi must be losing his mind," they agreed. "He wants us to choose a simpleton—an idler!"

"We might as well pick Nakhum the Sea Gull to be our rabbi." They all laughed.

The sweet smell of the newly thawed park tempted her more than the spectacle of wealth across the street. The stone wall on her right had opened onto a road cutting east-west across the park, with dirt footpaths visible just yards in.

"Let's go to the blacksmith," said the tall one. "He's simple enough. But he has stature—such a giant!"

"And a strong, powerful voice," agreed the next, in a strong, powerful voice.

"He's so hairy," said the hairy one, "you can hardly tell where his beard ends and his chest begins."

"Good enough. We take shifts at the bellows, all the Jews in Chelm, so that our blacksmith can prepare for *yontev*."

Bessie strolled through the trees, nostrils open wide, eyes full of beams from the setting sun somewhere out beyond the leaves. Within five blocks' distance she would have to find her way back to the sidewalk to exit for Mt. Sinai Hospital and the world of gut anxiety, but all that seemed far away now, as her senses stretched and yawned and embraced the dusk, with every stirring squirrel or bird pricking her hope that she would meet someone, a child, a girl, to whom she could tell her story: how the old rabbi died and was mourned; how the blacksmith became rabbi and the people of Chelm took over his forge; how they were all late for the Rosh Hashana services because their horses were improperly shod and their carriage wheels had fallen off; how the blacksmith scolded and cursed them for their impiety; how Nakhum the Sea Gull laughed at them all, laughed and laughed until his insides were aching...

A yellow bird flitted low across her path and up, bouncing on the air, into the shimmering treetops. Bessie was flabbergasted by her own sniffling sounds and stopped in her tracks, flooded by vivid recollections of Ukrainian wheatfields, of the panoramic smells and sounds of her childhood. They drenched her like a cloudburst, made her head heavy, and streaked her heart with old, wistful yearnings that her solitude could not satisfy. Bessie plodded to a dry patch of ground and sat, first brushing away loose dirt to keep her white stockings clean; losing, in that activity, her initial surge of grief, then recalling it with a simple act of surrender, a deep breath and sigh. Then she wept freely....

Ohhh for the blood-soaked land of her birth, for Tsil's bones, for Nakhum's watery grave . . . Ohh for the stubborn world that had swallowed her girlhood and vomited it out in violence, in endless marching and shouting and ducking and planning . . .

Ohh for Momma Greenpoint, fading to the edge of life amid dreams of Zion and a peaceful, lovely *shabbas* dinner with a reunited family . . .

And for the darkness that engulfed Bessie's lonely bed each night. For the two children whom she so, so often had wanted to wake to share her day's regrets. For the warm men who had slipped from her grasp into the grave ...

A twig snapped, the moment slapped her. She sobbed again and looked up.

"Don't make noise! Just give me money!" A chisel-faced monster in a red hunting jacket rushed at her like a flame from the trees.

Three times before, they had made love, gone all the way, in places unprivate enough to justify Janet's tenseness: by Turkey Lake in Bear Mountain Park at the height of summer; in a cheap hotel in Greenwich Village, where she could not bear to spend the night; in her own house, with Jacob on the roof, always about to come down ... "Wait, Willy! Is that him?"

This time there was no excuse, yet even in the hallway of Jerry Levy's building Janet felt, despite her hopes, despite the affection she had sworn to Willy, that same unbearable fear, bordering on panic, that craved noise, and activity, and food, even cigarettes. Willy was ahead on the landing, jiggling keys in the lock. Janet climbed on the balls of her feet like a thief to preserve the dormancy of the building, which had not shown a sign of life in its walls for four flights.

The hush in the apartment made her ears ring. She hurried to the kitchen and ran the faucet, more to break the silence than because she was thirsty. Willy was standing by Jerry's lamplit desk, smoking. "Why don't you sit down?" she called to him. "Would you like something to eat?"

"Not right now. Quiet in here, huh?"

"Yes," she agreed, too loud. (Loud! Your big ugly mouth!) "Is there a radio?"

"In the bedroom, I think. Jerry is so lucky to have a place like this, I can't get over it, I'm green."

Janet rushed to the radio console, past the single bed with bolsters, and spun the dials through zones of static until a clear voice came across. "Too loud," Willy complained, following her in.

"I feel weird about leaving the demonstration, don't you?"

"Hell, no. I feel great." He replaced her at the radio and tuned it to some classical music. "How's that?" She listened uneasily to the distant, muffled call of the reeds. Willy stretched out on the bed and yawned. "Jan, you look beautiful."

"There's no light in here."

"I can see you by the radio light." He patted the mattress at his side.

"I've got a perpetual siren in my mind," she muttered as she sat. "It never stops!"

"Shh. We'll look for the switch." He put his arms around her.

The music was still tugging at her guts, hinting at too many painful feelings. "Air raid, air raid, I don't like this." She rose up and flicked off the radio.

"Hey, what's cooking, Jan?"

"I don't know." She ran her fingers across her scalp. "Look at this crazy mop of mine."

"I love it."

"You love me?"

"You know I do." He held out his arms again.

"I wonder," she said, crawling to him across the mattress, "how lovers make out in Great Britain—always expecting air-raids . . ."

They kissed. His tobacco breath was warm and good. She closed her eyes and gave him her tongue too suddenly, felt his back stiffen, but relaxed him with her whimper. Then they broke for breath. He tugged her shirttails from her pants and pressed his fingers into her belly, into her navel as her pants snap popped. She licked his ear and returned to his lips, good good good, don't stop; the air was filling up comfortably with her rambling thoughts, faces and names marching through the walls, memories uncoiling like loose springs: campus men desiring her, approaching her for a word; soapbox crowds admiring her, marching off to strike . . .

Willy found her breast under the cup of her brassiere. He said he loved her, "so, so much," as Janet arched her back and pressed harder, harder against his hand.

"Brother! Comrade!" Bessie shrieked. She had time only for incantations before the fury slammed into her, caught her by the shoulder before she could fall, and smashed her jaw. Her plunge to earth was a dream flight as her consciousness blinked on and off like a loose light bulb.

Moments glided into whole minutes. He was long gone with her silly pocketbook. *Get up.* Her nose was oozing painfully into the ground and her mouth was a ruin of fragments and blood in hard concrete. *Get up.* The uniform, keep it clean. *I can't move.*

Chapter Nineteen / 1949

"How many beatings can this little stinker take and still be alive? This is what you're wondering. Let me tell you something—I wonder myself! Excepting this was the last time I really took a beating. Sure I got mugged a couple more times, like every old person that they don't live in a fancy neighborhood. I shouldn't even say 'mugged'—you know, they took my purse, big deal. The way people say 'mugged' these days, you'd think they got run over with a truck when all that happened was someone said 'Boo!' and took a few pennies.

"But I never got beat again, not even from the police. In fact, it's an amazing thing but I never even got arrested after that first time in Siberia. Once—I'll never forget this—we had the war in Vietnam, and I went to a protest in Washington with the Women's Strike for Peace. I saw there a young man with long hair, and a cop had him by the hair and was beating him with his stick and trying to drag him behind the buses, y'see, so there should be no witnesses. Well, I don't know what got into me—here I was, more than seventy years—but I got an old feeling and so I bashed that cop with my pocketbook, just one good shot, and the boy got away. And then, it was like you should feed a little fish to a big fish, the crowd moved all together and they, like, sucked me in the middle, and one person gave me a different coat and another gave me a hat instead of my red kerchief—lace, yeah, I wear the vest on my head now. There's not much left of it. Anyway, so even if this cop could've got to me, he wouldn't recognize me, y'see. And this was all spontaneous, just with the people—there was no leader.

"But I got it good from that *momzer* in Central Park. He broke both my nose and my jaw—one would have been an improvement, maybe, but not both! And he knocked out my teeth so I had to get the kind that I wear now, the kind that they live in a glass of water. All this was his way of saying 'Please' before he took my pocketbook. You think he was trying to tell me something?

"I do this, y'see, it's a little *shtikle* of mine, that you should interpret misfortune. So that everything should have a lesson. Of course, for me the lesson's usually the same: revolution. So my mugger friend shouldn't have to act like an animal to get his bread. But maybe I'm wrong, y'see. Maybe I'm not telling the truth. 'Cause when I look what's doing these days, believe me, I get scared. F'rinstance, if my grandson visits me and goes home at night, on the subway, alone, I worry until the next morning when he calls me.

"There's a sickness in life today that it makes people vicious. It's like those movies that you see late at night on the television, about those that they're dead but actually they're not. Not vampires, no . . . zombies. Yeah. I don't like this kind of a movie especially, but it's something to do at night if I can't sleep, I'm still working the night shift. And they're ridiculous, these movies, a real *potchky* job. But the reason you watch is they remind you in a terrible kind of a way of real life, of the life we got now. People that they got nothing left to them but teeth and nails. People that the only thing that makes them feel alive is to fight and kill.

"So I got two minds about this question. The part of me that's socialist says the muggers do it 'cause they're poor. The part of me that's an old woman that she might get mugged tomorrow and she already got mugged yesterday says they do it 'cause they're vicious. So why don't we go ask the muggers?

"This I already did, y'see. I think I told you, these apartment buildings where I live, mostly it's black, plus we have the *alte khalyeras* like me that we didn't run away with the rest of the

white people. So one day I was looking out my window and I
actually saw a mugging. Down where you can see the playground—it was a black woman walking there and three boys
came. I saw them run off with her bag. And one of the boys I
recognized, even from here on the seventh floor, 'cause he had
on a particular coat that I myself gave to his mother—it used to
belong to my grandson. It's a coincidence, the kind of coincidence that gets you hanged.

"Well, I got so mad, I got dressed even though I wasn't feeling so good and I went right over to his house. I got there before
the boy. And I told his mother—I knew her already from the
Tenants' Council—I told her what I saw.

"She nearly cried. They're a nice, middle-class Negro family,
y'see; They got the father and the mother and not too many
kids; they make a good living—you don't expect this kind of
a kid to do this kind of a thing.

"And next she got real mad, you know, and she says she's
going to beat the kid good. I can't argue with her about that;
I'm not against it that you should hit a kid sometimes. But I said
to her, Mrs. Jameson—this is her name—Mrs. Jameson, do you
mind if I first say something to your son?

"I had to wait for maybe half an hour, so me and Mrs. Jameson
have a cup of coffee and we talk about the world, you know,
and then her son comes home. And when he sees me, a white
woman, he nearly *plotzes*. He felt so guilty already, y'see. Sure
he knew me, but young people don't remember old people
one from the other.

"Anyway, I said, 'Hello, I was watching you and your friends
in the playground. The jacket,' I said, 'it looks good on you.'
That's all. Just to let him know I saw. And then his mother
tells him to walk me home so I shouldn't get mugged! She's a
smart woman, y'see. 'Cause she didn't embarrass him by yelling
in front of me. It's never good to humiliate a person—it serves
no purpose. You don't want to take from him the very thing he
needs to become a *mensch*.

"Now, this kid, the Jameson boy—Robbie—he still visits me
sometimes. He's going to college now and he wants to show me
that he's making good. And we never so much as talked about
that thing that I saw. Well, I'm glad—it should only be so easy
with the other kids that they're out making trouble. But the
point is, I'm not scared of the blacks. Many progressive people

are. They think that the blacks are something special, something holy, 'cause they suffered so much. They're the chosen people now! So even if you think a black comrade is acting like a fool, or this one is anti-Semitic, or this one is in the movement only so he can meet girls, you don't say nothing. Why? 'Cause the blacks got to have self-determination!

"Phooey. This is discrimination, not self-determination! I don't go for it. I never did. I expect the same from the black that I expect from the white—respect, and that they should have self-respect. And with these conditions, I'm willing to go all the way for revolution, for freedom. 'Cause that's the other thing about working with black people that makes the whites scared: You can't be a social democrat, you can't be wishy-washy if you want to make a struggle against racism. It's gonna be hard—there's gonna be cops, there may be guns, there's gonna be Ku Klux Klan. You're gonna have to do more than just vote and write a check for your organization and read a newspaper.

"Now, after the war, we had, like, a purge in the Party. Lots of comrades got brought up on charges that they're discriminating, what we called 'white chauvinism.' F'rinstance, remember that girl Shirley that she was such a greenhorn at the Madison Square Garden when we fought Spanknoebel's bunch? She got taken up on charges 'cause she wouldn't dance with a black man at a party. Now I myself saw what happened: The man was drunk, he was stinking from liquor, so he should've been danced out the door, never mind dancing with Shirley!

"Of course, many of those that they got taken up on charges were Jewish, since there was always plenty of Jews in the Party. So I said, 'Why don't we instead teach these Jewish people about their own history, about their own oppression, so they can have a *personal* reason not to discriminate and to identify with the Negro people? Let them read some of the Yiddish writers, some of the proletarian poets. They'll begin to understand that being Jewish and being progressive, it's like having wings and flying.'

"'Cause this is what I did when I lay in the hospital for three months, y'see: I read Sholem Aleichem, I read Winchevsky, and Morris Rosenfeld, Avrom Reisen, Peretz, Raboy, all the great writers. Their words, they gave me nourishment that I very badly needed it. Y'see, that man, the mugger, he took a lot more than my bag. He took more than my teeth, even. He actually took my heart and my mind. I began to say to myself, What the hell am I doing with my life, working all the time for socialism? Maybe human beings aren't worth it. Maybe they're all like this bastard that he was ready to kill me for a few pennies. Maybe they all deserve the kind of a life they'll get under Hitler.

"I was very depressed, that's all. First, I didn't get the supervisor job. That very night when I dragged myself from Central Park and I became a patient instead of a worker at Mt. Sinai, there was a young woman there, a nurse, and she was the one that she actually cleaned me up and put me to bed, a very nice girl—and it turns out that she's in training to take Mrs. Malincott's job. A young girl, direct from college. Now, this hurt as bad as my broken jaw. I could never know for sure, y'see, if maybe my politics had something to do with it. The fact that I was always at meetings and demonstrations and coming to work sometimes late and maybe with a little smudge on my uniform, this didn't help when it came time for a promotion.

"I had two careers, and I felt like a failure in both. As a nurse, I wasn't going anywhere; and as a revolutionary—well, let's say that the fascists were getting promoted a lot faster than the Communists around the world! Plus now Jacob was gonna go into the navy since I didn't get the money to pay his radio school. I even asked Momma Greenpoint—I wrote her a note, I still couldn't talk, my jaw was actually wired shut—I asked that she should please call my friend Captain Owen in Nebraska to find out maybe he could do me yet another favor and get my son into a nice part of the navy—a good ship, a safe job, something.

"Well, Captain Owen was dead. He died just a week before we called. He remembered me in his will, too—how do you like that? He left for me his boat-in-the-bottle, a model of the *Black Eagle*. But I regretted that I postponed calling him. I was full of regrets.

"I was going a little crazy, actually. I remember the time Mrs. Gittins came to visit me. She came nearly every day. She would sneak out from the laundry room, and she did lots for me, lots of favors. But this was the first time, and I couldn't yet talk, so I wrote her a note. First I wrote, 'You know I didn't get the job?' And she nodded and said, Yeah, she's real sorry. And she cried, 'cause I really looked terrible, all bandaged up and black-and-blue in my face.

"So then I wrote a whole little *meise* for her, to express how I'm feeling. I wrote that a poor Jewish man, he prays every day, he prays every night, he's a very religious person and he's very poor. Then one day he wins the lottery and overnight he becomes a millionaire!

"This is how I felt about Janet getting married, y'see—like a million dollars! I wanted everything for her.

"So, first thing in the morning, this rich man goes and he buys a new suit, a new hat, a new pair of shoes, a new coat, all new, and he steps out into the sun and he gets hit by a truck!

"Up in heaven he screams at God. 'How could you do it? A whole life I was poor and miserable, and still I prayed to you. Now you saw me, a rich man, and look what you do to me!'

"And God says, 'Was that you in those fancy clothes? I didn't recognize you!'

"Now, Mrs. Gittins, she thought this was very funny, that I should be writing for her a joke while I'm laying in the hospital. And when I saw her laughing, that's when I started to cry. I couldn't hold back.

"Other things I wrote, too. I wrote down the story that I was making up about the rabbi and the blacksmith in Chelm, and this they printed in the *Freiheit*. So I began writing more, and poems, too. I wrote and I wrote. I became crazy with words. In my mind, y'see, I began to take all these things that they're happening to me and to try to figure out *Why*. And the ideas I got were crazy. F'rinstance, this lousy mugger in the park, the way he came from nowhere and then he was gone, I began to think he was, like, an angel, that he broke my jaw so I would be quiet for a month and I would begin to write, 'cause my writings would be very important to the world, y'see. I had a mission. It wasn't exactly religious like I'm saying now, but everything began to have a reason, a meaning.

"Sure it's crazy! So how can I begin to explain to you the journey that I took with my mind, the kind of *mishugas?* It's too complicated, I can only give the feeling, bits and pieces. I had years, years, and years of suffering inside me, but I was always a rock. Now the rock cracked open.

"So I was reading the great Yiddish writers, and I felt their power inside me. Especially Sholem Aleichem. He writes in such a personal style, it's like you're writing the story yourself—excepting you're having better thoughts and funnier jokes than you ever had in your life! And since I met him, y'see—not only met him, I fed him, I took his temperature, I was one of the last people on earth to see him alive—maybe the *meise* he told me was the last one Sholem Aleichem ever told to anybody!—so this got in my mind, this idea that for some special kind of a reason I was the nurse to Sholem Aleichem the night before he died.

"So like I told you, I wouldn't talk. Even after I got my teeth, I wouldn't say anything. Not a word. I would only write. And when I did begin to talk, it was only in Yiddish. In my mind this was, like, a protest against what was going on with the Jews in Europe. When you feel helpless about something, sometimes you get a little cuckoo, so you think you actually got influence just by sitting there thinking. F'rinstance, when I watch the president on television, he has his press conference, and you can just tell when he's lying, you know. So I pretend that I can make him speak the truth just by sitting there in my rocking chair and concentrating with my mind. If I think hard enough, he's gonna suddenly drop his hands and say, 'Boy, am I sick of telling lies!'

"That would be something! He would take off his tie, maybe open his belt, let out a big belch, and then he would denounce the corporations!

"Now, Mrs. Gittins, she sees there's something funny going on with me that I won't speak no English, not to her and not to anybody, not even when she brings me newspapers and tells me what's cooking in the Party and all that kind of a stuff. So she gets an idea to help me. She says one day that she wants to learn Yiddish so she can read for herself all the stories she sees me writing. Now, your crazy friend Bessie Sainer, she liked this idea very much. Mrs. Gittins is gonna be my missionary, huh? So I started giving lessons to Mrs. Gittins, every day. And with this she got me talking English again. She's a smart cookie! Who knows, maybe she even learned a little bit the *alefbeys*.

"One thing I remember, years later, maybe 1948 or 1949 when they were persecuting the Party in America: Mrs. Gittins helped to hide me for a couple of weeks in Harlem when the FBI came looking for me, and I remember saying to her that it's a lucky thing I went crazy in the hospital, 'cause it gave me a taste of what we're going through now. 'Cause at this time, y'see, people's lives were being ruined just by words. A man would be called a Communist, or he would be named as somebody's friend that he shouldn't be friends with, or he got mail from a progressive cause, and this was enough to put him out of work, out of his house, out of his mind. The whole thing was a terrible game of words. A lot of *khaveyrim* had nervous breakdowns at this time. So me, I was just ahead of my time!

"But let's not get too far ahead. Right now I'm lying in the hospital having *my* nervous breakdown—and I got to tell you about my daughter's wedding. *This* is a story, and I didn't write it, and neither did Sholem Aleichem.

"Janet and Willy, they set the date for May Day like good Communists. But I still had the bandages on my nose, y'see, and I had no money to give for a wedding party or even for a present, and I wasn't myself. So I told them to please go ahead without me, and then I spent the whole night crying.

"May Day comes and I got the surprise of my life. In walks Janet and Willy, right into my hospital room. Janet's wearing a beautiful suit—the young radicals, they didn't go in for wedding dresses and fancy stuff—and Willy looks very handsome. And I cried out loud 'cause they had come to see me right after they got married in City Hall. This is a place for a honeymoon?

"Then Janet shows me she's got with her my red vest that I wore it for special occasions. And then Momma Greenpoint and Poppa Greenpoint come in through the door. 'What's this all about?' I said. 'So many visitors at once—am I dying and I don't know it?'

"And then begins a parade! I gotta take a deep breath so I can name them all for you! Belle-Brokha and her husband and Laibl. Max Markish, that's Belle's brother, Momma Greenpoint's other child, and he came with his wife, Gertrude, and their children . . . and Ruchel came, and Feivl, and Nat with his girlfriend, a gentile girl, and Elaine with her husband David and their two little boys . . . and Herschel, and Paul Dropsky with some guys from his band, including the young man he was in love with—and they brought their instruments, no less! Yeah, all into my hospital room! I must've had five people in bed with me! And then—it almost raised me to the ceiling—in walks my brother Julius with his wife, Fanny, all the way from Chicago!

"Momma Greenpoint, she's the one that she organized the whole thing with Janet, and she looks like she belongs in the bed next to me, not on her feet, but instead she puts her arms around me and she says, 'Come, Buzeleh, we're having a wedding party on Mt. Sinai.'

"This was a gift that the hospital gave me for being with them more than eight years. They gave us a big room, and the kitchen sent in coffee and cake, and we could make all the noise we wanted. And there came Mrs. Gittins and other *khaveyrim*, and friends, neighbors, nurses and people from the hospital—everybody! They wouldn't let Momma Greenpoint bring in no food from the outside, that was the only thing, but besides this, it was a regular party, a wonderful party, better for me than a blood transfusion.

"Everyone did a little performance. Herschel, he liked to sing, and he had a voice like a cantor, actually. And Jacob made imitations of radio personalities—he was hilarious! And Momma Greenpoint's daughter, Belle-Brokha, she wasn't a youngster no more but she was a wonderful folk dancer, light on her feet, so she led us in dancing. This I couldn't do—the floor was too hard and I was afraid of falling, and when I bounced, it made my mouth hurt. Eh, but still I danced! I had to. How could I not dance with my beautiful daughter, that this should be the last time I hold her in my arms as a little girl? How can I not dance with the *khosn* so he should know what kind of a woman he's got for a mother-in-law? And with Julius I had a waltz—we went round and round and he said to me, he said, 'You never got dizzy, did you Buzie? You never got tired. You always kept your eye toward the revolution, while me, I went for *parnoseh*, I went for the American dream.'

"And I said, 'Give some of your money to the *Freiheit*. And when the revolution comes, we're gonna need engineers, so you can teach us all.'

"He was a good man, my brother Yeshua. He remained not so active, but committed. And during McCarthy, he gave jobs to quite a few *khaveyrim* that they couldn't find work no place else. Julius would sneak them into his company in Chicago. He was never even a Communist, he was more an anarchist, but he was brave, y'see, and this I already knew, 'cause Julius was the first Jew to get a job as an engineer in his company.

"And then came my beautiful sister, Momma Greenpoint. We did a Russian two-step together, and we were both holding the other one up, and we were hugging more than we were dancing, and crying! Crying! And I looked at this woman, that we never had a political agreement about anything but she took care of me no matter what, and I loved her no matter what, and I knew that this was my victory: I had a family that nothing could break. I was not alone, not even if the Communist party should melt like wax.

"And I said to her, 'Remember when you slapped my face on Ellis Island, Leah? Remember? Well, now you can do it again, y'see, 'cause I've just arrived, I've just come back into my mind and into my new life.'

"So what does she say? '*Nu*, it's about time—you're nearly fifty years old already.'

"Then I laughed at her, 'cause she's so down-to-earth, you know. And she almost got mad at me 'cause she didn't know why I was laughing.

"Then the band played their last song. This I still got in my mind, bright like the sun. It's called, 'Firn di Mekhutonim Aheym,' which means 'Bring the In-Laws Home.' It's got a part that the clarinet hits such a high note, if there's a God in heaven, boy, he heard it. We were all very quiet, listening. I had my *kinderlakh*, my daughter on one arm and my son on the other arm, and I watched this beautiful young man with his clarinet pointed to the ceiling, and Paul Dropsky stands there smiling and winking at me 'cause we share his secret, you know. At this moment I felt so much goodness, so much joy, so much of how the world should be! And there I am with my broken nose and with the *mishugas* in my mind . . . and there's the world outside—Europe bleeding, the fascists marching, the Jews getting shot . . . and that clarinet just hung up there, crying . . . *Gottenyu!* By the time that young man ran out of breath, we were all crying!

"So then I made a goodnight speech. Not just a speech, no— it was more a poem. It came to me like a dream, I don't know from where. It was like Morris Rosenfeld should stand whispering in my ear. Who knows? I brought my daughter and her husband to stand in front of me, and Momma Greenpoint tells everybody to listen, and meanwhile I can hear Ruchel, she's complaining like always. She says, 'Who does Bessie think she is, a rabbi?' And Julius is the one that he answers her this time. He says, 'She takes after our father—but where *you* came from, Rucheleh, it's still a mystery!' So everyone had a good laugh. Then I waited for quiet, and I said this thing:

" 'Who are you, my children? Are you still the ones that I raised with my love and my tears? I wanted the world to be better for you—you would count life in pleasures, not years. Your father and me, we planted a garden. We wanted that you should have flowers. But who knows the weather? The clouds came and washed out the dreams, the joys, that were ours.'

"Well, this is not it exactly. I just talked, you know. Then I said: 'We wanted a world, a communist world, so our children won't suffer from need. For this poppa died. For this momma cried....'

"All right, I'll stop. It's awful—but it sticks in my mind! Like jelly, yeah. Listen, if you don't behave, I'll say the whole thing and you'll turn to jelly!

"Anyway, what I talked about, I talked about how good it felt to see my daughter thinking like I'm thinking, doing like I'm doing. That she doesn't have to be against my ideas just 'cause I'm her mother, y'see. Instead we can be *khaveyrim*. So this means I succeeded, 'cause I gave her my ideas, and these ideas, they're the seeds for the new world. So now we'll work together to plant those seeds, to make a new family and a new world. All this I said to her.

"And then I took a look at Julius's face—he looks like a smart old bird sitting on a pole, so I found more to say. And then I saw Momma Greenpoint—she's so pale, I felt like I got to find words just to keep her alive! So finally Janet steps up and kisses me and she says she loves me, and that's all I got to hear! I started to cry so much that the poem came to an end finally and everyone applauded.

"After I got out from the hospital, it was a good summer, despite that I had to get used to having artificial teeth. The four of us—Jacob, the kids, and me—we moved together to the Lower East Side, East Seventh Street, number thirty-seven. It gave us more room, it was a big place, and it wasn't expensive. We couldn't afford something expensive, 'cause Janet was still in college, y'see, still a baby, and Willy was just starting out to be a chemist with a drug company that eventually went out of business. So we really had just my income, maybe fifty dollars a week. I was back to work, but someplace new: Beth Israel Hospital. It was closer to where we lived now; I could save carfare.

"It was the first time for years that I lived so far from Momma

Greenpoint, but Janet's wedding meant now that *I* was becoming the *balebusteh,* if you know what I mean. And I was hoping the new neighborhood and the excitement, maybe it would make Jacob change his mind about going to the navy. Maybe he would meet a girl and get hooked for a while! This is exactly what I thought. But that's not what happened. He joined, or he tried to. He had to lie about his age by a couple of months so he wouldn't have to come to me for permission. And when I found this out, y'see, I went to the navy office and I made such a stink that by the time it got all straightened out, it was winter already, after Pearl Harbor. So then I gave my permission—I figured he'd be better off joining so that he shouldn't get drafted and end up instead in the army or who knows where.

"Meanwhile, even before we had Pearl Harbor, Hitler was invading the Soviet Union. So the Party got very busy calling for what we call the Second Front. We said that England and America should go into France so Hitler would have to fight on both sides, east and west. Listen, it was a good idea—it would make the war shorter, it would save many, many lives. Even Eisenhower wanted to do it. But that sonofabitch Churchill, he was still following his idea to wait, wait, wait as long as he can so the Soviet Union should maybe be destroyed. Let Hitler do the dirty work! So instead they waited until 1944—and by then, Warsaw was destroyed, Auschwitz was eating up thousands and thousands of Jews every week, all Europe was red just like Churchill was afraid it would be—excepting it was blood that ran everywhere, not communism.

"I remember we had a demonstration in the Union Square to call for the Second Front. And we had there for a speaker Mr. Charlie Chaplin—for him you don't need an introduction, right? You know, there's certain people, like him and like Pete Seeger, f'rinstance, that if ever in your life things get so bad that you think you might commit suicide, all you got to do is think about them and then you won't, 'cause they give you such hope with just a smile, a song. Anyway, so Charlie Chaplin comes up to the speakers' platform, and he's about to climb up there, he puts forward his left foot and then—whoops!— he catches it and puts forward his right foot instead. And then he says, almost to himself, he says that he doesn't want to put his foot in his mouth. I'm standing close to the platform and I'm laughing and laughing! And he gives me a look like he's surprised that I should be laughing, and then he winks at me. At least, this is what I saw.

"But the right-wingers in America, McCarthy and his bunch, they kicked Charlie Chaplin out from the United States. In 1952, he went to Europe and he didn't come back no more, 'cause they were calling him and everybody else that wrote or acted in good movies, all of them got called Communists. Hollywood had what you call a 'blacklist.' I don't want to jump so far ahead, with the Hollywood Ten and with Paul Robeson getting kicked out—that's already in the Fifties. But the point is, any country that it starts kicking out the artists, it's committing suicide. It's letting its own blood run in the gutter.

"Hitler, he also kicked out many of the great artists and the great scientists from Germany and from Austria, 'cause they were Jews or 'cause they were progressives. And when he did this, he kicked himself right in the teeth—thank God!—'cause otherwise, y'see, the Nazis could've got the atom bomb before anybody else. Sometimes I think about this—about these nuclear weapons, that they were actually made by the refugees from Nazism, and now they hang over the earth like the air itself. It's like a curse, a warning, from the six million Jews. From their grave. And I think we better listen.

"Because of the Nazis, more than twenty million of the Soviet people died. A number like that, it's just words, but can you imagine? It was a wall to stop Hitler, a wall of human bodies. And we in the Party in America, we stood on that wall in a certain kind of a way. For the first time since the Bolshevik revolution, the American people got a real look at socialism, y'see, and they saw the Soviet Union as friends, as allies. And the Party got popular again. In fact, we were maybe *too* popular, too chummy with the big cheese, if you know what I mean. F'rinstance, during the war, the Party wouldn't support any strikes. Our idea was that the workers and the capitalists have got to work together to stop the Nazis, to save the Soviet Union, to save the Jewish people, to save the world, to save save save. The workers should save everything but a little *gelt*, hmm? While the corporations, they themselves did big business with the Nazis!

"We even dissolved the Party and called it, like, a 'club,' an 'association,' so that we shouldn't give Roosevelt bad dreams about revolution at night. Roosevelt should get a good night's sleep so he can wake up and fight Hitler. Fine. It was Hitler we were after, not Roosevelt. With Roosevelt and the capitalists, we could have peaceful coexistence, but not with Hitler. But it's not right to give up the idea that we ourselves are a political party! You might have to go to bed with the capitalists, but you don't have to kiss them!

"Anyway, I. didn't need no 'club.' I already belonged to a club, of all the mothers in America that their sons went off to war. First went Jacob. I was scared stiff. He ended up with his radios, sure, he was always on secret missions in Europe! At least, this is what he told me to explain why he didn't write. And he came out with medals to prove it. *Oi,* I was nervous all the time. And when I would see a young man, maybe on Second Avenue, that from the back he looks like Jacob, so I would run to him and then it was like waking from a dream to see this stranger's face. . . .

"Next went Willy. He got drafted. But since he was a chemist, they kept him in the United States to work on stuff here. He was in Amarillo, Texas, and Janet went with him—she worked for the government doing public relations. They were there for maybe a year when one day a sergeant that he was a friend to Willy, he comes and he says there's a guy from the Army Intelligence—'G-two,' they called it—so there's a guy from G-two and he's asking questions about you.

"Then maybe a week later one of the big cheese, a captain, he calls Willy into his office and on his desk he's got a file as thick as the Bible. He starts reading to Willy from letters that he wrote to me, to friends, about how the Soviet Union needs a second front, how there's still Jim Crow in the army—things like that. And the captain says to Willy, 'Did you write this stuff?' And Willy says, 'How come you got copies of my personal correspondence? Where are we living, in Nazi Germany?'

"A week later he gets transferred, without a word, to Kansas. There's no more science work for him—they put him instead in a pharmacy. And they kept after him, with nagging and with punishment. They made him sign a loyalty oath that says you love America and you don't belong to a group that it wants to overthrow the government. But he already signed one in Texas— anyone that's doing important work or secret work had to sign a loyalty oath first thing. But when they made him do it again, he said, 'No, it's unconstitutional.' So they took away his stripes—

he was a corporal, and they made him a private—and they transferred him again, to Wisconsin. It was very cold there, but his
records, they stayed in Kansas, or maybe they got lost in the
mail? 'Cause for the rest of the war, Willy was left alone. Excepting he had Janet with him, so he wasn't really alone, hmm?

"And me, I wasn't alone either. I had now another fellow,
Paul Vogel. I met Paul when he was a patient at the Beth Israel
Hospital. He had that certain kind of a blood disease that the
Negro people get—it's the sick cell—no, no, the sickle cell, like
the hammer and sickle, that's how I remember it. Paul's mother
was a Negro woman, y'see, and his father was a Jewish man.
They were from Canada, Montreal. So later, when Paul and
me got close, he says it's not the sickle cell he's got, it can't be,
'cause both parents got to be Negro for the disease to come.
But it *was* the sickle cell, y'see. Paul was just an exception in
this like he was an exception in everything.

"I met him in the hospital, and then a month, maybe two
months later, I put an ad in the newspaper for boarders, 'cause
I had so much room in my apartment with the kids away. So
this guy shows up at the door and I recognized him right away.
He had skin color like a chipmunk, with some freckles, and hair
all bushy and gray. He was a husky guy, too. So I invited him
into my kitchen, and he began by saying, 'The last time we
talked, Mrs. Sainer, you were saying ...'

"I don't even remember what I was saying, I just remember
how impressed I was that *he* should remember my words. So
he moved in, he became my friend, and later he became my
boyfriend, too. And the neighbors became very mad, that a
black man should be living with a white woman on their block.
Everywhere there was prejudice, no matter whether they're
Jews or Ukrainians or Irish, all of them. So I ignored them and
I used to tease them. To the Jews, f'rinstance, I used to say,
'He's not so black, he's a Jewish man, only his freckles are
Negro.' Or I'd just tell them that he's circumcised—that would
make them turn red!

"But Paul sees that he's making trouble. When I gave out
leaflets, f'rinstance, about something or other, and nobody takes
them from me anymore. Or once we got a swastika painted
on our door. So he says, 'I got to leave now,' and I said, 'Over
my dead body! You got to stay,' I said, 'even if you get sick of
me, 'cause we've become a political cause now!' In fact, I used

to tease him: I would say that this was all a plot to keep him with me, that all my neighbors were in on it.

"But Paul didn't stay so long anyway. He couldn't belong to anything for long. It's funny that his name was Vogel—this means 'bird.' Who knows, maybe I got attracted just to his name when I read it on the chart in the hospital. I was still kind of crazy with words—I still am!

"He had a certain feeling of tragedy, and it attracted me. I know this about myself. When I see people of mixed race, especially from two races that they've suffered so much, the Jews and the blacks, to me it's like seeing a lovely flower that it blossomed too early. You just know that the frost is gonna kill it. 'Cause these are people of the future, y'see. His parents were those that they broke with prejudice, they found love, the most genuine kind of a love, 'cause you got no model, no movie, nothing to imitate. But if you have children, they can never fit into the world. They meet with discrimination from both sides. From this they might become strong, but they're always . . .

"Well, look, let's not talk about always, let's talk about Paul. He was a lonely man. F'rinstance, he never joined the Party, even though his ideas were progressive. And he used words like they should be silver dollars, that you shouldn't spend them. And his words *were* silver—he was an educated, intelligent man with a poet's tongue. For a living he drove a cab, so there was no one to bother him. When he wasn't too moody, he was like a cat that it can sit with you a whole day doing nothing. The room would have a different feeling, like the clock is slowing down and the street is miles away. And sometimes I would say, 'This is no good, to lounge like a philosopher a whole day.' And I would leave him, maybe go for a visit to Party headquarters or go do some work as a volunteer for the *Freiheit*. Or anything, just to go.

"We had a funny, moody kind of a relationship. If I got mad at him, he wouldn't yell, he'd just go for a walk, or go to his room, or something like that. He would never raise his voice to me. And once in a while we would sit and he would tell me about his life, and I would learn who he was, how he traveled. . . . It came out very slowly. He had a wife, a black woman in Kentucky. Her family was freed from slavery a few generations, so she had a bond with Paul, 'cause his mother also came from free Negro people that they escaped to Canada on the Underground Railroad. Anyway, Paul met her—he was handling racehorses for some rich man, and she lived in the country where the horses were, in Kentucky.

"This is the nineteen twenties I'm talking about. Paul wanted to become a veterinarian, but they had Jim Crow back then like you got pigeons today—everywhere! But he met this girl and they were in love, so they had a wedding on her land. Some of the neighbors came, black and white, but more came just to watch, and they didn't like what they saw: Jews mixing with gentiles, blacks mixing with whites. So there was plenty of gossip about this wedding.

"They should've got married in Montreal. 'Cause the next week—or maybe it was the next month; who remembers?—there was labor trouble in the coal mines in the eastern part of Kentucky, and there was lots of fighting that it spread all over, and Paul's wife, she fell into the hands of the Ku Klux Klan. They were out looking for her. She was a beautiful woman and she had a progressive mind. She was a fighter.

"The Klan! They're worse than cannibals! She wasn't herself for the rest of her life 'cause of what they did to her. They made her to be an invalid, actually. And Paul took care of her for ten, fifteen years, until she got tuberculosis and she died just before the Second World War. They had one daughter together; she lives now in Florida.

"But that's enough about Paul Vogel, yeah? I shouldn't spend so much time talking about him. It's a good story, maybe, but it was not so good a relationship. Too much of what we shared was tragedy, pain. It's like we came from the same homeland—sometimes you don't want to be reminded so much.

"I was also very careful that I shouldn't get involved with a man that's sick so much. When his health was very bad, I would ship him to the hospital and take care of him there. Not at home.

"But when I felt lonely, he was good for me. He taught me how to sit still. He made me feel not younger, no, but that it's not so bad to get old. And certain hours we had together, they were delicious. We both worked nights, y'see, and that one hour before we're supposed to go to work, we're both getting dressed, having a bite . . . We almost got fired, the two of us, for being so late to work! It was hard to leave each other.

"Right after the war, like I told you, we had in the Party

a campaign that none of the comrades should have racist ideas. And since I was living with a Negro man, or a man part Negro, and he's educated and he's easy to get along with, so all of a sudden people begin to come more and more to my apartment. People that they got brought up on charges and they want to make good, or people that they feel guilty 'cause they got no Negro friends. Paul became everybody's Negro friend! And he hated it.

"Plus by then my kids were home and we all lived together. Willy was going for training so he could qualify for a license to be a pharmacist—he wanted this instead that he should be a chemist, 'cause he couldn't stand to work for big companies. Plus there was a union, Local 1199, that it was very active for the pharmacists, very militant, even during McCarthy, and Willy was a founding member. Later this union also organized the hospital workers. Anyway, this was Willy's choice, and he was smart—soon there would be a blacklist in the companies that they did science. But he still had a living, y'see.

"Jacob wasn't so lucky. He worked in radio, and when the purge came he had nothing to fall back on. Of course, he blamed it on me, my son. He wasn't even in the Party no more, but he had a past, and he had me for a mother. Here he was a war hero, that he went on secret missions in Europe, and he comes home only to be persecuted. He could never understand it. We're just lucky he wasn't any kind of a big shot in the radical movement, 'cause if they called him in front of the House on Un-American Activities Committee, he would give out names. He told me this. We had one hell of a fight!

"But the point is, I had my kids again, and it was hard for Paul, all the activity, all the people, me being busy—I didn't need him the way I did before. So the next time Paul got shipped to the hospital for his anemia, this was in 1946, and when he came out, he says he's going to Florida to visit his daughter. The winter in New York was too cold for him—this is what he said. But I knew, it was *me* that was too cold.

"So we celebrated his fifty-third birthday. And I got him to come with me to the first demonstration that we ever went together—a demonstration for Israel, that there should be a Jewish state. And then he left. For years we wrote, back and forth, but I never again saw him. He died from the sickle cell in 1955.

"I gave Paul what I could. But he gave me more. It's true. He was a bridge for me across a few very difficult years. I was lonely. I felt old, what with my false teeth and with all the little aches and pains. And I felt disillusioned. I was very emotional. Partly it was just my age—I was just beginning with my change of life. But mostly it was the world itself, the way it was going. I mean, here you had the Holocaust, that we were just learning all the details—the trains, the ditches, the ovens, the gas, the millions. Much worse than we ever imagined—who could imagine such horrible things? And I would say to Paul, 'How can the world go on like this? Why isn't everybody crying, all at once? Why isn't everybody making it change, forcing it to change? And now, after such a war, we're gonna have the cold war? After so much persecution, we're gonna have *more* persecution?' And with Paul I could cry about these things—about my mistakes, about my son, about everything—'cause Paul knew great pain, y'see.

"So he helped to teach me to find something that it's inside me: that even without optimism, without activities, without even hope, I can heal. It's not even an idea, y'see, it's not some kind of a faith—it's more just a way that you sit, you breathe. The world is spinning, the tea tastes good, the birds are singing, you're alive. It sounds crazy or maybe boring to you? But there was a time after Paul left me that I was actually living underground so that the FBI shouldn't find me, and many days I thought about Paul, how he taught me to sit still. And now, as an old woman, it's the same thing: I can't live on passion all the time. I got to save my strength for when there's actually something to do.

"Look, I'll say it this way and then I'll be finished: We had fascism, the real thing, the worst thing, and from it we got the Holocaust. And then we got Hiroshima. And then we got the cold war. And then we got McCarthy. What was the use anymore to talk about communism, socialism, brotherhood? Let's just talk about survival."

❀

What had roused her? She awoke worried. The window rattled again, bathing her face right down to the collarbones with a cold, wet draft. Tomorrow night she would remember to sleep in the opposite direction—or was it worse to have cold feet? Who knows? Ask your dreams.

She guessed it was snowing outside and not yet dawn, for the house seemed exceptionally hushed, as though newly carpeted. Perhaps she had time yet to snooze? But there were crevices now between her quilt and sheets, through which the damp cold was pricking sections of her flesh. Damn that Dr. Greenbaum for stinting on heat! The people will feel no warmth in their old bones until the supper soup is in them. And if they freeze to death one night? He'll label it a heart attack. Bastard, he deserves one himself.

She raised her face to the leaky window, dragging her quilt with her. The scruffy yard and parking lot were spread thick with snow that was still falling in slow, fat flakes. At the near edge of the lot, the Bayside Nursing Home sign, cursive black letters on a whitewashed board, glowed beneath its hooded display lamp. Like a wedding invitation, Bessie thought; their sons and daughters should only know, it's actually a grave marker. Behind it rose a tall pine strung with blue and red Christmas lights. The streetlamps along the boulevard were also lit, shooting beams of color through the icy branches of oak trees. She'd gotten used to an autumnal scene out there; the new wintry look made her feel intolerably lonesome.

Bessie pulled her robe from under her pillow and wrapped it around herself before the cold reached under her pajamas. She padded across the floor, promising to buy herself a pair of slippers on her day off, then peered out the door at the pay telephone on the wall outside the Greenbaums' bedroom. For two consecutive days she had called Janet from there, forgoing her more cautious habit of phoning only from the public booth at the diner, two blocks away. Now the taboo lingered as she dialed and flinched with each ring, five in all. Janet answered in a panic: "Hello?"

"Hello, my daughter." Bessie huddled over the receiver, touching her forehead to the wall, speaking quietly. "What time is it?"

"Mom? What? . . . Oh, wait. It's five-thirty. Why are you calling so early? Is something wrong?"

"I didn't know the time. I'm sorry."

"When your grandchild comes," Janet said with a yawn, "I'll get little enough sleep. Shame on you, mother!"

"I couldn't sleep. How are you?"

"I can't hear you. Why are you whispering? Wait . . ." The phone clunked down as Janet had words with Willy in the background. "What's going on, momma?" she said, picking up again. "Is something wrong?"

"Nothing's wrong, Janet. How is Momma Greenpoint?"

"The same. She's very weak. Willy says she's very prone to infection, so we're bringing her in today."

"To which hospital?"

"Montefiore."

"You couldn't pick one where I *didn't* work?"

"Oh, mom! We had to pick one where Poppa Greenpoint can visit. Believe me, the FBI is not going to stand guard at her room on the chance that you might visit."

"They told you personally?"

"Stop it. How many years back in your record do you think they're going to go?"

"They haven't got enough clerks to do the job?"

"Oh, be reasonable, will you?"

"Janet. They came to Beth Israel with their questions. They came to Mt. Sinai. They came to our house. They came to our friends."

"I don't believe you're *that* important to them, mother!" Janet insisted with rising impatience. "You haven't been that active in many years, unless you've been doing things that I know nothing about!"

"You know exactly what I'm doing. For fifty-five years I've been doing the same thing."

"You make it so hard for everyone, momma—for yourself the most."

"*I* don't make it hard, Janet. It's the FBI that's making it hard. Remember that." The simple utterance of the federal agency's initials made Bessie shudder and catch her breath. Likely there were agents listening in on their conversation right then and there, no matter what Janet or her husband thought! "Look, you'll pick me up tomorrow at the station, yeah? Tell your husband, please, that I'm taking the early train. Otherwise they start making work for me here. Now, I'm sorry I disturbed you. Go back to bed." Bessie hung up and hurried back to her room.

Doubts plagued her like buzzing flies as she climbed back into bed to keep warm. Janet's skepticism had time and time again provoked her to review events and take stock of her decision to go underground. Perhaps she *was* overreacting, even playing directly into the FBI's hands by lying low and ceasing her political activities. But would she better serve the movement by rotting in jail for refusing to testify to some government committee? Though there had been no direct word from the fractured Party leadership about what to do, she herself had read the warning signs, too numerous and blatant to be ignored. Beginning in July: Returning from a twenty-four-hour virus to the picket line at Foley Square to protest the prosecution of eleven key Party members under the Smith Act, she'd brushed eyes with a grinning cop. "We missed you here yesterday, Mrs. Sainer."

"How do you know my name?"

"Are you kidding?"

Cossack pig!

And all through that trial, right up to the conviction on October 14 for "conspiring" to "advocate" the overthrow of the government, the newspapers had screamed at her from their racks: FBI REPORTS 12,000 REDS FOR FUTURE PROSECUTION . . . HUAC CITES RED INFILTRATION IN PUBLIC SECTOR . . . NY BOARD OF ED PROMISES INVESTIGATION AS SCHOOL TERM BEGINS . . . S.A.G. PRES. REAGAN BLASTS HOLLYWOOD RADICALS . . .

"You're not thinking of leaving Beth Israel, are you, Mrs. Sainer?"

"Leaving? To go where?"

"Well, this young man was here this afternoon. Very nice young man. He was asking all sorts of questions about you, Mrs. Sainer. Me and the girls, we figured he was checking references for another job."

"What kind of questions?"

. . . GALLUP POLL SHOWS 68 PERCENT SUPPORT OUTLAWING CPUSA.

"I'm gonna have to raise your rent, Mrs. Sainer. Cost of everything's going up, you know."

"Like hell you will. We got a lease."

"Yeah, but you don't want to go talking to no judge, do you? Like I was saying the other day to the government fella—he came snooping around with some questions, see, and I said, 'Cost of everything's gone up, buster, even information.'"

"You sonofabitch. Step back before I slam this door right in your ugly face!"

"Whoa! You watch your language, Mrs. Sainer. This is a nice building. We got nice people here."

. . . SCREENWRITERS LAWSON, TRUMBO GUILTY OF CONTEMPT . . . CPUSA BURNS MEMBERSHIP LISTS . . .

BETH ISRAEL HOSPITAL
Board of Advisors
216 East 16th
New York, New York

Sept. 1, 1949

Dear Mrs. Sainer,

It has been brought to the attention of this body that certain of your nonprofessional activities may be interfering with the proper execution of your obligations to this institution. To examine this charge, a board of inquiry has been convened for Oct. 1, 1949, at 1:30 p.m. at our office. Your presence is required at this time. You may bring an advisor, family member, or legal counsel if you so wish.

Sincerely yours,

Fred Gallatin
Board of Advisors

And how it had escalated, like the summer heat! ROBESON CONCERT PLANS SPARK PEEKSKILL RIOT. WOMEN AND CHILDREN ATTACKED AT LAKELAND . . . POSTPONED CONCERT SET FOR SEPT. 4. DEWEY PROMISES STATE TROOPS TO GUARD ROBESON . . .

"Janet, you stay home. You're in a family way. That's reason enough."

"Nothing will happen to me, mom."

"Why, you wear some kind of a halo? Nothing will happen! This is exactly what they said about Hitler! These are fascists they got up in Peekskill!"

"And you're going to go?"

"Janet, I sold tickets. I helped organize. Of course I'm going."

"Wonderful. My old mother goes and I don't."

"Watch your language! I'm too old to be pregnant, that's all. If Paul Robeson's singing, I'm going."

"I just want to go, too."
"You're not!"

. . . ROBESON CONCERT-GOERS AMBUSHED BY MOBS ALONG HIGHWAYS;
SCORES INJURED. . . . . REDS CHARGE POLICE COMPLICITY IN PEEKSKILL
INCIDENT. . . . .

And now Janet's disappointed in me, thought Bessie, standing
wrapped in her quilt and staring out the oily window at the
spreading daylight. You built yourself such a reputation, Mrs.
Sainer! Your daughter expects you to make a speech and everything'll be okay! *Oi*, what does she know? A child of the Party
—she lived, she played, she breathed inside the movement. She
thought we owned the world. She didn't live through the Palmer
raids, she never in her life met a real-live fascist, she never in
her life got socked in the teeth. *Oi*, Jannie, Jannie, you got to
deal on their level now, and with no idealism whatsoever. Pretend we got the Bill of Rights here with us in the underground,
folded up like an old letter from your boyfriend. That's your
idealism! We got to stay free for the sake of freedom, ours and
America's, okay? It's true! And when they hunt, we hide. They
come, we run. . . . Now, I'll tell this to Janet—I should maybe
write it down. . . .
"Six o'clock, Bess! Good morning!"
"Just a minute, I'm getting dressed."
Mrs. Greenbaum pushed open the door and ducked her head
in. She was disguised as a worker, as usual, in a blue kerchief and
overalls. "No dawdling now. We don't want to be late with
breakfast."
"Close the door, please," Bessie said. "It's cold enough in your
house."

The work in the nursing home lacked purpose, a sense of
progress toward healing or at least an institutional commitment to the patients' comfort. Bessie found nothing positive to
offset the suffering, decrepitude, and human helplessness in
which she had to wallow each day. Of course, Mrs. Greenbaum
dished out cheery words and pats to the thinning hair of her

patients as she made her supervisory rounds through the Victorian mansion, but these were impersonal, abbreviated gestures to show how busy she was. Only those desperate old souls who would have mumbled their troubles and life histories to a flickering light bulb would try to make conversation in response to her niceties; the rest of the "inmates," as Bessie liked to call them, knew Mrs. Greenbaum as the enemy, whose true interests were revealed more by the cold radiators than by the warm platitudes.

"Bless your soul," grunted Mrs. Guinness, an ancient but fit Irishwoman, as Bessie paused in the distribution of breakfast trays to fetch a blanket that had slipped from the woman's bed. "Bless you." Her fingers alighted like a spiny insect on Bessie's cap. "You're an angel in my eye, you hear? An angel in my eye."

"Sha, sha, it's my job."

"Oh, no!" Mrs. Guinness cried, face flushing. "It's your heart! Your heart, deary. You're an angel in my eye. Not like that cold bitch with her phony-baloney face—"

"Shh," Bessie cautioned, laying a tray of oatmeal and coffee across her lap, then moving to another bed in the suite of six.

They were starved for affection and respect, most of them feebler of speech and gesture than Mrs. Guinness, and showered Bessie continually with praise. "Take this pin for yourself, Bessie. It's from my daughter—you know how often she comes?" "I saved a banana for you, Bessie." "I'm praying for you, Bessie. All day long I pray to Jesus." But how much of their gratitude could she tolerate while serving them soggy oatmeal? How many weak caresses could she endure when their fingers were icy cold? How many gold trinkets could she accept from women whose sheets stank of urine but went unchanged for lack of clean ones? Bessie knew too well that she was not a nurse but a narcotic, the lone amenity that the Greenbaums tendered these helpless women and men while fleecing them of their savings and dignity.

"Mrs. Harlow, we get such fine reports about you from our residents." Dr. Greenbaum would address her by her pseudonym each payday as he unlocked his desk drawer to take out his enormous black checkbook. "Mrs. Greenbaum and I are so pleased that you were recommended to us by our friend Mr. Bronstein."

(Aie, Bronstein, you never were a judge of character!)

"We hope you'll stay with us a long time." Pen uncapped, he would hesitate deliberately over the checks. "Excuse me, I can't seem to keep it in my mind. Do I make it out to your daughter?"

"Yes."

"Janet Sainer, is it?"

"No, Dr. Greenbaum." And she would have to spell Willy's family name letter by letter, counting the links of her chains. How many times would the bastard repeat this ruse to remind her of her enslavement?

Mrs. Sainer, are you now or have you ever been a member of the Communist party?

"Mrs. Harlow, I need to bathe."

"I'm sorry, Mr. Serban, there's no hot water this morning."

"Can't you get some? Please."

"I'm not a plumber, Mr. Serban."

More and more often she was walking away without apologies. More and more often she was drawing boundary lines, refusing the constant call of conscience beyond duty, learning not to see what she could not cure. More and more she felt rage and revulsion at the victims themselves: their sickly bodies, varicose veins, wispy hair, eggshell skulls, trembling voices, paralyzed lives.

More and more she felt less and less.

Jacob picked her up in Willy's car at the railroad station in downtown Brooklyn, explaining that Janet was having a rough morning of nausea and nerves. Yesterday's snow had already turned to slush along Atlantic and Flatbush Avenues, but the side streets on either side of the broad boulevards looked peacefully snowed under. "I wish it would snow more," Bessie said as they accelerated onto the upper rampway of the Manhattan Bridge. "Everybody should take a nice vacation at home."

"Someday," Jacob said, switching lanes with a quick glance over his shoulder, "they're going to put a huge dome over the city and control the weather."

"You sound like your uncle Julius. He used to say the machines will bring socialism—every day will be like today, a quiet Sunday, with machines doing all the work. Instead, look what we got. A place like Auschwitz. An atom bomb."

"Look at that skyline!"

"It's beautiful," she agreed without enthusiasm. "I remember how it looked my first day in America. . . ." But why was she playing the nostalgic greenhorn with him? "I'm starting to sound like the *alte khalyeras* in the place I work. . . ."

"I wish my company would move to the Empire State Building," Jacob said as the car swooped onto Canal Street.

Too quickly they'd come to Manhattan, where the cat-and-mouse game would begin. Every young man in an overcoat would make her nervous. All right, she coached herself, so the worst that happens is you get a court paper—a subpoena, yeah. At least they have no concentration camps in America.

She glanced at her son for comfort. "Jakey, you grew a moustache!"

He smiled, a quick flex of his lips. "You're very observant, mother."

"It looks very natural. Really. Like it belongs there."

"That's why it took you this long to notice?"

Maybe, my son, I have more important things to worry about? "I'm sorry, *ziskayt*," she said. "I got—"

He suddenly braked at a red light. "You know I'm quitting the Party?"

She hadn't known. "It's too much for you," she quickly agreed. "Are you having some kind of a trouble?"

"No trouble. Face it, ma, I haven't been active in your movement since the YCL."

"What's there to face?"

"Once the Party burned its membership lists, I wasn't going to stick my neck out. I'm not going to go around making a monkey out of myself—I don't want to end up in a cage."

"You don't have to explain, Jacob. I wish sometimes that your sister and Willy would quit, too, so I wouldn't have to worry for them."

He ignored her conciliatory words, but seemed intent on reigniting the long string of explosives that tied them together. "Now they're passing out loyalty oaths at my company."

"*Nu?* I'll embroider one on your tie."

"They're fair-weather friends, all your comrades. If one day you don't buy the *Daily Worker* from Mr. Bronstein, the next day you're persona non gratis."

"What does this mean?" she asked in a half-mumble as the

familiar signs and stores along First Avenue distracted her, concern fluttering in her belly, ringing in her ears, as though the
Lower East Side were under foreign occupation or with a
pogrom raging through its streets. She would have to skulk along
the walls, talk to no one. . . .

"And if HUAC ever has reason to subpoena me, boy," Jacob
rattled on, "I'll name names and spell them, too. Instead of losing
my job, boy, I'd engineer one hell of a radio broadcast!"

"Jacob," she finally shot back, "will you please shut up? I
don't care about the filth in your mind! I'm nervous! Do you
understand?"

He sat with a moustachioed smirk as he turned the corner at
Seventh Street and sped west toward home. "Oh, shit, I forgot—
Janet asked me to get something at Ratner's. Would you mind
hopping out, ma?"

"Stop here! Stop! *You* go to the bakery. I'm going home!"
She backed out the door, drenching her feet to the ankles in
slush. "You're a vicious beast, Jacob. You ought to be ashamed
of yourself." She slammed the door.

Bessie wept in Janet's arms in the back room of their apartment, then slept restively, with pressure in her sinuses, for over
an hour. When she came to, she breakfasted with Willy and
Janet—Jacob had delivered the bakery goods and disappeared—
and tried to catch up with political and family news.

Both of the kids insisted that she was overreacting to the
FBI investigations and the Smith Act trials. Momma Greenpoint
was very ill, Janet pointed out. She was in and out of the hospital—how long could Janet continue to make excuses for Bessie's
erratic visits?

"Then I'll tell her," Bessie declared. "I never before hid my
activities from her."

"She doesn't need news like yours," Willy argued. "She's a
very sick woman, Bessie. I'm sorry to say it. She needs her
family, her flesh and blood, close by. Very close."

"I won't be close if I'm in jail," Bessie reiterated with slow
emphasis. "Now, we'll visit her today and that's all."

But Janet looked miserable, her face hanging over the half-
eaten muffin on her plate. "What's the matter?" Bessie said.
"You're not satisfied, either?"

"I'm sick to my stomach, ma," she moaned. "And I don't understand why after seven months I should still be this way!"

"I'm sorry, *mein tokhteh*."

"You're part of it, too," Janet crabbed. "All through this pregnancy, I not only have to take care of myself and Willy, I also have to worry about you. I have to answer to all the relatives about you. I have no peace!"

"Now look," Bessie said testily, "you and your brother, both. You're not little children no more. I can't protect you from *tsuris* no more."

"Protect us!"

"Don't raise your voice to me! You're not my boss!"

"Take it easy, Jan," Willy advised.

Janet slumped again onto her elbows. "From what did you ever protect me, ma? From the Depression?"

"I always made a living, yeah."

"And you always made us feel guilty about it! If we were going to eat, boy, then first we better make sure the neighbors' plates are filled! Wait, momma! Don't interrupt. You don't want me to yell? Let me finish."

"Finish," Bessie said haughtily.

"I'm going to!" Janet retorted. "And I'm not criticizing you, so take the chip off your shoulder! You know I've always admired you, momma. Every rent strike you led, I boasted about. And you were an exceptional mother, all things considered. You were. Haven't I been a part of your struggle from the beginning? Haven't I?"

"What do you want, Janet? I'm not a tin can that one minute you can drop me on the floor and then you expect me to open up—"

"Oh, please! Don't play the sensitive soul with me, mother, it makes me nauseous! If you were so sensitive, you'd take one good look at your son—"

"I took two looks!"

"—and you'd see that for him, at least, being a red-diaper baby wasn't such a bargain!"

"And neither time I liked what I saw!"

Neither was listening to the other, and they gave up at the same time, a collision of silence. "All right, before we go," said Bessie, standing, "I got to make some phone calls."

"Go ahead," said Janet with indifference.

"Where's my coat?"

"Use the phone in our room," Willy suggested.

"I can't use it here, Willy."

"C'mon, Bess. Don't stay angry with us. It's not so terrible an argument you guys are having."

"Willy, it's got nothing to do with an argument! I got certain kind of a calls to make and it's better that I should make them from the drugstore."

"Let her go," said Janet, pressing her husband's hand against the tabletop. "Please, ma, get me a Hershey's."

"You're gonna eat a muffin *and* a chocolate bar?"

"I only ate half the muffin. Besides, there's two of us." She patted her pregnant mound.

The overhead light inside the booth remained dead as she closed the door and dialed. Just as well: There was a young man at the counter, questioning Mr. Higgins, the proprietor, and he was simply too clean-cut, in Bessie's opinion, to be a native.

"Hello?"

"Hello, Bronstein?"

"Yes . . . this is Bronstein." His voice quavered from a thousand similarly uncertain moments. "Who is—"

"This is Mrs. Harlow."

Silence. "Who?"

"It's Bessie," she said gently.

"Oh! Hello. You caught me with my pants down, eh?"

"Well, pull them up. You shouldn't sound like it's the Gestapo calling every time your phone rings."

"Usually it is. Where are you now, Bessie?"

"Never mind, Bronstein." From the corner of her eye, she saw Mr. Higgins pointing in her direction. As the young man looked away to the candy rack.

"How are my friends treating you?" asked Bronstein.

"Like bloodsuckers."

He was incredulous. "What do you mean? They're nice people."

"They're bloodsuckers," she repeated.

"I don't believe it! Every day they bought a newspaper from me."

"*Mazel tov.*"

"So are you leaving them?"

"Where am I supposed to go?"

"I'd give you a place," he apologized, "but I get visits from you-know-who at least once a week. . . . My God, when is it going to end already? The workers should go on strike, you know, a general strike, to make these fascists crawl back where they came from."

"Sure they should. How's the club, Bronstein?"

"How can it be?" he said. "The leadership is on vacation. For Mr. Smith we have some money saved. . . ." Bessie guessed that he meant the bail fund for the Smith Act defendants. Then he mentioned a few mutual friends, but with pseudonyms and cryptic language that kept her mind whirring and drawing blanks.

"You sound tired, Bronstein. Are you doing a good job?"

"Sure. I'm an employment agent, a travel agent, a psychologist . . ."

"Good. Listen, my sister is very sick. I gotta go visit. I—" Still there, that young agent, with his back to her while Higgins rang up a purchase on his old wooden register. "I, uh . . ." She had nothing left to say, only to sigh.

"Did you hear this Senator McCarran?" said Bronstein.

"What, something new?"

"No, not new. Hitler already did it. He's putting up a bill in the Congress to make concentration camps for the progressive movement."

Bessie choked and fell into a coughing spell. "Goodbye," she croaked into the phone. "Goodbye."

She sat in the dark booth for whole minutes, turning over violent images of partisans fighting the Nazis in the forests of Europe . . . of herself holed up on Seventh Street, grenades hanging like fruits off her red lace vest as they came to drag her away. . . .

Pushing out the folding doors, she peeked everywhere at once, seeking her enemy.

"Ahh, Mrs. Sainer," Higgins hailed her. "I thought that was you in the phone booth. Long time no see."

Not behind the card racks . . . not outside the window . . . not near the pharmacy counter . . .

"Say, Mrs. Sainer." Higgins stepped out from behind his register. "That fellow up the block, William—he's your son-in-law, am I right?"

"Who wants to know?" she snapped.

"Well, I do! That's why I'm asking!" He slipped his hands into the pockets of his white jacket. "I understand the young man's a pharmacist."

She was backing off toward the door. "Where is he? He was asking you questions. . . ."

Higgins's brow creased. "Who?"

"While I was on the phone! You pointed!"

"Oh, oh, you mean what's-his-name, my surgical-supply man— by the way, Mrs. Sainer, we carry an excellent line, if you need orthopedic hosiery and such. But about your son-in-law . . ."

The door opened behind her and the draft seemed to blow her headlong into a rack of greeting cards. "Whoa!" Willy shouted, catching her by the arm. "What's the matter?"

Higgins took her other elbow. "Your mother-in-law seems a little upset."

"Our aunt is very sick," Willy promptly explained. "Very dear sister of hers."

"I'm sorry to hear that."

"C'mon, Bess, the car's running outside."

Higgins bowed away, hands slinking back into his pockets. "Well, I won't keep you then."

"Keep us about what?"

"Come, Willy," Bessie whispered, tugging his sleeve.

"I can speak with you some other time," said the druggist. "I heard you were a pharmacist, that's all. . . ."

"I am."

"Working?"

"I am."

"Is it worth your while? Good pay?"

"It's a union shop," said Willy with simple pride.

"Union's taking all the good pharmacists," Higgins complained, turning away.

"Don't insult yourself, Mr. Higgins."

"Taking them out of my price range, anyway."

"We barely make a living." Willy held the door open for Bessie, then chuckled as they walked across the wet curb to where the Chevrolet was double-parked. "I ought to get the union to throw a picket line around his store."

"He's working for the FBI," Bessie said. "I'm positive. You shouldn't talk to him no more."

"Who?" said Janet, bundled like an Eskimo in the back seat.

Chapter Twenty

Jacob's nastiness, the kids' skepticism, Bronstein's phone voice, and the druggist's suspicious behavior had kept Bessie on edge and stiff-necked throughout the morning, but as she drove with Willy and Janet along the Triboro Bridge parallel to the skyline, she began to feel the crampedness of her emotions and suffered a yearning to change everything, at once. She wanted to spend days, even weeks, with Momma Greenpoint, away from the children, away from activities, learning all her recipes, pondering her homilies, trying to feel the throb of her religious sense of life; to consummate, at last, a precious relationship made mundane by familiarity and beset always by other voices, other priorities.

"Kids," she said, "would you mind terribly that you should drop me first at Montefiore and then you'll go get Poppa Greenpoint?"

"Mother," said Janet in her half-cranky, half-scolding tone, "you can stay in the car when we get to the old neighborhood. Nobody'll see you at all."

"It's not that, Janet. Please, I would like to see my sister alone a little while. Please? Willy?"

"Sure," he agreed. "It's barely five minutes out of our way."

"Thank you." She resettled in her seat, then glanced in the rearview mirror at her daughter. "How are you feeling, *bubeleh?*"

"I'm all right." Janet was swallowing hard to keep down her nausea.

"I wish I had more than one day off to spend with you."

"I have to work tomorrow myself."

"How long will you wait before you quit? Are you gonna be like the peasant women in Russia that they give birth right in the potato field?"

"Right under the desk," Willy suggested. "We'll make a cradle out of the wastebasket. Teach the kid to type, first thing."

"Never mind," Bessie said, "you'll teach the progressive ideas first thing."

"Ugh, open your window, mom," moaned Janet. "I feel like such a wretch."

"It's too cold for you."

"Open it! I know what's too cold for me."

Bessie opened it a crack. "Look," she said, turning to look at Janet, "as soon as you make me a grandma, I'm coming home, okay? All morning I've been thinking about this. I'm gonna tell the Greenbaums to go to hell. And if HUAC sends me an invitation, so I'll send them a picture of the baby."

" 'Here, gentlemen, frame this instead of me,' " said Willy in a voice of pronouncement.

"C'mon, Jannie, give us a smile."

Standing at the foot of Momma Greenpoint's hospital bed, watching her sleep—perfectly composed, skin as pale and translucent as the wax pearls draped as a tiara across her hair—Bessie could feel the rush of life escaping from them both, moment to fleeting moment, from mouth and pore. Leah was dissolving into her own anemic bloodstream like the clay of a riverbank. And me? Bessie wondered. I'm chasing life, and I can never catch up.

Sit, old woman. Take off your coat. Make yourself at home.

Nobody in the hospital had recognized or accosted her, neither at the front desk nor at the nursing station. All the personnel were younger, much younger than she, and the halls and rooms had been refurbished almost beyond her recognition. The fear of persecution that had gripped her from the car to the revolving door at the entranceway was utterly vestigial, replaced by this irksome realization of her anonymity. She wanted to replace all the innocuous framed paintings in the hallways with snapshots from her youth. She wanted to project her memories like a movie onto the clean white walls. She wanted to be known again, in every room, every corner, at every desk.

Leah slept deeply, without snoring. Does she dream? Bessie wondered. We're a family of dreamers: Ruchel chasing her jewels, Julius his airplanes, Herschel after himself like a cat . . . and me, scheming always for a "better world." I'm scheming for a better world, and then I have to play catch-up with the daylight.

Now there's no daylight left. You live like a blind mole, underground. "Aiee, momma," she quietly moaned, then froze and guiltily held her breath.

Leah's eyelids lifted like thin shades.

Bessie lowered her lips to her sister's bloodless knuckles. "You know how much I love you, darling?" she crooned in Yiddish.

"Hello, Buzeleh . . ."

Oh, so weak! "What's the big idea, getting sick?"

Leah flipped her wrist slightly. "As usual."

"I want you to get better."

"God sends the cure . . . before the affliction. 'Better' means heaven . . . for me." She rested her eyes to amass strength for speaking. "Unless Mr. Markish . . . his connections. . . . He can make a bargain."

"Oh, silly."

"But I'm not bargaining." She arched her neck and slithered higher onto her pillows. Bessie fluffed them and Leah sank back with a smile. "Thank you. You do it better than Mr. Markish."

"I'm a professional with pillows," Bessie said.

Momma Greenpoint nodded heavily, her lips barely parting as she whispered, "And who will make the bed nice for Buzie?"

Bessie trembled on her intake of breath.

"You need a husband. . . ."

"Don't put men between us, Leah."

"Don't argue. . . . When you get old . . . there's nobody to look at you. . . . A husband . . . he looks. He doesn't always love what he sees . . . but he looks."

"Shh." Bessie kissed her temple. "You're working too hard for words. And I love *you* the same, with or without a husband."

"Love between two old women . . ."

"Hey!" Bessie cried in English. "Who are you trying to insult?" Leah shook her head but could not muster breath for words. Bessie lapsed into Yiddish. "I'm not even finished with half my hundred and twenty years. And already you call me an old woman! You'd better tell your husband to bargain for me, too."

Leah coughed her way to a voice. "You can bargain for yourself."

"Shh. You sound like a sick little frog."

"I never believed," she said, "you . . . an atheist . . . you're a believer, Buzie. . . ."

"Ha! That's for sure!" Bessie strayed from Leah's bedside to stare out the window at the silent stream of automobiles along the slick boulevard. "I remember how poppa believed. He actually did believe that he could make peace with the cossacks, with the czarists! Can you believe *that?* By being a nice guy . . . Well, we all get caught up in our ideas. Even when you grow up and see that everybody has ideas of her own. There's no one idea waiting like the sun behind the clouds. . . . But we do have to get rid of capitalism," she reminded herself, grimacing. "Then we can educate people to have a choice." She turned away from her vague, shimmering reflection in the window and had to squelch a surging impulse to weep out her fears and sorrows and gain from her enfeebled sister the sympathy that she was receiving from no one else.

Momma, momma, they're building concentration camps! It never stops, it never stops!

"Leah, won't you get better? You're such a comfort to us— it's like the old country is alive in you!"

"Alive," murmured Momma Greenpoint, unmoving. "Look what happened . . . the ovens. Every Jew is old now. . . ."

Bessie patted her arm atop the sheet. "Don't say that, please. What about Israel? Your Israel?"

Leah's shoulders slumped. "Israel . . . I worked my whole life . . . but it can't live in this kind of world. . . . Buzie . . . if God lived on earth . . . the *goyim* would break his windows. . . . The Jews can't have for themselves . . . until the Messiah—"

"Oh, stop with the nonsense! Please!"

Leah rolled her head and gazed directly into Bessie's eyes. "Neither can *your* dreams survive in this world, Buzie Kharlofsky . . . but I never tell you to stop."

"My dreams are not dreams!" Bessie insisted. "I still have the

Soviet Union to look to. *They* stopped Hitler, nobody else! *They* saved the Jews, actually."

Leah sniffed. "The old country . . ."

"No, the new country! They are, they're building socialism in the Soviet Union. Why do you scorn it, Leah?"

"They're building . . . in your mind . . . old widow . . . still talking about your honeymoon."

Bessie was amazed at Leah's strength for debate. "What's gotten into you, a dybbuk? You used to want to make peace instead of arguing."

"Peace . . . soon I'll have peace. . . ."

Bessie stroked her shrouded feet.

"Buzie . . . you do my job, Buzie. Organize the family . . . it's enough. Forget Russia. . . . It's the women . . . like Miriam . . . she saved her brother . . . Moses . . . gave birth to a nation. . . . Buzie, sit, sit on the bed. It's hard . . . looking up . . . my eyes . . ."

"Are they giving you any medication?"

"They give me kindness," she said, feebly squeezing Bessie's hand. "Human beings . . . they can still be kind. Today . . . the rabbi came . . . a young man . . . Reform. . . . We talked about Hanuka."

"Hanuka . . . It's Hanuka!" Bessie cried. "Is it? Yes! But where have I been?"

Underground.

Leah swallowed with difficulty. "I asked the rabbi . . . why the Torah portion this week . . . It's Moses . . . the burning bush . . ."

"Momma, momma," Bessie entreated her, "you've got to get home to light the menorah for us. It's Hanuka!"

"Shh. Listen to me . . . listen. . . . He said . . . the miracle of lights . . . and I interrupted him . . . a rabbi . . . I said, 'The miracle . . . the miracle of Hanuka . . . is one family, a Jewish family. . . .'"

"The Maccabees."

"They saved a nation."

"Shh," Bessie soothed her.

Willy waited in the frosted darkness of his car while Bessie picked her way across the sidewalk to the porch of the nursing home. From there she waved him off, signing repeatedly—Go, go

—then stood watching his taillights sink down the sloping, empty street.

Her heart was stuffed to burst. It seemed too frigid a night to stand and meditate—she had to pee—but there was no entering the home without losing her privacy to a dozen off-duty tasks. Exile among exiles. "And the children of Israel sighed by reason of their bondage." Momma Greenpoint had harped on that tale, the Torah portion of the week, Exodus 1:6–6:1: Miriam saving the baby Moses, who grew up in pharaoh's court until the fateful day when he struck the Egyptian guard ...

"*Then ... he went into exile ... a stranger ... in a strange land. ... This is you, mein shvesteh. This is Buzie. ...*"

But the burning bush, Bessie now recalled, had not been consumed by the flames. She turned her face skyward and silently cursed God for using her sister as a mouthpiece, full of sophistry and cryptic advice, while eating her up from within with "hemolytic anemia."

"It's congenital," Willy had explained following his consultation with Leah's doctor outside the room. "You can have it for years and years, then suddenly you have a crisis, an infection of some kind. ..."

The inevitability of the news after one look at Leah had made it seem soggy and colorless, a thing to be flung away. Bastards! Bessie thought with a cry in her throat. Bastards! They take everything away from us, even our tears! Fascist, Hitlerite bastards! And we're left with nothing but *bubbe meises. ...*

"*Then Moses ... put his hand ... with leprosy ... he put it inside his shirt ... and he came out clean. A miracle ... And God said ... go to pharaoh ... see pharaoh face-to-face. ...*"

Face-to-face. *Are you now or have you ever been a member of the Communist party?* Cold-blooded bureaucrats, you know the answer already! A plague on you and your committees! May all my suffering hit you at once like a giant fist!

Bessie stalked the length of the porch from light into shadow, flapping her arms and shivering as she wrestled with her sister's adages. *Nu,* burning bush, so give us some heat? To Moses you gave. ... What, you discriminate against women? Come, I'm better qualified than Moses was. I'm older, twice I've been in exile. So just show me one sign, anything, a shooting star, any-

thing, anything to make me believe this nonsense about redemption! I'll forget Hitler, forget the crematoria, forget her
hemolytic anemia and Paul Vogel's sickle-cell misery and all
your other careless curses. The Lord of the Universe—another
Hitlerite! I buried you with Smulevitch! For good!

She trembled at her sudden, vivid remembrance of Siberia: the
tears that froze in the ducts, and the blood that froze in the
veins. How did we keep body and soul together then? One
little star shining through a crack in the roof. Remember? And
Babushka's smelly warmth in the brittle straw. Lessons of revolution whispered at night: If we're given guns, she said, we make
revolution with guns. If we're given only snow and sick women
. . . sick old women . . .

We make revolution with *bubbe meises*.

"*Ma nishtano haleilo hazeh* . . ."—while Hannah the prostitute's tears ran down her throat—". . . *miko halyelos?*"

(Aiee, these memories, such memories! But only the dead
have no memories. . . .)

"Ouch!" Bessie bumped her hip against the railing at the
porch's end and then glimpsed her burning bush: Dr. and Mrs.
Greenbaum's Christmas tree, blinking in the backyard, illuminat-
ing the side of the house, red, blue, red, blue, purple.

Disrupting the place, placid as a stagnant pond, would have
been easy. Merely her hurried steps through the hallways, from
bedroom to bathroom and back down the stairs, were enough to
draw cries and whimpers from the darkened rooms. "Nurse.
Nurse. Nurse." They were starved for care, for sound, movement, and stimulation, and would respond to any of it like a
swarm of guppies. But her goal was not chaos or revenge.

Her goal was simply remembrance: the tending of her
Hanuka flame, the ingathering of her Siberian exiles. She needed
to organize herself bit by bit, extend her day's worth of oil to
eight, and recapture her hope from the Greenbaums' grasp.
Venturing step by step into the past, step by step into the future—small steps, little shuffling steps, beneath the notice of
her taskmasters, yet rising, no longer belly-to-dust. The most
difficult part would be controlling the raging, manic energy in
her veins. She could feel her pulsebeat throbbing in her skull
as she trod gently on the staircase.

In the dark, humming kitchen she collected a book of matches, two juice glasses from the prepared breakfast trays, and two of the small votive candles stored in the supply room in case of power failure. With the glasses clinking in the folds of her blouse, she remounted the stairs. What next in the Maccabean battle plan? On impulse, she entered Mrs. Guinness's room.

The old Irishwoman's crackling lilt greeted her before she'd even closed the door. "Hello, deary. They got you on night shift?"

Bessie thrilled to her voice. "You're awake! Mrs. Guinness, I need your help."

"You need *my* help. Can you beat that? Anything, darling."

"Shh, please. Are your roommates awake?"

"They're never awake. They're always awake. You're too young to know what I mean, God bless you. Gertie! Selma! Mrs. Petersen! Look at the angel that's come to us."

Bessie rushed from one bed to the next to ease their awakenings. "What, what?" "Bessie! . . . Did someone die?" "It's dark. . . ." "Oh, Bessie, oh, Bessie, oh . . ."

Three were bedridden and lay flat, breathing huskily as Bessie knelt at the center of the room and lit one of the candles inside a glass. The three others were sitting up, dry and skinny as the cornhusk dolls of her childhood. She could see their eyes, luminous in the faint arc of candlelight.

Mrs. Guinness's voice leaped from the darkness to rally her. "Look at this angel, God bless her, I love her so! She comes to visit a bunch of old bags and she's dressed up like she's meeting a gentleman."

"If one of you has a man under the bed," Bessie replied in a hushed voice, "bring him out. Probably it'll be Dr. Greenbaum, spying."

"That sonofabitch," growled Mrs. Guinness.

"Shh . . . Now, I didn't dress for anybody excepting you, the six of you. And for my family—I visited with them today. Once a week I get to vist them, just like all the inmates in this rotten place. How come they only let your kids come once a week?"

"Shoo, they wouldn't come more anyway," scoffed Mrs. Guinness.

But Bessie's words were unalterably in flight, like cannonballs. "Once a week. Once a week we get heat and good food and hugs and kisses and all kind of a things that human beings should have every day to feel like human beings! Well, now, ladies; you're gonna have a whole week of visiting, okay? From me! I'm visiting everybody at night like this, and it's not 'cause I got the night shift. I don't. Fact of the matter is, I'm visiting 'cause it's Hanuka, and I'm a Jewish woman, and Hanuka is the Jewish Christmas—we call it the Festival of Lights. And I'm gonna make this festival come alive with you. So . . ."

She held the candles in her palms, high so that they brightened the ceiling. "This is my menorah. The Greenbaums got their fancy-shmancy Christmas tree shining outside, so all the neighbors should forget what's going on *inside* this place. But they got no menorah, y'see, 'cause they're ashamed of themselves. In their hearts, they're ashamed. So this is our menorah—to hell with the Greenbaums—and we're all gonna make wishes over these candles . . ." Shh, Bessie Sainer, not so loud, not so fast, this isn't Union Square! But her ghosts had returned through the walls, and her memories were ricocheting everywhere. "Eh, I only wish I had my red lace vest. . . . One of these days in Union Square," she said, "I'll be wearing it again." And with a bullhorn to holler into and little marbles in my pockets to throw at the police horses' hooves when they charge. Down they go!

The intimacy of the gathering persisted long after Bessie's eloquence gave out and her makeshift candle lamps burned down. Four of the women spoke publicly—Mrs. Guinness had to be toned down repeatedly for security's sake during her outrageous reminiscence!—but the two others had strength enough only to whisper feebly to Bessie while she sat holding their deathly-cold hands.

Dead husbands. Dead children. Negligent sons and daughters, off to California, off to Long Island. Hardfisted landlords. Evictions. Broken hips. Cataracts and near-blindness. Stolen money. Lousy food. Bedsores. Bedbugs. Cruel words. Crueler silences.

"But behind all that misery, ladies—at the center of your lives—what kept you going? What keeps you going? Tell us—there's something warm. Something good."

Christmases past. Dear old friends, pausing in their lives to toast the future. An infant at the breast. Youth and beauty in the mirror. Parents in rocking chairs. Good smells in the oven. Men in the living room. The golden glow of sun on skin. A little bit of savings, a new car, a reupholstered sofa. A new house! A song...

"I would have died tonight," sobbed Mrs. Petersen as Bessie kissed her forehead. "I was planning for it. I was praying for it."

"Are you sorry to see another morning come, dear lady?"

Her answer drowned in her tears. Bessie peeled her off the mattress, wondering at her lightness, and hugged her goodnight.

"Mrs. Guinness?"

"I'm here, deary."

"Mrs. Guinness, will you do me a favor?"

"Do you still have to ask, angel?"

"Mrs. Guinness, will you do me a favor and pray for my sister?"

At two in the morning, Bessie stole into the kitchen to return the juice glasses and crept upstairs to her own icy room. The Christmas tree cast artificial moonbeams into her window, and her sense of achievement was likewise flickering as she lay sleepless beneath her comforter until dawn.

After lights-out the next night, she visited a second women's ward, with a genuine brass menorah that she had purchased on Hillside Avenue during a surreptitious lunch break. The night was warmer than the last, and Bessie found the women more active, less clinging to the scant warmth of their beds. She had to hush the meeting repeatedly, even at high emotional pitches, for fear that Mrs. Greenbaum or others of the skimpy nursing staff would be aroused.

She tried to tame the energy during the candle-lighting by speaking at some length about her own life and survival in Siberia. "Babushka was about as old as I am now, come to think of it . . . and she helped everybody survive, the cold, the food ... everybody..."

Then six tales were told, all terribly similar in plot: the slow dissolution of motherhood into dependency, ending in some catastrophic schism due to death, departure, rejection, or lovelessness. "Until finally you're dead," concluded the last, an intensely verbal, crippled leaf of a woman named Rose Peltzer. "But I'm still waking up every day. And I see my daughter's telephone number right on the ceiling. Plain as I can see your face, nurse. TWining 7-8371. I want to call that girl and tell her to get me out of here. I want to call that girl. TWining 7-8371. But I can't even walk to the phone. Every day I ask someone on staff to take me to that phone! I asked you, nurse, didn't I? Didn't I ask you?"

"Shh. Quiet, please, Mrs. Peltzer."

"Quiet. All the time I'm quiet. I'll be quiet in my grave. And they ought to print that number on the stone. TWining 7-8371. What time is it? I want to call her right now."

"Shh. It's too late."

"It's not too late. I want you to bring me to that phone, nurse."

"I will," Bessie agreed, to pacify her.

"TWining 7-8371."

"I'll remember for you."

"I'll remember for myself! You just carry me!"

"Tomorrow, Mrs. Peltzer. I'll bring a wheelchair."

"You can't get a wheelchair around here!"

"Yes I can. Tomorrow you'll call your daughter, all right, Mrs. Peltzer? I promise."

"Tomorrow," said the ornery old woman, bitterly.

"It's not allowed," cautioned one of her roommates. "You can't make calls unless you get permission."

"Shh, *I'm* giving permission," Bessie said. "Tomorrow we *all* make phone calls." Then a noise in the hall startled her to silence. "Shh. Everybody, shh." She glided to the door and peeked into the bright hallway. Mrs. Greenbaum was standing outside her room, hair in curlers.

Bessie slipped out to intercept her. "Mrs. Greenbaum. Hello. I heard something in there. . . ."

Greenbaum nodded curtly. "I did, too. It sounds like hysterics. What's going on?"

"Just a bedpan emergency. Don't worry."

She raised her eyebrows. "Are you on night shift, Mrs. Harlow?"

"Hmm? No." This was unbearable, to verbally fence while the six old women resonated with emotion and grief behind that thin door. Bessie wished she had words blunt enough to crush the boss lady's skull and be done with it. "Look, I—uh—how do you say it? I'm burning the midnight oil. Y'see, I'm writing Hanuka cards to my friends. It's Hanuka, Mrs. Greenbaum. Did you know?"

"Yes, yes. It's also a workday tomorrow, Mrs. Harlow. I'd suggest you put out that midnight lamp now and get yourself some rest."

"Well, I got a lot of suggestions for you, too, Mrs. Greenbaum." The words leaped off her tongue before she could trap them.

"What did you say, my dear?"

"How come we don't have a menorah in this house?"

Greenbaum folded her arms across her chest. "Are you—intoxicated, Mrs. Harlow?"

"We have a Christmas tree!" Bessie's voice cracked. "How come we don't have a menorah!"

Then the telephone rang like an alarm. "Christ Almighty, I don't believe this!" Greenbaum exploded. "It's one o'clock in the morning! Hello! . . . What? Sainer? Sainer who? . . . Bessie? Oh!" She slowly lowered the phone and smiled maliciously at Bessie. "Mrs. Harlow?" She dropped the receiver so that it dangled on the wire.

"Not my sister!" Bessie charged forward. "Not my sister!"

Chapter Twenty-One / 1956

"Not my sister, no! It was my grandson! I got a cradle instead of a coffin! How do you like that?

"But we didn't have an easy time, my family. We never do. There's a Jewish saying that if a man was meant to drown, all he needs is a spoonful of water. For a while I thought this was written just for us.

"Janet gave birth more than a month premature, y'see. It

was a very difficult birth. The baby was so small that we almost lost him. When Willy called in the middle of the night to the nursing home, there was nothing but pain in his voice, no *nakhes*. And I was completely *tsedreyt!* You know what it means, *tsedreyt?* It means cuckoo.

"The FBI came to our house on Seventh Street, y'see, on the same day that I went to see Momma Greenpoint in the hospital. Willy drove me back to the Bayside Nursing Home and meanwhile Janet gets paid a visit. Two agents. They were with her more than three hours with their questions and their threats, until Willy came home and kicked them out. You can do this, y'see. You don't have to say nothing to the FBI, you don't have to answer any questions unless they bring with them a warrant. But Janet was very scared, trying to cover up for me, trying to protect herself. And then two days later, she goes into labor.

"Willy blamed all this *tsuris* on me. Not because the FBI came looking. He understood this; he was a comrade himself and he knew there's nothing we could do but fight them or hide or do whatever's got to be. But Willy, he was hysterical 'cause the baby was in trouble, y'see, and Willy came out with all this stuff how Janet never really wanted to be in a family way 'cause she didn't want to be a mother 'cause she was too dependent on me, or I was too dependent on her—I don't know! You think I know? He had all kind of a things to say, right there when I met him in the hospital. He blew up at me like a bomb.

"All right, so what was he saying? My daughter, y'see, she gives and she gives, all the time, to other people. I used to think this is a wonderful thing—she's a real Communist, a real social person. If you need help with something, Janet will help. If an organization needs a secretary or a president, Janet will lead and she'll sharpen her own pencils. So I was proud of my daughter. I never thought, How come she gives so much? What's she looking for? Fact of the matter is, when there's too much of something, there's something missing. If there's too much food at the table, someone's not eating. If you got too much laughter, someone's not listening.

"My Janet admired me. She thought I was the greatest revolutionary in the East Bronx, if not the whole world. But she didn't admire herself so much, y'see. And I didn't really recognize this. She was a leader in the YCL, after all, and she was a wonderful speaker, and a beautiful girl, a popular girl—how should I know that inside her heart she's just a scared little kid?

"At least, this is what Willy said. According to Willy, Janet was afraid to be a mother. According to Willy, she gave birth premature just to make me come home from the underground. And according to Willy, I even *told* her that I would come home as soon as she gave birth—I gave her an invitation to do it premature. Now, I don't remember saying this to her. Why should I say such a thing when I'm not sure myself what's happening with the FBI and with my own future? But Willy insisted and he insists to this day that I said it and she heard it and she did it. So if he still says this now and I'm eighty-eight years, it's my memory against his—who would you believe?

"All right, so maybe it's better to get an honest slap than a dishonest kiss. Certainly Jannie and I were very close, maybe too close, and Willy's the husband, so I can understand that he resented me. Even if I don't take blame for Janet's problems! Fact of the matter is, I appreciated Janet's feelings for me, especially compared to my *meshugeneh* son that he would explode and get very ugly just from seeing me! And then later he would be full of apologies. Him I never understood and I stopped trusting him a long time ago. I'm sorry, you can criticize me all you like if I know you're my friend, but if you don't have some love or even respect for me, then who needs your criticism? And this was Jacob, y'see. He was in a boxing ring with me all the time, fighting, fighting—and believe me, he could fight dirty! Finally I had to give up about having a son, that's all. But that's another story, I don't want to waste my breath—I'll give you his number telephone, you can call him up.

"Anyway, I heard what Willy was saying to me and I saw that I'm coming between them, so I decided, Okay, Bessie Sainer, it's time to move. . . . But then Willy says, 'Never mind, we're planning to move ourselves.' Turns out that a few young couples that they're in the Party, they got young children or babies and they're all gonna move to a neighborhood, St. Albans, in Queens. It was a white neighborhood, working-class, and a couple of black families came in, so now all the white people were running —a stampede, you know. So the Communists went in to try to make stable the neighborhood. They would show the whites that other whites are moving in, not just out. Then maybe the neighborhood could be truly integrated instead of all just one or all the other.

"Now, let's see . . . there was Janet and Willy, and a couple named the Friedmans, and another, the Zackheims, that they had a beautiful baby girl—you know, my memory's not really so bad! Anyway, they were all Jewish people, young, progressive people, and they bought for cheap 'cause the whites were so anxious to get out.

"I supported this project. I thought it was a progressive idea, and they got a nice house with a big porch and a backyard where Janet could be with her boy a whole day. He would sit in his little sandbox and build all kind of a things! And so I moved to the Bronx to be with Poppa Greenpoint, 'cause Momma Greenpoint was already very, very low, one foot in the grave. Her own kids visited plenty, but they couldn't come to live, 'cause they were already with their own families—Belle-Brokha in Long Island, Max in Pennsylvania—and Momma Greenpoint couldn't go to them, 'cause she had to be near the hospital.

"In a certain kind of a way, it was good for me to live with them. It continued the life I had, the way it was in the Bayside Nursing Home, excepting *that* place was a zoo, you couldn't do good work there. But here I was taking care of an older person—Lester was already seventy-five years, older than Leah— and I liked this. I did this kind of work for the rest of my life. I was a private nurse for old people, for sick people, until I myself was seventy-five, and then I retired.

"Listen, I didn't abandon those old women in the Bayside Nursing Home either! Sure, I quit. I had to. First, I wanted to be with my daughter. Second, I knew I was gonna get fired, and personally accompanied out the door by the FBI. Those Greenbaums were real *gonifs*, y'see. Instead of waiting for payday that they should have to pay me, they went first thing in the morning to the telephone and gave me out to the FBI.

"But I did my share of work with the telephone, too. Everybody was agitated, y'see. The old women and men that they could walk were coming out into the hallway, and Mrs. Peltzer is shouting her daughter's number telephone, and those that they're senile are mumbling and crying—it was what you call 'bedlam.' So while everybody's busy, I went and I phoned the daughter of Rose Peltzer. This was in the middle of the night—

I wanted to give her a good shock, like I myself was shocked when Willy called. So I let her listen to what's going on so she should get scared. It must have sounded like a real death camp to her. And I told her how her mother was feeling, how rotten the place was, how she ought to come and visit her mother not on Sunday when everyone's cleaned up but on the Jewish sabbath when they got no heat and everything stinks. This is what I told her. And I left her weeping on the phone.

"Then, during the week at home, I tracked down as many of the children of the inmates that I could, and I gave them the same treatment that I gave the Peltzer girl. Some of them got mad, sure, and some of them didn't give a damn, so if I helped make them a little more, miserable, I'm glad. But there were some that they really appreciated what I said to them. They were fooled by the Greenbaums, y'see—those two put on a good show: He was a doctor, she was good with words, they were both polite and with enough *shmaltz* that you think they got some kind of feelings. Or else these kids were embarrassed about their parents: What's their friends or their boss gonna think to meet a father or a mother that she's senile or that she's wearing diapers?

"I'm not saying that kids should take care of their very old parents. It's a full-time job, and people live longer these days than they used to—they used to die before they could become a burden. But the thing is, you can't forget that they're human beings, these people. They got *tsuris* now, but once upon a time they took the time to give birth to you, so now at least you should take care that they should be comfortable.

"Am I scared that I should someday go into a nursing home? Yes, I am—I'd be faking if I said different. I look in the mirror and I see an old woman there, and I know my health is very delicate, that tomorrow I might slip in the bathtub and break a hip and then I couldn't live alone no more. Sure, the kids would take me into their house, but it wouldn't be a party, I'll tell you that. They got their lives and I got mine, y'see, and there's a lot of history between us, that too many times I interfered with their happiness, with their privacy and their plans. In this way I'm just like any old person—I don't want to be a burden on my kids, ever.

"Anyway, life is full of accidents. Life just kind of happens to you while you're busy with your pots and pans, if you know what I mean. Who knows, I could be left all alone in this world—all we need is a little bit of a tragedy to happen to my kids. And then what? Without your family, you got no other community in America. Your family's supposed to take care of you, and you just be sure to pay your taxes, right? This is what you call 'rugged individualism.' I call it loneliness.

"But am I gonna sit here worrying? I am not. You know, back when I was first getting to know Yasha, he introduced me to a guy that he worked with in Coney Island. He was a tight-rope walker—Ted Mulligan was his name. Ted Mulligan used to walk the rope without a net, and I would ask him, 'How do you do it?' And Ted said to me, 'We all do it, Bessie. The thing is just to walk natural and walk tall.'

"There you have it. And even if I'm someday walking with a walker, believe me, I'll still be waving my fists in the air and organizing people. The nursing-home *gonifs* better look out if Bessie Sainer comes into their place! They better be as scared of me as I'm scared of them.

"The Greenbaums, f'rinstance. It was many years later, but eventually they went too far with their cheating and they got put out of business by the government. Now, I didn't do it, I just wrote a letter and I hope it helped. It was my great pleasure to sign my name, my real name, to that letter.

"So after Bayside, I went to live in the East Bronx again. And I was very nervous, 'cause everyone knew me there. And sure enough the FBI came. Two young men that they looked like they just stepped out from the dry cleaners. They came to Momma Greenpoint's and they asked me all kind of a questions, mostly about other people, leaders in the Party. But I didn't answer no questions, and they didn't have a what-you-call-it, a subpoena. I was under Party discipline again, y'see—I was keeping close contact with my comrades, and this gave me a certain kind of a confidence to stand up to the FBI. There was a network of people—people to help, people to hide you if you gotta be hid. Even if I went to jail, I'd still belong to a movement, with a movement lawyer. I wouldn't be alone. Look, even if I died, I'd be buried in an IWO cemetery and the undertaker would be a *khaver!* The radical movement today should only provide so good for its people!

"So they came back every week, these two from the FBI, and we became very familiar. They would tell me all about my life and I almost enjoyed to hear it. And if I saw them following me out on the street, I'd bring them to all kind of a places—Harlem, f'rinstance, where I felt okay but they, two white men, they stuck out, they looked like cops. Or else I'd lead them into the moving pictures—it's just too bad there were no progressive films, Hollywood was having its purge, y'see.

"Actually, I don't really remember where I brought them, and it wasn't fun like I'm making out now. But the point is, I made peace with the idea: All right, so I'll go to jail. Better to curse the judge than curse my family if they should slip up. Better to sit in jail than to hide in a closet, yeah? And I felt alive, very alive. A child comes into this world, it gives you hope: that for this one, this generation of babies, life should be better. To hold that fresh life in your hands, it's like taking a bath in sunshine. I felt reborn. Y'see, I had a taste of what it means to be old, and I swallowed it and I said, 'Okay, one of these days, but not yet. . . .'"

"I myself was not arrested. There were not so many actually arrested during the time of McCarthy, only the leaders—the state chairmen, people like that. And our organizations were smashed up. And people like Ethel and Julius Rosenberg got taken for scapegoats. Them you know about, yeah? A Jewish couple with two small children, and the government says they're spies that gave out the atomic bomb to Russia. So they got fried in the electric chair. I remember the day they were executed just like I remember the day my Hannah died. Both things, they still make my bones ache. We were desperate—we had a rally in Union Square to scream for amnesty for the Rosenbergs. I remember, grown men were crying, they couldn't stop. The Rosenbergs were like your next-door neighbors, y'see. If the government can kill these two, then nobody's safe!

"But even when McCarthy did the worst he could, carrying on about the Reds this and the Reds that—and with Nixon and other reactionaries following him like the flies follow a bull—still, it was only a teensy part of the Party that we went to jail or to the underground. The rest of us, we kept on with our activities. We fought to save the Rosenbergs from the electric chair. We fought against the cold war and against atomic bombs. We fought against the Korean War, especially that it shouldn't become a war with China or with the Soviet Union. And we fought that Israel should be protected, and England and France and the United States should stop interfering with the Middle East, and there should be peace with the Arabs. And we fought that Germany shouldn't get weapons no more. And the Nazi war criminals should go to jail instead of going on social security.

"Plus there was the civil-rights movement, and I got very involved in it. In 1954, the Supreme Court said that the schools got to be integrated, and this started an enormous, a tremendous, wonderful campaign against discrimination.

"So we did a lot, y'see. And still with our May Day parades and our summer camps and *shules*. And we had hope for the future, like a vision, for as long as the Soviet Union was alive and strong, we had hope. Like heaven is for a Catholic, this is what the Soviet Union was for the Party. We believed that socialism was flourishing there and that the people were being, like, reborn. We knew that anti-Semitism is against the law in the Soviet Constitution and we believed that the law was real life. Why shouldn't we believe? Stalin put on a very fancy show for us.

"It's a funny thing, you know—if you look at what's going on in the Soviet Union the same time that you have McCarthy here, it's the same thing. Stalin and McCarthy would be very comfortable in the same room with each other. But it's not funny—it hurts, actually, it hurts. But I told you I would tell the truth. So we're gonna talk about Stalin.

"I already told you how life was good for the Jewish people when Lenin was in charge. There was, like, an affirmative action for Jewish culture. But Stalin destroyed all that. In the 1930s, he was already pulling it apart. F'rinstance, you had Birobidzhan, in the East. They called it the 'Jewish autonomous region.' It was like a state in the United States. Here the Jews could develop and preserve Jewish identity and culture, and still be a part of the bigger nation, the entire Soviet Union.

"In 1937, Stalin liquidated the entire leadership of Birobidzhan. Then in 1952—August twelfth, you should remember the date— in 1952, he killed twenty-four Jewish writers, actors, trade unionists, the entire creative leadership of the Jewish people in the Soviet Union. Stalin says they're 'cosmopolitanists'—they're not loyal to the Soviet culture—and when Stalin points the finger, that's goodbye! Dovid Bergelson, Peretz Markish, Itzik Feffer—it's unbelievable when you look at the list. It's like America should lose I don't know who—Albert Einstein? Leonard Bernstein? All the best actors and musicians and scientists and thinkers that they're Jewish—some you wonder 'cause they changed their names—it's like they should all be wiped out in one night.

"But not only that. Not only do they get killed, but the newspapers don't talk about it. Not in the Soviet Union. They just give the weather report, and they probably give credit to Stalin for making the weather, too.

"Can you imagine in America that such an important bunch of people should get killed and you don't even read about it? In America, you find out what color underwear they're wearing when they die. And I'd rather have this, I'd rather have all the gossip than have nothing at all.

"Look, I'm only getting started with Stalin. Never mind what he did to the Jews. Half his own Party he killed when he made his purges! Stalin executed maybe a million people even before the World War. Millions he sent to Siberia. Half the leaders in the army he killed, including the chief of the army. No wonder he had to make a pact with Hitler—you can't grow new generals as fast as you can kill them!

"So here I meant to talk about McCarthy and the Smith Act and the blacklists and all that stuff in America and instead I talk about Stalin. 'Cause Stalin destroyed my Communist party, not McCarthy. I feel like I should have a heart attack for saying such a thing, but it's true. And the truth I'm still learning, y'see. 'Cause the truth didn't come to us until 1956. That's already three years after Stalin died! Finally, in 1956, Khrushchev made a speech and told about Stalin's terrible crimes. It was a secret speech, of course, but we had in Poland a paper, the *Frei Shtimmer*, that they printed Khrushchev's speech, so here we had for the first time a Communist paper saying what the right-wingers were saying all along.

"And here I spent a whole life building the Party that it should be healthy, and democratic, and progressive, and with culture, that we should be able to give leadership to the struggles of the working class and improve ourselves, improve us all, as human beings—then suddenly I find out such things about Stalin. It's like getting a phone call one day that says your son is in jail for murder or rape or some kind of a terrible crime. The first thing you do is you ask yourself, How can this be? And you look back at your whole life, and suddenly it feels worthless. You've been blind with your eyes open. You've been following orders like a dancing monkey. Even if you had a disagreement, you just figured there was something wrong with *you*—you're bourgeois, you're not revolutionary enough—or else you kept your mouth shut so you could keep your friends, and you maybe became a little less active, that's all.

"There's this story that says when Khrushchev made his speech, someone in the Party Congress called out, 'It's easy to criticize Stalin when he's dead. How come no one came out against him while he was alive?' And Khrushchev says, 'Who is that speaking? Come forward.' And nobody comes. And Khrushchev says, 'There's your answer, comrade.'

"We were not scared of our own Party leadership that we should be executed for disagreeing—don't be ridiculous! But there was no democracy in the Party. I could tell you lots of stories—too many stories—of people that for one reason or another they got expelled from the Party, and suddenly they got no friends whatsoever. All their friends, all their social life, was in the Party, y'see. Even sometimes they married inside the Party. So now nobody's even talking to them, and their wife or their husband maybe leaves them—they're poison to everyone they meet. So they're not killed, no, but what kind of a life . . . ?

"Take Albert Bronstein, f'rinstance. He was coordinating for people that they went underground, and every day the FBI would come to his store or to his house to ask their questions. Finally, it was 1952 or maybe 1953 and Bronstein says he's going to move to Israel. He's got relatives there and he can't stand to be bothered no more. You should've heard: Party people called that man all kind of a names! Zionist, cosmopolitanist, police spy, renegade, Trotskyist! And they expelled him from the Party, so all he's got for company is the FBI men. And eventually the FBI got to him, sure. It took them another year to break him down, but eventually he gave out names. But this was the fault of the Party! They should've sent Bronstein with a round-trip ticket to Israel, and instead they sent him with a one-way ticket to hell!

"Me, I went to visit him, the week after he's expelled. He's still a human being and he's still my friend even if he's a *shlemiel*. And we had a long talk about political life. He was very bitter, like a man that he gives up whiskey *after* he's already got cirrhosis. He said, 'If a Communist can't live as a human being, how can we teach anybody else to live? If a Communist can't live as a human being, then what kind of a revolution are we gonna make?' It reminds me how my father used to say, 'Where there's no bread, there's no Torah; and where there's no Torah, there's no bread.' For me, when there's no democracy, there's no communism; and when there's no communism, there's no democracy. So you haven't got communism in the Soviet Union and you haven't got democracy in America. And in both places they'd like to put a person like me into jail!

"Now, in St. Albans—eventually I moved there with Willy and Janet and the baby, y'see, 'cause Janet wanted to go to work, and Momma Greenpoint died, and Poppa Greenpoint went to live with Belle-Brokha. . . . What was I saying? Oh, yeah, about St. Albans. We used to organize 'brotherhood festivals' in the neighborhood, with singing and dancing and good food and speeches. It was a wonderful day for the whole neighborhood. So I got very involved in this, and I got very involved in the movement for Negro equality. And this helped me to stand it when the news came out about Stalin, 'cause I was up to my ears in a new movement that it had a passion of its own. And it was an American struggle, it had nothing to do with the Soviet Union.

"Maybe I didn't get as disillusioned as other Communists that they dropped out of the movement entirely 'cause I didn't have so many illusions to begin. I was already more than sixty years, remember. My sister Leah, that she was a mother to me, finally she was dead, and I could still feel this loss, another loss. I had all kind of a little aches and pains in my body and also in my spirit, and these reminded me every day how hard is life. I knew life, y'see. People had to go work in factories in the Soviet Union, yeah? People get old in the Soviet Union, yeah? Women still go in labor to give birth, and men still die in war, and these things—birth and death and love and hate—the system, capitalist or socialist, it doesn't change so fast the reality of life.

"This doesn't mean that the political struggle is not so important to me anymore. Capitalism is no good, that's all, 'cause it's stupid. Why should we compete when instead we can cooperate? But just 'cause you start cooperating, it doesn't mean the job gets done so easy. I didn't have so many foolish ideas that everyone eats cake in the Soviet Union and everyone eats sawdust in America. In both places there's good and bad, happy and sad. Like Yasha used to say: We're all a bunch of monkeys.

If you remember that, then every little bit of progress that we make becomes precious, and you don't talk so easy about bombs and guns and revolution.

"Anyway, I had my own little monkey: my grandson! And through him, I was looking at the world with new eyes. I had my old eyes and his new eyes—this is wisdom! F'rinstance, when he was just four or five years, he liked to wake up early on Saturday, when his mother and father would sleep late—they could sleep a whole morning if you let them!—and he would come onto the porch in the summertime, 'cause he always loved birds. I would find him there in the morning when I was coming home from work. And if it was cold, he'd be inside playing in front of the television. We got for the first time a television in 1952—maybe 1954?—and we made it that my grandson had to ask permission to watch. But when his parents were sleeping . . . I didn't mind. We would watch together, me lying on the couch, him lying above me on the bolsters. He liked to have me with him; I didn't give rules—this is the privilege of being a grandma.

"Or maybe he would take out his armies—he had little soldiers that they're made of iron; he called this playing 'men.' And I would pretend that this one is George Washington—Sure, I got right down on the floor with him, what do you think? So this one is George Washington, and then I told him stories from the Bolshevik army that I would fit them to American history. It wasn't history, actually, just stories, but it gave him the ideas, y'see, about freedom. Then later on, when I was tired so I couldn't stay on the floor, he would carry them to the table and he would tell *me* all kind of a stories. I don't know who told bigger stories, him or me!

"And he made a name for me. In Yiddish, you say *bubbe* for grandma, but he couldn't say it right, so instead he called me Bobbie. And this is the name that stuck, and he still calls me this.

"I think these Saturday mornings in St. Albans were the happiest times in my life. The house got very beautiful sunlight in the morning; you could play with the shadows from the venetian blinds and you could see little bits of dust floating in the sun like a million planets. This I remember. When I sat with my grandson, I felt content. He was an affectionate boy, he hugged me all the time, and I would hug him right back. And

I hug him to this very day. I get more exercise from hugging him than I do from anything.

"And when I came home from work in the morning, I would sit on the porch and I fell asleep most of the time in one of those beach chairs—how do you call it? And I would see my grandson with his friends: Black and white, they were playing and yelling and running around. And these sounds would come into my dreams—I must've looked like a real old lady, sitting on the porch fast asleep!—but I would have these wonderful kind of a dreams, about a new world where everyone is playing, everything feels good, and people are all kind of a colors: white, black, brown, red, green, purple. It's true, all kind of a colors, and it didn't make no difference, I wasn't even surprised, I wouldn't even think about it until I woke up."

❀

July 14

Dear Janet,

I'm writing instead of calling because it's too soon to call—I'm scared but not yet in trouble, and if I call now you'll worry your heart out until I get home. If I do actually find trouble here, what are you going to do from New York, call the police? The distance makes it unimportant whether I call or write, and this way, at least, I put my mind to rest and keep myself busy and I make a record of what's happening—I'm going to write this whole thing in Yiddish, I want to be fluent—and in a couple of days we can sit together and have a good laugh.

I'm in North Carolina, in a place nobody ever heard of called Bluestone. Dr. Kingsley's car broke down on the highway a couple of miles from here, so we ended up here waiting for its repair. I'm separated from the doctor now— he's at the gas station, I'm at a little war memorial outside the post office, there's a bench. He said if we were seen together too much, people would start wondering. Right now they assume he's my chauffeur! Can you believe it? He told me even before we left his garage in Atlanta that I had to sit in the back seat because if anywhere in the South a white woman was seen driving in the front seat with a Negro man, it would mean trouble for them both. When I'm in the back seat, he looks like my chauffeur, and he's got a handsome enough car for the part. But I've never felt so ashamed in all of my life.

My accent makes it even more complicated. Anti-Semitism is as much a part of racial bigotry down here as salt is a part of the ocean. You should have heard the name-calling at our demonstration in Atlanta. You would think that every one of the five thousand was a Jew, and every Jew is a homosexual or a prostitute or a devil. And we're all Communists, of course. The Party should only have such success with recruitment! So Dr. Kingsley advised me to make out that I'm from Bulgaria, because the local people here are so ignorant that they won't know where Bulgaria is and they'll be too embarrassed to ask. So far he's right.

They were all impressed with me and treated me like an aristocrat from Europe. One fellow who was visiting his friends at the gas station when we arrived insisted on giving me "hospitality" by taking me to a place in town where, he says, it won't be so hot. Summer is pretty bad down here. But the place turned out to be a bar, all these men drinking beer under a great big fan. When they saw me, they began to roll down their sleeves and pull on their jackets and snuff out their smelly cigars and pay lots of attention—you'd think I was half my age. I was exotic, so I made my accent sound even thicker and my vocabulary got weaker by the second and I pretended to understand only bits and pieces of their conversation. Believe me, Janet, I didn't have to pretend so hard, with their southern accents. But one word I heard over and over: "Nigger . . . nigger . . . nigger."

So I took a chance—maybe I was foolish, but they were being so polite to me!—I put on a thick accent and I asked them, "What means 'nigger'?"

It was difficult to say the word even once! Do you remember what a campaign we had in the Party to teach comrades that a Negro man is not a "boy" and a Negro woman is not a "girl"? So you can imagine how these natural-born racists talk: "Boy" is a word with some dignity as far as they're concerned—better than "monkey" or "nigger" or all the other curses they've made up for Negro people.

So the guy who brought me there says that my "boy" is a nigger. He was talking about Dr. Kingsley. But I said, "My boy? My son . . . is 'nigger'? What means?" And they all had a good laugh. One man says he can't believe I've been in the South ("Dixie," they call it, like Israel is "Zion") if I don't know what "nigger" means.

"I guess the Klan is not doing their job," he said.

I had to control my anger and it exhausted me. And I had to become more and more elaborate about my own story—I'm very glad that Willy made me study that map of the southern states before I left. And meanwhile I kept pushing for explanations about "nigger." I was forcing them to explain to me their attitudes about Negroes, you see, and by being naïve, by "not understanding," I could challenge their prejudice. But you can imagine, Janet—it's not my usual style.

Then one man, the one with the foulest mouth, he says he's got to go and he walks over to the wall and straps on a gun and a jacket that's hanging there, part of a uniform. I couldn't believe what I was seeing. This guy was the sheriff of the town.

It hit me, then, Janet, more than any time the whole weekend, more than the entire demonstration with all the signs and the marching and the slogans, it occurred to me just what Rosalee Ingram is up against as a black woman trying to resist white men like these in their hateful little world of power. That man, the overseer who tried to take her in the field, he could be best friends with any man in this bar. I hate to generalize about people, you know—the Party has done this in a sectarian way much too much—but the culture in the South is so mean-spirited when it comes to the Negro people that whatever kindness and gentleness there are in these people gets ground to dust. I can just see it in my mind: the overseer comes up to Mrs. Ingram—a mother of eight who sweats in the field a whole day—and he comes up with all the confidence of that sheriff with his hanging belly and his hanging guns. And he expects her to submit. Of course. How many times I heard of this kind of thing happening to Jews in Russia!

Not in the fields so often, we were not an agricultural people, but rape was there as a constant club over our heads. Sure it was.

And sure it was a shock to him when Rosalee fought back like a human being. Sure he was shocked by her strength—what does he know of childbirth and slave labor in the fields? He was shocked enough to have a heart attack like he deserved, and good for him. This is Mrs. Ingram's story, and I believe every word of it. There wasn't a stab wound on any part of that guy's body. The Ku Kluxers who came to testify against her couldn't go so far as to desecrate a white man's corpse, I guess, otherwise they would have manufactured some evidence by sticking a knife into his back.

But they don't have to bother! Mrs. Ingram's crime is resisting the white man's will, nothing more. And for this, my daughter, she faces the electric chair. Ach, there's so much sickness, Janet, I can't begin to tell you. When I contrast what I see down here to the way we live in St. Albans, trying always to mingle, to build a feeling of community with our Negro neighbors, it makes me wonder how it can be that we all exist in the same world.

When I get back home we're going to start a big campaign in our neighborhood to get everyone to send telegrams to the governor of Georgia to demand a pardon for Mrs. Ingram. The Defense Committee decided that we can't afford to stand on principle and not demand a pardon because she committed no crime; now our job is to save her life, later we can prove her innocence. It's just like the Rosenbergs—we had to scream for a pardon, even beg for a pardon, and the press treated this as if we were admitting their guilt. Well, we can't have the Rosenbergs' lives any longer, but we'll fight to have them vindicated for as long as we live, right?

It's interesting, Janet, I've been thinking about it the whole weekend: The struggle for emancipation of the Negro people in America is very much like the struggle for Jewish emancipation under the czar. And I'm not talking about a theoretical idea, I'm talking about how the struggle feels. Many who were on the train to Atlanta, they still have no idea of how the society of the South works. All they know is one hour they were in New York or Philadelphia or Washington or whichever stop they boarded—the whole train was ours!—and then a few hours later they're in Atlanta, Georgia, just another city, not really so different. But me, because I stayed with Dr. Kingsley overnight, I'm really in the middle of it—up to my neck! And it's Mogilev-Podolsk all over again.

For instance, when I went back to the gas station to see about the car, Dr. Kingsley was having a conversation with the two white men inside the garage. They were mechanics, all greasy in their overalls, and there stands Dr. Kingsley in his suit—he's a dignified-looking man with glasses and gray hair and a gray moustache—and these two are talking down to him, insulting him, actually. They kept calling him "boy." And he's not only standing for it, he's smiling foolishly and keeping his head bowed.

How many times I saw this in Russia, where a Jewish man, even someone like my father or like Gideon Blum whom I've told you so much about—men with dignity—they'd be walking in town and some stupid brute of a peasant would try to humiliate them. Yank a beard. Push them out of the way. Insult them with anti-Semitic vulgarity. Pinch their daughter. And we couldn't resist, because there were always the Black Hundreds, and the pogrom mobs, and the police, hovering behind that peasant like his shadow. And this is the Ku Klux Klan today, you see. In the South you see billboards advertising the Klan along the highway. And you don't know if you should speed up or slow down, if you know what I mean.

And then the whole world holds it against Jews for walking with our eyes to the ground, for having hunched backs, for being nervous, for sneaking, for staying close to each other. And if we dare to resist, *this* is the crime! You watch, Janet: Will the FBI investigate the Ku Klux Klan? Yeah, with one flashlight and no extra batteries. And will the FBI investigate the NAACP? Yeah, with a hundred torches burning.

I could hardly keep up my Bulgarian act, you know, I was so mad to see Dr. Kingsley being humiliated! I spoke only to him, I snubbed the other two plus the one who brought me there. I put on a truly aristocratic air. Big deal! The

car was still not ready, and Dr. Kingsley was very nervous
that these mechanics were going to cheat us or make us
stay overnight—in separate hotels, of course. It's that kind
of town—the mayor is probably the brother-in-law of the
sheriff, whose best friend is the judge, who owns the
hotels. A real democracy. (I just hope that Dr. Kingsley
brought some extra money along. I'm very low. Meanwhile he calls me "ma'am" as if he were really my chauffeur. I can't stand it.)

The final indignity came when he needed to use a bathroom. They had no "colored" bathroom. They said he
would either have to go in the bushes or else take a walk
to the Negro part of town, maybe three blocks. Janet, if
they had only a ditch to live in, they would make it segregated! And when I made as if I were going to go with
him to the Negro district, he said in a loud voice, "Why
don't you take a nice stroll through Bluestone, ma'am?
I'm sure these gentlemen won't be long in fixing the
car."

So that's how I ended up here at the post office. Bluestone is only ten blocks long, and that's if you include the
great big junkyard which begins where the pavement
turns into a dirt road. There's nothing to look at, just
a hardware store, a place with some dresses in the window,
two churches (one on each side of town so you either
have God or the sheriff accompanying you through), a
candy store where I didn't see any kids—it's Monday, I
guess they'll be out of school pretty soon. (I hope you
don't mind my rambling like this, Janet, it helps to calm
me. I don't know why I'm nervous. . . .)

There's nothing. The air is so hot and sticky . . . and
all the whitewashed buildings are so bright they hurt your
eyes to look. Here where I'm sitting at least there are some
trees for shade. At first I thought the war memorial was
for the Civil War, but I took a look at the plaque: "To
make the world safe for democracy." Fourteen names.
Fourteen dead men from Bluestone, North Carolina.

How can I begin to care about these people? How are
we going to take these minds that have been so poisoned
and flush them clean? Or do we do like Stalin did with the
peasants, just round them up and force them into integrated

schools, integrated farms, integrated factories? That's no solution.

The thing that amazes me is the understanding and the patience that so many of the people at the demonstration seemed to have. When I first met Dr. Kingsley and his wife at the first-aid station, he said to me that I had to be willing to treat *anyone* who came, black or white, even if it was one of the racists who stood around shouting curses at us. None of them came—no one used the infirmary except a few children with bruises or a few lost ones. But I was tremendously impressed by this sense of charity. So many of the Negro people whom I met on the train and in our ranks—your old lady walked five miles in Atlanta!— they seemed to bear no hatred or bitterness. I suppose they feel their own liberation, they smell it in the air, more than they feel their burdens right now. They've got no time to curse the ground when they're reaching for the sun. If the white people were only smart, they would recognize this strength, they would see the invincibility of a people who have compassion for their own oppressors. And then we'd get an equal-rights bill passed in Congress this year and the start of something wonderful in the South.

But if the white people are not smart—and my experience here with the peasants of Bluestone gives me little hope—then they'll interpret this nonviolence as a sign of weakness, and they'll scorn that mercy. And then it'll be like the story of Sodom. You know, when God couldn't find any righteous people to spare, not one, it was goodbye to that city! All the ferocious anger of three hundred years of slavery will rip apart our country.

That's another thing: The Negro people here are for the most part religious, so I can talk about Judaism and the Bible, which is fun even though I don't believe. I was up late last night with Dr. Kingsley and Mrs. Kingsley, talking about God, about Marxism, about the differences between these views, all that. (Their daughter who Dr. Kingsley is going to see is a religious worker in New York—she works with homeless women.) And I kept on thinking how Momma Greenpoint would be involved in this movement if she were still with us.

* * *

Surprise! I'm in the car again and we're driving along the highway going north. The doctor created a little revolution in Bluestone: He made some friends in the Negro part of town, including a mechanic, and he was with them for a while, giving all kinds of advice. He says they haven't seen a real doctor ever, some of these poor people. Finally he got to talking about our demonstration for Rosalee Ingram and other things in the movement that are going on. And then he described his own situation—our situation—with the car, and how he thought we were going to be cheated or worse. Well, it took them quite a while and quite a few drinks, he says, but finally four Negro men piled into a pickup truck and they drove Dr. Kingsley to the gas station. Then they simply took his car from the garage and fixed it right there on the street. And that was that.

Dr. Kingsley is very nervous and has been driving sixty miles an hour for the past half-hour. . . .

Chapter Twenty-Two

Janet heard her mother's wild tale with only one ear, asking questions to show interest but listening more intently for the squeaking hinge of the front screen door that would signal Willy's return from the real-estate agency.

"So that's my letter. You want it, or should I throw it away? Maybe Willy should see it first." Janet shoved the letter into a utensils drawer amid savings coupons for the supermarket. Her mother was miffed. "You'll put it away for safekeeping and you'll forget where it is."

"I don't want it getting stained," Janet explained with a dismissing wave of her hand. "Later I'll find a permanent place for it." Refilling their coffee cups, she sat with a sagging face. "So what else, momma? You and Dr. Kingsley stayed with the Ostermans in Philadelphia . . ."

"Yeah, and then this morning he offered to drive me to Queens, direct. Instead I said he should come during the week for supper. With his daughter. I didn't know if you and Willy would feel like having company in the middle of the day."

"We wouldn't," Janet agreed.

"You look tired, *ziskayt*."

"I *am* tired, momma."

"Why are you so tired?"

"Must I have a reason?"

"Sure!" Bessie chuckled. "Otherwise I'll bring you up on charges!"

But Janet's glum expression deflected Bessie's kibitzing as effectively as it had eroded her enthusiasm for storytelling. She strained to conclude. "Anyway . . . I thought when Dr. Kingsley comes we can get together for a house meeting, a block meeting. We can make a committee to raise funds for Mrs. Ingram. Dr. Kingsley is a very good speaker—he could make the appeal. We should do this," she urged her unresponsive daughter, "so people start to think about the struggle. Even the Negroes, you know, if they own a house, they start thinking right away they're middle-class—"

"We'll see, momma."

"What's there to see? We've got to make plans for this kind of a thing, Janet. Dr. Kingsley is only gonna be here a few days. We can't be lazy."

Nodding, Janet carried her cup to the sink and coaxed herself to remain patient. "I'm not getting lazy, mother. But you're all excited because you just got home. I need to go a little slower." She peered through the narrow horizontal window into the backyard.

"Maybe we can do it at the Zackheims' house," Bessie conceded. "It's a little bigger. . . . You're looking for your son?"

"No, just looking. For birds, squirrels, I don't know. He

wouldn't be out there—he ignores the sandbox these days. Half the time I don't know where to find that kid at any given moment."

"Sure, he's independent like his Bobbie! I tell you, *mein tokhteh*, it was really something for me to just pick up and go to Atlanta. I couldn't do it a few years ago, not until you kids were settled."

"Yes, momma, you were the rock of stability in our lives," said Janet sourly.

"Never mind. Even when I was in that stinkhole in Bayside, I used to be looking out the window, just like you're doing now, and I would worry about my kids."

"I'm not worried! What makes you think I'm worried?"

"Not that you're worried *now*, Janet. This is not what I meant."

"Well, you'll have to learn to speak English, mother."

Bessie's patience ran out. "Janet. Are you gonna bitch a whole afternoon? If you are, I'll go find your son and we'll have a good time calling you names behind your back. What's the matter with you today, you're not glad to see me come home?"

"Nothing. I'm sorry." Where the hell was Willy? Why couldn't *he* break the news? Janet could not stand to stonewall any longer and decided to drop a hint. "I'm sorry, momma," she repeated. "We received a class photo from school in the mail today. . . ."

"Your son looks a little cockeyed?"

"Do you want to see?" Janet led her down three steps into the living room.

The photo on the glass coffee table showed the full class assembled in three rows, kneeling, seated, and standing, flanked by the teacher, gargantuan next to all the kids. Spotting her grandson, Bessie hurrahed. "Look at that, he's wearing the sweater I knitted for his birthday!" She looked up at her daughter. "I think he looks very nice."

Janet sank onto the couch and looked at her distrustfully. "Are you telling me that's the *only* thing you notice about that picture?"

"The Zackheim girl is not in his class?"

"Oh, come on, momma!"

"What? *Shrei nisht*, Janet." Bessie fingered the photo's edge and snickered. "Heh, he looks like a little pimple with all the Negro children."

Janet threw up her arms. "Hallelujah! So you're *not* getting blind in your old age! Look at it, momma. Two Caucasian children in the entire class!"

"I see." She scanned the picture again, nodding slowly. "To me, he looks happy."

"Well, his father is definitely not happy," Janet replied. "We had one of our real brawls this morning, a real humdinger! If your grandson is hiding in a closet somewhere, I wouldn't be surprised, the volume levels we reached! . . . Look, momma, I'm not going to pretend it's all William's fault. I'm not delighted with that photograph myself. This is not what we bargained for when we came to stabilize this neighborhood five years ago."

"For what did you bargain? You got a beautiful home, you got wonderful neighbors. . . ." Bessie rapped the photo with the back of her hand. "And to me, your son looks happy!"

But Janet seemed as distraught as a little girl with a full bladder, unfit to be scolded or preached to. Bessie realized how wide was the gap between her own exaltation from the weekend and her daughter's state of mind. "It was a bad fight you had?" she asked, hoping to be able to soothe her. "Where's your husband now, working?"

"No, he's off Mondays," Janet said in a bruised voice. "We were at it for hours, momma, it wasn't just a squabble over a cup of coffee."

"So where is he now?"

"He'll be home soon," she said.

"All right, so I'll leave you two to make up. It won't be so bad, you'll see. Where's your son?"

"I just finished telling you, I don't know, momma!"

"All right, Janet! Don't be so nervous! I'll go find him, that's all."

He wasn't far, just down the block on his red tricycle, riding in circles. Spotting her on the steps of the house, he cheered and waved and pedaled furiously. She had to stand aside on the sidewalk as he shot past, showing off his prowess.

She bent to hug him as he straddled his tricycle. "Look at you,

you're past my *pipik* already. I think you grew just this week-end."

He flexed his arm to make a muscle that she tenderly squeezed. "Wow!" Then he rode at her side down the block, asking questions, at her prompting, about her trip south. She loved recounting her experiences in the simple terms and broad strokes that he required; his sense of hurt and of justice always restored a pristine quality to her own moral convictions. The day was hot and bright, but the maple-lined streets were a patchwork of sun and shade with an animating, cooling breeze. Traffic was nil; the boy could ride from curb to curb without her guidance. Here and there an elderly neighbor or housewife waved from a porch or yard, but by and large the neighborhood belonged to Bessie and the boy.

". . . So if you and your friend Gary, or that girl you said you liked—Laverne?—or any of the Negro children from around here, if you all lived in Atlanta, you couldn't go to the same school together."

"How come?"

"Like I told you—segregation. They don't let the Negroes and the whites mix. This is what we're fighting against, y'see. This is why your Bobbie went to the demonstration. We want *integration*, that whatever color you got you can all go to the same school."

"My school's like that, right?"

The naïveté and sincerity of his question provoked her doubts. How did he really feel, belonging to such a tiny minority in his class? Did the white teacher show favoritism that might spoil him? Did the Negro children tease or insult him? For this we need a family conference, Bessie thought, to discuss, not to yell.

"Your school is a good school," she replied noncommittally. "In the South, the Negro children get rotten schools, with no books, no blackboards, no toys. . . ."

"How come?" he asked again, concentrating on lowering his tricycle from the curb to the gutter.

"Because," she said, "the Negro people used to be slaves in the South. And if you're gonna make someone a slave, you can't treat him like a human being. 'Cause you might start to feel guilty. Do you know what I mean?"

He nodded without conviction. She felt curiously gratified by his innocence. "Maybe you never in your life did a cruel thing," she explained. "But let's say, f'rinstance, that you had a dog."

"Yay! A puppy!"

"For your birthday," she elaborated. "Then every day you give it a beating."

"No way!" He dismissed her idea with a flick of his wrist and executed a figure eight in the street.

"*A leben ahf dein kup!*" she cheered, applauding.

"That's easy," he bragged. "I need a two-wheeler. But I'd rather have a dog! Will you really buy a puppy, Bobbie?"

"Would you really take care of it?"

"I'll be your best friend. . . ."

"You're already my best friend. Anyway, the dog should be *your* best friend, no?"

"I'm gonna name him after you, Bobbie."

She laughed and stroked his head. "Such an honor! We'll see what your parents have to say, all right?" Not all right. He was utterly disconsolate at the thought. "But I don't see why not," she added encouragingly, though she felt nervous about preempting Janet's authority.

"Shirley's got a dog named Clipper," he said. "She says she's going to keep him when they move."

"Sure. I'd keep *you* if I moved."

He eyed her hopefully again. "When we sell the house, do we have to sell the dog, too?"

She laughed again, and then a sudden fear struck her still. "What are you talking about?"

His eyes were downcast. "Mom said you'd get mad." All at once he pedaled away like a bandit.

By the time she reached the porch, Bessie had compressed her anger and fear into a tight package for storage inside her aching skull. She could hear Janet talking with the boy about dinner plans while the telephone rang on an end table just inside the doorway. When Willy picked it up, Bessie coughed to make her presence known to him, then took refuge in her rocking chair, thinking, Let them come to me! Nothing is different until they come to me!

She watched the rustling trees and kneaded her thoughts into arguments while the passing time mocked her. When the phone rang again, she imagined with horror that it was Dr. Kingsley.

"*We're moving from St. Albans. The kids think there's too many* shvartzes *living here.*"

What excuse could they have for running? After remaining in the movement this long, through McCarthy, through Stalin—*oi, kinderlakh*, he was a murderer and we called him God! But it's getting good again, don't you see, kids? It's in the air again, the progressive spirit, the spirit that moves us. This struggle for Negro rights—how can I begin to tell you how it feels to reach across the barriers, to share such dreams? This is life! We're gonna give it up for a photograph?

What about the others? she wondered. So-called comrades! The boy had mentioned the Zackheims—were they giving up the struggle, too? Over and over Bessie cursed them all, most especially Willy, as homebreakers, bigots, Social Democrats, cowards, meanwhile listening restlessly for Janet to have an "accident," to drop something or burn herself on the stove so her mother could come running....

(Go to her now, Bessie Sainer. Who do you think you are, the pope? She'll listen to you, she always does. Read your letter to her again, and to Willy. Go talk to them!)

We shall not, we shall not be moved. Just like a tree that's standing by the water ... Let them come to me! she resolved again. Let Janet find the courage to explain her bigotry to me—that's exactly what it is, bigotry! Bessie imagined sitting in her rocking chair on the porch for a whole year. The neighbors would come and fan her in August, ply her with hot coffee in November, dig her out of the snow in February. Throughout the civil-rights movement, all through the South, she'd be known as the Righteous White Woman, the *Yiddishe Bubbe* who embraced all Negro children as fondly as her own....

So an hour passed, and Bessie sat ignored, gripping the armrests of her rocking chair, belching and swallowing her rage, until the long weekend caught up with her and tipped her over the brink of exhaustion into sleep. Quick, agitated dreams began to hop all over her, fleeing from memory each time her head snapped upright, then swarming back on her eyelids as they lowered....

"Momma is asleep, Jacob, I told you." Janet's voice roused her. The swishing trees nearly pulled her back under with their lulling rhythms, but she sat upright, blinking her eyes, listening intently to her daughter on the phone just behind the screen door. "No, I will not wake her up! She's completely exhausted from her weekend."

"I'm awake," Bessie grumbled.

Janet ignored her. "Yes, she went all the way to Georgia and back. Yes . . . yes, she's quite incredible. . . . No. No. You're not listening to me, Jacob. . . . You're not listening, Jacob! Just because you're tanked up and repentant about the last time you shat on your mother's head doesn't mean I'm going to let you talk to her! How many times must we go through this routine with you? Go talk to a psychiatrist instead! You're a fucking tease, you know that?"

Such language, *mein tokhteh!*

"You don't have to listen, dear brother! We can just hang up now, you're perfectly grown-up! . . . What? Yes, yes, I'm glad you found yourself a new job, Jacob. I'm very glad. . . . No, I'll tell her for you. . . . Yes, I am being her guardian at the moment, that's right. We all need it sometimes, Jacob. . . . She's safe and sound, yes. I'll tell her you were concerned, uh-huh."

Bessie was all ears, trying to pluck what information and consolation she could about her estranged son. Since Momma Greenpoint's death, Bessie's relationship with Jacob, as well as with many of the extended family, had disintegrated, lacking Leah's regular *shabbas* dinners and overt acts of intervention and reconciliation to keep them all accountable to, if not affectionate toward, one another. Unmediated, Jacob's outbursts had reached insane pitches, which Bessie could only muffle with distance—distance that she maintained with a stubborn hostility of her own against his occasional repentant overtures. If Jacob belonged to her family at all anymore, it was to Ruchel's camp that Bessie had consigned him as an *alrightnik*—frivolous, acquisitive, caring for nothing but himself, beneath her scorn.

Yet her resentment and her yearning were slugging it out for mastery of her heart as she eavesdropped on Janet's conversation: "No, sweetie, we can't have you for dinner, not in the near future. . . . Don't jump to conclusions, Jacob! It's got nothing to do with momma. She doesn't have to be with you if she chooses not to be—she's an independent gal, as you well know. . . . What's that? . . . Yes, we're trying to sell the house."

The screen door whined open and banged shut. "Bobbie? Will you watch 'Popeye' with me?"

"Shh . . ."

". . . Fourteen-seven, the same as when we bought it. The agent told Willy we'll be lucky not to lose a thousand, can you believe it?"

The boy repeated his question in an urgent whisper. "If you watch with me, mom'll let me turn it on."

"Sha, be quiet!" Bessie's words broke like a thunderclap over the child's head.

Janet was simultaneously hollering: "Oh, keep your racism to yourself, Jacob! We don't use that word and we don't talk to people who do, do you understand me? . . . Oh, damn it, call me back when you're sober!"

As Janet slammed the phone down, her son began to bawl out on the porch. Bessie was squinting at him, fully noticing him for the first time. "What—what's the matter?" she said. "Hey!"

"You yelled at me!" His voice cracked with hurt.

"I'm sorry, *ziskayt!* I'm sorry. I'm not mad at you. Nobody's mad at *you.*" He rubbed his eyes as she lifted him onto her lap. But Janet swept onto the porch and plucked him from Bessie. "Your hands are better than mine?" Bessie spat. "Mine got dirty handling the nigger children, hmm?"

"I won't even dignify that, mother." Janet turned back into the house, riding the boy on her hip and running her fingers through his hair.

"*Ahf tsu lokhes, mein tokhteh.* Just because you can curse your stupid brother, you think you're a progressive?" The words fired from Bessie's lips as she pursued Janet into the living room, which seemed like a dark lagoon after Bessie's sustained exposure to the bright daylight.

Janet set her son down on the carpet. "Go play, sweetie. Do whatever you want."

"No!" cried Bessie. "Let's ask him instead what he thinks about moving! And about leaving his friends, his sandbox, everything!"

"It's not up to the child to decide," Janet said firmly. "Nor is it up to *you,* momma. I'll deal with his feelings—Willy and I will deal with his feelings."

"If you'd calm down a minute, Bess, we could probably deal with you as well."

She'd not seen Willy, behind her in an armchair, as her eyes were adjusting to the gloom. "Ah, here's the *ben toyreh!*" she raged at him. "The Communist in his armchair."

Willy stood. "If I leave the armchair, you get off the soapbox. A deal? At least take in a little information before you've already got a picket line going! We're not looking for a military coup here, Bessie! It so happens that events occurred simultaneously and quickly this weekend, and you happened to be away."

"And we happened to be worried sick about you!" Janet interjected, though half-reluctant to confess it.

"Why?" said Bessie, skeptically. "I called you from Dr. Kingsley's house, no? I told you I wouldn't come on the train."

"Yes, mother. And when you're ready for hand-to-hand combat with the KKK, I'm sure you'll leave us an inspiring suicide note."

"Don't be fresh, Janet!"

Willy played the peacemaker. "Whoa, Jan. Let's not make your mother out to be a criminal, either. Nobody's a criminal."

"You're wrong!" Bessie said. "If we move from St. Albans, it's like you should desert your wife when she's pregnant. The movement is pregnant now, don't you see?"

"Can I watch 'Popeye'?" asked the boy. "I'd rather watch him fight than watch you guys fight."

"We're not going to fight," Willy insisted.

"Yes, you can watch," Janet hurriedly assented. "Just keep it low."

The three adults watched him plant himself in front of the television. "Very nice," Bessie muttered. "From this he gets no Negro faces excepting Amos 'n' Andy. But *this* . . ." She picked up his class photograph, still exposed on the coffee table. "This is the only place he gets something that's not full of racism! And this you want to stop!"

"Bessie," Willy gently urged, "please listen. That photo is only one factor. The more important one is that I've been offered a terrific deal. Didn't Jannie tell you? I've got the chance to buy a pharmacy, just two blocks from where I'm working now. You know what kind of business my boss does? It's fantastic. And this house happens to be all we've got for capital. You know," he added, "it's one thing to commute to the Bronx when you're an employee, but it's another when you've got ultimate responsibility for the whole place."

"Fine," Bessie huffed. "You'll hire a Negro porter and you'll call this the 'civil-rights movement.' I hope your own union puts a picket line in front of your store. I'll march at the head!"

Willy sank back into his chair and reached for a cigarette. "You not only offend me, Bessie, you disappoint me. I thought we three could come to an understanding. I only want to give something to your daughter! But you'll have to give up something in turn."

"No!" she retorted. "I never made no deals with social democrats! Not even when Gompers wanted that he should have me for a speaker, and he paid more than all your drugstores! I told him like I'll tell you: *Gey kakhen afun yom!*"

Janet seized her mother by the shoulders and jerked her silent. "You stupid, arrogant woman!"

"Ow! Let go of me, you're hurting!"

"Are you senile already? Give me that picture!" She tore the photo from Bessie's hand and shoved it into her field of vision. "There, look at it! Maybe I wouldn't react so violently if I had a few other pictures from my life! Pictures of my father—do I have any, momma? In my mind only—with a bullet hole in his head! And what about Sainer? I have one picture, momma, one!"

Bessie shook her off and shrank away from her fury. "What are you giving me with pictures, Janet? I got no pictures. Who had a camera?"

"That's right. Who had a camera? Who had time? Who had interest? What about my own wedding, mother? I have no pictures from my own wedding! We were too busy transporting it to *your* hospital room so *you* could have a little *nakhes!* For God's sake," she screamed again, "I am sick to death of having every step I want to take be measured by you to see if I'm in step with the masses! When did I ever receive any guidance from you about my future except that I should have the correct political line about things that I don't even really give a good goddamn about!"

Bessie trembled, blinking rapidly, stammering for words, groping for a clear, whole thought instead of the shards and fragments that were cluttering her mind. This was all a terrible mistake, she decided. Jacob was the one who said these things, not Janet. Not Janet!

Willy intervened again. "C'mon, Jan, back off a little. Let's not go in for hyperbole."

"Oh, Willy!" she wept. "Let's stop pretending this is *not* a political capitulation. It is! For once in our lives we're upwardly mobile, just like it says in the *Wall Street Journal*. And I'm going to hang on for the ride! We're not lynching anyone—"

"Of course we're not."

"We're not gassing anyone, we're not denying anyone's rights! I'm just not *bleeding* for someone else."

"All right, all right," he soothed her.

"I'm sorry, honey," she said, rolling into his arms. "I'm sorry we wasted our time arguing this morning. If I didn't have so many illusions about my mother, I would have put up the 'for sale' signs before she even came home. To hell with subtlety and to hell with discussion."

"She didn't want me to see the realtor," Willy explained to Bessie, "before you got home. So we battled—"

"Never mind explaining to her." Janet's voice froze over again. She strode to the screen door and pushed it wide open. The theme music to a "Popeye" cartoon wafted across the room, all rhythm and horns. "Why don't you just hit the street, momma? There are plenty of rooms for rent. You're a very popular lady, as you well know. And you won't have to be embarrassed by our bourgeois ways."

"Turn that television down," Willy ordered the boy.

"Don't look at me with such shock, momma," Janet taunted her.

"C'mon, honey," said Willy. "Take it easy."

Janet paid him no mind. "They're finished with Stalin in the Soviet Union, mother, and I'm finished with Stalinism in my house. You hear?" Her arm tired and she let the door spring shut. "If you plan to stay," she warned, "you'll have to act your age. Slow down like the rest of us."

"Bobbie?" The boy was standing, facing all three of them. "Bobbie, come watch with me. You lie there"—he pointed to the couch—"and I'll lie there"—on the bolsters. He bounced on the spring mattress. "C'mon, it's real comfortable." On the screen, Popeye was bullfighting.

Bessie turned her head slowly back to Janet. Tears were welling in Janet's eyes even as the lids narrowed to bar Bessie's scrutiny. Bessie saw her daughter's luscious lips tightening, her cheekbones quivering, her struggle not to yield but to win this moment forever. They looked away from each other, Bessie with a deep breath and slow nod, then shutting her eyes to record the image of her daughter's bitter grief in her mind.

Nishtgedeiget. Bessie almost mouthed the word. *Nishtgedeiget.* No more worries. Salt tears stung her eyes. Her head remained bowed as she trudged toward the couch. Her grandson was mounting the bolsters. "So?" Bessie said, in a croak. "How did you know your Bobbie's getting tired?"

Chapter Twenty-Three / 1963

"Human beings learn early how to talk, but late how to be silent. This is a Jewish proverb. My daughter taught it to me without ever saying it.

"Momma Greenpoint used to say the same thing a different way: 'If God meant for us to say as much as we see and hear, he would've given us two mouths like he gave us two eyes and two ears.'

"And now I'm saying it to you, *kinderlakh:* You can't go through life thinking you know everything, 'cause you end up learning nothing. And you end up alone, with all your words like a fence around you. And with all your books sitting on the shelf collecting dust. And with all your ideas turned to curses."

❀

"*Nu?* For how long do I have to sit?"

"Bobbie, don't move!" the boy shouted as his Brownie camera shutter clicked. "Aw, you blinked!"

"You ought to move closer to the window," suggested his father, still digesting at the table. "That's your source of light."

"I'm using the flash," objected the boy. "I don't need the window."

"You still got that going?" Bessie pointed to the tape recorder's slow-turning reels.

"Oh, yeah!" He knelt by the machine and efficiently shut it down.

"He's got the same feelings for gadgets like your brother had," Bessie noted to Janet, who was staring dully at the silent picture on the television screen.

"I wish you wouldn't speak about Jacob in the past tense, momma," she replied. "He's not dead."

"This is true—the way his wife gets pregnant like a rabbit."

"She's a Catholic, momma!"

"She's worse than that."

"Are you going to turn into a religious bigot in your old age?"

"Why don't you just drop the subject?" Willy advised.

Bessie got up to clear the landslide of dishes from the table. "You left so much food, *kinderlakh*. Everything you got to take home."

"With pleasure," Willy agreed. "Only be sure to keep what you want for yourself, Bessie."

"When you cook," she said, "the smell fills you up. You take everything."

"May I turn the sound back up?" Janet asked around the room with her hand on the television volume knob.

Her son was not finished with his project. "C'mon, Bobbie." He patted her chair.

"What, more?"

"C'mon, we're rolling!" He picked up his microphone and squatted on the carpet. "Okay . . . we're still interviewing Bessie Sainer, folks. I want to ask you, Mrs. Sainer: How come you didn't get along with your brother?"

"Who?"

"Uncle Herschel."

"You little *gonif*," she chided him, "you want that your whole class should see your Bobbie's dirty underwear?"

"What do you mean?"

"You ask too many personal questions."

"But I want it to be personal! Mrs. Markish said we shouldn't just list the dates and stuff. C'mon, Bobbie, this is my whole summer project! Didn't you ever read in *Reader's Digest*, 'My Most Unforgettable Character'?"

"When your teacher hears the things I'm telling you, she won't forget." To Janet: "Is she a progressive?"

"She's a Kennedy liberal, momma. But it's a good class, she teaches well."

"Son, if you want to be an interviewer," Willy said, "you can't harangue people. You've got to take what they give you."

Clucking his tongue, the boy shut off his machine.

Bessie relented. "No, I'm a mule. I'm sorry."

"I just don't get it!" he cried. "You're supposed to be bringing all these people together, right? Like, uh—"—he glanced at his notepad—"the Unemployed Councils. The *Shnorers . . .*"

"Hey, you talk the *mameloshn* like a real professional!"

"But you don't even get along with your family! Except for Mom."

"And Momma Greenpoint," Bessie reminded him.

"Yeah, but she wasn't even what-you-call-it, left-wing. But you said that Uncle Herschel was."

"*Is*," Janet reiterated. "He's not dead, either!"

"And he's still a social democrat!" Bessie retorted.

"But aren't the Democrats the good guys?" asked the boy. "President Kennedy's a Democrat."

"And President Kennedy is not such a good guy," Bessie replied. "Look at what he did with Cuba. Everyone forgets, we got missiles in Turkey, in Persia, it's a ring-around-the-Russians. But when they put a missile that it's a hundred miles from the *alte khalyeras* in Florida, we *plotz*."

"He's still a liberal, momma," Janet said. "And he inspires people."

"He believes in physical fitness, Bobbie."

"If he wants a real physical fitness, let him give jobs to all the people that they're unemployed. Let him go chase after the Ku

Klux Klan and the racists that they're throwing bombs into churches."

"Well, I like Kennedy," said the boy feebly.

"And I like *you*," Bessie said, not wishing to press too hard. "But now I got to do the dishes, okay? . . . Sit, Janet! You're my guests."

"We're your guests every week, momma."

"Good! So I got the whole week to wash dishes for the next time."

She shuffled into the kitchen with a stack of them. Her dinner had been a blockbuster that left her family groaning with delight, and now cleanup time would cap her proprietary satisfaction. She enjoyed sponging her old china under hot running water until the veins in her hands were coursing with warmth. She found pleasure in stacking dishes in the drainer, row by row and up into a delicately balanced heap. The kitchen was for her the most intimate room in her apartment; nowhere else did she feel more youthful, independent, and competent.

Janet transported a few serving dishes in to her. "That was just delicious, momma."

"Put them right there." Bessie indicated the stovetop.

"I wish you'd let Willy put up a few shelves for you."

"Janet, please." Bessie's tone was sharp and dismissing. This was a worn-out dialogue. "I don't want any *potchkying* in here. I don't need shelves." She resoaped her sponge. "*Kinderlakh*, I love it so when you come. It gives me such *nakhes!* I feel like I'm living."

"You've got a beautiful home, momma."

"In your house I would feel like an old piece of furniture."

"Who's inviting you? We're strictly Danish modern!"

Bessie laughed. "And your son, your son is a regular Edward R. Murrow. Only with some of his questions, I feel like the FBI's coming for a visit, if you know what I mean."

"You handled it fine, momma. There's no need to go into names and dates. But he is picking up a tremendous amount of political wisdom from you."

"Political wisdom nobody's got," Bessie said. "But your son has got a good head."

"Sure," said Janet with a smile, "who do you think he takes after? So, mother . . ." Janet's hand went into the pocket of her pants. "It's going to be your seventieth birthday."

"If you don't tell anybody, I won't say anything either."

"No, no," Janet assured her, "I know you don't want to make a whole shebang out of it. But this is for you. From your family." She was holding forth a plain white envelope marked "Bessie."

"What's this?"

"Just take it."

"My hands are wet."

"No excuses, mother!"

"What, what have you got?" Bessie peered into the envelope at what appeared to her an untold amount of money. "Are you kidding, Janet? This is more than I had to escape from Siberia! Take it back, I've got all that I need."

"It's not a matter of need. We want you to treat yourself to whatever you want."

"I'm making a living, Janet!"

"Can't you be gracious, mother? Save it for your old age."

As she slipped out of the kitchen, her mother was in pursuit, still protesting. Willy shushed them both with a curt gesture. He and their son were at attention in front of the television, watching a news broadcast. Screams of distress and chaos mixed in with the barking of dogs and the broadcast buzz of the television set. On the screen, scores of Negro people were being flung head over heels by jets of water from high-pressure firehoses held by groups of white men standing like wartime bazooka squads. "Look at that!" gasped the boy. "What are they doing?"

The sound track cut to Walter Cronkite's amber-toned narration. "This was the sight one month ago in Birmingham, Alabama, as civil-rights demonstrators were met with violence in the state's largest city. The entire nation watched as long-simmering racial tensions . . ."

"So?" Bessie talked back to the screen. "Why don't they do something about it instead of watching?"

The scene cut to Cronkite at his new desk. ". . . as the Southern Christian Leadership Conference held a press conference yesterday to announce their final plans for a mass demonstration in Washington, D.C. Stuart Koppleman has the story. . . ."

"For the first time in one hundred years," a black man was saying behind a barricade of microphones, "America is awakening to the fact that segregation is evil and must be destroyed in all forms. But we ask today, which side of this struggle is the federal government on?"

As Stuart Koppleman's voice overlay began, Willy took Janet around the shoulders. "It's after seven, honey." She nodded. "Bessie, I want to thank you for another extraordinary dinner—"

"Just a minute," Bessie said, "I want to hear this."

"Can I stay here a while? Ma?"

"Ask your grandmother. It's fine with me."

". . . We call on President Kennedy to undertake fundamental solutions to the race problem in America. It's not enough for him to hop from one crisis to the next while Negro lives are languishing. This is the message of our demonstration next Sunday. . . ."

"I'm going to Washington," Bessie flatly declared, pointing at the screen. "Who's going with me?"

"I want to!" The boy shot up his hand.

"Momma, it's not a good time—"

"It's never a good time to fight, Janet, but you got to do it anyway!"

"Let me finish. I meant only that it's not a good time to *discuss* it when we're halfway out the door."

"So what's there to discuss? I'm going to Washington even if I got to walk there."

"I'll ride you on the handlebars of my bike, Bobbie."

"*A dank! Dos iz alts.*" She raised her chin to Janet. "And you should come, the two of you."

"What's the date?" asked Willy, consulting his wallet calendar. "August twenty-seventh . . . the twenty-eighth."

"Sunday," Janet said. "I would like to go, sweetheart. . . ."

"The store's open Sunday," he pointed out. "People buy beach articles until Labor Day."

"For one day you'll let them burn on the beach!" Bessie said.

"We'll see, momma." Janet winked at her.

"Not only that," Bessie added, "but you should pay your help if they'll come to the demonstration."

"Mother . . ."

"All right." She turned from them, waving her hands. "You'll see, you'll see."

"Where's the food you wanted us to take?"

"It's ready to be wrapped, in the kitchen."

"Hey, you guys, can I stay?"

Bessie tousled the boy's hair. "You can stay, *tatenyu*."

"I'm still going to ask you about Uncle Herschel," he warned.

"*Oi, a leben ahf dein kup!*"

The daylight was fading quickly as the crickets' cry rose from beneath the window ledge and a night breeze, perfumed by grass and damp brick, aired the apartment of food odors. Bessie felt tender, almost romantic, sitting in the shadowy living room with her grandson, and kept poking and petting him as she answered his questions.

"In the First World War we fought 'cause Herschel believed 'My country, right or wrong,' and I believed 'No, the working people should not fight unless they're fighting to make their country *better*.'"

"It seems pretty silly—you guys would fight about whether or not to fight!"

"So? I've heard you with your friends fighting about which games to play! I remember once I heard you and your friend Gary, in St. Albans—"

"C'mon, Bobbie, that's ancient history."

She laughed and patted his knee. She would have preferred for him to do the talking—she could listen for hours—about his hopes, his anxieties, at thirteen. He was an openhearted boy, instinctually progressive; his bar-mitzvah speech in December (the family had thrown a grand party without synagogue services) had delighted everyone, coordinating comments on the nuclear-arms race with reflections on Jewish history and the Holocaust—all points covered. Yes, he was a true red-diaper baby, and, to Bessie's undying pride, the *Freiheit* had reprinted the entire speech on its English pages as an "example to youth." But what about his inner world, his yearnings, of a kind only recently hinted at by his bouts of moodiness, his wild enthusiasms for loud music and tight pants, his long bicycle rides to who knows where, his fervent admiration for the Freedom Riders, as he wished he could be older, just a little older. . . ?

Maybe, Bessie thought, if I had spent more time with Jacob like this . . . and she felt a rare urge to go to the phone, to dial that number that she still knew by heart. . . .

"Bobbie, did we lose any family in the Holocaust?"

"No—no, we were all here in the United States—excepting on momma's side of the family—my mother. She had sisters with children, and children's children, like that. . . . Also the Kaminskys, your uncle Feivl's family, most of them remained in Mogilev-Podolsk and Odessa. . . . Also Poppa Greenpoint, remember him?"

"Well, sort of. He had a beard."

"Not just a beard. He had a younger sister, Malke, and two brothers."

"Wow, we lost a lot. That's really a lot."

"Every Jewish family," Bessie agreed. "Every Jewish family has a grave dug by the Nazis. Momma Greenpoint used to say this all the time. She felt it in her bones. . . . You want a glass of milk?"

He nodded somberly and shut off the tape recorder.

"What are you gonna do with all this?" Bessie asked as she shuffled toward the kitchen. "Maybe you ought to write what *you* think and never mind your *alte kranke bubbe*."

Pouring the milk, she glanced at the phone, a black box on the wall, but she knew its instantaneous voice was not the right medium for reaching back across the years, across the chasm. . . .

"Herschel? Herschie, we're having cookies and milk. I want you to come. We shouldn't meet only at funerals, Herschel. . . ."

"Jacob? Jacob, how's my grandchildren?"

"You know, it's really important to be Jewish," said the boy, standing in the foyer outside the kitchen. "I don't know why—I mean, I don't even understand why the Jews always got persecuted. It's real stupid." He took a swallow of his milk, breathing noisily. "I would fight, boy, if they ever just started to take away my family. I'd go crazy! . . . You think there could ever be a Holocaust for Negro people, Bobbie?"

The phone rang and cut into her reply. "That's your mother," Bessie predicted, though she felt oddly apprehensive about the call, as though her imagination could have evoked real-world results:

"Mom, it's your son. I wanted to wish you a happy birthday."

"Tell her we're not finished yet," said the boy.

Bessie shushed him with an upraised hand. "Hello?"

"Yes, my name is Johanna Ross, and I'm calling for the National Alliance Against Racism?" A Party organization—Bessie received their newsletter each month. The caller sounded like an educated black woman, who seemed to be reading from a text as she described organizing efforts for the forthcoming march on Washington.

"I'm making plans with my family to go," Bessie said.

"Oh, you are? Good!" Miss Ross strayed from her script. "I've had no luck today—guess I've been calling some very *old* people."

"A lot of comrades were in the struggle many, many years, even if they can't always go here and go there."

"Uh-huh."

"I myself, I'm seventy years."

"No kidding? Really? Well, we've chartered a couple of buses. They're scheduled to leave from Gun Hill Road about six-thirty in the morning on Sunday. What about you, Mrs. Sainer, would you like to make reservations for your family?"

Bessie tried to slap her grandson's hand as he picked up her birthday envelope from the counter beneath the phone. "Give me that! . . . No, excuse me—what's your name? Miss Ross. Please give me your number telephone."

"Holy shit, look at all this money! Where'd you get it?" He swiftly counted. "Two hundred dollars!"

"Just a minute, Miss Ross, I need a pencil. . . . Will you give me that?" she snarled at the boy as he pretended to be a gold-struck miser, huddling against the wall with her money.

"We could rent our own bus!" he whooped.

"Okay," she said, returning to the phone, "give me your number telephone. I have to call my kids first." She repeated the number, digit by digit, while jotting it down.

"We could take an airplane to Washington! Hijack!" He blew gunshot sounds out of his mouth and collapsed to the floor. "Uhh, you got me!"

"The Alliance is also asking for contributions," noted Miss Ross, "to pay the fares of those who are too poor."

"How much is the fare round-trip?"

"Twelve dollars—and we're having a picnic lunch, boxed chicken, available for a dollar."

"Hoo boy! All right, put me down for a contribution."

"If you want to make your reservations now, Mrs. Sainer, we'll give you a week to cancel. That way, the women who are cooking have some idea—"

"You're a real saleslady!" Bessie complimented her.

The boy was rolling over slowly, a reviving corpse, groaning: "I am the spirit of Uncle Herrrrrschel. I have come to haunt you...."

"All right," Bessie said decisively. "Put down for me, my daughter, my son-in-law, my grandson . . . and my brother Herschel."

The boy bolted to his knees. "Bobbie! You said—Bobbie!"

"Who else?" she asked him casually. "Laib and his wife? Sure, they would come. And maybe your uncle Jacob?"

"Bobbie! She's still on the phone!"

"How much does thirteen dollars go into two hundred? . . . Miss Ross, how many times does thirteen go into two hundred?"

"Fifteen," said both she and the boy at once.

"Good. So put me down for fifteen seats. And if they don't get filled, so you'll give them to people that they can't afford. Tomorrow I'll send the money. I got the address on your newsletter."

Johanna Ross was bubbling with appreciation as she said goodbye.

The boy was still on his knees and wide-mouthed. "You wanted your family to have a get-together?" Bessie said, before he could find words. "Now you're gonna start writing invitations."

Chapter Twenty-Four

It gladdened Bessie to see her grandson playing catch with two Negro boys, even though their recklessness at chasing the rubber ball between cars and into the street kept her nervously glued to their movements. Janet likewise was closely watching Bessie, who had let slip that she had an excruciating headache, not to mention—and she hadn't, but her pasty complexion clearly indicated—an upset stomach that made her dread the long bus ride.

The buses were late. Rumors were flying that the bus company was betraying its contract, probably under pressure from the FBI, but the organizers and bus captains kept assuring the crowd that they had been in phone contact with the company and were expecting the buses to arrive any minute. "Please, everybody," announced one imaginative woman, "can you imagine Harriet Tubman deciding to go home 'cause the underground railroad is running a little late?"

"Who's going home?" Bessie said to her daughter. "You got here such a group, I could stand and watch a whole day!"

They were Negro and white, including several whose gray hair and spindly legs made Bessie feel like a youngster, cranky in her illness. There was a contingent of nuns in their clean, dark linens, keeping sedately to themselves on the steps of their church; an orthodox rabbi and several black ministers; an anomalous business-suited man with an attaché case; a woman in hair curlers and sunglasses; five teen-agers with transistor radios tuned to the same station.

You think you lost your love . . . ?

She saw familiar faces, too, of *khaveyrim* she'd known in various struggles for years. They kept gravitating toward her with hugs and inquiries about her health, her work, her general welfare, with admiring comments about her old red lace warvest, and "Do you remember, Bessie, when we . . ." She in turn was friendly but not very communicative, relying on Janet's gift of gab. "You're satisfying the customers," Bessie told her as they stood briefly outside a group conversation. "Who can stand to make with the memories when you're expecting the memories themselves to come?"

"Expecting or hoping, momma? Don't expect, you'll be disappointed."

"Hope, expect—when did you ever know me to make this distinction, Janet? What time have you got?"

"Willy's wearing a watch." But he was yards off, conversing with a pair of 1199ers whose union caps he'd spotted in the crowd. Janet touched Bessie's arm. "I think you'd better concentrate on taking care of yourself, momma. You don't look well to me."

"I'm okay," she insisted impatiently. But her mood of exhilaration was darkening, sealing over, as she felt unsteady on her feet and increasingly out of place in the expectant, chatty crowd. *Alte kocker, altvarg,* she cursed herself, you can't even stand on your own two feet, let alone march through Washington! The tinny music from those teen-agers' radios buzzed annoyingly in her ears.

Then a hurrah went up, and bodies mobilized with many sighs and groans of relief, as the buses appeared at the corner and lumbered up to the curb. Time's up, thought Bessie, swallowing gall. "I'll get your son."

"Stay here, momma."

"Please, Janet, I can't get on the bus yet." She stepped into the street where she'd last seen the boy and his new friends.

He was at the window of a car, talking to the occupants. Bessie called his name and he waved to her, bouncing up and down. "Come, *ziskayt,* hurry up. I can't stand to be at the back of the bus."

The door at which the boy was lingering swung open. "Yoo, Aunt Bess!"

Belle-Brokha! "Belle!" Bessie cried, holding up her hand, one finger raised. "Belle!" She rose up on her toes with pleasure.

"Are we late?"

"No no no!"

Two young men—Belle's sons, yes, and so tall!—unfolded from the car. Bessie's fatigue dropped away from her like a veil to the ground as she bustled to the car with wide-open arms. "Belle!" She gave a strong kiss to the heavyset woman.

"We had to come all the way in from the Island," Belle apologized; then turned to Bessie's grandson, playing usher at the door. "That was such a sweet letter you wrote. You're a real writer!"

"Who else, who else?" Bessie bubbled, leaning into the car. Laib was at the wheel. "Laibl! *Oi, a leben ahf dein kup!*"

"Hi, Aunt Bess," he crooned. "How you doing?"

And another figure sat in the back seat, bundled against the window, not yet stirring, looking like a somber old rabbi seated on the eastern wall. "*Vi geyts*, Buzie? You think I can get myself out of here?"

"Oh, Herschel. *A gezunt dir in pipik!*" She was in his lap as he lowered his feet to the street.

"Everybody out!" Laib said. "We've got to go park."

Paul Dropsky, shriveled but spry, was with Janet and Willy when Bessie returned with her entourage. Unaccompanied, he had traveled by subway, the glad possessor of the bus ticket that Bessie had mailed, without much hope, to her sister Ruchel. "My harmonica just pulls me," he explained as Bessie and Janet praised his vigor and stroked him with affectionate words. "This morning it said to me, 'You're gonna go to Washington, Dropsky, you're gonna go and play with all the great Negro musicians.' And there you have it. It took ahold on me, I won't tell you where, and it pulled me right out the door."

He was a sly, salty old man with trembling hands that never quit gesturing. Bessie felt dizzy with joy, unbelieving of her success at rounding up—how many? One, two, three, four, five, and Laib makes six, plus her own family—ten people! "We got enough here to form the Jewish Bund all over again!" she told Herschel, hugging him again.

"How many blocks will we have to walk on this march?" he fretted.

The buses were taking on passengers. As soon as Bessie mounted the stairs behind her grandson, smelled the leather seats, and saw the rows of eyes glancing at her, at each new passenger, she remembered where they were going and why, and her family pride widened to embrace the entire crowd. The moment was at hand again, redemption in the offing; like a professional, she sobered up, settled into her reverie, fists clutched in her lap.

"I want to sit next to you, Bobbie."

"Come, *ziskayt*."

"Let Bobbie have the window so she can look out," said Janet in the seat behind.

In her thoughts, Bessie kissed her darling daughter. Then she pressed her face to the glass to watch the street, to watch for Jacob.

The bus captain began to make announcements while an aide collected tickets. The boy kept up a steady commentary like an excited duckling. Janet pressed her nose into the space between the backs of their seats. "You all right, momma?"

Bessie gave no reply. The bus's engine roared and, with an air-cushioned lurch, they were rolling. Already someone at the back was strumming a guitar and singing sweetly, "We shall overcome . . . we shall overcome . . . we shall overcome someday." The tune was picked up by a dozen humming voices. And Paul was quietly playing his mouth harp, first in spots, then with steady-streaming breath and a tonguing technique that gave the sound, for those who had ears to hear it, a plaintive Jewish flavor. The apartment buildings of the Bronx were filing past, saluting the bus convoy with flapping curtains and an occasional human face. Bessie imagined her son chasing the bus exhaust, one arm waving.

"One of the best slogans that it came out during the 1960s was from the Cuban leader Che Guevara. 'Revolution,' he said, 'is an act of love.' And I believe this, y'see. I would like to have on my wall a poster with these words.

" 'Cause when I think about my life—and I do this a great deal, *kinderlakh*. Let's face it, it's not so easy growing old. There's not so much to fill your time, to keep occupied your mind and your hands. There's not so much that it really belongs

to you anymore, that the world should really touch you, that
your mind should suddenly echo, or your heart should suddenly swell up so you want to go write poetry or something.
When you're old, living is more a habit, everything is more a
memory, and your body, with all the little aches—this part gets
stuck, and that part doesn't work right—your body talks louder
than your mind. Me, I'm always groping like a blind woman
to find that part of me that she's still young, still thinking about
questions and hoping for answers.

"I wake up in the morning and first thing I do is I talk to myself. Hello, what's the matter today, don't worry, the headache
will go away, goodbye. And then I can first look around the
room, how the light's coming in, and the plants are growing. I
always try to wake up slow, with appreciation for life. This is
my way that I can almost pray, I pray for the Messiah.

"Only the Messiah's already here, y'see. This I believe. I'm
not religious, I'm too much a rebel to believe that someone else
already figured it all out and all I gotta do is like they say, pray
a certain way, vote a certain way. I can't believe that God is a
Republican, or a Catholic, or a Jew. I don't believe there's a God
at all—and if there was, y'see, and he makes the world that it
should be so miserable, then I'm gonna stand there and curse
him to his face and march right into hell. I promise you.

"So don't think I'm getting religious in my old age when I say
that the Messiah's already here. If you read Karl Marx, you'll
know what I mean. It's true, he said that religion is the opiate
of the people. But that's not all he said. He asked the question,
Why do people take a drug like this? It's because they feel their
pain, they feel it and they don't want to submit to it, just like I
don't want to give in to my headaches and my blood pressure.
Marx said that religion is—here, I'll give it to you exactly: 'Religion is the sigh of the afflicted creature, the soul of the heartless
world.' You didn't know Karl Marx was a poet, hmm? There,
that's another poster I would like to have on my wall.

"Why do you think people go to church or to synagogue?
You think it's because they believe all the *meises* about God and
sin and all that kind of a nonsense? I don't think so. I think it's
'cause they want to be together, they want to sing together,
they want to share a feeling that life is worth living, together!
They want to get away for a minute from the life that they
can't control at all. Who knows, any second an atom bomb

might fall in your backyard. Or a chemical that it gives cancer might spill into the water you drink, if it's not there already. Or the stock market might crash on all our heads all over again. Or a computer might get a little rusty and the whole world will disappear. Isn't this what life feels like today?

"It's like everybody in the world should be as old as Bessie Sainer. We all go to sleep and we're not sure we're gonna wake up in the morning. So we become desperate to believe in something, y'see. And if we get scared enough—if the economy gets *fahmisht,* if we can't tell where to go, where to live, where we belong—if this kind of a alienation grows big enough, then the entire population becomes ready to take up horrible political ideas. A Hitler comes along and everybody's ready to call him the Messiah, just so they can feel a part of something, of a movement. And then they'll be able to strangle little babies with their own two hands, 'cause when you believe crazy ideas, you're ready to do crazy things.

"But there's another kind of belief: the belief in human beings. It's the feeling that you have when you're a child that you want to play with other children, you want to make, like, a gang, a team, you want to be with them all the time. It's the understanding that human beings can be responsible for each other, to share and to give and to learn, and from this we're gonna gain, we're not gonna lose. It's the belief that there's nothing the Messiah can do for us that we can't do for ourselves.

"It's true, *kinderlakh.* I know it's true. I was there, a dozen times, I saw the miracles that human beings can do. It's like Martin Luther King said: 'I've been to the mountaintop. I've seen the promised land!' He was talking about America—an America that forgets about profits and thinks instead about people. An America that forgets about punishment and thinks instead about solutions.

"But sometimes I worry that Martin Luther King and the civil-rights movement was the last chance for America to have a peaceful revolution and become the promised land. Here you had the Negro people, that for two hundred, three hundred years they were slaves, so terribly oppressed. But they were ready to say to America, 'We forgive you.' And they weren't carrying guns, they were carrying only their pride, their history, their dignity. Martin Luther King was saying to America, Let's forget all the *tsuris.* Let's unite. What was his dream, what did he say, do you remember? He said that his dream was for the children of slaves and the children of slaveholders to play together. Even if you yourself had Negro people for slaves, Martin Luther King was ready to forget it.

"So the civil-rights movement was America's mirror. We stood before it, each one of us, and we saw ourselves. We saw how we are part of the system, how we participate in the system. And what did we do? We didn't smash the system, we smashed the mirror.

"It's like pharaoh denying to Moses and the Jews their freedom. He had his chance for a peaceful revolution and he said no. So then came the plagues. Now America's got its plagues. There's nothing but hatred ruling in this country. The miracle, I think, is that after Vietnam, after the riots in the ghettos, and with all the assassinations, and with radiation and cancer, and with inflation and unemployment—with all this, we can still act like human beings, we can still manage to have hope. The miracle is that most people are not murderers. Most people don't mug. Most people don't commit suicide. Most people still love their children and try to love themselves. And we're not yet saying '*Sieg Heil*' to an American Hitler.

"Sometimes I ask myself, Why am I still alive? I survived so much, but for what? I mean, if you ask my daughter or if you ask my grandson, they got an answer, sure—they like me! They like the cookies I bake, the kreplach and the Jewish penicillin, the stories, the jokes. They want someday to have a photograph of me with my great-granddaughter. They see me and they know they got a heritage, something that it wasn't made in Hollywood, it wasn't on television, they can't buy it in the department store. I help them to feel human. I help them to feel Jewish. I help them to feel progressive.

"And I guess *this* is my job, that I should be everybody's Bobbie. To show you that you can live the way you believe and you won't end up a bum. You can join with other people to win back a part of your life from the system. My generation, we were fighters and poets. We worked for twelve hours in the sweatshops and still we had the strength to stand up and sing and remember who we are. We never made a revolution, no, but at least we never lost the spark of life.

"So we can talk about mistakes if you like, but I'd rather talk about what we learned from our mistakes. And we can talk about disillusionment, but I'd rather talk about the beauty of our ideas, y'see. We can talk about failures, but I'd rather talk about a heritage, a legacy to the younger generation.

" 'Cause let's face it: I'm not gonna finish the job. I'm not gonna retire from it, but I'm not gonna finish it. I mean, just to blow out all the candles on my birthday cake takes a dozen young people to blow! And revolution means a lot more than just making wishes and blowing out little candles.

"But it starts there, y'see. And it doesn't end when my candle, Bessie Sainer's candle, goes out. There's a Jewish saying that to a doctor and an undertaker you shouldn't wish a good year. Fine, so I'll tell them to have a good *yontev* instead, 'cause on *yontev* they don't work. The point is, I'm not gonna hide in my closet and hope that the Angel of Death passes over me without coming for a visit. I never hid in a closet before and I'm not gonna start now. You have to be realistic if you want to get old and still enjoy your life, y'see. You have to know that to a certain age you'll come and then you'll start decaying whether you like it or not. And if you look straight at it, you know that this is the way of life and this is the way it's gonna be—you can't make a revolution against old age. Then you accept it. And then you're not old, you're young, 'cause your time is now. I'm not afraid."

May 31, 1981
Brooklyn